COPYRIGHT

The Graveyard Club: The Death of Diamond Slim

Copyright © 2025 by Kenneth M. Harrell

Book cover design by (ebooklaunch.com)

Interior book design by (KM. Harrell)

Editing and proofreading by (Two Birds Author Services)

Wonder Boy Publications

 ISBN: 978-0-9997144-8-5 (Paperback)

ISBN: 978-0-9997144-2-3 (ebook)

Library of Congress Control Number: 2025901633

Series: The Graveyard Club; 1

First Paperback Edition 2025

ALSO BY K.M. HARRELL

Nyira and the Invisible Boy

For Aunt Lee Bessie
Who introduced me to the world of books

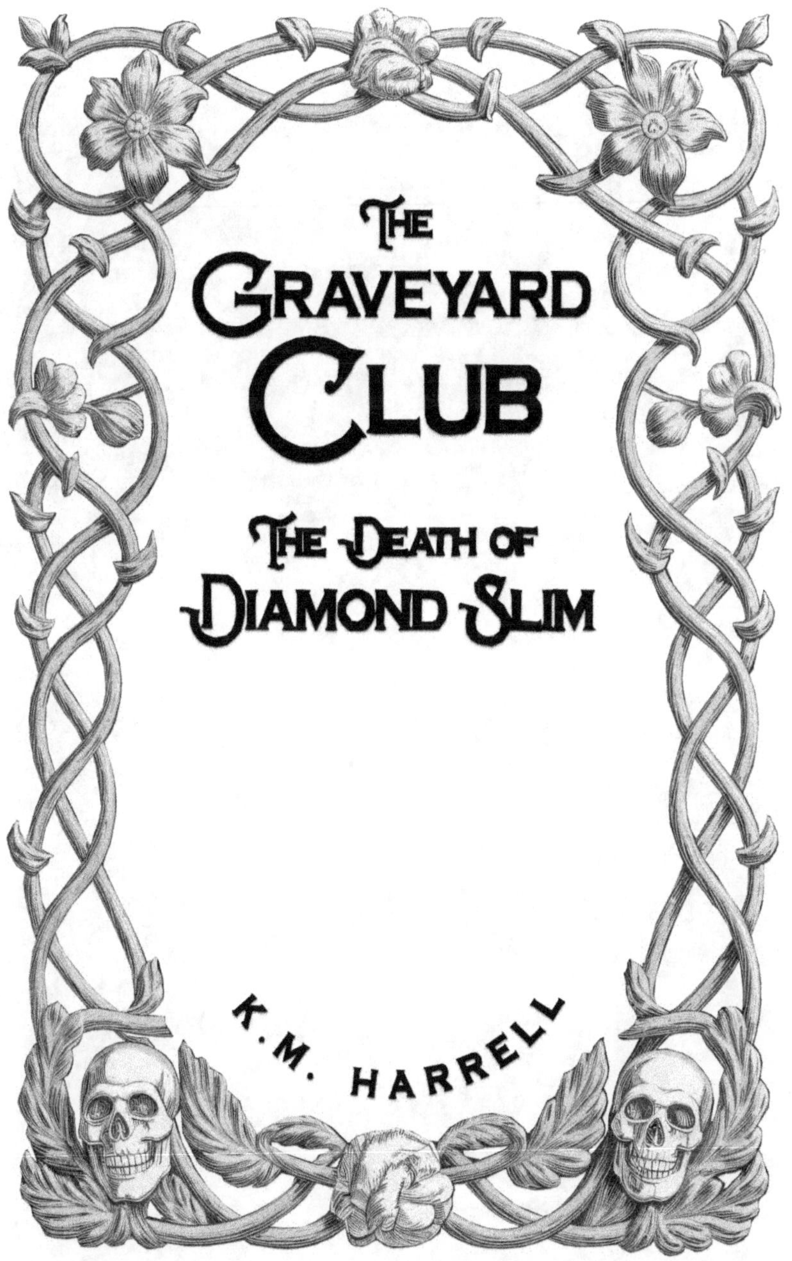

THE
GRAVEYARD
CLUB

THE DEATH OF
DIAMOND SLIM

K.M. HARRELL

SCENCE CONTEST

🎬 **JOIN THE GRAVEYARD CLUB SCENE CONTEST!** 🎬

Think you can bring *The Graveyard Club: The Death of Diamond Slim* to life? Here's your chance!

📖 **How to Enter:**

• Pick the most exciting, chilling, or thrilling scene from the book.

• Record yourself (or a willing friend) reading the scene—max **3 minutes.**

• Start your video by introducing yourself and showing the book cover.

• Email your clip to **k7476777@gmail.com.**

What Happens Next:

We'll post your video on the author's Instagram for everyone to enjoy. The most captivating performance—judged by audience engagement and a touch of author magic—will win a **signed Graveyard Club T-shirt!**

It's simple. You read. We share. The magic happens.

Don't wait—start filming your scene today!

CHAPTER 1
SHE WHO RAISES THE DEAD

That day, after Besa got out of Sister Gerard's School for Magist Children, Felix, her guardian, allowed her to walk a little way up Chartres and receive the attention of the enchanted magnolias, which often shuffled out of the yards of homes to offer shade to those who stroll Chartres. Besa encountered three that day, as they all knew her—she came this way often. No one remembered when the trees became enchanted, but it was a fun attraction for anyone who visited this area and shopped at some of the Magist shops on this street. There was also a dress shop, whose mannequin spun around in the window if a patron stopped to look, and if you stood there and watched long enough, the mannequin would go change dresses and show you something else. There was a pie shop not much further down that would float you out a sample, if it sensed you were hungry enough and the door was open. But Besa was going to Antoine's Sweet Shop, which had the best macaron cookies. Her friends, Margaret and Dickey, were strolling along with her when a black horse and carriage pulled up beside them. The horse looked more like a thoroughbred than a simple walker; he pawed the ground when they stopped. The girl at the reins was a few years older than Besa. She wore a yellow chemise dress trimmed in silver ribbons and lace—a younger girl in a similar blue dress sat beside her.

"Are you the Negress?" the older girl asked. She was obviously Creole. Besa knew that only they could look at someone dressed better than they were and still see only a negro. Besa's dress was striking; made of moiré, it had a lustrous sheen accentuated by its violet-shaded, applied chenille flowers and sparkling buttons. Pleated trimmings stood out along the bottom edge and seams of the wide pagoda style sleeves. The back of the dress fell in shimmering folds over the dome-shaped petticoat worn underneath. Besa was tall for her age, and her dark skin and regal carriage gave her dress's color some depth.

"No," replied Besa. "I am not the Negress. I am a person with a name."

Both Margaret and Dickey stood staring at the two girls —while Besa kept walking toward the shop.

"Please excuse us, mademoiselle. She meant no offense," said the second girl. She looked younger, possibly fourteen, like Besa.

"Shut up, Angeline!" said the older girl. "She's just a negro!"

"You will not tell me to shut up!" cried the younger girl. "I stole Papa's horse for you!"

Besa made it to the shop and opened the door.

"Please wait!" cried the younger girl.

"Stop it, Angeline," said the older girl. "Or I will pull your hair. Is she your slave?" she asked Dickey. "Please tell her to come here."

"She is not my slave!" declared Dickey, who then

sprinted to hold the door open for Besa. "I'm hers." Besa disappeared into the shop. "And hers too," continued Dickey when Margaret followed her inside.

"Wait for me, mademoiselles and I will serve you your treats!" said Dickey, entering the shop with a grand manner.

"Not a chance, butter boy. You're not touching my cookies," said Margaret.

"You, mademoiselle, have no sense of decorum," said Dickey, sitting down at their table with a pout.

The shopkeeper was in the back as usual, but the enchanted pastry case knew the kids and their preferences (they came there almost every day after school). So it bagged up three bags full of cookies and sent them out to their table.

"You may call me whatever you like," replied Margaret. "Just keep that big stomach of yours away from my cookies. I haven't forgotten about last week."

Besa stood at the shop window, watching the two Creoles arguing.

"What do they want?" wondered Margaret.

"I don't care," said Besa. "I have to go. Felix will get impatient."

Besa opened the door and she, Dickey and Margaret moved quickly toward the carriage situated behind the two Creoles. They moved so fast the trees couldn't keep up with them.

"Stop!" cried the older girl. "You will stop when I am speaking to you, girl!"

Besa slowed down for a moment to give her a look and then proceeded to and boarded her own carriage. The younger girl jumped from their carriage and pursued her.

"Please, mademoiselle! I beseech you. Please forgive my

sister's rudeness. We are in desperate need of your services!"

"Angeline!" admonished her older sister. "Do not shame yourself. She is nothing but a—"

"Marie Simone!" said the younger sister. "If you do not stop and apologize, we will never see him again!"

Besa looked from the tearful Angeline to her older sister.

"See who again? What do you want?"

"I first want my sister to apologize."

"Why would I apologize to a servant?"

"She is wearing one of Madame Jarré's designs! She is not a servant! "

"How is that possible? Her dresses cost almost as much as Papa's stallions!"

"She does all my dresses," said Besa. "But you still haven't told me why you have accosted me on my way home from school."

Angeline said something to Marie in German.

"Why would your father beat you?" asked Besa. Both girls looked at her, surprised that she could understand them. But German was one of twelve languages Besa spoke.

"It's time to go, Marie," said Angeline. "Papa will be angry enough as it is. And we have accomplished nothing."

Marie began to cry.

"Please, my angel! Do not be angry with me! You know I can be such a fool sometime."

"I am not angry. And I am not the one to whom you should apologize."

Marie climbed out of their carriage and stood before Besa's.

"Please, mademoiselle! You are so obviously a lady. Please forgive my insolence. We have come here at risk of a beating, hoping you are she who raises the dead. We have lost someone very close to our hearts and have recently discovered where his body is buried."

"What is his name?" Besa asked.

"No, Besa," said Felix, finally speaking up. "It's too soon for that."

"It's been almost a month, behike. I can't stay home forever. People need us. "

"I'm ready," declared Dickey, his thumbs in the sleeves of his tweed vest, to puff himself up. "As long as it's not too dangerous."

"That's not true," replied Margaret. "You're never ready. The last time you almost got her killed."

"What are you talking about? Mokheer distracted me, and it snuck up on us."

"That's why you set the wards, Dickey!"

The incident Margaret was referring to happened during their last case. But it started with the boy at the French Market...

BESA'S FAMILY COOK, Miss Maymi, often took her along when she went to the French Market. A number of the vendors there did not speak English. Or not the kind of English Miss Maymi understood, so Besa was often called upon to translate should any haggling take place.

"You talk Choctaw much better than I do, Besa," she said. "My mama spoke it good, but not all us chidren learnt it."

Miss Maymi was also afraid of the Cajuns, who brought fish to the market. Their accents reminded her of the overseer on the plantation she grew up on. She had been allowed to hire herself out to other plantation families, and with the money she earned, purchased hers and her family's freedom. She might still sound like a slave, but Miss Maymi was probably the best cook in Newald. Besa didn't know what her papa paid her, but she was worth every note.

After they'd made all their purchases, Besa liked to stroll about the market on her own, smelling the French bread coming out of the stone ovens, the Portuguese pastéis de nata tarts that were some of her favorites, the Swedish kanelbullar desert that she loved with a cup of coffee from the Ethiopian brewers, and any number of amazing local and international fruits, while also listening to the various languages being bantered back and forth.

Besa saw the boy standing by a wagon about a yard from the market boundary, staring but not moving any closer, as if he were afraid of all the people he saw. He was a light-skinned boy of about nine. His hair was a curly sandy color, but the rest of him looked filthy. His pants were dirty and worn at the knees, and the left sleeve of his shirt was torn at the seam and hung off his shoulder. Besa purchased an apple and took it to him. He looked at her strangely and shook his head, backing away like a shy colt.

"Please take it," she said. "No strings attached." He snatched it and turned his back to her while he bit into it. When he finished, he turned around and said, "Thank you."

"What's your name?" asked Besa.

"It's not a good name. You don't wanna know it," he said, turning a bit away from her.

"If I buy you another apple, will you tell me then?"

"I will if you add a piece of bread with that apple," he said, smiling.

She delivered the apple and a sweet roll.

"They call me Stinky where I come from," he mumbled, looking at his feet.

"What place do you come from that would give you such a name?"

"Diamond Slims' Pleasure Palace."

"You came from a brothel?" asked Besa, surprised.

"I ain't there no more. My sister Sylvie is missin', and I need to find her," he replied, looking up at Besa.

"That's terrible. Do you think someone took her away?"

"I do. I believe it was Diamond Slim that done it."

"Where would he have taken her?"

"I won't ever know. He was killed in a duel fo' dawn this morning." And then he began to cry. "I don't know what to do. Sylvie all the family I got left."

"What will you do now?" asked Besa, approaching as if to offer comfort, but he backed away.

"I been livin' wild for a month now, lookin' for Slim. I s'pose I could still do that till I find some place to be."

"I could ask Felix if we need another stable hand."

"Why would you do that? You don't know me. I ain't no charity case!"

He turned to leave.

"Wait! I think my friends and I might be able to help you. We attend Sister Gerard's School for Magist Children, up on Chartres."

"What can magic do for me?"

"Me and a few of my classmates have been going into graveyards at night, opening tombs, to try and raise the spirits of the dead."

"That sound crazy. Why would you do somethin' like that?"

"That's what my papa did for a living. I'm just trying to follow in his footsteps."

"Your papa makes a livin' diggin' up graves at night?"

"My papa is a necromancer."

"Your papa Pierre Melponte? The richest, most powerful Magist in the city?"

"I'm Besa Melponte. If my friends and I can raise Diamond Slim's spirit, you could ask him where your sister is."

"But I ain't got no money to pay you."

"We don't do it for money. If you'll meet us at Antoine's Sweet Shop on Chartres in three days, I'll discuss your case with my friends."

"I guess I can meet yo' graveyard club, Besa Melponte. See you in three days."

He then trotted off toward Place d'Armes. The name he'd called their group had a truthful ring to it. They'd not called themselves anything up to that point. They'd also not had much success opening tombs and rousing the bones. Their parents had no idea they'd taken up this gruesome hobby. But if they did, they'd have Besa to blame—or more specifically, the hurricane that had struck over a month before...

CHAPTER
TWO

The night of the storm, there was a hard rain as the hurricane raged out in the gulf. Besa's papa took no notice to storms, not when he was focusing on her studies. This was their nightly ritual. They had already gone over social studies, mathematics, and physics.

"Now it is time for your Latin," he said, as lightning blasted a swath of light across his serious, but handsome face. Besa began to recite the opening passage of Plato's Republic. She made it all the way to the third paragraph before she noticed that Papa's attention had wavered. She'd made a minor mistake, but he hadn't noticed. That's when she saw that her papa's eyes were ablaze, and in the shine from the silver tea service that Felix just laid out on the center table beside them, she noticed hers were too. Papa's skin also gave off a glow. This only happened when something terrible had occurred.

Suddenly, she was pulled into a vision. Instead of being in their parlor, she stood on the deck of a ship in the midst of the storm. The vessel held a number of wealthy passengers in the midst of a grand dinner party; and as if in defiance of the weather, they took no notice of the storm raging about them. The slaves catering to the partygoers were the only individuals on the ship affected by the storm. They startled when lightning struck or thunder boomed, and dodged away when a wave rose up above the ship's rail, as though it might be trying to view the goings-on of the lavish gathering. The partygoers soon grew impatient with the nervous slaves.

"Where is my champagne?" asked a bearded man in a gold-buttoned tweed suit.

"Our plates are empty!" cried another man in a luxurious velvet suit and a beautiful Top Hat.

"Massa," said a slave delivering a replenished plate to Top Hat. "The storm is getting worse."

"What storm!" laughed Top Hat. All the other partygoers laughed as well. A beautiful, dark-haired woman in a blue silk dress and wearing a diamond tiara screamed for her young slave attendant to bring her more brandy. A girl of about ten finally came from below deck, clutching a large bottle to her chest as if it were a lifebuoy. "What took you so long?" demanded Tiara. But the girl was shaking so much, she spilled half the liquid.

"Your girl looks a bit piqued, Mary," said the man sitting at the table with Tiara. He had a large diamond pin in the lapel of his silk suit coat. "Maybe she needs a drink."

Besa knew this was just a vision, but as she walked under the canopy shielding the partygoers, she smelled the food, felt the spray of the waves and the rain. And when a heavy gust slammed into the starboard, she even smelled the fear of the trembling slaves, but no one noticed her. Then a girl of about eleven turned from filling a glass at a table not far from the starboard rail and caught sight of her. The girl dropped her large decanter and screamed,

"Death! Death has com—"

As if in answer to her call, a large wave rose above the rail and swept her away. The wealthy partygoers couldn't care less; they laughed louder, drank harder. The storm wouldn't dare disturb their fun. But the storm was hungry too, and one dark girl wasn't nearly enough to satisfy it. Next, an aggressive wave rose up and swept Top Hat into the depths. Next, it swallowed Tiara before she could finish her tenth drink.

"What is happening?" cried an inebriated Diamond Lapel.

"This is not right!" shouted a handsomely dressed man with an impossible beard. His lovely companion was swept away just as he was about to suggest they move midship.

"Where is Captain Saurvet?" demanded another partygoer. "This is his vessel!"

The storm didn't care whose vessel it was, and then took the outraged complainer too. The partygoers stopped laughing, and fear was on the menu. The storm served a heavy dose of it, as it toyed with the ship for the next few minutes. Everyone soon moved belowdecks. This decision only seemed to enrage the storm as its powerful winds easily spun the vessel around, and when it could contain its hunger no longer, a giant wave rose up and swallowed the ship and all its passengers. Besa soon found herself back in the parlor, with her papa standing quietly before the fireplace.

"It appears to be your bedtime, little cacica," said Felix, gathering up the remnants of their informal dinner in the parlor.

"But why, Felix?" Besa complained. "I'm not a child. I'll be fifteen soon."

"You know that's a few months away, Besa," replied the

behike. He could be as severe as Papa when it came to her bedtime.

"But I want to help Papa. I, too, saw Captain Saurvet's ship go down in the gulf. Soon they will deliver the news to Madame Saurvet and her children."

Pierre turned from the fireplace. His green eyes blazed with knowing, but his face was shadowed by the glow of the lamplight.

"The fact that you are in knowing before your fifteenth year is troubling," he said. "And you know I can't allow you to participate in an enchantment ceremony. But if you want to come and watch a spirit rise, I suppose it couldn't hurt."

"I think she may still be too young, Pierre," replied Felix.

"It's all right, my friend. I'll make sure she's safe."

CAPTAIN SAURVET OWNED many slaves and numerous enterprises throughout the colony. Normally, this would be of no consequence to Pierre. But Saurvet chose to keep secret the amount and location of his wealth from his family and business associates. And while "decent" folk condemned him as little more than a demon worshipper, those in need of a particular bit of information that only the dead could supply knocked on the Necromancer's door.

Besa and her papa knew that Madame Saurvet would stall for as long as possible as she pondered her limited options. But in the end, she would send someone to fetch Pierre.

BESA WATCHED her father put on his green, purple and black robes and then take the book of Taalu out of the safe in the library. Pierre was tall (over six feet), broad shouldered, strong as twelve stevedores and dark as the night. People feared him. Besa was afraid of him, too. But she took solace in having his love to protect her.

They sat in the shadow of their enormous library. Their mansion, the largest in Faubourg Marigny—stood three stories, including a locked third floor level that Besa had been trying to get into since she was seven—was not hard to find. They waited together, not speaking. Pierre's large, dark hands draped over the book as it lay in his lap. It was like no other book in their library, or in any library Besa had ever been in. It was kept in a case of gold-lined goat hide, with two onyx buttons fastened by loops of silver. The Taalu was a little smaller than the Christian bible; but how heavy she didn't know. She'd only seen it twice—this was the second time.

AT MIDNIGHT, Felix came to the study to say someone was inquiring at the front door.

"Okay," said Pierre, as he rose and exhaled. "Here are the rules. The first one you break will get you sent back to the carriage: One, stay in the background. Two, do not look directly at the Taafli. Use this." He pulled a large hand mirror out of the desk drawer. Three, keep your head covered. Four, don't, under any circumstances, try and engage the Taafli. Five, do not scream. If it comes towards you and you become frightened, simply look down at your feet. Are we in agreement, young lady?"

She nodded her assent. And while she had every confidence in father's skill and his ability to protect her, she was still a slight bit afraid.

ONE OF THE CAPTAINS' many Newald mansions was situated between Ducayet and Crete streets. Pierre had been down this street leading to the captain's mansion many times in the dark. He had been there for a Creole ball during last All Hallows Eve. But the white men sent by Madame Saurvet seemed to feel it was necessary to escort him. Besa found this amusing. The illumination from the gas lamps along the way lent their trek a stage-like air, and the sky above was bursting with stars. The storm and rain had cleared, and as they made their way only the horse's hooves sloshing in what remained of the flooding, along with an occasional drip off the streetlamp, gave any hint of the recent storm violence that had visited the city. When Besa tried to make light of this needless procession, her papa quickly shushed her.

A MINIATURE of the palace of Versailles, the property at The Chateau de Saurvet, took up more than four hundred acres between Ducayet and Crete streets and contained over a hundred rooms. The gardens and grounds required a crew of more than two hundred slaves to maintain it. The Zulu warrior guarding the gate at the beginning of the drive was a powerful looking African, almost as powerful looking as Pierre. The warrior took no notice of the white men and directed his words toward Pierre.

"Sorcerer, state your business here!"

The white men did not like being ignored.

"Boy, go inform the house that we have brought the big witch doctor."

Pierre bristled at this description, but Besa placed her hand over his and looked up at him.

"You are big, you know."

"And you are yet a handful."

The path to the mansion's front salon took them through two levels of nine intricately graded gardens, six fruit groves, twelve ponds with sculpted fountains, and four manmade lakes. They entered the house at the door of the grand salon, which consisted of a 35-yard-long gallery of mirrors and an extensive art collection. They were greeted at the door by a distinguished-looking Black butler. Pierre knew him.

"Dooley, it's good to see you again, my friend." They shook hands.

"Indeed," Dooley replied. "You look well, Necromancer. But these are not good circumstances. And I must warn you; you won't have many allies here."

He turned and addressed the men who'd escorted them. "I will take responsibility for the doctor from here."

One of the men, a beefy red-faced fellow who seemed to take offense at having to retrieve Pierre, took issue with the term: "doctor."

"He ain't no damn doctor. This negro's just a—"

"Shall I inform the house that you have an issue with an invited guest?" replied Dooley.

The Saurvets were known for a brutal attitude towards all in their employ, slave and white. The white man shut up and moved away from the door; the others followed. The misty night closed over them like a dark blanket as they stomped away.

"They await you in the War Salon," Dooley informed them.

"I'm familiar with it."

"Bishop Delacroix will be in attendance."

Pierre's face lost some of its color. He kneeled down and took Besa's hands in his.

"Besa, perhaps tonight is not the best time for your first spirit experience. I fear this will be a difficult ceremony. Why don't you go back to the carriage? Old George will get you home. He knows the way."

"But Papa, please!" she implored. "I promise I will be all right. I'm not a child, Papa."

"I don't like the feeling I'm getting about this, Besa. Dooley, can you send someone to escort my daughter home?"

"I'm afraid not, my friend. All servants have been confined to the house. And I don't have to tell you the danger to a negro on the streets at night, especially a girl."

Pierre looked at her, and for the first time in Besa's life, she saw fear in his eyes. She placed her hands on his enormous shoulders.

"You will not always be able to protect me," said Besa. "I am your daughter, but I'm strong, too. Please. Let's just go and finish this."

This seemed to give him some comfort as he stood, apparently resigned to their present situation. They again began to move towards the Salon.

The War Salon was decorated in homage to the captain's service and heroism during The Battle of Newald. The paintings and lithographs that adorned the walls depicted scenes of the various battles, along with weapons and medals mounted as tastefully as was possible for implements still bearing the blood of the conflict. Along with the artifacts, the pièce de résistance was a mural on the ceiling that portrayed the captain as a saint leading the battle in which he earned his rank, his reputation and eventually his enormous wealth.

～

WHEN THEY ENTERED THE ROOM, the first person they encountered was the bishop, André Delacroix.

"What are you doing here, witch doctor?"

"I have been summoned, priest."

The bishop turned around and scoured the room with his glare.

"Who is responsible for summoning this devil monger?"

A thin, severe looking man stepped forward.

"That would be me, your Excellency," replied Miles Bradford, the Saurvet business manager. "No disrespect to your abilities with the rosary, Your Grace, but we needed to take some fairly drastic measures."

"What type of measures? The church forbids any such satanic rituals practiced by the likes of this negro. Madame Saurvet, does this ceremony have your blessing?"

Geneviève Saurvet was so pale, she looked dead, too. She could barely make eye contact with the bishop.

"André, I am sorry. But Jean was a difficult and secretive man. We have no means of support if this negro is not able to—"

"I forbid it! The church will not sanction such unspeakable practices. Think on your husband's soul, madam. On your own soul!"

"Your Excellency," replied Mr. Bradford. He took a very calm, just slightly condescending tone with the bishop, whose face showed he did not care for it. "We are trying to be practical. There is no access to the captain's resources. And unless there is a way to communicate with him, the business and the family are not the only ones who will suffer."

He had the bishop's attention then.

"What are you saying, Bradford?"

"I'm saying that unless we can locate the captain's gold, there will be no way to underwrite the construction in the new chapel and rectory."

"But surely there is another way," sputtered Delacroix.

"I'm afraid not," replied Bradford.

"So, you are saying the holy body's fate lies in the hands of this Satanist?"

Pierre glanced at Besa and waved her toward the door.

"I'm going to bid you all good evening," he said, giving a gracious bow and turning to follow his daughter.

"Wait, Mr. Melponte! Please try and be patient. I apologize for the bishop's—"

"The church needs no one to apologize for it. The church is—"

"Just a pile of bricks at the moment, Your Grace," replied Mr. Bradford. "Unless you allow this man to do his job, and cease your insults!"

"...Very well then," replied Delacroix. "Am I allowed to at least perform the absolution over the captain's body first?"

"By all means," replied Pierre.

Bishop Delacroix performed a half hour ceremony of prayer and singing that ended with holy water being sprinkled onto the captain's corpse.

"I suppose now you can do...whatever it is you intend to do...negro," sneered the bishop.

Finally, Pierre was able to begin.

"I will need everyone to move back at least twenty feet," Pierre directed.

Pierre had warned Besa that until she reached full knowing, it was not safe for her to look directly at the Taafli. But there was no danger to non-Magists, as long as they did not touch the Book of Taalu or interfere with him during the enchantment ceremony.

Pierre took the chalk made from ground jackal's bones and powdered boar's tusk from his bag and drew a ten-foot circle around the ebony table upon which the captain was lying. He then took out a vial of blood—his own blood, actually—and placed a drop at each of the four corners of the table. He then stood at the head of the table inside the circle and between two points of the blood, and began to chant his incantation. When he removed the Book of Taalu from its covering, the book was glowing. Pierre then placed the goat hide over the head of the captain and closed his eyes as he opened the book. A light flew out of the book: A large, golden dragonfly-like creature flitted around the room, and for a second hovered over Besa's head and said: "Hi little one."

But as Pierre directed, she did not look directly at it. She simply watched through the mirror as the Necromancer continued to chant. The Taafli hovered over and then merged with the captain's corpse. The body gave off a glow and then a brilliant white eminence ascended from the flesh. It was at this point that Geneviève Saurvet fainted.

Mr. Bradford went about the process of trying to revive her with a glass of brandy. But Bishop Delacroix was transfixed. He, in fact, had started moving slowly towards the table, until he stood right at the foot of the circle.

"Not in all my years of service," said the cleric, "have I witnessed such a miracle."

Pierre opened his eyes.

"Stand away, priest," he ordered. "There is little time for chatter."

Mr. Bradford, having restored Madame Saurvet, helped her to approach the table.

"Oh, my heavens, Jean!" she cried. "What has become of you, my love?"

"Geneviève, mine beloved," replied the spirit. "Why are thou so far from me? You are but a ship that floats in the distance. I long to behold thee."

"Jean, we are lost without you. And if you do not..." She descended into tears. Mr. Bradford whispered something in her ear. "...Jean, my love," she continued. "We are bereft; our home and the children suffer in your absence. How are we to be maintained? You must reveal the location of our means."

The spirit seemed to ponder this for a moment.

"The locket I gifted thee," the spirit declared. "There be the key to the wine closet vault." The spirit then receded once again into the body, and the Taafli ascended to flutter around the ceiling. But then the unthinkable happened: Bishop Delacroix snatched the book of Taalu from Pierre's hands.

"I claim this item as an artifact of the church!" he declared.

"Priest! You are in grave danger! You must return the book at once!" cried Pierre.

"This document should be a part of the holy sacrament. It is too powerful to be in the hands of a slave!"

"Don't be a fool, priest! This item is not of your blood. You have no understanding of what you've done!"

The bishop seemed crazed, as if some unearthly thing had gotten hold of him.

"We can speak to the Saint!" he said. "This is not the kind of power that should be in the hands of a mere negro!"

A horrifying screech erupted, like a thousand eagles screaming: The Taafli had turned its fury upon the bishop. Bishop Delacroix gripped the large cross hanging from a chain around his neck and held it toward the creature. The Taafli did not seem to like this gesture; it gave off an even louder screech. Besa's mirror cracked from the decibel of it. Bishop Delacroix began to recite the rosary: "Hail Mary, full of grace, the Lord is with you..." The Taafli lit upon the metal of the cross, and as it rose, a thin strand of molten metal was gripped in its claws. It then took the strand and wound it around the outstretched arm of Bishop Delacroix, who could only scream in agony; he then collapsed as the creature descended upon him.

PIERRE WAS able to prevent the Taafli from killing the bishop by securing the Book of Taalu from his unconscious grasp, and allowing the entity to return to it.

When Dr Robichaud arrived and removed the bishop's frock and topmost garments, he gave a cry at the clergy's wounds.

"My God! What type of beast could have done such damage?"

When no one had the words for a reply, the physician became incensed. "Are you all a bunch of mutes? Someone tell me how this man came to this state!"

"It—It was not a beast, sir," replied Mr. Bradford. "It was like a little light."

"A light, you say. But how could a little light have done this kind of damage? And how could such a thing have gotten in here?" As the doctor spoke, he continued to take items out of his medium-sized black bag. "Blast it! I am going to need my bone saw for this." He turned and addressed a solemn younger man dressed in a short-fronted tailcoat, tight pantaloons and Hessian boots, who'd lingered near the door, as if in anticipation of just such a request. "Mordecai, please run back to the hospital and retrieve my saw."

Mordecai was gone almost before the doctor could complete his sentence.

Once the assistant had exited, Dr. Robichaud, a portly man with dark hair and a significant beard, did not bother to remove his black frock coat as he went about the task of cleaning and prepping the wound. "Bradford, please have one of your servants prepare a large pot of boiling water, along with a small pot of warm water, for the opium and laudanum solution. I will also need a few of them to help restrain the bishop. We can't have him moving too much once I get going with the saw. And you have still not told me what caused the need for that blasted saw!"

"As I said, it was a little light that—"

"A light could not do a thing such as this, sir!"

"It came out of the Necromancer's book."

Pierre had, until this moment, maintained a safe distance from the incredulous white man, keeping Besa out of sight behind him. "The Taafli is not a simple light," he offered. "It is a powerful entity."

"Who is this negro and what has he to do with this incident?" demanded Dr. Robichaud.

"He...The entity belonged to him, sir," replied Mr. Bradford. "We hired him to raise the captain's spirit."

"This man is a Magist?" exclaimed the doctor. "Why would you allow such a creature into this gentleman's noble house?"

"It was my idea, sir. We were at our wits end. And I—"

"You will stop talking now, sir! Or you will find yourself the object of this poor man's lawsuit! Leave me, as I prepare to remove this man's badly damaged arm. And make sure this Magist remains on the premises for when the police arrive."

After this statement, the doctor requested that one of the bishop's priests—who were attending him—summon the Gendarmes, as he continued preparations for the bishop's operation.

Pierre took the opportunity before the police arrived to have a word with Besa. The girl was already crying.

"Papa, what are we going to do?" she asked.

"The first thing you must do, Besa, is calm down," said Pierre, kneeling and grasping her by the shoulders.

"But Papa, the police..."

"Never mind about the police. I need you to be calm and clear-headed for both of us, because I need you to do something for me. Something very important."

"What is that, Papa?"

"I need you to take the Book of Taalu back to the house and place it in the safe. Felix—"

"But I don't want to leave you, Papa! I'm afraid of what might happen to you!"

"That is precisely why you must leave, and leave now, my child."

"But, Papa, I—"

"Go now, Besa. Right now. Before the Gendarmes arrive. I don't even want to think what they'd do to you, if they got their hands on you." He approached his friend, Dooley, who stood by the door. "Please make sure she gets out to the carriage, my friend."

Dooley was initially apprehensive, but finally he opened the door and led the girl out of the room. When they got to the door leading out of the grand salon, Dooley gave Besa a warning.

"You must take care to move as quickly as possible, child. And under no circumstances are you to lean your head out of the carriage. Just hold on to the reins and let the horse get you home." Besa stepped out of the door without replying.

She was determined not to let her father down. But when she reached the carriage, she breathed a sigh of relief, because Felix was already seated at the reins, with the horse he'd ridden to get there tied to the back. "Felix, how did you—"

"Hurry and get in, Besa! No time to explain."

Just as she was about to mount the carriage, she remembered something. "I must go back! Papa forgot to give me the combination to the safe!" When she turned to go back, Felix reached over and grasped her arm.

"There's no need, Besa. I have the combination. Get in! We must hurry!"

When Besa mounted the carriage, Felix handed her a black cape with a hood. "Put in on and keep the hood up." With Besa seated and so attired, the carriage took off at a brisk pace. They slowed when they passed the Gendarmes, who were on their way to Captain Saurvet's residence.

Besa burst into tears when she saw them.

"Besa, please!" whispered the behike. "We must not call attention to ourselves!"

"But what will become of Papa? That doctor called him a creature!"

"We can't control that, Besa. But I know that Pierre would want you to be safe," replied Felix, as they pulled into the stable yard of the Melponte residence. Once Juan took possession of the carriage, Felix and Besa made their way into the house. When Besa came through the front foyer, she handed her cloak to one of the downstairs servants and turned toward her father's library, hugging the book of Taalu to her chest.

"If you will give me the book, Besa," said Felix, "I will make sure to place it into the safe."

"No," replied Besa, going past him. "Papa charged me with placing it into the safe."

Felix simply sighed and followed the determined girl into the library. She yet clutched the book to her chest as the behike entered. When he opened the safe, she reluctantly placed the book of Taalu inside. She then burst into tears and ran up the stairs to her room.

A bit later, Miss Maymi knocked on Besa's door and informed her that her dinner tray waited outside. She got no reply, but when one of the kitchen assistants returned a few hours later, the tray sat in the same spot, but empty.

Felix didn't receive the full story of the evening until the next morning.

~

HE BROUGHT her breakfast later that morning because Besa was too upset to go to school.

"Your father wouldn't be happy that you're missing school, Besa," he told her, as he sat the breakfast tray down on the side table beside her bed.

"Papa is probably unhappy about a lot of things right now," replied Besa, grabbing a piece of toast and stared at it as she spoke. "The least of which is whether I attended school today."

"You know that's not true, Besa," replied Felix, taking the toast from her hand and spreading jam on it. "Pierre would be very much concerned about your studies."

"Can't you understand that I can't just go and sit in class?" replied Besa, taking back the toast but not eating it. "Not when I don't know if Papa is being treated well?"

"Can you tell me what happened once the doctor arrived?"

This request helped to keep Besa from crying again. She picked up her cup of tea, but soon set it aside too.

"When Dr. Robichaud arrived and saw the bishop's injury, he asked what type of beast had caused it. When Miles Bradford told him that some type of light had done it, the doctor refused to believe that a light could cause such damage, while Mr. Bradford insisted that it had. Throughout this whole exchange with Dr. Robichaux, Papa kept himself well back away from the scene, but for the sake of clarification, he stepped forward and explained that the Taafli was not simply a light, but was a powerful entity. But the doctor did not listen to Papa's explanation; he took issue with Papa being a negro and asked Mr. Bradford what Papa had to do with the bishop's injuries. When Mr. Bradford explained that they'd hired Papa to raise the captain's spirit, the doctor flew into a rage, saying they should not have allowed such a creature into a noble gentleman's house. After that, he sent for the Gendarmes and ordered them to not let Papa leave until they arrived. That's when Papa gave me the book and sent me to the carriage."

"You have carried yourself very well through all this, Besa, and it's time you learned that the book of Taalu is not really a book; it's a gateway into the Taafli's realm."

"So when the bishop grabbed the book, he was blocking its path home?" asked Besa.

"Yes," replied Felix. "You must be strong, Besa. For Pierre's sake. You can stay home for a couple days, then you must return to school. Eat your breakfast before your tea gets cold."

"Will you try and find out if Papa is being treated well, Felix? Otherwise, I won't be able to eat or go back to school."

"I promise to do the best I can, Besa."

Two days later, when Besa returned to class, Margaret noted that she was not herself. She had not remembered to do her homework and offered no explanation to Mr. Willoughby, their dark studies teacher, and she barely said anything when she came to their usual spot at recess—the wooden table near the back wall of the playground. "Besa, are you ill?" asked Margaret.

"No," said Besa. "Papa took me to one of his enchantment ceremonies the other night."

"But I thought he... Isn't that a good thing?" Margaret was shocked when her friend burst into tears. She'd never even seen Besa get angry, so tears caught her off guard, and she didn't know what to do.

At that moment, Dickey and a group of the third years ran by, oblivious to Besa's crisis.

"Dickey!" yelled Margaret. The boy stopped and looked at her and also noticed Besa. He turned and ran to the table.

"Hey...I...Besa's crying? I—I don't understand."

"Sit down and shut up, Dickey!" Margaret told him. Dickey did as instructed.

"But—Besa doesn't cry. Does she?"

"Obviously she does. We're looking at her. She told me her papa took her to an enchantment ceremony the other night."

"But—. What? Really? But that should be a good thing. Shouldn't it?"

"I'm guessing that it wasn't," replied Margaret. "Or she wouldn't be crying."

"You're right," said Dickey. "It's still strange seeing her like this."

"If you give her a moment, I'm sure she'll stop and tell us why."

When Besa finally calmed down, she told her two friends everything that happened on that night.

"But that's not right," said Margaret. "Your father didn't cause the bishop's injuries."

"That's not how the doctor saw it. He said they never should have let a creature like Papa—"

"Okay, Besa," replied Margaret, wrapping her friend in a hug to keep her from crying again. "Dickey, give me one of your handkerchiefs."

"But I've only got one!" cried the boy.

"Dickey! I swear, I'm going to—!"

"All right! You don't have to threaten me!" He took a monogrammed cloth out of his vest pocket. "I want her to stop crying too. I'm sorry about your father, Besa. Do we know where he's being held?"

"Probably at the Magists compound on Chef Menteur road," replied Margaret. "That's where they keep the most powerful Magists."

"Will they at least let you see him, Besa?"

"Stop it, Dickey. You know they don't allow visitors."

"I don't know why. Other prisoners' families get to visit their father, brother or mother. "

"But those people aren't Magists, Dickey."

"But how do we know if he's all—"

"Shut up! You're not helping!" said Margaret.

"Oh! Sorry!" replied the teen, when he noticed Besa on the verge of tears again.

When Besa got home from school, Felix still had no information about her father's status.

BESA RECEIVED a visitor in her dream that night. She, Dickey and Margaret had paddled deep into the cypress swamp—a trip her father would've never allowed her to take while awake—when a giant, golden dragonfly fluttered out of one of the cypresses and hovered above them.

"It was good to finally meet you, Besa," said the Taafli. "Hopefully we will have lots of fun together."

Its voice was a chorus of many.

"What's your name?" asked Besa. The creature shifted into different shades of gold, possibly a sign of delight.

"We are too numerous to name. But tell us, what is your favorite color?"

"I'm fond of violet," replied Besa. The creature quickly shifted into the most brilliant violet gold Besa had ever seen. "That is beautiful."

"Thank you," it replied. "We shall be violet for you."

Then fluttered off toward the trees.

"When will I see you again?" asked Besa.

"Only you can decide that," said Violet, and disappeared. That's when Besa made a decision.

CHAPTER 3
THE IDEA

One of Besa's two closest friends at Sister Gerard's School for Magist Children, was a tall, pudgy blond Irish boy named Dickey O'Brien. Dickey had earned the nickname, butter boy, from his classmates, because his mother, Sofia O'Brien, doted on her youngest child and feared he might grow hungry while at school. So, every day she brought freshly baked bread and a jar of butter. Even after Dickey pleaded with her to stop.

The second was a slim, red-headed, slightly freckled, light-skinned creole witch-in-training named, Margaret Claiborne. Margaret's father was an Episcopal minister who became distressed when his youngest child could fly almost before she could walk.

Besa had pondered her decision for a week, before she decided to broach it to her friends at recess.

"I have decided that I cannot be sad anymore," she told Margaret, as they lounged on the wooden bench near the back wall of the playground, watching Dickey play a game of Catch-the-Sprite, with a group of third years. "Felix told me that I must be strong, for Papa."

"Okay. That sounds like a good idea," replied Margaret.

"I have also decided that I will not be afraid of the Gendarmes, and I will honor Papa in the best way I know how."

"What do you mean?" asked Margaret, with half an eye on the action. "This is a stupid game!" she said. "Sprites are almost impossible to see in the daylight. I'm sorry Besa. What was that about your papa?"

"I said I will not be afraid of the Gendarmes, and I want to honor Papa in the best way I can."

"Really?" said Margaret. "How are you going to do that?" Suddenly something buzzed past Margaret's ear and landed on the table. It was a Sprite. It was no bigger than the size of a child's thumb. It made eye contact with Besa and gave off a musical hum, and then Dickey landed on the table in pursuit of it. He slid over the side as the Sprite escaped just in time.

"Dickey," said a perturbed Margaret, "aren't you a little old to be running around like this? Besa was about to tell me something amazing."

"I'm sorry," said Dickey, dusting himself off. "But isn't this recess?" And then Besa gave him a rueful smile. Something about it made Dickey pause, "Oh, hi, Besa. Margaret said you have something amazing to tell us?" Besa repeated her announcement.

"Wow!" replied Dickey. "How are you going to do that?"

"I'm going to be a Necromancer!"

"What?!" said Dickey and Margaret together. It was at that moment the Sprite landed on Dickey's hat and an eight-year-old sorceress whacked him over the head with a butterfly net.

"Ow!" cried Dickey, who extricated himself from the net and informed the children and the sprite that he was quitting the game for today. Margaret gave him an it-serves-you-right look.

"But aren't you afraid that the Gendarmes will come and take you away too?" asked Dickey.

"I suppose I should be," said Besa. "But the only Magists in danger of that are those who cause harm. I'm not going to do that."

"That makes sense," said Margaret.

"And even though the ceremony ended badly, it showed me what Papa is and what he does, so now I know what I am and what I'm meant to do."

"That is very courageous of you, Besa," said Margaret.

"I'm a necromancer. It's in my blood. The Gendarmes can't stop that. So I'm going to raise the spirits of the dead, just like my papa did. And I want you two to come along with me."

"How's this supposed to work?" asked Dickey. "What are we going to be doing?"

"I figured the best way we can perform this task is to go into graveyards at night and open some tombs. There are a lot of graveyards here in Newald. We won't have to worry about subjects to practice on."

"Oh, my," replied Margaret, with an excited look in her eyes. "I'm all for practicing. I will definitely go with you, Besa."

"Why would we have to go to graveyards?" asked Dickey. "Those places are spooky. Why don't we just go to people's houses, like your father did?"

"Because I don't want many people to know I'm doing this, Dickey."

"Why not? Wouldn't you be performing a service to the community?"

"You are such a dough head, Dickey. She needs to be careful not to draw attention to herself."

"Then maybe she shouldn't do it? I, for one, don't want to go into graveyards at night. Those places are scary!"

"I can't believe you're a Titan," said Margaret. "You are the most cowardly Magist I know."

"I am not a coward! I'm just being practical. Graveyards are full of dead people. I don't like dead people!"

"I just realized something. You are nothing but a gigantic stuffed chicken, full of butter and bread. Which is a weird image, because it would make you totally delicious."

"Stop it!" cried Dickey. "Now you've made me hungry!"

"Can we please focus on what we were discussing?" asked Besa, exasperated by these two.

"I say we vote on it," declared Margaret. "I vote yes!"

"I vote yes, too," replied Besa.

"Wait a minute! That's not fair," complained Dickey. "I was going to vote...something different. Can we vote again? We also need Mokheer's vote."

"Do you really think Mokheer is going to vote against Besa?"

"You don't know that, miss quick-voter-person. We should at least get his opinion."

Mokheer wasn't a day creature, so they would have to wait until dark to bring the idea to the Warlock boy. He'd been Besa's friend since she was two, and he floated up through the window of her playroom and kept her company at night.

After school they all congregated at the benches under the magnolia tree in the garden behind the Melponte house.

That and the lofts above the horse barn, had been their favorite places to meet. Mostly because Pierre hadn't allowed Besa to venture very far from the house. That was different now. A kitchen assistant brought them a tray of Miss Maymi's delicious tea cakes. She always managed to rustle something together when Besa's friends came over.

When the moon came up, a tall, brown boy wearing long breeches, a tail coat and vest, appeared right behind Dickey.

"Of course, I'm going to vote yes," said Mokheer. Dickey startled.

"Why do you do that?" cried Dickey, almost choking on his fifth tea cake.

"Because you shouldn't wolf down your food like that," replied Mokheer.

"What do you know about food?" retorted Dickey. "Do you even eat?"

"Of course, I eat. You should come to one of my family dinners. My mother would love to serve you."

"Never mind. I don't want to end up in a cauldron."

"Pity. My mother has a platter that would just fit you."

"Why do you come here? Shouldn't you be locked in a crypt somewhere?"

Mokheer always smiled when Dickey tried to take a low blow.

"Like I said. I am voting yes."

"How do you even know what we're voting about?" sneered Dickey.

"Okay. Let's say I don't know. What's your vote?"

"Nunya business, ghost boy," replied Dickey, folding his arms and looking smug.

"For the record: Whatever Dickey votes, I'm going the other way."

"Then I vote yes!" replied Dickey, with a smile.

"I vote yes too," replied Margaret.

"I'm voting yes, too," said Besa.

"And I'm voting no," said Mokheer. "I guess you win, Dickey."

"Yeses win!" declared Margaret, who ran over and gave Dickey a hug. "I knew you'd come to your senses, butter boy!"

Dickey only stood there and moped, knowing he'd been outflanked by Mokheer again.

"I like your idea, Besa," said Mokheer, coming to touch her on the nose (this always gave her a strange type of charge). "I guess it's time you took hold of your legacy. But are sure you want to be out that late? Because it will have to be midnight when we do this."

"What?" cried Dickey. "If the people are already dead, what does it matter? Eight o'clock should be good enough. It's dark by then."

"You're a Magist too, Dickey," said Margaret. "And we all know that most spells work better after midnight."

"Can anyone tell me who decided that? This is insane!"

"That's because it's been that way for thousands of years, you stuffed chicken!"

"That reminds me, I need to get home for dinner," said Dickey, trotting off towards the stable to retrieve his horse.

"It doesn't matter what time we do it," said Margaret. "He's still going to be scared."

"First of all," Besa told Mokheer. "I will be fine being up that late. I'm up that late reading most nights, anyway."

"Don't worry my little princess. I will protect you," said Mokheer, his arm around her shoulder.

"Don't do that," said Besa, pulling away from him. I don't need protecting. I'm not some damsel in distress."

He didn't respond, just raised his eyebrows—or what passed for eyebrows on an entity such as he.

"I said I liked the idea. What's a damsel?"

He was serious about that. Even with the support and friendship Mokheer gave her, Besa couldn't tell where he came from. He called himself a warlock child, but she knew other warlock children who walked in the daylight.

He'd just appeared in her playroom one day, and it never occurred to her to be afraid. And now, she didn't know what she'd do without his calm, knowledgeable presence.

"It's decided," said Margaret. "We go at midnight, starting when?"

"All Hallows Eve is coming up in a week," replied Mokheer. "Midnight on All Hallows Eve will be perfect."

"Dickey's going to faint when he hears that."

They all laughed then, knowing that he would.

"There's just one more detail you have to help me with, Mokheer."

"What detail is that, my princess of the night?"

"You have to help me steal The Book of Taalu from my papa's safe. I know you can walk through walls of granite, but what about steel?"

"Besa," said Margaret. "Maybe we can find you a book of your own."

"The bishop is already trying that," replied Mokheer.

"He is?"

"Yes. With limited success. But you won't have to."

"How do you know that, Mokheer?"

"Because your power is different from your father's, Besa."

"What do you mean by that?"

"I can't explain everything about why or how I know

something," he said. "But I've known this about you since you were very small. It has something to do with why I was drawn to you. At least that's how I understand it."

"That's a bit strange, don't you think?" asked Margaret.

"Stranger than going into graveyards and breaking into tombs?"

"I guess not. When you put it that way."

At this point, Felix came out and informed Besa that her dinner was ready. She wanted to say, "I'm not hungry," so she could stay out later. But Felix would see right through that.

"I guess I'd better get going too," said Margaret. "I get a little floaty when I'm hungry."

She'd started to hover off the ground a bit.

"Good night then," Besa told her, pulling her to the ground with a gentle embrace. "I'll see you at school tomorrow."

Mokheer wasn't much for hugs. He just disappeared when he was ready to leave.

"So much for goodbyes," said Besa, looking at the spot where he'd been just a second ago. "I guess I'll see you when you show up again."

DICKEY THE TURKEY

Dickey was not a chicken. He didn't care what Margaret said. Okay, he did care. But only when she said something nice about him. This was rare, so he settled for her not saying anything bad. Tonight, would not be counted for that. And he definitely was not a chicken. He was really a fat juicy turkey, as his brother Francisco referred to him, when they were in their uncle's fencing Salle.

"You are so easy to skewer, Ricardo." His uncle Diego preferred referring to Dickey by that name, rather than Richard, which his father had chosen. His father often lingered at the courthouse well into the evening. That's when his mother's brother would take him under his wing —he and his fourth oldest brother, known as Francis when the judge was around. But in their uncle's care they were both Francisco and Ricardo.

Don Diego had been a swordsman in the court of one of the Spanish Kings. Dickey couldn't remember which. Even Don Diego had said it was one of the ones not named Phillip. He'd lost track of which one. But it didn't matter in the Salle.

His uncle only required that he use circular parry against Francisco, and hold his ground. But Francisco was faster than he. And thank goodness uncle Diego had not allowed him to strike Dickey above the neck. But the foil had poked and jabbed him everywhere that the plastron on his chest left an opening. Worst of all, he was a better swordsman than Francisco, who rarely practiced and had a lazy "en garde" stance, as his uncle called it. But he was a lot taller than Dickey, and thirty pounds of muscle heavier. "Use your skill, Ricardo!" his uncle called when they were in a bout. "Don't let him insult you with his slovenly technique!"

In the beginning, Dickey had gotten in some good strikes. But that only angered Francisco, who made sure to punish his younger brother.

"Don't show him your fear, Ricardo! He is a sloppy fighter and is making you look bad!"

"You are a turkey, Ricardo," his brother taunted under his breath. "That's why you will never get a kiss from sweet Margaret! You are a fat turkey on a skewer. Like father makes in the fireplace during Christmas."

It was a silly taunt. Margaret was anything but sweet. But it still stung—because it was true. He would probably never win a kiss from his fiery red-headed witch. Dickey had gotten him with a good strike to the shoulder for that one and had even dodged his brother's awkward retaliatory charge. Dickey struck him again in the side.

"Bravo! Ricardo!" said his uncle. "Stay one step ahead of him. Good job, son! That's showing him!"

But Dickey knew that Francisco would simply ambush him in the hall at home. Right before they went to bed, while his mother wasn't looking. Francis would catch him in a stranglehold from behind and start punching him in his back and his side.

"Every time you do that, you're going to suffer, you fat turkey!" Francis would say.

This is the life I have, thought Dickey. I can't even defend myself properly.

He could make himself bigger and fight back, but mother told him he shouldn't do that in the house. "You shouldn't use your extra strength against your brother, Dickey," she'd told him. "You might hurt him. And then you'd feel bad." Dickey was thinking that he wouldn't feel any worse than his brother did when he hurt him. And if he cried, his brother just called him a whiny cry-baby. "A cry-baby turkey!" Francis would say, proud of himself for coming up with that barb. There weren't many paths out of a life like this. His only option was to shift and drive Francis into a wall and tell him to cut it out! He wasn't prepared to take that step yet, and Francis benefitted from his apprehension.

This was why he played so hard at recess. The third-years wouldn't question him about his tortured home life. Their only requirement was that he simply play. That was good enough for him. He could oblige them. The only one bothered by it seemed to be Margaret. He could ignore her criticisms, though, because Besa was amused by all the fun he had. That gave him a cushion against Margaret. That added a bit of joy to his gallivants with the third-years. And with the way Besa's life had gone lately—

her father locked up—it was the least he could do.

He often had vigorous and rewarding training sessions with his uncle. "You are getting a lot better, Ricardo," he'd tell him. "Your en garde and parry are almost perfect. You should have no problem with Francisco in your next bout. Just hold your ground and defeat him." Dickey knew it wasn't that simple. But he liked to hear his uncle say it. When Francisco came, he would turn it all around on him.

MARGARET AND THE RICH GIRL

Margaret rarely spoke during supper in the evenings. Her three brothers did most of the talking when they sat down. Alfred, the oldest, was apprenticing with a carpenter that attended her father's church. William, the second oldest, was a clerk for a prominent solicitor in town, while Joseph, the youngest next to her, had nearly finished with school and would attend the crown's service-academy for a life as a military officer. Her father could not afford the price of the commission, but Maximillian Larue—a wealthy friend of her father's—was acting as his sponsor. "And what do you want to do, Maggie?" her mother once asked her.

"I haven't thought about it, mother. I'm only fourteen," she replied.

Madam Clouseau, a dress designer and also a member of her father's congregation, had already offered Margaret a path to follow. "All the other girls your age have started an apprenticeship. But you want to spend all your time with that rich girl."

"She is not rich, mother. She is wealthy. That is better than rich."

"And how does that help you, Maggie? There is nothing she can do for you, but remind you that she will never need to work."

"She's doing no such thing, mother."

"Then what is she doing for you?"

"She is being my friend, and I am hers."

"That's won't put food on your table, girl! Friends have a way of interfering with your future, child."

"If you want, mother, I can do the after-dinner cleanup alone," said Margaret, by way of changing the subject.

"All right," her mother replied. Unable to turn down the offer. "But this discussion is far from over."

Most of the time, her mother would've stayed and helped, anyway. The fact that she didn't spoke to how tired she was. Betsy Claiborne was a lean, mixed, middle-aged woman who worked six days a week cutting and designing patterns for Madame Clouseau. She then went on her church's sick and destitute mission in the evenings. Margaret didn't know what she wanted to do with her life, but she certainly didn't want her mother's path.

She'd had a chance to tag along with William a few times during the summer as he went about his clerking tasks for Hoffman, La Salle, and Delisle. Her brother was impressed that she'd understood the complicated briefs they often filed with the Judge Magistrate's office. "So, do all these documents go to Dickey's father?" she'd asked.

William had laughed at the suggestion. "I should hope not. Judge O'Brien presides over criminal, civil and some family law. Hoffman, La Salle, and Delisle focuses on wills and trusts–formally referred to as probate."

"I like these brief things," she replied. "Maybe I can be someone's clerk someday."

"You've always had a keen mind, Maggie. But there are

no female barristers. Not that I know of. And most clerks are just awaiting their chance to read the law."

"Is that what you're doing, William?" she asked. "Waiting for your chance to read the law?"

"That is exactly what I'm doing, Maggie. And take heart. If you marry your friend Dickey, you will more than likely be a barrister's, and eventually a judge's wife."

"Or I could be a clerk at your firm," replied Margaret.

William had a big laugh, like their father.

"You've always been such a precocious little sister! We will have to see. Let's go find some tea and beignets, my treat!"

Already a tall, strong man, he lifted her off her feet and spun her around as they walked up Royal toward Bourbon Street. She would love to work with William; he was the first to recognize her mind and gave her books to read that challenged her and made her think. Her mother often cautioned him when she heard him complimenting Margaret's intelligence. "Reading will come in handy at Madame Clouseau's," she'd said.

Margaret's heart sank when she contemplated such a dreadful future.

"You'd think she'd want a better life for her only daughter," she'd whispered to William, as they sat at the dinner table that next night.

"I don't think she expected a girl when you came along," he replied. "Especially one as smart as you are."

Margaret had smiled and then looked down when her mother scowled at her.

"Putting ideas in her head is only setting her up for disappointment, William."

"William is going to let me clerk in his law office one day," said Margaret.

Her mother just rolled her eyes.

"The court sentences you to clear up and put away the dinner dishes," her mother replied. Richard and Joseph couldn't help but laugh. Their mother wasn't known for her humor. Margaret didn't see anything funny, and moped as she went about her task. She would give anything to have servants like Besa. She definitely wouldn't say something like that around her mother. Ordinarily she would whisper a spell, and the dishes jumped into the dish tub and began washing themselves. Her mother scolded her if she caught her skating by like that.

FOUR

A month after the incident at the Saurvet residence, there was an insistent knock on the front door of the Melponte mansion. When it wasn't answered promptly, a loud banging ensued, possibly with some type of object. The noise echoed so that Besa came onto the landing of the stairs of her room on the second floor and requested someone get the door. Miss Maymi, the cook, hustled out of the kitchen, furiously wiping her hands on the apron at her waist as she approached the door, intending to put herself in between whatever might cause her employer's family further harm. She reached the door at the same moment as Felix. The behike regarded the short round, tignon-headed woman as if she'd run out of the kitchen in just her under things.

"You can't be serious, woman. This is a matter for my department. Return to your stove."

"You best get yourself to that door before I do," Miss Maymi replied. The pounding increased, and she made to go past him, but he blocked her path and pulled open the door.

Constable Picard stood on the doorstep, a wide, heavy-gutted man, who on most evenings such as this, could be found chugging "le petit goyave" at Thiot's Café on St Philip's. He was not happy being sent on such a mission. Cajuns would not approach Magists if they could help it. He was sweating like a bull, but had three men with him and was determined not to show his fear.

"We have a document for the child and her guardian."

"That would be me," said Felix, aware that Miss Maymi was perched just off his left shoulder, looking for any sign that she should intercede. "I'm her guardian."

The Cajun pulled some papers out of the breast pocket of his coat, looked at them and then presented them to the butler.

"You've been served," said the Cajun. "The bishop is suing her."

Miss Maymi sprang.

"You must be out yo'—"

Felix snatched the papers and shut the door.

"Are you trying to get yourself taken to jail, Miss Maymi?" Felix asked. "Because negroes cannot speak to white people in such a way in this city. Please go back to your kitchen and let me do my job. This is going to be hard enough for Besa."

Miss Maymi conceded his point with a sigh and retreated back to her ovens. More knocking was heard at the door.

"You must sign the certificate of acceptance, sir!"

Felix opened it calmly.

"I shall make sure the child receives it."

THE BISHOP SUES NEGRO MAGIST FOR DAMAGES!

Read the next day's headlines

Felix had initially attempted to shield Besa from the lawsuit, not wanting to exacerbate the fragility of her grief. That lasted a week until Besa caught part of a newspaper that blew into the carriage as they drove home from school one day. Felix would have liked to take it out of her hand, but there was a newsstand along their path as well.

"It says here that this bishop is suing me," Besa said, looking at Felix.

"Not really you, just your father's estate," replied Felix

"How could you even say something like that to me?" replied Besa, glaring at him. "I am my father's estate."

"I didn't want to upset you, Besa. You were already grieving."

"Please drive over to Mr. Lexington's office."

"You want to do that now? Shouldn't we go home first?"

"This paper is a week old," she said, holding it out to him. "Were you waiting for them to drag me into court?"

"I guess I didn't handle it well," admitted her guardian.

"Turn left here," Besa directed. "Hopefully, his office is still open."

When they entered the office, Mr. Lexington stood up, seeing the girl was in distress. "Benjamin," he said to one of his assistants. "Please bring Miss Melponte a cup of tea.

Would you like some cookies with that, mademoiselle?" he asked, as he presented her with his own chair.

"Thank you," said Besa, sitting down.

"What can I do for you?"

"This blew into our carriage as we were going home," said Besa, handing him the section of newspaper. Benjamin arrived with tea and cookies. "Thank you, Bejamin," she said, setting the cup on the desk and taking a cookie from the tea service tray.

"Oh, my goodness," replied Mr. Lexington as he began to read. He was a somewhat portly man with mutton chops and a goatee. "We need to be very careful with this, Besa. Where is the copy of the summons?"

Felix pulled it out of the inner pocket of his coat and handed it to the gentleman.

"I should have received this document within hours after you did, sir. Was it your intention to ignore this?"

"I don't know," replied Felix. "They can't sue a child, can they?"

"They are not suing the child. They are seeking redress from the estate! And since she is the only living heir, they can most definitely sue her! You have not made this easy. We have three days to reply, or they could've ruled against her and seized her assets!"

"What? I never intended any harm to—"

"From now on, I am to receive any legal documents right after you do!"

"In Felix's defense," said Besa, taking a sip of tea. "He was just trying to shield me from reminders of Papa's confinement."

"He almost caused another disaster. Why don't you both go home while I draft the appropriate response," suggested Mr. Lexington. "It's a good thing you caught that newspaper, Besa," he told her.

"Yes, it was," she replied.

~

Mr. Lexington finished drafting the response by the next morning and had his assistant file it with the court. The date was set for the case to go to trial by the end of the month. And while her guardian had attempted to shield her from this matter, as the sole Melponte heir, she would be compelled to attend the trial, and possibly be called as a material witness.

~

Mr. Lexington spent the rest of the mouth coaching Besa on courtroom etiquette: How to properly address the judge. How to stay calm and engaged if she was called as a witness. "Don't dress too flashy. Choose something pretty but respectable."

"What do you mean?" asked Besa. "All my clothes are respectable."

"What I mean is, don't wear one of your ball gowns," replied Mr. Lexington. "You must always look like you're interested in the proceedings. Don't pout or look bored."

"You're giving these instructions to Felix as well, right? He is my guardian."

"No. I will not," replied Mr. Lexington. "Felix is not a witness. The only thing Judge O'Brien will need Felix to do is escort you to the courthouse."

"Dickey's father is the judge?" cried Besa.

"Yes. There is no way to change that. He's the Magistrate. Since you and the estate are on trial, the plaintiff gets to call witnesses first."

~

ON THE DAY of the trial, the lobby outside the courtroom was crowded with people.

"Is there a big murder trial happening today as well?" asked Besa.

"No, Besa. I think we are the only case on the docket today," replied Mr. Lexington. "The bishop is a very influential person in this city. They're probably here to see him get justice."

"But what about, Papa?" asked Besa. "When does he get justice?"

"Unfortunately, we are not trying that case today. Let's go inside."

They pushed through the doors and entered the courtroom.

When Besa attempted to take a seat among the spectators, Mr. Lexington informed her, "You and Felix must sit up front with me, Besa."

Once the judge entered, Peter Fontenot, the bailiff, ordered,

"All rise for the honorable William O'Brien, magistrate of the crown's sixth judicial district!"

"You may be seated," said the judge as he took his own seat. "Before we begin," he said. "I would ask the two solicitors to approach the bench." Both attorneys obliged.

"Good evening, Miles and Darwin."

"Your honor," replied the solicitors in unison.

"I've called you both up here so that I might set the tone for these proceedings. This is obviously a fraught situation, with one man maimed and the other jailed because of it. I would ask that you both control your client as best you can. I know everyone wants to be whole."

"Respectfully, your honor," replied Mr. Fairfield. "My client has lost a significant part of himself."

"Respectfully, your honor," replied Mr. Lexington. "My client has lost a great deal as well."

"She has all of her arms and legs, your honor! At least, she appears to."

"What does that mean?" demanded Mr. Lexington.

"It means that I see how this is going to go," said the judge. "I had hoped we could do this in a cordial manner for a change. I guess not. Meeting adjourned, gentlemen. Back to your tables. Mr. Fairfield will start first.

"Thank you, your honor," replied the church's counsel. I would like to call Besa Melponte, your honor."

"Miss Melponte, please take the stand," directed the judge.

Besa looked every bit the upper-class young woman in her elegant but understated periwinkle dress and brown leather ankle boots with silver side buttons. She cut quite the confident and serious figure as she took her oath, sat regally and regarded the solicitor with her steady green-eyed gaze."

"Miss Melponte," began Mr. Fairfield. "On the night you and your father injured my client, were you aware—"

"I object, your honor!" cried Mr. Lexington. "Please inform the Church's representative that this is not a criminal trial! And even if it was, this girl is not implicated in any wrongdoing!"

"I concur with Mr. Lexington's statement. You are here to gather information in a case for material damages, sir. Not to indict a witness."

"If it pleases the court, I shall re-phrase my question," replied Mr. Fairfield. "Miss Melponte, on the night you and your father entered the salon of Monsieur Saurvet, were you aware of Bishop Delacroix's presence there?"

"Yes sir, we were aware," said Besa.

"How did you know? And wasn't your father angered by his presence?"

"Your honor, I object!" said Mr. Lexington. "Counsel is trying to set a trap for my client!"

"I will allow it," said the judge. "But I'm warning you, counsel. These tactics are not strengthening your case. Answer as best you can, Miss Melponte."

"Thank you, your honor," said Mr. Fairfield.

"Yes, we were aware that the bishop was in attendance on that night. And my father wasn't angry that the bishop was there. He was afraid."

"And why was that, girl?" asked Mr. Fairfield.

"Because Papa knew the bishop had a negative opinion of Magists. He even tried to send me home, but I convinced him I would be fine. And even though the evening ended badly, I was never afraid. Papa did everything he could to prevent what happened to the bishop."

"I seriously doubt that," replied Mr. Fairfield. "Isn't it true that you made hateful statements to the bishop on that night?"

"I certainly did not!" said Besa. "I barely saw him. Papa kept me in the background. I was only allowed to view the proceedings through a hand mirror Papa gave me."

"That sounds unlikely," retorted Mr. Fairfield. "So, you concede that the actions your father took that evening ended badly for the bishop? Those were your words. Were they not?"

"It doesn't matter how you twist my words, sir," replied Besa. "My father took the action he was hired to take. And the Saurvet family was happy with the results. Mister Bradford will attest to that. Papa had no control over the bishop's actions and all that occurred after."

"Thank you. That will be all, girl. I think we have proved our case. The plaintiff rests."

"You may return to your seat, Miss Melponte," said the judge. Besa did so without comment.

"You may call your first witness, Mr. Lexington," said the judge.

Mr. Lexington stood up and looked at the courtroom.

"Your honor, I would like to call Bishop André Delacroix."

The bishop entered the court room accompanied by a large contingent of priests.

When he sat on the witness stand and saw Besa sitting in the seat next to Mr. Lexington's chair, he knew this was likely the necromancer's daughter, so he made sure to scowl at her.

Then Peter, the bailiff, approached him. The bailiff of the court had been a young altar boy in Delacroix's parish when he was still a priest and had received numerous beatings at the cleric's hand; and he appeared yet afraid of the looming, dark frocked figure.

"Will you...uh, raise your h-hand...?" requested the bailiff.

"Will I what, Peter?" replied the bishop. "What is this for, son?"

"F-for you...to uh, sw-swear on the...uh, bible, sir?"

"Is this necessary?" snapped the bishop. "Why am I

swearing to the God I represent? This is preposterous! I was injured trying to intervene in a demonic ceremony performed by this child's father. Is that in doubt?"

"Calm yourself, André," ordered the judge. "You are not the authority in this venue. I am. And you will abide by its tenets, or I will dismiss this matter."

The bishop grudgingly consented to the oath, and was thanked profusely by Peter, the bailiff. This caused Judge O'Brien to eye his subordinate suspiciously.

This was the first time Besa had gotten a good look at the bishop since Doctor Robichaud took his arm off. She found him very distinguished looking in his black hooded cowl and gold crucifix around his neck; and he was almost as tall as her papa. Mr. Lexington approached:

"Good afternoon, Your Grace. I just have a few questions that should help us settle this matter. Your excellency, are you asserting that you were injured on Aug 29th, during a ceremony performed by my client's father, Pierre Melponte?"

"I do assert," replied the bishop warily. "And I have a missing limb to prove my assertion."

"Can you give us the details of that evening, sir? To the best of your recollection."

"I most certainly can," replied the bishop. "It was the night of the horrific hurricane and shipwreck out in the Gulf. And I received word that among the casualties was a parishioner and gentleman of the highest character, Monsieur Jean Saurvet. Once Monsieur Saurvet's body was retrieved and returned to his family, he lay in state in the war salon of his residence. As his spiritual counselor, I was, of course, summoned to administer last rites and perform the Absolution. I was in preparation for this process, when the negro witch doctor intruded upon the scene."

"So, you are asserting that Mr. Melponte was an uninvited guest that evening?" The bishop sat glowering at Mr. Lexington.

"He was an unnecessary guest, sir."

"But was he there at the behest of Madame Saurvet?"

"The poor woman was in shock, and had obviously been coerced by a corrupt business associate of Monsieur Saurvet."

"But you were the church's representative at the ceremony."

"A demonic ceremony, sir. With Satan's practitioner conducting it!"

"But I am confused, Your Grace," retorted Mr. Lexington, his gaze now sternly upon the bishop. "How could such a ceremony have occurred—with you, the church's highest appointed official, in attendance?" The bishop's face devolved into the consistency of stone, and his eyes projected death. "Were there perhaps some words between yourself and Mr. Bradford that made you consent to this demonic ceremony? I, in fact, have signed statements from Mr. Bradford and Geneviève Saurvet, attesting to that very fact. And if it pleases the court, I would like to enter these documents as evidence."

Delacroix's expression went very pale. "I am calling a recess!" he declared, standing up. "So that I may consult with my attorney!" He moved quickly toward the door out of the courtroom, as Mr. Fairfield—looking just as surprised as the judge—got up to go with him. But the bishop had a desperate trick up his sleeve. He spun around, wrapped his one arm around Besa's throat from behind, and snatched her up out of her chair.

"Don't anyone move!" he directed. "Or I will crush her

throat! I can see the way this is going. I will not get justice here!"

Another older priest, who came in with the entourage, raced across the courtroom toward the bishop.

"André!" cried the man. "Have you lost your senses? Unhand that child at once!"

"Shut up, Michel!" replied the bishop. "This has nothing to do with you!"

"André. You can't seriously be considering harming a child," replied Michel. "You're the bishop, for Christ's sake! Think of your standing in the community. You could be excommunicated!"

"Not for one negro, Michel. The church will not care one way or the other. This will be my justice against the vile man who took my arm. I lost something, and now he will lose something too!"

"You will unhand me, sir," said Besa. "Or you will pay a higher price!"

"You're in no position to threaten me, girl!" And he tightened his grip, choking her a bit.

"You obviously don't know who I am. I'm my father's daughter, and I am not threatening you!" Suddenly a Taafli rose into the air above them.

"André, look out!" cried Michel.

The entity let out a horrific screech, like a thousand eagles had descended upon the courtroom. When the bishop looked up, the Taafli gave a second screech and shot toward him. He dropped Besa and stumbled backward, running over the spectators situated behind him. He tripped over them and took half the row with him and landed in the third row behind them. He literally stepped on them in his stumbling frantic effort to get out the courtroom door.

"Keep it away from me!" he cried, ducking and dodging, and then reached out and snatched open the door. "You'll pay for this, girl! I don't care what it takes! You'll pay for this!" He could be heard as he ran screaming from the courthouse.

"What was he so afraid of?" the judge asked Mr. Fairfield.

"I'm sure I have no idea, your honor," he replied, as shocked and confused as the rest of the spectators.

"Motion to dismiss, your honor," said Mr. Lexington.

"Do you object, counsel?" asked the judge.

"I guess not, your honor," replied Mr. Fairfield.

"Then this matter is dismissed!" declared Judge O'Brien with a rap of his gavel.

Felix approached Besa and helped to her feet.

"Besa, how did you do that? I didn't know you knew how to call the Taafli. Where did you learn that?"

"Are we allowed to leave?" Besa asked Mr. Lexington.

"Yes. The case is dismissed," he replied. "Have a good evening, Miss Melponte."

"Then let's talk outside, Felix," said Besa, pushing through the courtroom door.

"Besa, are you in knowing?" asked Felix when they got outside. "How did you manage to call a Taafli?"

"No, I am not in knowing," said Besa as they made it to the carriage. "And I did not call a Taafli."

"But I just saw you do it. Everyone did."

"Not everyone, Felix. It was not for everyone to see. Only you, the bishop, and Michel saw it. To everyone else, he just looked insane."

"What are you talking about, Besa?"

"It is called a projection, Felix. The image came from the

bishop's own fears, his own mind. It only frightened him because he allowed it to. I learned it in Dark Studies."

"You learned that in school? That was impressive."

"No, it wasn't," said Besa. "It was just useful. Can we go home now?"

"Yes, we can," said Felix, slapping the reins a bit, and they headed home.

CHAPTER 5
MAGIST COUNCIL

One of Miss Maymi's kitchen assistants wheeled a serving cart into the dining room as Besa and Felix sat down to dinner that evening. She then dipped into the large pot sitting on the serving cart, filled a bowl with the delicious gumbo stew, and set it before Besa.

"Thank you, Clara," said Besa.

When the girl filled a heaping bowl for the guardian, he dug right in.

"Pass me the cornbread, please," he told Besa. She obliged, and he noticed that her food wasn't touched. "You know how Miss Maymi feels about you not eating, Besa." He took a bite of his cornbread. "This is delicious. What's the matter?"

"The matter is, I am getting behind in my studies."

"Please take a bite before it gets cold, Besa," he implored. Besa put a spoonful in her mouth.

"Happy?"

"Yes," replied Felix. "I don't want your food to get cold. If you send it all back untouched, Miss Maymi will think it's something she did."

Besa began to eat in earnest then. "I knew you were hungry."

"I am hungry," said Besa, taking a bite of her cornbread and a spoonful of gumbo. "But I'm still getting behind in my studies."

"This is a dangerous situation, Besa."

"You're the one who said Papa would be concerned about my studies," said Besa, rising to get another serving from the large pot. "Wow! There's a lot in here. Too much for just us."

Suddenly, a portal opened and sucked in Besa, Felix, and the dining table, along with all the food, and sat them down in the middle of some kind of cave-like structure. It was massive, with gas lanterns all around the bare stone walls, a clean, flat, decorated stone floor, and a massive crystal skull chandelier suspended from the twenty-foot ceiling. In between the normally formed stalactites, and on the left side of the cave, was the fully intact skeleton of a gigantic ancient beast. And even more amazing, twenty beings were seated inside the massive rib cage—literally in the beast's belly. Some of them were creatures, some were humanoid, but they were all members of the governing body called the Magist Council. And seated within the intact skull and tusks of the ancient beast, was a giant white werewolf—Septimius Seuz, the council president. At the sight of the monster, Besa gasped and ran to hide behind Felix.

"Good evening, Melponte family," said Seuz.

"What is the meaning of this, Seuz!" demanded Felix.

"I don't know about you, Septimius," said a slim black man dressed in a blue silk tail coat, cotton twill trousers, and a cut-velvet patterned vest. "But they got here just in time!" He approached the serving cart. "Is that gumbo? I am starved!"

"Stand back fool! We were in the middle of dinner!"

"Sorry about this, behike," said Seuz. "We have a question for you and the young lady."

"Who already hasn't been eating well lately," replied Felix. "And you aren't helping that by dragging us here like this."

"She's not eaten much," said Tarum, gazing into the pot. "They've barely touched it! May I have some, little lady, please?" Septimius looked perturbed.

"Mr. Vice President. Why don't we stick to our agenda?"

"But it's going to get cold if someone doesn't eat it," whined the vice president.

"I guess it's alright," said Besa, peeping out from behind Felix.

"She wasn't eating it anyway," said Felix.

"I was too," retorted Besa petulantly, as the vice president served himself a heaping bowl of gumbo and two pieces of cornbread.

"Tarum," said Septimius. "Would it be possible for us to continue with our meeting?"

"Oh! Don't mind me," said the vice president, skipping back to his seat behind the white werewolf.

"What is this intrusion about, Seuz?" asked Felix, "You can see we were in the middle of dinner."

"I'm sorry about that, Felix. But questions need to be asked."

"I'm not sure what questions you're referring to."

"Oh God! This roux is divine!" cried Tarum. Septimius turned and gave a growl. "Oh! Sorry!" said the vice president.

"Questions regarding the bishop!" snapped the wolf, who was really snapping at Tarum.

"Those are questions you should ask the necromancer, since I wasn't a witness to the incident."

"These questions are for the girl," said the werewolf.

"This child is not subject to the authority of this body, Seuz!"

"For goodness' sake, Felix. We're not going to bite her!" cried the council president. "We need a bit of information."

"And I'm not biting anything but this gumbo!" Tarum piped up. "Oh, if only I could have seconds." He waved his empty bowl over the council president's head.

"I suppose it will be all right," replied Besa, "Seconds, and to answer your questions, Mr. president." She stepped out from behind Felix.

"Besa, you don't have to do this."

"We're already here, anyway."

"Yes!" squealed Tarum, as he raced past the outstretched arm of the council president, trying to block his path to the gumbo pot. Tarum took another heaping bowl.

"Would you like a bowl of gumbo too, Mr. President?" offered Besa. "We could sit down at the table and talk over dinner."

Seuz sat pondering the offer for a moment. He then stood up. "That is most hospitable of you, child. I would love a bowl. That is, if the vice president hasn't eaten it all."

"I don't think so," said Besa. "Miss Maymi made a lot. Please have a seat," She pulled out one of the armless red velvet and cherry wood chairs.

"Thank, young lady. I'd always hoped to sample some of Miss Maymi's cooking."

He took one of the bowls from the serving cart and

served himself from the still steaming pot. "It's interesting that she made so much just for the two of you," he said, taking a piece of cornbread. "It's almost as if she expected you to have company."

"Yes," replied Besa, sitting in the chair next to him. "And here you all are. What questions did you want to ask me?"

"Just a moment," replied Seuz, taking a bite of gumbo and cornbread. Besa handed him a cup of tea to wash it all down. "Thank you." Seuz took a couple sips. "How were you able to call a Taafli against the bishop, when you're not yet in knowing?"

Besa smiled then. "Because it wasn't a Taafli. It was an illusion from his own mind. It was easy to initiate while he was holding me, and only Felix and his friend Michel were affected by it."

"I can attest to that," replied Felix. "The judge asked what the bishop was afraid of, as he ran screaming from the courtroom."

"They taught us about it in my class at school," said Besa, serving herself another bowl of gumbo. "It's called projection."

"That's amazing," replied the council vice president.

"That is amazing," replied Seuz. "Are the other students at school as proficient with it as you are?"

"Probably Margaret. She's my best friend, and usually good at everything," said Besa, spooning gumbo into her mouth. Seuz reached over and passed her the cornbread plate. "Thank you," she said, taking a piece.

"We should invite the council to dinner more often," said Felix. "She hasn't eaten this well in weeks."

"Really?" said the council president. "Why is that, Besa?"

"I've been worried about Papa. They took him and he didn't even do anything wrong."

"I understand," replied Seuz. "I have a brother who's been missing a while as well."

"I'm sorry," said Besa.

"Tell me, Besa," asked Seuz. "Is Margaret your only friend at school?"

"No. My other best friend is Dickey. He's not as smart as Margaret. He doesn't like to study, but he's really very sweet."

"Oh," replied Seuz. "Is he also your future beau?"

"Oh, no. Dickey is going to marry Margaret."

"You all sound like quite the trio," replied Septimius, looking pleased.

"There's also Mokheer," replied Besa. "He only comes out at night though."

"A perfect quartet," mused Tarum.

"The reason I wanted to ask you these questions is so we can figure out a way to protect you all."

"Protect us?" replied Besa, a bit incredulous. "But I told Felix, I already know how to protect myself."

"Yes. But what about the rest of your friends?"

"I guess we could consider it. I shouldn't speak for all of them, anyway. Though Mokheer is insubstantial. Nothing can hurt him."

"Good to know," said Seuz.

Besa leaned down and removed two pecan pies from the second shelf of the serving cart. "Would you like some pie, Mr. President?"

"What?" piped Tarum. "Wait a minute! There's pie too?"

"I think you've had enough, vice president," replied

Seuz. "We should perhaps offer some to the rest of the council members."

"Would any of you like some pecan pie?" Besa called into the rib cage. "We have three!" When Besa looked up, a beautiful, emaciated black woman stood before her holding out a plate. The girl was startled, because the women was there so suddenly.

"Yes, please," said the woman, who looked like she hardly ate anything, never mind pecan pie.

"Don't be alarmed, child," said Seuz. "That's Obsidia. She's a Seer, so she's probably had that plate all day. An epic sweet tooth."

"Oh, my God! I can't believe I'm being denied pie!" complained the vice president, as the council members who enjoyed sweets lined up behind Obsidia.

While Besa served, Septimius outlined a plan to dissuade any of the bishop's followers from attacking Besa or her friends. "You won't ever see them, Besa, but throughout your day and on your way home, there will be a security Dreid watching you." Besa served Septimius a piece of pie on the plate he was holding.

"Thank you," he said. Besa sat down to her own piece.

"But how will I know if it's a security Dreid, if I've never seen one?" she asked, taking a bite of pie.

"This pie is amazing," said Seuz. "Tarum, would you call in one of the Dreids, please?"

"Okay," said the vice president. "Then can I have some pie?" Seuz looked at Besa.

"Absolutely," she said, and smiled. Tarum pulled out a small object that hung on a chain around his neck and blew into it. It made no sound.

"Is that a whistle?" Besa asked Seuz.

"In a manner of speaking," replied Seuz. "But it's really a security mechanism. Watch." Besa saw a bright glow rise up from the floor, and then a large black entity rose up from it. The thing had the consistency of mist. There was a suggestion of a head, but it had no eyes, and its appendages, such as there were, looked like insubstantial tentacles.

"That doesn't look like it could protect anything," replied Besa.

"Besa! Be nice," admonished Felix.

"I'm just giving my honest impressions."

"I suppose a demonstration is in order," said Seuz. "Tarum, would you–"

"Nope," said the vice president, holding the slice of pie Besa gifted him. "I'm eating my pie." He took a seat at the dining table as well.

Seuz sighed, got up and went to his desk, and pulled a chain dangling behind his chair. A massive eight-foot ebony beast that looked like an ox in the shape of a man, opened a door at the back of the chamber. The door was tall too, but the man ox had to dip his head to account for the two-foot towering horn on each side of his head.

"You rang, mister president?" boomed the ox man.

"Yes, Lucius," replied Seuz. "Would you bring in something heavy and made of metal?"

"Right away, sir," said Lucius. He ducked backed through the door and returned clutching a large anvil in one hand like it was a potato. "Where would you like it, sir?" he asked.

"Right there in the middle of the floor will be fine, Lucius."

There was a boom when Lucius put the thing down. Besa could feel the weight of it from where she sat. Seuz pointed at the block of metal and said, "Hebron, erase."

The entity turned toward the object, reached out one of its tentacles and shot a bolt at the anvil. It was a short burst, but the anvil turned white hot, then collapsed in a pile of ash.

"Wow!" said Besa. "I have one more question."

"What's that?" asked Seuz.

"May I have one of those whistles?"

"You can have mine for another piece of pecan pie," said Tarum.

"Okay," said Besa.

"I assume we're done," said Felix.

"I guess we are," replied. Septimius.

"Then kindly transport myself, Miss Melponte, and our dining table, back to our house. Besa still has homework to do."

"But I—"

"No buts. You know the rules. And I will take that whistle to keep until you leave for school tomorrow."

A portal took them all back, minus one full pie pan. But it showed up empty on the dining table the next morning.

DELACROIX (DELLY)

The bishop was not accustomed to losing. And as far back as his catholic school days at Father O'Keefe's, he didn't recall ever having done so. He had been a heavy child in his youth. Some went so far as to call him fat. But after the first five or six times he convinced them to change their minds, no one repeated their mistake. He had become a much-feared bully by that time, and everyone just called him Delly; and not in some sissy kind of way. Woe be unto some new kid who made a reference and then snickered about it. They didn't snicker after Delly found out about it, and caught them in the school-yard. They were usually too busy trying to catch their breath after Delly drove his massive fist into their solar plexus. Delly was tall and big at that time too. But he wasn't a vicious bully. Not right away, at least. He mostly stood and watched the kid after he'd 'plexed him, and asked questions.

"Is that painful?" he'd asked. The kid was heaving and often couldn't respond, not able to catch his breath. "I asked you a question!" growled Delly.

"Hurts," the kid croaked.

"Good. It's supposed to. But I ain't no meany, so I don't want to do this to you again. But I gots to make sure you learned your lesson. So after school today, you got chalkboard duty with me. We got a deal? Answer me!" shouted Delly. He'd gotten his insistence on understanding from his father. A ship's cooper. Aubrey Delacroix was quick and vicious with his fists. His temper had hindered his promotion to first mate. Sailors wouldn't follow a man who might attack them over any provocation. That didn't help Delly, of course. He was more considerate of the kids he had to beat up, offering other options for penance. And when the penitent showed up, they cleaned the boards with him. Once the boards were clean, he'd have them write something along the lines of: "Delly is the toughest guy in the school," maybe a hundred times, and leave it up until the next day, just so the other boys would see it and attest to its truth.

The writing was always gone before the Father saw it. Everyone knew who the real toughest guy in the school was. Father O'Keefe carried a fifteen-inch hickory stick dangling from a loop on his cowl. And the fool boy who'd accepted a dare to steal it from the loop had been beaten so bad with it, he hadn't come back to school for a year. Even then, he hadn't remembered any of his friends and was never himself again. To say Bishop Delacroix came from a background of brutality was an understatement. If any of the kids he'd known from his school days could see the man glaring at himself in the mirror of his private chambers, they'd have said, "Man, Delly is on one now. Somebody's gonna pay." Delly would want revenge after losing such a major part of himself. But the other guy, this bishop guy, had to be careful. There was another friend from school who was with him.

He'd met his dear friend and confidante, Father Michel Guidry, while they were in seminary together. Michel had come from an entirely different background, one of peace and love and forgiveness. It was through Michel's influence that Delacroix learned to temper his anger and use his intelligence and incredible drive. He'd kept Michel close all these years, because there were many times when Father Guidry had convinced him to keep Delly in check. To seek a better, kinder, compassionate way—a forgiving way. That's why he'd kept his distance from Father Guidry since the night of the attack. Delly was back, and he only cared about smashing, yelling, and throwing, giving pain for pain.

"You ain't sippin' on no holy water tonight, boy! That negro did this to us!"

Delacroix left the diocese for a few hours and just walked. He didn't want to be among the many engaged in the promenade along the levee facing the cabildo. Too many would recognize him there. He chose to walk along the docks instead. Delly appreciated this route. This was where he'd been headed if not for a family friend sponsoring him into the seminary. His father had laughed at the obvious waste of money, and had confidence that a son who was starting to mirror him in size and temperament would soon follow him onto the decks. "This galoot ain't no priest," his father had scoffed. "He won't make it two months in that place before smashing some Father's foolish face. I'll see you in the cargo hold soon enough, sonny. Don't let them black dresses make you too soft. Stevedores need brute strength."

Ironically, it wasn't André Delacroix who didn't make it two months, but Aubrey Delacroix. His father was crushed to death when a large container slipped free of its netting and fell on him and the three other stevedores waiting to guide it into its place among the other ships' cargo. The one person who saw Delly cry was Michel—the first and only time. It sealed their bond. The old brute had not been much of a father, but he was the only influence he'd had. He knew what Aubrey would have said to him if he saw him this way: "What's wrong with you? Get out my house and don't come back until that negro is lying dead in the swamp somewhere!" It was during times like these that he missed Aubrey. All he could to do now was stare at the ships that had taken him from him. He would love to pick up one of the boxes stacked next to him. He still had his strength. Lifting a small crate would've made him feel closer to Aubrey, but all he had of him was loss. As surely as if he'd been on the docks the day his father died, all he could do was scream, "Aubrey! Aubrey! Aubrey!"

And then out of nowhere as if Aubrey decided to answer, an arm snaked around his neck and snatched backward. The smell of sweat and unwashed body made the bishop momentarily ill.

"That's a lot of noise coming out of a one-armed priss," said a voice in his ear.

"Unhand me, you stinking brigand!" demanded Delacroix, and then immediately regretted it. It wasn't something Delly would have said, and it got him a knife to the throat.

"That's pretty tough talk comin' out a priss about to get his throat cut," said the individual at his ear.

"That's mighty strange talk comin' out a priss, Nate," said a voice who was accompanying Stinky Knife. "I don't know what no brigam is, but I believe you been insalted."

"It's insulted, you morand!" said Nate.

"I think you mean moron," supplied Delacroix.

"Ain't you a know-it-all priss," replied Nate, pressing the blade so hard it drew blood.

The second man reached over and touched Delacroix's garment.

"Them some fancy clothes the priss is wearing, Nate. Oughta get us a lil' somethin' from the Cajuns what come to the market."

"Shut up, Emory! I'm runnin' this here robbery. We'll dump his body—"

"He got some kinda chain around his neck, Nate. It feels like somethin!"

"Well, I'll be. You are full of surprises, mister priss. Strike one of them tapers you stole from the parish, Emory."

"I ain't got but six left, Nate. Gone cut his throat so we can get them clothes off him!"

"I'm gon knock you over the head if you don't do what I tell you! Light it!"

Emory used the flint spark he had probably also stolen from the parish and lit one of the long matches customarily used to light candles at the parish altar. He then held it up before the bishop's face. "Oh, sweet Mother Mary!" cried Emory. "Let him go, Nate! Let him go!"

"You don't tell me what to do!" said Nate and stepped

in front of the bishop as he held the knife to his throat. "I'm in—Ho-ho-holy Mother Mary!" cried Nate, who dropped the knife, and then dropped to his knees. The bishop turned his steely gaze upon two of his parishioners, as he drew himself up like a giant, vengeful raven.

"I assume you procured those tapers at your last confessions," growled the bishop. "And should one word of this episode reach the light of day, I will see to it that both of are commuted to the very bowels of hell!" Delacroix snatched the lit taper.

"Now give me the rest of them, and follow me so no one else decides to ambush me."

Delacroix knew he was lucky that these were some of his own people. Because it could have gone badly otherwise. As it was, Nate and Emory followed very dutifully with heads lowered in a posture of contrition. When the bishop dismissed them and entered the diocese, the first person he encountered was Father Guidry.

"André, you're bleeding!" cried Father Guidry.

"Then kindly provide me a handkerchief, Michel!"

The priest quickly fished one out of the pocket of his cowl.

"How did you receive such an injury?"

"It's nothing," said the bishop, pressing the handkerchief against his neck. "I was watching stevedores load cargo into the hold of a ship, and a splinter must have caught me in the neck."

"That must have been a mighty big splinter. And you smell. Were you helping to load the cargo? Where did that odor come from?"

"You are the picture of decorum, Father Guidry. Please yell the fact that the bishop stinks after a long walk, so all the staff can hear it!"

"Please forgive my rudeness, your excellency. I was worried because you were gone so long."

"Get used to it, Father Guidry. Because for the foreseeable future, the bishop will be taking long walks well into the evening."

"But André, I don't know about that. Is that even safe? There are some bad people on the streets of this city at night."

"Yes. And a number of them are parishioners."

"What?" cried Father Guidry.

"Goodnight, Michel. I will take a carriage back to the residence."

The bishop would have liked to take another walk after he changed out of his bloody clothes and cleaned the cut at his throat. But Father Guidry would not sleep until his carriage pulled into the stables of the residence.

CHAPTER 6

FIRST TRY

Besa and her friends' first task was to pick and explore a potential site for raising the dead. After wandering around Newald's graveyards for a week, they settled on the crypt of a wealthy plantation family at the St Loomis Graveyard. The size of a small house, the structure had a large angel perched on its roof. Dickey was charged with conjuring a skeleton key that would open any lock. while Margaret hovered overhead, looking around the grounds in case there were gravediggers or graveyard attendants who might interfere with them.

"It's all clear," said Margaret when she landed. "The cemetery manager's shack is at the other end of the property, and no light showed in the windows or smoke from the chimney."

The grass around the structure had been manicured by careful hands, and the marble had not been allowed to get dirty. But as expected, the front door was locked. Wealthy people were often afraid that grave robbers would strip their loved one's resting place of the family heirlooms buried with the corpse. This was a relevant fear, because the remnants of the Batavian Pirates were still wandering around. A tomb laced with treasure offered easier pickings than fighting past the cannons on the decks of merchant vessels. Dickey's key worked so well Margaret was speechless. They entered the structure, to find it was designed like the occupants were coming home to a cozy dwelling. Marble shaped chairs sat throughout the building, with a few situated before the coffin area where the bodies were laid to rest. The name of the occupant was etched on each family member's section. They pried one of the compartments open with a little flat tool that Margaret had in her possession. Besa was a little perturbed with herself for not thinking of the detail.

"Don't be so hard on yourself, Besa," said Margaret. "It's a witch's trade to come prepared."

Once the compartment was pried open and the corpse tray slid out, Besa's body became weak.

"Your eyes are glowing," said Dickey. "Are they supposed to do that?"

"This is my first time doing this," replied Besa. "I assume that they are. I'm also feeling very sleepy."

"I think this might be the point where you chant your incantation," said Mokheer.

As Besa began her chant, a deep voice hummed a long monotone note. She had not heard that during her papa's enchantment ceremony. "Go away!" shouted the voice. She was startled out of her chant for a moment, but Mokheer told her,

"Don't listen to it. Concentrate. We'll handle all the outside distractions."

When Besa closed her eyes, a warm glow swept over her, and she was floating in a river of golden light, like she was in a dream. In the dream, the river's current carried her toward a giant golden cathedral with no doors but a lot of large open windows. Besa couldn't believe what she was seeing—the structure rose so tall and bright it seemed to reach all the way past the sky, which was also composed of various colors of light, like millions of golden and purple, and yellow, and silver, and pink and white rainbows had managed to meld together into something beyond description. The river of light carried Besa through one of the open windows of the cathedral, and inside was a congregation of millions of Taafli, each perched within their own individual little sanctuary. The cathedral was composed entirely of them, each etched with a different shade of light. Besa didn't realize there could be that many colors, but the cathedral was filled with it, from the bottom where the river came in all the way beyond the sky ceiling. But in the middle of all the multitudes of perched Taafli, sat one creature composed completely of a white golden light. As Besa floated before them, the white lighted Taafli floated toward her.

"Greetings, golden one," it said. "We are so happy to finally meet you in person. You are obviously well ahead of your time for knowing. But we must warn you that this enchantment ceremony is not safe. You and your comrades must leave quickly. We will help you awaken."

When her eyes opened, Besa heard someone screaming: "I can't believe you locked us in here, Dickey!"

It was Margaret. Both Margaret and Mokheer were holding her up as things flew at them. Not things—pieces of one of the marble chairs were flung by some strange invisible entity. And something else was screaming, "Die golden one. Die child of light!" She would not have known the invective was directed at her, were it not for the Taafli. Violet hovered just above them, using some kind of shield to deflect the chunks of marble being tossed at them. She noticed that Dickey's arm was thrusted through the bars that trapped them, as his hand worked at a key stuck in the lock.

"Will you calm down, Margaret," replied Dickey. "You're making me nervous!"

"Excuse me if I'm a little agitated! Something is trying to kill us! Get that lock open, or I'll turn you into a toad!"

"You'd better not!" said Dickey. "I almost got—" An explosion erupted and blew them through the door. "I did it!" cried Dickey. "My key worked!"

Margaret was anything but impressed.

"Come here, so I can thank you. You butter-brained ninny!" She had an evil look in her eyes and Dickey was having none of it.

"Now, Margaret. You control yourself!" he said. Margaret was rolling a charm between her two hands.

"I just want to thank you for saving our life, Dickey. Come here!"

"What's that in your hands? That don't look like a thank-you charm!"

He turned around and fled just as Margaret rose up and flung the charm.

"Ow!" cried Dickey as he ran, the sparkles pricking him all over.

"Margaret! Ow! Get this stuff off me! Just for that—Ow! No more bread for you! Ow!"

"Margaret, that's not really going to hurt him, is it?" asked Besa.

"Not really. It's just a frustration charm. It'll go away soon."

"Tomorrow during recess, I would like to talk about

what happened," said Besa. "I'm quite exhausted now, and only want my bed."

"Do you feel like you will pass out?" asked Mokheer.

"I should be fine once we reach the horses."

They made good time putting some distance between themselves and the mausoleum. Dickey made sure to give Margaret a wide berth. When they got to the horses, Besa knew Night Rain would find the way home, even if she passed out. When they made it to the Melponte residence, both Mokheer and Margaret helped float Besa up to her second-story bedroom window, and watched as she climbed safely inside.

Her room was just as she'd left it, but she got a sense that Felix had been there. This wasn't something she possessed before the failed enchantment. She wondered whether the sense was permanent, and what other new senses she'd acquired?

BESA'S SENSES grew more defined during the next school day. She discovered that she could hear what people were saying in the classroom next to hers, even if they spoke softly.

When they were released for first recess Besa, Margaret, and Dickey staked out the benches on the back wall of the school's large outside quadrant. If you walked behind the building, you wouldn't see it. The grass was well trimmed and there were benches to sit, and implements for the younger children to play on, and the sun shone from above. They all wondered how Sister Gerard had managed that, because the space was obviously enchanted. No dirt got on your shoes, no matter how much you ran, or on your clothes if you fell. You also couldn't hurt yourself, even if you jumped from the highest level of the play tower. The children found this the most fun detail. They often took a running starts and leapt off the thing. Besa and Margaret watched as Dickey broke away from their group to take his turn. He did a little flip in midair before landing on his bottom, then ran over to them breathless.

"Oh, boy! That was fun!" he cried. "I'm going to do that again!"

But when he turned to go, Margaret caught his arm.

"Dickey," said Margaret. "We're supposed to be talking about what happened last night."

"Wait a minute," said Dickey, going a little pale. "You're not blaming me for that, are you?"

"No, Dickey," replied Besa. "We're not blaming you. I just need to know what happened after I blacked out."

"First off, that thing flew out of your chest," said Dickey. "It looked like a giant golden dragonfly."

"It's a Taafli," said Besa. "I learned that from Papa."

"We didn't see it until you passed out, and we eased you down to the marble floor."

"Is that how it's going to be from now on, Besa?" asked Margaret. "Because we need to bring something to lay your head on."

"I guess so," replied Besa. "This being my first enchantment."

"Go on, Dickey," said Margaret.

"When the being came out, it said: 'Do not be afraid, young ones. I am here to protect you and the Golden One. This location is not safe. So please remove yourselves and the Golden One immediately.' And when we looked at you, Besa, you really were golden. That's when something we couldn't see started throwing chunks of marble at us."

"It's amazing no one was hurt," said Besa, sitting on the bench near the back barrier.

"Only because the golden dragonfly covered us with some kind of shield. The pieces of marble just bounced off it," said Dickey. But Margaret had a strange look on her face after he said that.

"I just realized something, Besa. That creature was you."

"I was unconscious. How could it be me?"

"Because it came out of you. Essentially, you were protecting us, even though you were unconscious. How did you even know you could do that?"

"I didn't know. It was Mokheer who told me I wouldn't need my Papa's book."

"But what is he, Besa? We only know him because he's always with you."

"I've known him since I was a small child. He told me that he thinks he was drawn to me because of my powers. But I didn't know what they were until last night."

"So, when you see bones, or a dead body, your body just knows what to do?" asked Dickey. "That is amazing. What else can you do?"

"My hearing has become quite keen," replied Besa. "I can pick up what others are saying from quite a distance away. For instance, Charlie Doyle over there is planning to run by and snatch your hat off."

Sure enough, Charlie was racing toward them, but before he could take the hat, Dickey snatched it off himself and swatted Charlie in the chest with it. Charlie was so surprised he stopped and looked at Dickey.

"How did you know I was going to do that?" asked the boy.

"Because I can read minds, you little wart!" cried

Dickey. "So, watch it! Or I'll be waiting in the coat room to wrap your suspenders around your neck!"

"What?" said Charlie, backing away with a horrified look in his eyes. "How did...? You keep away from me!" The boy ran off. Besa had also picked up that Charlie had this fear.

"That was evil of you, Dickey," said Margaret. "You didn't have to do that to him."

"So is dunking my hat in the horse trough. He and his little friends are always hitting me with spitballs in my Dark Studies class. This will give them something to think about before they plan another attack on me."

"Don't tell him anything else, Besa. That is too much power for him."

"Not even that Millicent McGillicuddy is coming to drop a spider down his collar?"

"What?" said Dickey, getting up quickly. He was deathly afraid of spiders. He kept his eyes firmly on Millicent as she approached. The girl was two years older than Besa and her group, a tall, gangly girl with a head of bright red hair, and covered from head to toe in freckles. She was a passable sorceress and had chosen Dickey as the object of her malicious nature.

"Hello, Dickey," said Millicent, smiling at him as she sat on the corner of their table. She would've been prettier without all the freckles.

"Don't you come here smiling at me!" cried Dickey, pointing an accusing finger at his tormentor. "I know what you're up to. You'd better keep your spiders to yourself!" And he took off before she had a chance to reply. Millicent looked disappointed. She usually had the upper hand on Dickey with her pranks.

"How did he know that?" she asked.

"He knows you're always at him," replied Margaret.

"Yes. But how did he know I had a spider?" asked Millicent. "I didn't tell anyone. Are either of you mind readers? Something tells me it's you, Besa. Since no one can seem to classify exactly what you are. She walked away, eyeing Besa, making sure to keep a safe distance from her.

"Besa," said Margaret, after Millicent left. "You read her mind?"

"I don't know. If I did, I wasn't aware of it."

"That is an amazing power! People are going to be so jealous of you!"

"I don't want you assigning powers to me, Margaret. It could have been a lucky guess. Everyone knows Millicent has evil designs on Dickey."

"That's true. You think maybe she just likes him, but can't find a way to tell him?"

"Now you're being ridiculous," said Besa, chuckling. "At least for Dickey's sake, I hope you are!"

The school bell gonged, and they headed back to class.

CHAPTER 7
DICKEY

On some nights, Dickey had clerk duties in his father's courtroom. The problem was, on this night, so did Francis. Dickey's heart sank when his mother informed him that the judge requested that both his youngest sons participate.

"Your father feels bad that he can't always see you both," she'd said. "I'm sure you'll both learn a lot and make the judge proud."

"I'll do my best, mother," replied Dickey.

"No, you won't, turkey boy," retorted Francis, under his breath. But his mother heard him.

"Yes, he will, Francis. Richard's been doing these tasks for a while and always does a good job." She came up and gave Dickey a kiss on the cheek. Francis just rolled his eyes. "Don't you be mean to your brother. Your father won't be happy about it."

"Yes, ma'am," replied Francis. "I'm sorry, Richard," he said, and tried to reach over and give his brother a hung, but Dickey flinched and moved back."

"Can we go now, mother?" asked Dickey.

"Yes." She ushered them out the back door, into the stable yard.

"Richard always does a good job," said Francis, sarcastically, as they went to their respective stalls to retrieve their horse. "I should pop you one for shrugging off my apology. You'd better not make me look bad in front of father."

"I doubt you'll need much help with that."

"As long as it's not you," He feigned hitting Dickey, and the boy flinched. "Watch it, turkey boy." He eyed his younger brother menacingly as he trotted by on his horse. Francis had always preferred the big black gelding their father had named Caesar, while Dickey liked the gentle chestnut mare his mother had named Constance. Dickey liked her because she kept her head no matter what happened, while Caesar was a big coward that would bolt at the slightest surprise or provocation.

The judge had come home shaken one evening after a long day of cases, and warned the boys, "Be careful on Caesar,"

"Did something happen tonight, William?" asked their mother. She'd been setting the table for dinner, but stopped to come listen to her husband. He hardly said anything when he came home. Dickey discovered that sometimes his father sounded hoarse, as if he'd been shouting all day.

"It wasn't anything I couldn't handle," said his father. "But the new gelding, Caesar, startled and reared when a squirrel ran across our path on the way home. He would've thrown me off if I hadn't been holding on tight."

Dickey chuckled a bit, which caused Constance's ears to perk up, and she gave a short whinny.

"You were thinking the same thing I was, Constance. It's good we don't know what path Francis took. We might be tempted to arrange a two-squirrel obstacle course for dear brother. It would be a humbling start to his evening." Constance gave a blow and bobbed her head. "I didn't say I was going to do it. It was just a thought, sweet Constance," he said, and gave her a gentle pat on the neck. "Don't you tell on me."

When he got to the courthouse stable yard, one of the older grooms, Malcolm, greeted him with a smile. The lean, wiry-looking, Black man had silver along his temples like the judge. "Good evening, Mr. O'Brien," he said, grasping Constance's bridle. The groom usually had a treat for her, so she was always happy to see him. "Your brother is already inside, getting to work."

"I doubt that," snorted Dickey. "Thank you, Mr. Williams." He dismounted and stroked Constance along her muzzle. "I know she's in good hands." He stopped before he got to the back door of the courthouse and took a deep breath—to collect himself. Dickey had done this duty a few times for his father. It wasn't difficult, but having Francis along would be a bit more taxing. This would be a strange evening. Of that, he had no doubt. "Taking care of courthouse documents is an important task," his father had told him when he first started. "Everything needs to be filed properly and on time." That's why the inclusion of his competitive, moody brother was puzzling. He turned the door knob and stepped into the old stone courthouse. He didn't know much about stone, but he believed it was flagstone, unlike the cabildo next door, which was made of granite. His father had told him that granite held its temperature better than flagstone, which explained why the courthouse was so cold in the winter and hot when the temp went up. The clerk's offices were narrow winding corridors, decorated with a brown wood paneling. They'd put more money into the judge and barrister chambers up front. His father's chambers had better quality wallpaper than they had at home. His mother loved flowers. So everywhere she inhabited—the kitchen, the dining room and the parlor, along with the sitting room—had a floral motif, with paintings of flowers, flowers on the tables, even a floral pattern on the side chairs and the settee. The only place with no floral motifs was his father's study. He'd chosen a rich, dark paneling for the books of his library. Although he must not have had any say about his chambers, the walls there displayed hunting scenes. Dogs running, and men on horseback pursuing something that you couldn't see. Nothing that Dickey could see, at least.

When he stepped into the clerk's office, he encountered Mr. Norris, the chief clerk—a thin, neatly dressed man with mutton chops and an overwhelming bald spot. It took up most of his head, leaving a small island of brown hair that began with fluffy patches over one ear and stretched in a hopeless line all the way around the back of his head to the fluffy patch on his other ear. Mr. Norris always looked nervous, only now his face and head were red, like he'd been slapped. But when he saw Dickey, he actually smiled, which meant something terrible had happened, or was about to happen.

"Your brother—Mr. O'Brien—has decided to help with the court docket," declared the chief clerk, wringing his hands.

"But sir, why didn't you just take—" Dickey stopped when he realized something: Mr. Norris was afraid of his brother—the boss's son. Dickey knew he would probably get punched for this later, but he had to intervene. Francis was hunched over the important ledger, and appeared to be making notes in it.

"What are you doing, dunderhead?" asked Dickey, as he pulled a desk chair up to sit beside his older brother.

"Helping, turkey boy. What are you doing?"

"Watching you get in a lot of trouble. That is a permanent court document. Father will skin you and your horse if you mess that up."

"What!" said Francis, almost dropping the massive book.

"Whatever's written in this book will be a permanent record kept forever."

"Then it's a good thing I never touched it. You did. Didn't you?" said Francis, making a fist and holding it under Dickey's nose.

"Yes," replied Dickey. "Yes, I suppose I did. If you will kindly give me the inkwell so I can—" Francis had a malicious look in his brown eyes as he tipped the inkwell over and damaged the other documents on the desk.

"Oh, no!" he cried. "Look what Dickey just did!"

Mr. Norris rushed over to the desk. "What happen—" He stopped when he saw that they were blank sheets of paper. Dickey placed his finger over his lips, telling Mr. Norris this was a secret. "Don't worry, Mr. Norris. I'll re-copy every last one of them." I need something un-important to copy, whispered Dickey. We need to occupy him with something. Before he damages something important.

Oh, I know, whispered Mr. Norris. I have an old will you can use.

"Do you think your brother might help with this important task?" inquired Mr. Norris.

"Nope" replied Dickey. "He's not good with stuff like this. It's too complicated." Dickey set about the task in earnest. Francis soon showed up and looked over his shoulder. "What's too complicated, turkey boy?" he asked, giving Dickey a shove in the back of the head.

"Some documents that father needs."

"Don't worry about it, Mr. O'Brien," Mr. Norris informed Francis. "Your brother writes very fast and doesn't make mistakes."

"I know I can do it faster than him. Let me do it."

"I don't know, Mr. O'Brien. The judge needs these done by the end of the night." Mr. Norris was a good actor, because he was really selling the task to Francis.

"I'll show you," said Francis. "Get up, feather head, and let me do it right!"

"I don't want to get blamed if you mess this up," said Dickey.

"Get up or else, turkey boy!"

"All right!" said Dickey, relinquishing his chair to Francis.

"Don't worry, Dickey," said Mr. Norris, handing him some important documents. "I have some simpler stuff for you to do."

"Yes, give him the simple stuff," said Francis.

Mr. Norris gave Dickey a thank-you pat on the shoulder for helping him control the situation. Dickey smiled and headed to the file room to label and file what Mr. Norris gave him.

At the end of the evening, after the courthouse closed, and they were riding home, the judge asked, "So, were you boys able to be useful to Mr. Norris?"

"I certainly was!" declared Francis. "I don't know what silly thing Dickey was doing, but I finished all the documents you needed, father."

"Documents?" replied the judge.

"You know, father. The ones you needed for that big

case?" said Dickey, with his finger to his lips as he peeped past Francis.

"Oh, that case," said the judge. "Thank you, Francis. They will definitely come in handy." He gave Dickey a look that said, you'd better explain later.

"He did what to the docket?" asked the judge when he and Dickey were alone.

"Don't worry, father, I got it away from him before he could do much harm. Me and Mr. Norris made up some harmless tasks to keep him busy the rest of the evening."

"Sounds like the clerk's office is not the right place for your brother."

"Mr. Norris would agree," said Dickey.

MARGARET

Besa suggested that Margaret stay open-minded with her mother and to cherish the time she spent with her parents. Margaret was thinking of her friend's heartfelt words when her mother suggested she accompany her on her next visit to serve the sick and destitute.

"I'd be happy to go, mother," said Margaret.

"I understand that this is not something you're usually interested—"

"I said I'd be happy to go, mother," replied Margaret, with a smile. Her mother looked shocked.

"Open your mouth, if you're really my daughter."

"What?"

"I said open thy mouth, demon!" cried her mother, coming at her with a cross she snatched off the mantle of the sitting room fireplace. "They say demons don't have tongues; they lie so much they've been burned out. In the name of the Lord, open thy mouth, demon!"

"Mother, please," replied Margaret, pulling the cross out of her mother's outstretched hand.

"You will not defeat me, demon!" She pulled a small

bottle of what looked like holy water from the pocket of her sweater and splashed it on Margaret's face.

"Mother, you're scaring me!" replied the girl, backing away.

"Open thy mouth, you vile beast! I want my truculent, selfish child back!"

"All right, mother, here!" said Margaret, as she opened her mouth.

"Margaret! Oh my God, child!" cried her mother, pulling her into a bear hug. "Thank God that you're back, child!"

"Don't you mean your truculent, selfish child?" said Margaret, backing away from her mother.

"I didn't mean it, Margaret! I was just trying to get the thing's attention."

"There was no 'thing,' mother. It's just me!"

"But you've never agreed to go on any outings with me. What else was I supposed to think?"

"I'm sorry, mother," she said, giving her mother a hug. Betsy grabbed the crucifix from the mantel again.

"Open thy mouth! Open thy mouth! You foul thing! I command thee!" she cried. brandishing the crucifix almost on top of Margaret's nose.

"This will be a long evening if you continue to do that."

"My daughter never gave me a hug like that!"

"Please stop talking like I'm not right here, mother. When are we to leave for the visit?"

"Oh my God!" cried her mother.

"Okay," said Margaret, opening her mouth and sticking out her tongue. "See. It's me. I'm right here! What time are we leaving?".

"All right, I believe you," said her mother. "We have four

other mother-daughter pairs to pick up and get some food and other sundries from the church. Then we'll go."

"But eight other people won't fit in our buggy, mother."

"I've done this a few times, so I know how it works," said Betsy. "We always take the church carriage."

Margaret had often ridden in the cavernous thing when they picked up kids for bible study a few years ago. The words "Humble Blessings" were stenciled on one side of the dark blue vehicle. The other, more important fact was the thing had no seats, other than the driver's. All the passengers sat in the rear. There were runners down the center and loops for chains at intervals along each side, which confirmed everyone's suspicions that it had come from a funeral parlor.

Margaret was lucky on this outing, because she got to sit next to her mother, who sat next to Mr. Hemings, the church driver. But the mother-daughter sets they picked up didn't seem to mind at all. "Tis a blessed evening, Sister Claiborne," they'd all said. At least that's what the mother part of the pairs said. The daughters just peered at Margaret. Some of them spoke to her and some of them didn't. They each tied themselves to the metal loops with a length of rope.

"Who are we visiting first, Betsy?" said Mrs. Norwood, the previous minister's wife, before he passed away and Margaret's father took over the congregation. She always wore her Sunday best, even when shopping at the French Market, or strolling along the levy for promenade. She was still spry at fifty-five. She had been very young when she and Reverend Norwood started Humble Blessings over forty years ago. The child she had with her was Jenny Talbot—a thirteen-year-old non-Magist girl with blue eyes and lustrous blond locks; she was so beautiful that when Dickey and the rest of the gang met her in town with her mother, he was speechless, and instead of stating his name as Besa had done, he started to babble so bad Margaret had to elbow him in the side to help him collect his thoughts. "Pleased to meet you, Dickey," the girl managed, before blushing and hurrying to catch up with her mother, Henrietta Talbot, who'd already walked into Ms. Duschoff's Tailor's Shop.

"We will first stop at The Un-wed Mother's House over on Annette Street. After that, the indigent camps near Congo Square. Then we are stopping at the McElroy's on Burgundy." Alice McElroy was a generous soul, and often provided meals for saints who were going out on missions in the evenings. Margaret prayed she'd made one of her sweet potato pies—which was almost as good as Miss Maymi's.

"After that," her mother said. "We will proceed to the Poor House on Chartres, and also make a stop at The House of Refuge on Lafayette. The house was run by the Ursulines, but not all who were served there were of the Catholic faith.

The Unwed Mothers House really was just a house. It did not have institutional connections like the Poor House or the House of Refuge. Even the indigent camp received visits from the Ursulines from time to time. But fallen women and girls received no dispensation. Margaret always found that odd. The house was only a large one-story cottage. She wasn't sure why the structure wasn't painted white like all the other old houses on the street; it was a bright shade of yellow. The wooden porch they walked upon was blue, as if to offer contrast. But it looked like a fresh paint job, as if someone might mistake it for a regular house if the paint started to fade. The facility usually housed eight to twelve girls. The term "girls" fit them very well, because most of them were barely eighteen, and some were as young as thirteen. The proprietress of the house was named Wilma Mahoney. Rumor had it she was a former fallen woman herself—with a brothel background. But she had purchased this structure with her own money and had been providing this haven for lost and abandoned women for more than ten years. Mahoney was a thick, freckle-faced woman with an unruly mane of red hair. She had a good face, Margaret thought, but a questionable smile—chewing tobacco had badly stained her teeth. But she always had a smile ready when Humble Blessings showed up on her blue porch. Her smocks hung loose and flowing, which looked comfortable to Margaret. She liked the look as well when she went to school, preferring a belted smock. But her mother shoved her into a corset and bustle when she went to church.

"Welcome! Welcome! Ladies of Humble Blessings!" Wilma declared. "Always wonderful to see you. Please come in." She stood back and ushered them into the front foyer, which looked like it had been recently wall-papered. Margaret posited that it was probably due to Wilma's resourcefulness. The home did earn some small revenue from quilts and baskets produced by the girls, but not enough to support fifteen people in the house. Wilma also had an unpaid assistant named Daisy Wheeler, who lived and worked with the girls. The story was, Daisy had escaped from a laundry bondage run by one of the Catholic orders. Mahoney had offered her a refuge, and she never left. "Please come in and sit down," said Wilma, guiding them to the structure's only parlor. Daisy appeared out of the rear of the house. She always looked nervous when she saw strangers, as if fearing the nuns had come to retrieve her. She was a short, raw-boned, dark-haired woman who never wanted to look at you. The one time she did look up, Margaret noted there was something wrong with her left eye.

"Good evening, sisters," Daisy mumbled to her chest. "Blessings to you."

"Daisy," said Wilma, in a non-demanding tone. "Would you mind getting tea for the guests?" Daisy nodded once and fled into the back of the house. "Please sit down, ladies." The parlor furniture had been upgraded since Margaret had been there over a year ago.

There was a cherry wood, floral-patterned settee, a number of respectable looking floral-patterned side chairs, a nice oak circle table, good looking wallpaper similar to what was in the foyer hallway and a clean floral-patterned rug under it all. And everything seemed to match. "Thank you for your hospitality, Miss Mahoney," said her mother. "We just came to bring you the offering for the month." She pulled a small pouch out of her bag and handed it to the grinning woman. "Thank you, Mrs. Claiborne. We are always blessed by your visits here. Ah! And here is sweet Daisy with your tea!" Daisy placed the tea service on the circle table and disappeared.

"You must excuse Daisy," said Wilma. She is shy around new people. Please enjoy your tea while I install this offering in the house safe." She excused herself. The tea tray included sugar cookies that the girls were happy to dispose of—Margaret even had a few herself. Like the tea, they were delicious. When Miss Mahoney returned, her mother and the rest of the mothers stood to give their goodbyes. "The tea and cookies were delightful, Wilma, but we must be on our way," said Betsy.

"I understand," replied Miss Mahoney. "And it's so good to see you again, red," she said, looking at Margaret. "You've been quiet tonight." She brushed her hand through Margaret's hair—which always made her feel like a bashful little girl. She only managed a blush.

"Oh, she's probably got homework and other thoughts running through her head. You never know with my little fireball."

"It's always good to see you too, Miss Mahoney," Margaret finally said, with a smile, as everyone made their way back toward the foyer.

"Hopefully you'll come back the next time," said Wilma.

"We'll see," replied Margaret, stepping off the porch and making her way back to the carriage.

"She really seems to like you, Maggie." said her mother, as they climbed back into the vehicle. Then Margaret leaned over her mother and handed Mr. Hemings some of the cookies from the tea service.

"Thank you, Maggie," replied the driver. Her mother looked shocked.

"Calm down, mother," said Margaret, and stuck out her tongue. "See, it's me. It's really me."

The indigent encampment was also a refuge for runaway slaves. The camp was set up in four sections. The first one held the perimeter guards, who truly weren't guards as much as individuals of first contact. Negroes weren't allowed weapons in Newald, so the best way for the guards to do their job was to be grinning happy fools. They usually accomplished this by singing and drinking—or appearing to do so. When new runaways were being sought by their masters, the group of drunken singing black men was twice as large. The Humble Blessings missionaries were an approved, welcomed organization. When the church carriage approached, the singing and pretend drinking subsided, and Henry Leblanc approached the wagon. A tall, muscular man, Henry also led and organized the encampment. He was a free man of color, with a successful carpentry business in town. He was also a deacon with the Humble Blessings congregation. He looked distinguished in his brown tail-coat, black vest with pocket watch and twill cotton pantaloons on Sunday. He never looked cheap.

"Good evening, Sister Claiborne," he said when he saw Betsy. His smile big and bright. "How has your evening been going? Any trouble?"

"No, Henry," said Mrs. Claiborne, giving him a hug. "We are definitely safe now."

"Is that you out there, Henry?" called a voice out of the rear of the carriage.

"Yes, ma'am. It's me, Mother Norwood. How are you feeling?"

"I'm blessed the same as you. My feet hurt, but they still work—praise God."

"Yes, ma'am. Amen."

"We brought a few supplies for your camp, Henry," said Betsy. "Some smoked meat from the pantry, vegetables from the church garden, and some clean used clothes and blankets."

"Thank you, Sister Claiborne. You are always a blessing to our little hideaway. And as our thank-you, we'd like to invite you to our Calenda this evening. I know you said it's been a while since you've seen one."

"I don't know," replied Betsy. "We should be on our way."

"I don't know when we're going to have a singer like we have tonight. His people are from Dahomey."

Margaret noticed a strange look on her mother's face, one she never saw on Betsy Claiborne—excitement. "That's where my papa's people were from," said Betsy.

"Didn't you tell me he used to sing at Calendas when he was alive?"

"Yes!" said Betsy. "We can stay for a little while," and when was about to go farther into the camp, like there was no one else here but her. Margaret was shocked by this uncharacteristic behavior. She caught the woman's arm.

"Wait a minute, mother. Where are you going?"

"Oh! I'm sorry, honey. I lost myself for a moment," said Betsy. "I was just going to listen to the Calenda singer for a moment. I won't be but a minute," she said, smiling.

"I'm sorry, mother," said Margaret. "But I have to ask you to open your mouth."

"What?" said Mrs. Claiborne.

"In the name of the Lord! I rebuke thee, demon!" cried Margaret, falling to her knees. "My mother would never do something like this! Not in the middle of a missionary visit!"

"Stop it, Margaret," her mother told her.

"Thou shall not defeat me, you foul thing! I want my boring, pushy mother back!" cried Margaret. She pulled a cross out of the pocket of her coat. "Open thy mouth, foul beast! Open thy mouth!"

"All right!" said her mother, opening her mouth. "See, it's just me."

"Oh, my goodness, mother! Thank God you're back! I was so worried," said Margaret, pulling her into an embrace.

"Stop it, child," said Betsy. "This is not funny at all. And I am not boring or pushy."

"I didn't mean it, mother! I was only trying to get the things' attention."

Mrs. Norwood climbed out of the carriage. She was a petite woman with a long grey braid wound around her head like a crown, and a strong personality. "Goodness, Betsy, what is all the ruckus about?"

"Nothing special, Mother Norwood."

"It was too special, mother. A demon had taken hold of her!"

"What? What is the girl going on about?"

"She was just play—"

"My mother was in the grip of a demon!"

"That is not true. You take that back!"

"I cannot take back something that's true," said Margaret. "This demon would have her desert our mission tonight, so she could go dance in a Calenda."

"But that can't be true, is it Betsy?" asked Mrs. Norwood. "We're here because you brought us on the mission visit."

"I...was just—"

A scream erupted from the rear of the carriage.

"Help! It took her! It took the girl!"

Margaret, Betsy, and Henry rushed to the rear of the carriage, where the door hung open. There were only Mrs. Wilmington and her daughter, Abby, Mrs. Dupri and her daughter, Agatha, and Mrs. Marcon and her daughter, Marie.

"What happened, sisters?" asked Betsy. "And where is Jenny?" All the mothers were in shock, but Mrs. Dupri was able to give them the details of what they witnessed.

"We were sitting her waiting for you to come back,

when the rear door of the carriage was pried open. At first, we thought it might be Miss Betsy or the driver, but this yellow entity floated in among us. I was so frightened I couldn't even scream for a moment. It passed over us all like it was searching for something, and then it settled on Jenny, cowering in the corner by herself. It wrapped itself around her and she disappeared."

"But where did it take her?" asked Betsy, to no one in particular.

"I'm sure I don't know, Betsy," replied Mrs. Dupri. "But what are we going to do?"

"I think I know what it is," said Margaret.

"Is this something you've studied, Margaret?" asked her mother.

"Yes, it is. It's something called a grmlle. It's a request spirit. We need to search your camp, Deacon Leblanc."

"Why, child? What are we looking for?" asked Henry.

"We need to find the person who sent it."

"But if it's a mist, like Mrs. Dupri said," replied Mrs. Claiborne, "what will finding the sender do?"

"If we can find him quickly, he will still have mist around him," said Margaret.

"Hurry, men!" Henry shouted to his other guards. "We're looking for someone with yellow mist near them or on them! Let's go!"

Margaret was about to take off, so she could try to spot the person from above, when her mother grabbed her arm.

"Why would someone do something like this, Margaret? They released an evil spirit?"

"No, mother. That's not what the grmlle is for," said Margaret. "It's a request entity. And it's more than likely a child did this. An experienced medicine man wouldn't need something like this. And they can control them. But someone inexperienced, who's afraid, might try it."

"Let's go tell Henry we're probably looking for a child," said Mrs. Claiborne.

"I can see him from above a lot easier," replied Margaret, taking off.

But it wasn't that easy. The camp was a patchwork of various types of dwellings. Everything from shacks, rag tents and even discarded wagons the indigents had gotten hold of and transformed into a place to live. She recognized Henry from the way he pushed his men before him, directing them to spread out over the three acres of ground to locate the culprit. But Margaret spotted the mist well before they would've gotten to it. It wasn't associated with a tent or a dwelling, just a small campfire in the eastern quadrant of the encampment. She landed next to Henry.

"Whoa! Girl!" he cried. "I'm never going to get used to you doing that!"

"I'm sorry, Deacon Leblanc," Margaret said. "But I spotted a campfire at the eastern boundary of your camp."

"Okay, lead me to it."

She took off again.

"I have to see it from above," said Margaret. "Okay. I see it. Have your men move to the left side of the camp. Okay. A little further over and three rows down."

"Wait. I think I know where we're going." He seemed to know a shortcut and began moving through all the dwellings to arrive at the spot a few moments after Margaret. Three young girls crowded around the campfire. One of them—the youngest—quickly put her hands behind her back. Margaret landed not far away and walked over to her. The child watched Margaret come down, completely transfixed.

"Are you a angel?" the child asked. She wasn't more than six—shoeless, wearing rags, her face and hair filthy.

"No," said Margaret.

"But mama said only angels can fly."

"Then I guess I'm your angel," said Margaret. "What's your name?"

"Mary."

"Did you just call a spirit, Mary?" asked Margaret. The child looked a bit frightened for a moment. "I need you to point to where it went, Mary."

Henry finally got there.

"Is this the one," he asked.

"Yes," said Margaret. "The mist is still on her hands."

"But what did she do?"

"You made a request, didn't you, Mary?"

The child looked down at her feet.

"I was trying to get mama to come," said Mary.

"Where's her mother?" asked Margaret.

"Nowhere that she can come back from," said Henry. "How they managed to get here is a mystery to all of us."

"It's not a mystery to me," said Margaret. "She's obviously a Magist. Can you point to where you sent the spirit, Mary?" said Margaret.

"What good will that do?" asked Henry.

"We study these spells in school. A grmlle won't be able to consume Jenny, unless she passes away."

"So it hasn't killed her?"

"No. It doesn't kill. But when the request is sent out to it, it requires a price to be paid. That's why they are mostly used by small children, who don't understand the conse-quences of what they've done. If her mother were some-where it could reach, she would be here now. And the grmlle would ask its price. But since there was no way for it to fulfill the request, it stayed too long and got hungry. It only took Jenny because she was alone. Point where you sent it, Mary."

The child pointed south, in the direction of the plantations.

"Have you got some of the smoked meat my mother brought?" Margaret asked.

Henry turned and called to a man at the beginning of the section.

"Emile! Bring that bundle from the church!" The man trotted off and came back about five minutes later with the package. Margaret searched among the items, grabbed a large slab of meat, and took off south. She didn't know what the entity would have done when the sun came up, since it was exclusively a night spirit. She found it in the branches of a large live oak tree. Almost to the top. It was wrapped around Jenny, and the girl looked to be in a dazed state.

"Jenny," said Margaret, as she floated up a few feet from her in the branches. "Jenny, can you hear me?" The girl woke up.

"Wha...Where am I? How did I get up here?"

"Don't worry," said Margaret. "I'm going to get you down. But you need to grab onto that limb and hold on tight, okay?"

"Okay. I'll do my best."

When Margaret started to chant, the entity glowed intensely bright.

"What is this!" cried Jenny. "Help me! Get it away from me!"

"I'm going to do that, Jenny. But you have to stay calm and don't move."

Suddenly Margaret thrusted the slab of meat out before

her and rushed at the entity. It did exactly what she hoped it would do—let go the girl—and attached itself to the meat. The problem was, Jenny had probably never climbed a tree, and so didn't know how to hold on. When the thing let go, she fell. She didn't hit her head, but she got a couple scrapes from the branches before Margaret caught her. She wasn't a very heavy girl. Not yet anyway. Margaret flew her back to the carriage. Mrs. Norwood almost fainted when she saw the child, as if it just occurred to her that she was gone.

"Oh, my Lord, child!" she cried, running and picking up the girl, who was almost she same size as she was, but she had mother strength then. "Thank the Lord you are safe."

"No," said Jenny, in her beautiful, ethereal childlike way. "Thank Margaret."

"Yes," replied Mrs. Norwood. "We should thank her too."

"I think it's time we all went home," suggested Mrs. Dupri, hugging her own daughter protectively. So, they all climbed back into the carriage and went back to Humble Blessings.

MAGIST COUNCIL

When the Magist Council convened that evening for its weekly meeting, Septimius was friendly and very hopeful. "My, Jeyda, did you add a bit more color to your horns?"

The creature, a massive eight-foot-tall man with the haunches of a goat and huge curled horns, was caught off guard by the compliment.

"Why, yes, Septimius. Thank you for noticing," replied Jeyda. "I just added a bit more grit to the brine I used to clean them."

"You did a smashing job. And Tovar," he said, singling out a slightly hairy fanged female creature in a brown smock. "Isn't that a clean smock you have on? The blood-free look works well on you. And Tarum, that new brown suit looks impressive!"

"Did you happen upon a lame, whitetail stag in the woods tonight?" asked Tarum. "Because you are over the moon."

"Yes, my dinner was quite satisfying this evening. Thank you for asking, Tarum."

"What about Obsidia?" asked Tarum. "She must be

sneaking into the cake vault again. She's putting on a little weight, wouldn't you say?"

The emaciated women smiled and blushed a bit but did not make eye contact with anyone.

"As a matter of fact, Obsidia," said Seuz "You look...You won't look at me. What's the matter? You look like something terrible just happened. Did the bishop get his hands on the Melponte girl?" He sat down at his desk inside the skull and awaited the bad news.

"No," said Obsidia. "It's not anything that bad."

"Whew!" said Septimius, sitting back in his chair

"It's still bad, though, and complicated," said the Seer.

"What does bad and complicated mean, Obsidia? Don't be so evasive. We need to know the facts. What is it?"

"The kids have begun to go out at night."

"That doesn't sound so bad. Children go out at night with their families all the time."

"That's not what they're doing," replied Obsidia. "They're going out alone after midnight. Then they go into graveyards and break into tombs."

"That doesn't sound sane, but there's nothing dangerous in that," replied Tarum.

"Normally, that would be true. But the last tomb they opened, the entity inside rose up and tried to kill them. Thankfully, the Taafli was able to protect them."

As they talked, one of the members delivered Septimius his usual cup of tea. By the time Obsidia finished her report, the cup lay crumbled on the stone floor, and liquid dripped down the side of his broad oak desk.

"At least we started out well," said Tarum."

"And the last thing is..." said Obsidia.

"Uh-oh! Everybody duck!" cried Tarum

"They have no intention of stopping. No matter what."

The next sound they heard was the council president's wooden desk bouncing off the rock wall of the cave. The force of it shattered the thing and sent wood splinters flying everywhere. A splinter shot into the ribcage and stung Tovar, because she let out a howl and grabbed her face.

"I did warn you all to duck—did I not?" said Tarum.

"What is wrong with those brats!" roared Septimius. "Do they have a death wish?"

"Besa sees it as a way to honor her father," said Odsidia. "But they haven't raised a spirit yet."

Seuz just sat with his face in his paw, shaking his head.

"Isn't that just like a bunch of selfish, inconsiderate children?" said Tarum. "And now we need another desk for Septimius to throw. We should seriously consider something in cast iron next time."

THE NEXT TWO

The children's next two enchantments went much smoother, now that they knew to set wards, and that the Taafli would be there as well. But Besa could not get a spirit to rise the way her father had. The boy from the brothel therefore presented an intriguing opportunity, and when she told the group, or her club, about him they all seemed to agree—or almost all of them.

"This stinky boy you met on the street gives you a name and you accept it, like that?" asked Dickey. "I have some idea for names, too."

"Dickey," said Margaret. "This is not about the name. It's about—"

"No, wait," said Mokheer. "I would like to hear the names Dickey thought up."

"Oh, goodness gracious!" cried Margaret. "You know they're going to be dumb! You just want him to make a fool of himself!"

"I think you're being cruel, and unfair to Dickey," replied Mokheer.

"Of course, I am," said Margaret. "And you're suddenly

worried about his feelings! All right, Dickey. Let's hear your suggestions."

"I don't want to now," said Dickey. "Since everyone expects them to be dumb!"

"I didn't say that, Dickey," replied Mokheer. "You have a right to give your opinion."

"He's right, Dickey," replied Besa. "We all know Margaret can be a little severe sometimes."

Margaret rolled her eyes at this statement. They had set the club meeting up in the garden room at the rear of the house, with its high-backed rattan wicker chairs and sandy pine topped wicker table. This prompted Miss Maymi to whip up some of her delicious tea cakes, served with peach marmalade for added sweetness. Dickey had another eight on his plate after wolfing down seven already. He was still chewing as he formulated his idea.

"Whenever you're ready, Dickey," said an exasperated Margaret. And in true Dickey fashion, he stuffed another four cakes in his mouth. "Oh, for Pete's sake, Dickey!"

"Give me a minute," said Dickey, through mouthfuls. "I think better when I'm eating."

"That explains a lot."

"Okay…" said Dickey, now that his mouth was clear. "We should call ourselves…The Wolf Sneakers!"

"What?" said Margaret. "Wolf Sneakers? As in wolfing down your food, Dickey? I blame you for this, Mokheer!"

"Wait a minute," complained Mokheer. "How is his suggestion my fault?"

"Because you knew it was going to be dumb!" cried Margaret. "Thinking while chewing is not his best talent."

"You're right, Margaret," replied Dickey. "I'll stick to chewing." He snatched her last three tea cakes off her plate and wolfed them down." Margaret was livid.

"I'm going to turn you into a frog!" she shouted, jumping up.

"No casting within the house," said Felix, who appeared out of nowhere. "Or the grounds," he continued. Dickey got to enjoy his revenge without retribution.

"We have gotten off the subject of what the brothel boy is offering us," said Besa.

"What's that?" asked Margaret, still glaring at Dickey as he continued to chew.

"You think he's the solution, then?" asked Mokheer.

"Solution to what?" asked Margaret, finally paying attention.

"A solution to why the spirits don't rise for us, like they did for Papa," replied Besa. "Papa's enchantments were always in answer to a question someone had posed. Or a wrong that needed to be addressed. The bones we've been finding have no one to answer to. But this brothel boy has a question to ask the dead Diamond Slim."

"That makes sense to me," offered Dickey, and he placed two of his last four cakes on Margaret's plate. She smiled at him, and then he attempted to take one back.

"You are hopeless," Margaret told him, still smiling. "It makes sense to me too."

"And I guess The Graveyard Club isn't so bad for a name," said Dickey, wolfing down his last two cakes and eyeing Margaret's, so she stuffed both of them in her mouth.

"Good for you!" cried Dickey. "They taste better that way, don't they?"

Margaret couldn't speak but nodded her head in agreement. "Told you so," said Dickey, smugly satisfied.

CHAPTER 9

MEETING STINKY

They were already in the sweet shop when Besa spotted Stinky loitering out front on the walkway.

"Our brothel boy is here," she told Dickey and Margaret.

"Oh, my!" replied Margaret.

"Why, he looks...terrible!" cried Dickey. "Like one of those street children!"

"He actually looks better than the day I first saw him," said Besa.

"I hope you aren't thinking of bringing him in here. If his name fits, I might not be able to finish my cookies!"

"You not being able to eat?" replied Margaret. "I doubt that will happen. But it would be worth seeing."

"I'm not going to bring him in here. We're going outside to talk to him."

"I don't have to come, do I?" asked Dickey, gazing at the filthy boy pacing on the walkway outside. "I have cookies to finish." He stuffed one in his mouth for emphasis.

"Dickey," said Besa. "If you don't consider yourself a

part of our club, then of course you don't have to come." She turned and went out the door.

Margaret followed her out.

"Wow! That was kind of harsh. He worships the ground you walk on."

"I don't know if I agree with you on that, Margaret. But I want him to understand that I'm serious about this. He needs to make up his mind. This boy needs our help, and it shouldn't matter what he looks like. I believe his case is what we need to perform a successful enchantment."

"Hi," said Stinky, moving hesitantly toward them, as if he wasn't sure about Margaret.

"Hello, Stinky," said Besa. "This is Margaret, another member of The Graveyard Club."

"So you liked the name, huh?" asked Stinky.

"Speaking of names," said Margaret. "Is Stinky the name your mother gave you?"

"No," said Stinky, and then got shy and stared at his feet for a moment. "My given name is Cyrus. But no one ever calls me that."

"What if we call you Cy?" asked Margaret.

"Hey, that's not bad!" said Cy, brightening. "I don't know why I never thought of that." At that moment, Dickey came out of the sweet shop and walked over to their little group.

"Sorry. I'm in," said Dickey as he walked over to Cy. "Hello, Stinky," he said. "Want a cookie?" He held the bag out to the boy.

"It's actually Cy now," said Cy. "And I would love a cookie."

Margaret watched Dickey's face as the boy's filthy hand disappeared into the bag.

"Dickey is another member of The Graveyard Club," said Besa.

"Pleased to meetcha, Dickey," said Cy. "And thanks for the cookie."

"Why don't you just keep the bag," said Dickey. Margaret looked like she might faint.

"Why don't we go over to that bench across the street, next to the dry goods store, so Cy can tell us more about his case," said Besa.

They all walked over with Cy leading the way, when a carriage suddenly raced toward them. It must have been stationed somewhere close, because it caught them off guard. "You're not getting away with injuring the bishop!" yelled a non-Magist man who leaned off the side. "Your evil father won't recognize your dead carcass!" He threw a rope that looped around Besa's shoulders, and would have dragged her off her feet—but something grabbed the rope, sliced it in half and then snatched it and held it, so the carriage was held stock still. Besa saw that it was Hebron. The Dreid then shot a bolt that blew the wheels off the carriage and set it ablaze. The two men inside jumped off and ran for their lives. Hebron didn't give chase. He also didn't stick around for a thank-you. It was over before the kids realized what was happening.

"What was all that?" asked Cy.

"Don't worry," said Besa, smiling. "It was just an experiment from school."

Margaret and Dickey were also dumbstruck, but didn't contradict Besa's story. "Why don't you sit down and tell us about your case," said Besa, sitting down first and patting a spot for Cy to sit right next to her.

"You go to a strange school," replied Cy.

"You have no idea," replied Margaret. "Please sit down, so we can continue."

"Okay," said Cy, taking his seat on the bench. "What I was gonna say is me and my sister Sylvie lived on the street for a month after mama and daddy was took by the fever. Sylvie is pretty and could sing well. She also learned piano from our mama. Mama's family had money, but disowned her when she left home for my daddy. He made an honest living on the docks as a Stevedore. When he hurt his back and got laid off, we had it hard, with mama not making much from teaching music to poor children. Then they got the fever, and me and Sylvie took care of them the best we could. Sylvie was thirteen, and I was seven at the time. When mama and daddy died, we couldn't pay the rent on the house, so we ended up on the street. Sylvie wouldn't go to one of them orphan houses. She was afraid we would be separated. So she sang on the street in Vieux Carré. She knew a lot of French and Creole songs mama had taught her, and people gave her money. But that only lasted a few weeks, and then we started going to sleep hungry. We could've gone to one of the Catholic missions, but mama told Sylvie that some of them places take girls that ain't got family and make 'em slaves in they laundries. Sylvie didn't want that, 'cause where would that leave me. But one day this fancy dressed man in a nice carriage came by and gave Sylvie a whole five note. I was so hungry, I almost fainted. We could buy food for five days with that.

"'Where are your mother and father?'" asked the man. Sylvie seemed shy about speaking to him. He was a tall, skinny fellow in a black suit and diamond in the lapel. I told him our mama and daddy was took by the fever.

"'Please accept my condolences on the loss of your parents,'" he said then. He seemed real concerned about us.

But my sister was very standoffish, like she didn't want to talk to the nice man.

"'Thank you very much, sir,'" she finally told him. "'But me and my brother are doing fine by ourselves.'"

"'Don't be foolish, girl. You can't support your young brother by begging on the street. What will you do about his schooling and a place to sleep? I can offer you a job singing in one of my establishments. It pays twenty bills a month with room and board.'"

My sister didn't say a word, just stood there staring out in the distance, like maybe she saw our daddy coming. I was young, but I knew what a place to sleep meant."

The man told her, "'You can't think to raise your brother singing on the street.'"

"'Please, Sylvie,'" I said to her. "'Ain't nobody offered us a place to sleep before.'"

Sylvie finally looked at the man and said:

"'My brother may be little, but he can work, too.'"

"'All right,'" said the man. "'Five bills a month for your little brother. Do we have a deal?'"

He reached out his hand for Sylvie to shake, but she got shy again.

"'What's the matter, Sylvie?'" I asked her.

"'I don't know, Cyrus. This don't feel right. Mama used to tell me about men like him.'"

"'But what else we gon do?'" I asked. "'I wanna sleep in a bed tonight,'" I told her, with tears in my eyes. She pulled me into a hug then, and said,

"'All right, Cyrus. I'll do it for you.'" She was crying but went and shook the man's hand. "'You have a deal, Mr. Slim,'" she said.

"That was two years ago, and I swear fo' God that the first night we slept in that bed in Diamond Slim's brothel, was the last night my sister had any peace. You see, my sister understood where we was goin' was no place for someone like her—a young innocent girl. All I heard was money and a place off the street to sleep. But Diamond Slim was thinking about a different kind of bed. He let her sing and play the house piano, but there was never a night when some drunk john didn't grab her in the middle of one of her songs and try to carry her upstairs. Me and the house piano man was the only ones who tried to stop it, because Mama Stell, the madame, was hopin' one time she might give in. She fought and cried for almost two years. Until a month ago. Mama Stell said somebody else had rented our room. Unless we could pay the seventy bill a month that the new girl would be making, we would be back on the street. I don't know the details of the deal she made with Diamond Slim and Mama Stell, but she didn't want me seein' her after she started. Mama Stell sent me out the house on a detail that kept me away for half the day. When I came back, Sylvie was gone. I asked Mama Stell,

"Where did my sister get off to?"

"'Don't you worry about that, lil' man,'" she said. "'Big sister done took good care of you. You gon have food and a place to sleep as long as you want it. Now git out my office and git back to work!'"

"Everyone else in the house refused to tell me anything. Only the piano man, Murphy Jones, felt sorry for me."

"'You and that gal shouldna never come in here,'" he said. "'I don't know where they went, but she left outta here with Slim.'" "I been livin' on the street, sleepin' where I could, eatin' what I could find, searchin' for Diamond Slim. When I finally located him and was told he was headin' over to the Oaks, I was overjoyed. While we watched other people try to kill each other, I would beg him to tell me where he took my Sylvie. You can only imagine my surprise when I got there, and he was in the process of gettin' his self killed, and I was too late."

"I'm sorry for what you went through," said Besa. "Do you know where his body will be resting?"

"I don't know if you wanna do this thing you told me about," said Cy. "Cause he not gon be in no tomb you can open. He gon be dressed up in a box at the house Mama Stell at."

"He'll be somewhere in the brothel?" asked Margaret.

"He not gon be 'somewhere'. He gon be right down in the front room. A week from now, they gon have a party funeral for him. That's what Murphy Jones, the piano man, told me."

"What time do they do go to sleep?" asked Besa, already formulating a plan.

"Besa," said Dickey. "We can't go into a place like that. It's indecent."

"No more than breaking into a crypt and taking out the bones," replied Margaret.

"But they do awful things in places like that," said Dickey. "And it might be dangerous."

"They gon all be passed out drunk," said Cy. "That's the kinda party Mama Stell throw. The only one not drinking will be Slim."

"We'll make sure we're really quiet and won't wake them," Besa told Dickey. "We can sneak by a bunch of sleeping drunks."

CHAPTER 10

THE SHADOWS

For the second week, the bishop took similar walks out to the docks. That particular evening stevedores were actually loading cargo into the hold of a ship. When the bishop tried to explain why he needed to go there, Father Guidry asked,

"But, André. What are you looking for?"

"I'm not sure, something that I'm missing."

"Something that the Lord God cannot supply?"

"I don't need lectures from you about the Lord God! I'm the bishop!"

"Then act like it, André. I'm not some street brigand you're trying to intimidate. I'm a man of the cloth too, and also your friend. Why don't you let one of the priests take your confession?"

The bishop bristled at the suggestion.

"I don't need to take confession. God already knows how I feel."

"Spoken like a man who really needs to give confession."

The bishop turned and headed out the side door of the diocese, which lead to the street.

"I'm going out," he said.

"At least take a carriage, André," implored Father Guidry.

"No. I need to walk. I'll drive the carriage to the residence later."

"How late?" demanded Michel.

"Are you giving me a curfew, Michel?" asked Delacroix, with an amused look.

"No...I just. Why don't I walk with you?"

"Michel. You have never been one for exercise. The docks are two miles away."

"I won't make that," said Michel, sitting down with a stricken look at the thought of it.

"Then it's a good thing you're not coming." Delacroix closed the door and was off.

"Be careful, Your Grace!" called Father Guidry out of the window he'd opened in the study.

"Don't worry! God is with me!" replied Delacroix.

He had been doing these walks for two weeks now. He didn't dress down or try to conceal the golden cross around his neck. In fact, recently people had started to stroll along with him.

"I hope you don't mind the company, Your Grace," said a man leading another group who looked like they'd just come from digging the canal. "Me, Sean, Billy, and Jackie happen to be goin' your way."

"I don't mind the company, boys. But shouldn't you be heading to the dinner table about this time?" asked the bishop; he pulled a large gold watch from his pocket. "It's past six-thirty."

"We just want to get you to the docks safe," said Jackie. "Ain't no stinkin' low-li—"

Denny stomped on Jackie's boot.

"Ow!" howled Jackie. "What you do that for?"

"Mind your words, Jackie," said Denny. "We want the bishop to have a nice, calm stroll."

"Oh, sorry, Your Grace," said Jackie, a bit ashamed.

"It's all right, Jackie," said the bishop, and they strolled the rest of the way without uttering another word.

"Looks like we've arrived, boys," said the bishop. "All of you kneel down so I may bestow blessings upon you and your families."

"You ain't got to do that, Your Grace," said Denny. "We don't need payment."

"On the contrary," replied the bishop. "I would be remiss in my duties if I did not."

"He would be what?" asked Jackie, looking confused.

"The Lord would not be happy with me if I neglected to bless all of you, as you have blessed me," replied the bishop. "Please kneel down. It won't take but a moment."

The men all kneeled, and the blessings were duly bestowed, and just before Denny and the other men turned to leave, Denny said, "There might be some other fellows getting off shift at the shipyard when you're ready to go back to the chapel, Your Grace."

"Isn't that convenient," said the bishop. "Good night, gentlemen!"

"Well, whadda ya know. Ain't nobody never called me no gentleman," said Jackie.

"That's cause you ain't," replied Billy, giving him a playful shove in the back.

"Ain't nobody tellin' me nothin'," said Jackie. "I'm buyin' me a suit!"

Denny laughed. "You dirt rat. You can't afford no suit!"

But Jackie didn't say another word, which meant he was serious.

And true to his words, a week later, Jackie showed up at the bishop's stroll wearing a black tail coat, black pants, fedora, and had obviously had a bath and a shave to boot.

"Good evening to you, Jacques," said the bishop. The address stopped Jackie in his tracks. "Ain't nobody never called me that but my mum,"

"Yes," beamed the bishop. "I know her. She sits in the second pew right next to the stained-glass window." Jacques walked a little prouder after that, reveling in his shave and new suit.

The other men, not wanting to be outdone, started showing up in a black tail coat, black pants, fedora, and a shave as well. It was now an un-official pre-requisite. By the end of the fourth week of the bishop's escorted sojourns, forty men made up what was now referred to as the bishop's "Shadows."

As the Shadow force grew, they didn't just shadow the bishop on his long walks; they also performed tasks for him around the chapel and the diocese offices.

"André, " asked Father Guidry. "Who are these men?"

"They are friends and followers, Michel," said the bishop. "They just want to help."

"Help with what, André? We have deacons and priests for these tasks."

KIDS SCHOOL STALKING

All the men who followed and commiserated with the bishop knew the history of his injury—and who was to blame. They'd also heard how the man's daughter tried to hurt him again when he went to the courthouse to seek justice. The Shadows had their own way of seeking justice and knew where they should start.

So, when the students of Sister Gerard's walked toward the front door of the building, there were men in black suits —surly looking men—blocking their path.

"Which one of you is Besa?" one of the men asked. He was a thick angry-looking non- Magist."

"None of us are Besa," a girl in front spoke up. "She comes—"

"Don't say another word, Emily!" said Sister Gerard, pushing past the men clothed in her habit to get to her students. "What do think you're doing bullying innocent children?"

"We weren't bullying nobody, sister," said Beefy Guy, backing up a bit in respect. "We just have some questions to ask them."

"These children aren't required to answer any questions from any of you!" she said, ushering the children past the group. One of the men reached out and snatched one of the children—a seven-year-old boy named William Billings.

"You know, sister," said the man, twisting the child's arm until he cried. "Buildings like these get burned down all the time. And nobody knows why."

"Here comes the Gendarmes," replied the sister. "I'm sure they would be happy to talk to you about setting fires and hurting children!"

It was clear the Shadows wanted no part of the Gendarmes. They quickly let go of the boy and ran toward their horses. The interesting thing was, the Gendarmes weren't really coming. It was just a large carriage and driver rolling past the school. The driver waved at the sister as he went by. The sister smiled and waved back as she ushered the children through the door and on to their classes.

NEWS of the Shadows activities reached Father Guidry's ears at the diocese, so he forced the bishop into the confession booth to make contrition for the actions of the group.

CONFESSION

"Bless me father, for I have si—It's been two months since my last confession."

"Your Grace?" said the flustered cleric in front of him. "I-I don't know if I can—"

"Shut up and let me finish, Father!" growled the bishop.

"Yes, your excellency," replied the priest. "Sorry to interrupt, sir."

"No. I'm sorry, Father Doland," replied the bishop. "I confess I'm a little angry at being here."

"Why is that?" asked Father Dolan, calming as he allowed the confessor to continue.

"Because I've been angry at everything lately. I lost a part of me in that attack recently—and then got attacked again. And while I know it's beneath me, I still want revenge. I want to hurt the ne—person who hurt me. I will say the rosary a hundred times before bed tonight, and work on my sinful thoughts. Thank you for listening, Father Dolan." He left the confessional and walked back toward the diocese offices.

"My goodness," said Father Dolan after the bishop left. When the priest moved from the confessional, he went over and collapsed onto the nearest pew and uttered, "Sweet Mother Mary!" He got up, crossed himself, and walked to the back of the chapel.

SEEKS HIS OWN BOOK

And while pressure from Father Guidry went away after the confession, the Shadows did not, and they were still actively working on the bishop's behalf. A week following the confession, one of the Shadows opened the door to the bishop's office and announced,

"Herr Werner Von Boutin is here to see you, Your Grace."

Michel was suddenly confused.

"Who is Werner Von Boutin, André?"

"Someone who has a book I need to look at," replied the bishop, getting up and following the messenger into the chapel sanctuary, where a number of young priests and Shadows had gathered. When Father Guidry arrived, he noted a corpse lying upon a large table in the middle of the sanctuary.

"What in the name of the Lord is the meaning of this, Bishop Delacroix?" cried Father Guidry, observing a thin, dark-haired, short-goateed man in a black tail coat, black pantaloons and a gold medallion on his lapel, setting up items near the body.

"Please calm down, Michel," replied Bishop Delacroix. "Herr Von Boutin needs to concentrate."

"André, have you lost your mind?" He ran over to the table to look at the corpse as Herr Von Boutin arranged substances on the surrounding table. "Has this man been given absolution?" shouted Father Guidry. It was at that moment Herr Von Boutin removed a strange dark book from a doctor's bag. Father Guidry ran across the sanctuary, grabbed a small statue of the Virgin Mary along with a large gold cross, dragged it all over to the table where the corpse was lying and placed himself between it and the advancing Herr Von Boutin.

"In the name of our Lord! I command thee, cease! This ceremony shall not desecrate this man's soul!"

"Father—Michel, please come away from there," said the bishop.

"I shall not, André! I cannot allow such blaspheming in the Lord's sanctuary!"

"Father Guidry," said the bishop, coming toward the distraught cleric. "Why don't we discuss this in my office for a moment?"

Michel was hesitant at first, but the bishop gave him one of his gregarious smiles, like he did during their seminary days. This made it very easy for Michel to fall into step with his dear friend. The bishop even draped an arm around his shoulder as they strolled quietly toward his office door. Once they entered, the bishop said, "Please take a seat, Michel." He poured himself a glass of sherry from the crystal decanter sitting on the cherry wood side board beside his desk and passed Michel a wine glass as well.

Michel took a sip and asked, "What is the matter, André? Is this about the Magist's book?"

"Michel, you don't understand. The power of it was amazing. It would change the holy sacrament."

"André, can you hear yourself? Change the holy sacrament? The Holy Father will ex-communicate us both for this blasphemy. Please think about what you're doing."

After the bishop had been in his office for a few moments with Michel, there was a knock at his door.

"Don't move, Michel. I want to finish this discussion when I come back. I'll be just a moment."

When it took more than a moment, Michel grew suspicious and went back out to the sanctuary, feeling something terrible was about to occur. He had to push his way past all the deacons and young priests crowding the doorway to the sanctuary. When he broke through, he saw Von Boutin holding his black book as he stood chanting over the corpse; then he opened the book and a strange black thing emerged from it. Michel became disoriented and felt like he might faint, but still heard someone screaming, as the black thing floated toward the body. But suddenly Michel was tackled. He hadn't been aware, but the screaming was coming from him. He had charged at Von Boutin. He now lay at the strange man's feet, screaming, "No! No! This shall not be! This shall not be!"

As the black thing merged with the corpse, Michel was keening, "Heeelp! Heeelp! God please, no!" When the spirit rose from the body, it was gray and looked like a frightened thing.

"Spirit," said Von Boutin. "Speak thy truth!"

But the spirit didn't seem to hear him.

"Where am I?" it said, looking about itself. "I'm not supposed...Wait! No! Nooo! Help meee!" and the image disappeared.

"You vile—!" cried Father Guidry. He grabbed Von Boutin by the leg and bit him like a vicious dog. Von Boutin screamed and began hitting the priest on the head with the black book. It opened a wound in Michel's scalp that bled profusely, but he kept screaming, "Blasphemer! Thief!" and kept on biting the man. "To hell!" snarled Michel. "The same place you just sent that man's soul! If I have to send you there myself!"

He reached up, snatched the black book from Von Boutin's hands, clubbed the Shadow holding him down with it, rose and beat Von Boutin with his own book. He would've killed the man if all the priests and Shadows in the room hadn't pulled him off.

"Take him to my office!" said Bishop Delacroix.

It wasn't an easy task as the priest kicked and scratched and bit, as he tried to get back and finish off Von Boutin.

They finally got him through the door of the bishop's office and barricaded it so the crazed cleric couldn't get out.

"Stop this, Michel!" ordered the bishop. "What is the matter with you?"

Michel picked up the hat rack in the corner and charged the bishop. But Delacroix stood his ground. "You want to kill me too, Michel? Go ahead. I won't fight."

But Michel just tossed the thing aside.

"You understand that, don't you, André?"

"I don't know what you mean, Michel."

"That you respect violence. You don't respect sin or divine retribution. But you understood when I tried to cave that evil creature's head in, didn't you?"

"I don't understand where all this anger is coming from."

"Because you stood by while an innocent man's soul was ripped from his body; and you felt nothing. Just so you could test some un-holy book?"

"Michel, you're still bleeding. Please sit down for a moment."

The bishop pulled a handkerchief from his desk and gave it to his friend. Michel took the cloth and held it to his scalp.

"I've asked Deacon Montez, who was a doctor before he came to the church, to come and see to your injuries. But I take offense that you assumed I felt nothing watching that horror unfold. I had no idea the type of book this man would have."

"And yet you unleashed him on—"

"A corpse, Michel. The man was already dead, remember?"

"You saw what happened, André. He very likely sent that man to hell."

"I don't think a book from a strange man can do that. That's a bit presumptuous to think a book could subvert our Lord."

"I seem to recall, not long ago, someone I respect claiming that another book could subvert the holy sacrament."

"Now, just a minute, Michel. I never said that! You are making too much out of this."

"Am I, André? I don't think so. Because all of this is too much. This book lunacy, those Shadows, all of it is bad. And I know it's not going away. So, you have to make a choice. Either put away these evil pursuits, or I am leaving the priesthood."

"You would threaten me, Michel? How dare you!"

"I do dare, André. We are no longer doing God's work. That creature took more than your arm. It seems to have taken your soul. You're not the André Delacroix I've known for all these years."

"Please don't do this to me, Michel. I'll stop. I promise. Why don't you take a carriage to the residence? I'll be along soon."

"All right," said Michel. "But I'm telling you, André. Some of your 'Shadows' are not what they seem."

CHAPTER 11
MAGIST COUNCIL

The whole club had settled into Besa's parlor, as they discussed their plan for the brothel boy's case. Miss Maymi had really outdone herself for this meeting; there were four cakes and four pies, not to mention the four course feast she'd prepared leading up to the decadent dessert fest. Dickey was completely in his element, commandeering one whole cake and a pie.

"Dickey," said Margaret "Why are you such a—"

"Don't bother him, Margaret," said Besa, smiling. "Look at his eyes. He can't hear you, anyway."

"Oh, God! He can't!" said Margaret. "He looks like he's in a trance."

Butter boy had set up his own private heaven on a cherry wood coffee table in front of the settee. Dickey had fetched a serving knife from the kitchen, and waved off the coffee one of the kitchen assistants brought out to offer everyone. He leaned over the four-layered cake to cut his initial slice, when a portal popped open in front of Besa. She only had a chance to say, "Uh-oh!" before it sucked in the whole club—desserts and furniture—depositing them in the middle of the Magist Council chamber.

"Septimius!" cried Besa. "What is the meaning of this intrusion?"

Septimius just reclined in his chair, his paws folded on his stomach, gazing at them all for a moment without uttering a word. Tarum walked toward the dessert table, his eyes all aglow.

"I'm always happy to see you, Miss Melponte. Never mind old sour-puss over there. It just so happens that I—"

"...didn't have dessert," said Besa, rolling her eyes.

"Septimius!" cried Tarum, picking up a plate from the table. "This child is a mind-reader!" Septimius gave a pre-emptive growl.

"Don't mind me, Mr. President," said the vice president, slicing a piece of cake and cutting into one of the pies. "I'll be done in just a moment."

And then there was a blood-curdling scream. It was Dickey. Besa and Margaret rushed over to him. The boy looked like he'd been struck, his face was so red.

"What happened, Dickey?" asked Besa. "Are you hurt?"

"Yes!" said Dickey, finding it hard to breathe. "What happened? A horrible thing! Someone stole a piece of my cake!" cried the boy, pointing at the wounded confection. Margaret was furious. "Why, you gluttonous sack of—"

"Excuse me!" roared the council president. "I don't mean to interrupt your sugar-coated melodrama, but we have important matters to discuss!"

"You could've just invited us here!" snapped Besa. "And saved yourself the trouble of all this!"

"Oh, no," said Tarum. "This works fine for me." He stuffed his mouth full of cake. "MMM! Sugar-coating and all!"

"The question before us, Graveyard Club—that is what you're calling yourselves, right?—Is how are we going to protect you, and keep our end of the bargain, if you don't keep yours?"

"What bargain is he talking about, Besa?" asked Margaret.

"Oops!" said Tarum. "Fearless leader keeps secret."

"Isn't that interesting," said the council president, as he leaned back in his chair and crossed his arms. "Why don't you explain, madam president?"

"I never really gave it much thought," said Besa.

"What do you mean?" asked Margaret as Dickey let out another scream. "Shut up, Dickey! And eat what you've got!" yelled Margaret.

"But somebody stole another piece of my cake," whined Dickey.

"You were saying Besa?" said Margaret.

"I was saying," said Besa, sitting down at the dessert table. "They agreed to protect us. All of us."

"So that was what the thing blowing up the wagon was about?" asked Margaret.

"Yes," said Besa.

"And it was working out wonderfully," said Septimius, coming to slice himself a piece of cake and sitting down at the table. "Until our charges started going out at night, just so they can get attacked." He took a bite of the cake. "This is amazing!"

"Told you so," said the vice president. "Miss Maymi is a wizard!"

"Nevertheless," said Seuz. "The Graveyard Club is violating the terms of our agreement. Namely, that we keep you safe, and you try to stay safe." He took his last bite of cake. "I am having another piece of this." He stood up to take another slice.

"I caught her! I caught her!" cried Dickey. He had a hold of the Seer's left hand, which was still holding the serving knife. "I caught her red-handed!" he said. "She still has icing on her face!" Obsidia looked like a happy rag doll being jostled by the butter boy.

"Let her go, Dickey," directed Margaret. "We're their guests. So you are obliged to share." Obsidia gave a big smile at that statement, and then snatched her arm away from Dickey and sliced herself another piece of cake.

"Hey! That's a big piece!" he complained. "You can't possibly eat all—Oh my God! She stuffed that whole piece in her mouth! I've never seen anything like that!"

"We have," said Besa and Margaret together.

"Graveyard Club!" declared Seuz. "We will not follow you around all night! It's not practical."

"We understand," replied Besa.

"Wait a minute, Besa," said Dickey. "Our last case was dangerous! How can you turn down protection?"

"Be quiet, Mr. Can't-work-his-own-key!" said Margaret.

"But that wasn't...I mean, the thing...But still. How can we turn down protection?"

"You've been voted down, Dickey," said Margaret. "Two to one."

"But Mokheer should—"

"Mokheer doesn't need protection," said Besa. "So, we have an understanding, Mr. President? You can't protect us at night. Please send us back home."

A portal popped up and swallowed them all.

"But wait a minute!" cried Tarum.

"Help!" Dickey could be heard screaming. "Someone took my pie!"

BESA'S DREAMS had been quite active lately. And this night when she went to sleep, she had hoped for a chance to pose more questions to Violet, the Taafli, but this night's dream had an entirely new, though vaguely familiar visitor. A tall, dark, very beautiful older woman was standing on the banks of the swamp, and she wasn't wearing an expensive dress like Besa might prefer. She wore a tignon on her head and a wrap that most of the African dignitaries wore when visiting Newald. Some of them came to purchase the freedom of a kidnapped loved one, or to visit some family holdings of their own plantation. Her papa had called these lushly colored garments pagne.

"Might I come aboard your craft?" asked the woman in perfectly unaccented French.

"Who are you?" asked Besa, suddenly stubborn. "And why do you want to come aboard my boat?"

"Come on, child," said the woman, smiling. "Don't be difficult. Pull up to the bank so I won't have to get my favorite pagne wet and muddy." Besa obliged and pulled up to the little dock that just showed up out of nowhere and let the woman step into the boat. Once she was seated, Besa and the woman just gazed at one another.

"Finally," said the woman. "Do you mind if I hold you for a bit, Besa?" I have watched you from afar for so long. I would like our spirits to finally touch."

Besa leaned forward, and the woman with her father's face wrapped her in something she'd never felt: a motherly embrace. And though she hadn't intended to, Besa cried.

"I didn't get to meet my mother," said Besa, sniffling a bit.

"Neither did I," replied the woman. "And just like you, I was all my papa had."

"Did your papa tell you about your mother?"

"No. I was still very young when he was taken from me."

"Younger than I am?" asked Besa

"Yes. A lot younger," said the woman. "Have you thought about when he comes back and you're gone, Besa?"

"I don't know what you mean. Why would I be gone?"

"I was not unlike you. I, too, had a lot of power when I was very young. But I had no choice but to use my power to protect those I loved. You take unnecessary risks. This case you're going on tomorrow is very dangerous. Please think about whether it's the best thing for you."

"You're Papa's mother?" asked Besa.

"Yes. And I know you're missing him. I would hope to keep you safe until he returns."

"Will you tell me something about Papa, Grandmother? Something that he would never tell me?"

"This is not the dream for that, Besa."

"But this is my dream. I should get whatever I want in my own dream."

"I can't explain it," said her grandmother. "But something is definitely holding me back from offering you more. But I did send Mokheer. Does that help?"

"Thank you. Even though that is not enough and is the reason I'm going to continue doing what I'm doing. This is the only way I can try to understand and be close to Papa. He offered me one small glimpse of himself, and I'm not letting go of it. No matter what, Grandmother. I can only see him in my dreams nowadays, and yet he is still closed off from me. I don't understand why. Thank you for visiting my dream. I hope to see you again."

"Be careful tomorrow, Besa. And I do intend to come back."

Besa paddled back toward the little dock so her grandmother could step out of the boat, then worked her way to the other side of the swamp, looking for Dickey and Margaret.

Shadows

As a part of Father Guidry's conditions for remaining in the priesthood, the bishop dismissed all the Shadows working in the diocese and the chapel. No one complained or put up a fuss, because they knew it was all for show. The bishop convened a new Shadow committee in a large house in Vieux Carré. Although there was one complaint from the bishop when he had to give up his ecclesiastical robes for something a bit more clandestine. This outfit was also blue. Delacroix refused to budge on the color. But he was forced to wear a hat and also a cape.

"This is ridiculous!" declared the bishop, catching a glimpse of himself in a mirror he passed on the way to the house's large library. "I look like a villain in one of those Parisienne melodramas."

"It can't be helped, Your Grace," replied Denny. "You know this city has eyes and ears everywhere."

"You're right, Denny," said Delacroix. "I'm just being an old fuss-bucket. These measures are obviously unavoidable."

He took off his hat and cape, which one of the Shadows placed on the oak hat and coat rack by the door. When he sat down, Delacroix took an assessment of the surroundings. There was a giant polished oak desk, two-level floors of pecan wood shelves stocked with books, black leather chairs with clawed feet and a massive floral Turkish carpet covering the floors.

"This is a beautiful library and a wonderful house. Do we know who the owner is?"

"An anonymous supporter of our cause, Your Grace. Someone who shares your opinion of the Necromancer and his child."

"Please extend our appreciation, Morton. To the business at hand. Have your actions given you any opportunities to seize the girl?" asked the bishop.

"None at all, Your Grace," replied an extremely tall man with deep blue eyes. The bishop figured he must be new. "We've only managed to scare some of the children at her school before the Gendarmes showed up and chased us away."

"Does anyone have any ideas?"

That's when three men stood up, and Delacroix knew, just by looking at their deep green eyes, that they were Magists.

"We have a plan," said the man in the middle of the three. He hadn't spoken very loudly. In fact, Delacroix wasn't sure he'd spoken at all. But his words reached the bishop's ears from all the way across the library, which held fifty individuals.

"What kind of plan is it?" asked the bishop. "Tell me about it."

"We can't tell you about it, Your Grace, because it might hurt you should someone read your mind."

"What kind of nonsense is this?" sputtered the bishop. "No one can—"

"The girl can; and if she comes near you, she'll know our secret. The plan will take a bit of magic, but we know we can pull it off. We'll get back to you when we're done," and they all three vanished.

"Wait a minute!" someone said. "These are Magists? It was a Magist that injured the bishop. Why are we trusting them?"

"Yeah," shouted another voice. "These creatures are monsters! Why would we trust them?"

"All right!" said the bishop, slamming one of the large books down on the desk. "Everyone shut up!"

The room quieted. "I know that some of you are thieves and criminals, right?" Someone replied in the affirmative. "And yet we accepted you. And some of you don't go to church." The room got really quiet. "I'm not judging you. But I know this is a fact. And I imagine a few of you have done terrible things. But the one thing that unites all of you is the cause you share. My cause!" said the bishop. "And now we've come to a point where we need individuals with different kinds of skills. Otherwise, we will be stalled. And so, I'm going to allow these creatures to act on their plan. We don't have any other options, anyway. Did anyone get their names?"

"We are One, Two and Three," came voices that echoed through the room. "I am called One. And there is only one particular issue we need to clarify about the plan," said One's voice.

"And what issue is that, one?" asked the bishop.

"That someone may be dead at the end of it," replied a second voice. "I am Two."

"Obviously, as a representative of the Church, I can't openly sanction a murder."

"But what if it's an accident, Your Grace?" offered Denny.

"I think you have your guidelines, One, Two and Three,"

said the bishop. "The incident must appear to be an accident."

But Jackie apparently had a question, because he raised his hand.

"You have a question, Jacques?" asked the bishop.

"If they're dead, what difference will it make?"

"Shut up, Jackie," said Denny.

"And with that, I think this meeting is adjourned," said the bishop.

THE DEATH OF DIAMOND SLIM

The body was at the brothel, just as Cy had said. And whatever drunken wake Mama Stell had thrown for Diamond Slim was well over at midnight when the kids arrived. But the undertaker and his assistant had loaded the corpse into their wagon, and were driving off just as The Graveyard Club arrived. Besa and the group hung back, but continued to follow the wagon, knowing that if Henby's Undertakers locked Slim inside their establishment, Cy might never learn the whereabouts of his sister, Sylvie. The night was rather misty, so they had no problem following in the shadows. And to Dickey's chagrin, the smelly street boy was obliged to ride with him. Besa was familiar with Henby's, which sat on the corner of St Peter and Royal. But instead of making a left toward their shop, the wagon took a right, toward which cemetery they weren't sure yet. Diamond Slim had not been given absolution of his sins by a priest—as far as Cy knew—so there was no way Henby's could take him to one of the Christian burial grounds, like the St Loomis. So that left the All-Man's potter's field cemetery. Besa became quite nervous when she realized where the wagon was headed.

"Besa," said Margaret. "Are you sure you want to go in there?"

They hung back as the undertaker's wagon rattled through the decrepit little gate, with a wooden sign above that said, ALL MAN'S. Over the years, the sign had injured quite a few people, and killed one when it fell.

"Yes, Margaret," replied Besa. "I do want to go in there. How else are we going to raise Diamond Slim's spirit so that Cyrus can ask him where his sister is?"

"I don't want to go in there," said Dickey. "No offense, Cyrus."

"What are you all afraid of?" asked Mokheer. "It's no different from the three other graveyards we snuck into. There are no crypts to break into here. Everything is out in the open, and if we sit out here too much longer, we won't know where they buried him."

"From the looks of it," said Margaret, "he wasn't buried at all."

The undertaker's wagon came back through the gate, empty.

"What did they do with the body?" asked Dickey, looking perplexed.

"Wait a minute," said Mokheer. "I've heard of this place. Its other name is Prostitutes and Criminals Graveyard. And if I'm not mistaken, there are only two gravediggers for the burials here."

"They just leave the coffins out in the elements?" asked Margaret.

"What happens if it rains?" asked Dickey.

"I think this is a great opportunity," said Besa. "His

body being left out means we can finish this quickly and get Cyrus the answers that he seeks."

"The reason the bodies sit out so long is that no one wants to be in there at night, Besa," said Mokheer.

"Once again. That is perfect. We won't be disturbed. I didn't come this far to turn back. If none of you want to come, then Cyrus and I will do it by ourselves."

Dickey could feel Cyrus' heartbeat as he sat behind him on his horse, so he knew the boy wasn't excited about it either.

"What do you say, Cyrus?" asked Besa. Cyrus didn't respond.

"Are you afraid of the spirit, or are you afraid to know the truth?"

"I thought y'all worked as a team," said Cyrus. "How we gon do this with just me?"

"She won't be going alone," replied Mokheer. "If you are determined to go, Besa, I will be with you."

"Me too," said Dickey.

"You're just saying that so Mokheer won't make you look like a coward," said Margaret.

"It doesn't matter why I'm saying it. I'm going. Who's the coward now? Puck-puck puckaah!"

"You keep making chicken sounds at me and I'll—"

"I know. You'll turn me into one. Are you coming or not?"

"Of course, I am," said Margaret. "I'm certainly not going to let you make me look like a chicken."

"Why don't we all just flap toward the entrance," said Mokheer. "Before something makes off with old Slim's corpse."

"They're already spooked, Mokheer," said Besa. "And that did not help."

As they coaxed their reluctant mounts through the gate, everyone came to a halt, for the landscape inside All Man's was cloaked in a dense fog—or what looked like a fog. This was apparently unique to All Man's, because all the land adjacent to the graveyard had hardly any fog at all.

"I can't see a thing in here," said Dickey. "How are we to find Slim's body?"

"Henby couldn't have gone very far," said Besa. "I'm sure if we just keep to the little road and move slowly, we should come to it."

Besa's assessment proved correct, because about a hundred yards from the entrance into All Man's, they came upon a coffin sitting in the wet grass. The lid remained in place, but you could tell that someone or something had attempted to pry it open. The wood at the head of the coffin looked scratched and clawed at.

"Dickey, have you brought your lantern?" asked Besa.

"I didn't think we would need it. We were supposed to do this inside a brothel."

"I've been working on a spell that can ignite an object," said Margaret. "But it will only last a few minutes."

"Mokheer," said Besa. "Would you look around on the ground and find us a branch for Margaret to ignite?"

"Absolutely," said Mokheer, disappearing into the fog.

"Are we gon get to talk to slim, Miss Besa?" asked the boy.

"We should be soon, Cyrus," replied Besa. "We just need a good light to see by in this fog."

"Besa!" cried Dickey. "I'm sure I saw something move out—Ow! Something bit me! We need to get out of here! It's not safe!" He turned his horse toward the gate.

"Oh, for Pete's sake, Dickey!" said Margaret. "Just calm down. I'm sure nothing bit you."

"Oops!" said a cheeky Mokheer, walking past Dickey with the branch he was sent for. "Sorry. Just trying to find my way back. Here's your branch, Margaret. Hope it's big enough."

"This will do fine," said Margaret. "See, Dickey. You're overreacting again."

"You did that on purpose," Dickey told Mokheer.

"I said I was sorry," said Mokheer.

Margaret went about the process of igniting the branch.

"Can you maybe not bother him so much tonight, Mokheer?" asked Besa. "He's already a little antsy."

"You're taking his side?"

Margaret ignited the branch. Its brightness lit up the area about ten yards around them, revealing that all the graves in that space had been dug up, the coffins ripped open and lying empty on their sides.

"Finally, we can get to work," said Besa, dismounting and going to examine
the casket.

"This is unsettling," said Margaret. "Whatever opened up all those graves probably made those gashes."

"What kind of creature could dig up all those graves and put such deep gouges in the wood like that?" asked Dickey.

"Dickey, don't worry about that. Please dismount and set the wards," said Margaret.

But Dickey was slow to move.

Besa told him,

"The sooner we get started, the sooner we can leave."

When Dickey dismounted, he tried to help Cyrus down, but the boy waved him away and jumped off on his own.

"Dickey," said Besa. "Would you give me your pry bar, so we can get this coffin open?"

Dickey retrieved the short metal rod from his saddle-bags and handed it to her.

"Thank you," said Besa. The wood made strange screeching sounds that caused Dickey to jump, as Besa pried up the nails in the lid.

"How often do you have to pry a coffin open?" asked Cyrus.

"This will be the first time on a coffin," said Besa, puffing a bit as she worked on a difficult nail. "We mostly use this to pry the lid off a sarcophagus."

"What's that?" asked Cyrus.

"It's like a coffin made of stone," said Margaret.

"How far out should I set the wards?" asked Dickey.

"Normally, I would say ten paces," said Margaret.

"I'm not going ten paces into that fog!" cried Dickey.

"Okay, then five should do."

Dickey stood gazing into the dense fog as though trying to tell if something was in it.

"I think I saw something move out there," he said.

"Check to see where Mokheer is, Dickey," said Margaret. "Then please do your job."

"What are you talking about? I do my job!"

"Are the wards set, Dickey? Because they almost have the lid off."

"All right," said Dickey, staring fiercely into the fog. "Mokheer! I know you're out there trying to scare me! I am not—"

A pair of glowing eyes pierced through the fog and came toward him. Dickey fled back toward the coffin, saying, "Something! Something's coming!"

"What is the matter with you?" asked Margaret. "You're not helping, Dickey.

"But I saw—" Mokheer came into the light carrying two more branches.

"I thought you might need these soon," he said, handing the branches to Margaret.

Thank you, Mokheer. You've been helpful."

Just then the ignited branch went out, and Margaret quickly ignited a second one.

"But he's not helpful!" cried Dickey. "He's been trying to scare me since we got here!"

Margaret just shook her head and sighed, as she lent her free hand to help Besa and Cyrus remove the lid from the coffin.

"Tell me, Cyrus," said Besa as Margaret held the ignited branch over the coffin. "Is this the corpse of Diamond Slim?"

The corpse was dressed in an expensive black suit, with ivory buttons all down the front, and some glistening jewels at the cuffs of the shirt with Slim's arms folded across his chest. Besa wasn't sure it was wise leaving jewelry on a corpse being buried in a pauper's graveyard, but that was no concern of hers.

"Yes, that's him," said Cyrus, after close study. "I'd know that smug nose anywhere."

When the boy confirmed the body's identity, a strange light emanated from Besa's skin and her eyes glowed.

"Is this going to work?" whispered Cyrus to Dickey.

"It should, if you will be quiet," offered Mokheer. All the kids had watched Besa during all the other enchantment attempts, but this one was different. As Besa progressed through her incantation, she exuded a golden light, not unlike the glow that emanated from the Taafli, and she levitated about three inches off the ground. When the incantation was finished, she didn't have to be lowered down; this was accomplished by some outside force, which placed her head exactly on the pillow. The second her head touched it, the Taafli rose and hovered for a moment.

"Such a gloomy place you've found, young ones. Stay close," it instructed. And then it merged with the corpse of Diamond Slim. When the spirit rose, Margaret almost dropped the ignited branch.

"Why has thou summoned me?" inquired the spirit. Everyone looked for Cyrus, but he was hiding over by the horses.

"Cyrus, what are you doing?" asked Margaret. "You have to ask it your question. Dickey, bring him over before it departs."

"Come on, Cyrus," said Dickey. "Don't you want to ask it about Sylvie? Don't worry, we'll go together." Dickey put his arm around the boy's shoulders and guided him toward the spirit. The entity regarded him with hooded eyes.

"Cyrus, it is strange to see thee here. What would thou ask of me?"

But Cyrus couldn't speak, as he gazed at something beyond his comprehension.

"Say something, Cyrus," coaxed Dickey. "You're supposed to ask it a question." But Cyrus appeared thunderstruck, unable to utter a word.

"I go now," said the spirit, as it began to descend back into the corpse.

"Cyrus, you have to say something!" cried Dickey. But the spirit was fading.

"Where did you take Sylvie?" blurted Cyrus. The spirit stopped and turned to regard him.

"I have her on the Yankee, in cabin twelve," replied the spirit.

"Is she alive?" asked Cyrus.

"Life is still in her," replied the spirit, and receded back into the corpse. Then the branch went out. Margaret quickly retrieved the third one and ignited it.

"Dickey, where's Besa?" asked Margaret, as she shined the light on the spot where she lay just a few moments before.

"I—I don't know," said Dickey. "She was there a second ago."

"Did you set the wards, Dickey?"

"I—I intended to, but Mokheer kept—"

"Where is Mokheer, Dickey?" asked Margaret, as the Taafli ascended from the corpse and let out a horrific shriek, blasting the whole area with light.

"A dark thing has taken the Golden One!" declared the Taafli. "See there! The child of light battles the beasts!" It gave a second shriek and took off toward them.

"Dickey!" cried Margaret. "Go and get her! If that thing kills her—"

Dickey was already shifting when he took his first step. A group of the creatures were trying to corral Mokheer, as a fourth ran across the graveyard with Besa. The Taafli hovered above them, but seemed tentative. Dickey had grown to twelve feet and made quick strides toward the Taafli.

"What happened?" asked Dickey, in his booming giant's voice. "Why didn't you stop the monster?"

"My power will erase it, but the golden one will die too. I cannot harm her. You must take her away from it, Titan. It goes to the steeple!"

There was a small cathedral right at the back of All Man's, and the monster was headed for it, leaping the fence that separated the graveyard from church property. At this point, Margaret flew toward the Taafli, and Cyrus, riding

Dickey's horse, wasn't far behind her. Mokheer killed one of the three creatures attacking him, and the two others fled toward the church-yard after the gigantic Dickey, the Taafli and Margaret in flight. When the creature holding Besa leapt onto the roof and tried to disappear into the rafters, Dickey made an incredible lunge and grabbed one of its legs. When it turned to take a swipe at Dickey with one of its massive claws, Besa slipped from its grasp. When Dickey turned to try to catch her, the monster, a pale-skinned beast with a mouth full of teeth, jumped on Dickey and they both fell off the roof and hit the ground. The thing wasn't as large as Dickey, but it was huge, about eight feet to Dickey's twelve. Luckily for Besa, whose head struck one of the stone angels lining the chapel's roof, the Taafli managed to slow her descent enough for Margaret to catch her and lay her gently on the ground; she conjured a pillow and placed it under Besa's head—which bled a good bit. Margaret stayed by her friend and extracted some cloth from the pouch at her waist, using it to wrap Besa's head. The Taafli easily erased the two creatures running towards them, while Dickey snapped the creature that had taken Besa in half.

"Yuck!" cried Dickey. "What was that thing? It stank."

"That was part of chapter 26, in the Conjurer's Manual, Dickey, 'Ghouls and other flesh-eating monsters'," replied Margaret, adjusting Besa's pillow a bit.

"Oh. I guess I didn't get to that part yet."

"That's not the only thing you didn't get to!" snapped Margaret.

"I'm sorry," said Dickey, shrinking. "I don't know what else to say."

Mokheer finally caught up to them.

"Is Besa all right?" he asked, kneeling down to look at her. "She has a bruise on her face."

"She hit her head on one of the angels on the roof, when that thing dropped her," said Margaret. "I wrapped it the best I could. It's almost gone. The Taafli must be healing it. Goodness, gracious. How did he find us?"

Felix pulled up in one of the Melponte's family wagons.

"I'll take it from here, Margaret," said the Taíno, stepping down from the wagon to lift up his young cacica and lay her on the blankets in the bed of the wagon.

"How did you find us?" asked Margaret.

"I always know where Besa is. I have the same link to her that I had to her father. Her grandmother made sure of that."

"I guess this is the end of The Graveyard Club now, said Dickey. "Once Septimius finds out, he will never forgive us for this."

"He will hear nothing from me," said the behike. "My task is to keep Besa safe as she follows part of her destiny."

"Part of her destiny?" asked Dickey. "What is the other part?"

"We can't really know that, Dickey," said Mokheer. "Only when it presents itself."

"We have more than one destiny?" asked Dickey.

"Most of us do," replied Felix, climbing back onto the wagon. "Besa has taken ill," he said. "That's what you must tell anyone who asks where she is; she will be at home for a while."

"Okay," said Margaret. "I see. How long will she be at home?"

"About two weeks," said Felix. "You can all visit her after a week."

He drove the wagon out of the church-yard. They all

saw Mokheer appear on the wagon and sit down next to Besa.

"I hope Besa is all right," said Dickey.

"You'd better hope she is," said Margaret, glaring at him. "And you—Never mind. It's time to go home," and then she took off. The only person left besides Dickey was Cyrus, astride Dickey's horse.

"You want me to give you a ride to the docks?" Dickey asked the boy.

"No, thank you," said Cyrus. "The Yankee won't be back to shore for another two days."

"You know the ship?" asked Dickey.

"It's not a ship. It's a river-boat. It's where Slim done a lot of his gamblin'. I'll be waitin' when it docks." The night mist disappeared him as he walked back toward the road.

WHEN BESA AWOKE from her coma, a tall, broad-shouldered, blue-eyed man with thick spectacular blond hair sat in a chair next to her bed. He wore a blood red velvet tail coat, gold patterned vest and white silk pants. There was also a diamond and sapphire encrusted 'S' medallion on his lapel. Besa started when she saw him and moved to the other side of the bed.

"Who are you?" she asked. "And what are you doing in my room?"

The man sighed and looked at his hands and ran them through his beautiful hair.

"I'm Septimius, Besa."

"What!" said the girl. "But you look human."

"I am. For a little while, at least."

"You don't like being human?"

"No. I don't. It's complicated. But this is not about me. It's about you."

"What do you mean?"

"I never had children, so I can't really understand being a father. But I thought if I looked like...like you, maybe I could reach you. And try to...help you."

"This was very sweet of you," said Besa. "I don't know what so say. But my situation is complicated too."

"But Besa, this was dangerous. I'm a monster, so I know dangerous when I see it. I don't understand why you have to do this."

"I'm trying to understand my father," said Besa. "Because I never knew anything about him. Other than necromancy—it's all I have now."

One of the kitchen assistants brought in a tray of food—eggs, bacon, muffins and tea—and sat it on the mahogany tea table and pulled it to the foot of Besa's bed.

"Thank you, Millie," said the girl, getting up and preparing herself a plate. "Would you care for some breakfast, Mr. President?"

"I've never eaten more than when I visit you, Miss Melponte. Maybe some bacon." Besa gave him six pieces on one of the gold-edged custom Taafli plates. "Tea and a muffin?" she asked, placing a muffin on his plate.

"Thank you. I love blueberry."

They sat quiet for a long moment and just ate.

"You said you never had children," said Besa, sipping her tea. "Did you ever try?"

"Yes," replied Septimius, wiping his hands and mouth on one of the "M" monogrammed silk napkins. "But it was very long ago. I was married, but after my attack, I changed, and my wife..."

"She lost your child when she saw you?" asked Besa.

"She jumped out of the window of our castle—pregnant with my child."

"I'm sorry," said Besa. "You would've made a wonderful father. And I appreciate what you're trying to do. But this is my legacy, and like you, I can't not be what I am. No one knew what I was before Papa showed me. I don't have him, but I have this."

"Go ahead and finish your breakfast, before it gets cold," said Seuz. "And I do understand. I wish I didn't, but I do."

He got up and went toward the door. "Thanks again for the food."

"I'll be having breakfast again tomorrow," said Besa, smiling, "if you want to come by."

"Probably not. Tarum would try to come with me," said Septimius, grinning. "We don't want that."

"No, we don't."

"At least you won't be by yourself," he said, going out the door.

"I'm not?" asked Besa. "Who else is here?"

"That would be me," said Mokheer, appearing at her bedside. "I'm wounded you'd think I would abandon you in your hour of need."

"My hour of need? I'm in my room with all the food I want and a vigilant attendant. What need do I have?"

"Entertainment," replied Mokheer.

"So, do you sing?" asked Besa, cheekily.

"Absolutely not!" snorted the warlock boy. "But if you close your eyes, I can show you every single detail of what happened last night."

"Okay..." said Besa.

Two hours later...

"Good heavens!" cried Besa. "I could've been killed!"

"You noticed that, huh? Do you still think this Graveyard Club is a worthy endeavor, Besa?"

"Is that why you showed me all that, Mokheer? To get me to stop?" Besa rose to pour herself another cup of tea—it wasn't cold yet—and sat down on the end of her bed, sipping it.

"I want you to do something a little safer, Besa. That's all."

"Mokheer, let me ask you a question." She reached over and took a cookie off the tea tray.

"What's that, Besa?"

"I don't know very much about you. But you seem to know everything about me. What is my power for?"

"What is it for? I don't know what you mean."

She took a pillow from the head of her bed and stretched out on it as she retrieved another cookie off the tea tray.

"I've known you my entire life, and you say you were drawn to me because of my powers. If they're not meant for enchantments, then what do you think they're for? Because one minute you tell me something very important about them that helps me use them better. And the next minute you want me to stop. I don't understand."

"You saw what happened, Besa. Your life was in jeopardy. I just want—"

"To control me?" asked Besa, looking him in the eyes. "I saw what happened, and the one thing that stood out is you got Dickey so confused and frightened, he forgot to set the wards that would've protected me."

"Wait a minute. You're saying this was my fault?"

"You showed me every little detail, Mokheer," she said, still holding his gaze. "You didn't see that you had a hand in the chaos? And that it almost got me killed?"

Mokheer didn't say anything for a long time, as he seemed to consider Besa's observations. "You want me to go away?"

"No. I don't," said Besa, sitting up and taking the pillow onto her lap to lean her elbows on it. "But you can't continue to do stuff like last night and tell me you're trying to keep me safe. Because I'm still going to do this. With you, or without you. It would be harder, because I'm still learning things about myself. Things that you seem to know. So yes, I want you to stay with us. But only if you're helping me."

Mokheer didn't say anything, and then just disappeared.

"I guess I have your answer."

AFTER A WEEK of staying at home, Margaret visited and brought Besa's homework assignments sent by her teachers. Dickey came too, bringing bread made by his mother. This little gift had the effect of insulting Miss Maymi, who didn't take kindly to someone else cooking for Besa. Dickey apologized profusely and swore he would never do such a thing again. Miss Maymi graciously accepted and gifted him a large piece of chocolate cake. Dickey being Dickey, Margaret could see the wheels turning.

"Quit trying to think of other things you can apologize for, Dickey. Because I know you. At least I know your stomach."

"He can have all the cake he wants," said Besa. "Miss Maymi won't mind."

"Don't tell him that. He'll run through that kitchen like a Hun, wolfing down everything in sight."

"I will not!" cried Dickey.

"Really?" replied Margaret. "Let me guess your next thought...Where is the kitchen, right?"

"You're wrong!" said Dickey. "All I want to know is where Besa's father's library is located in the house."

"It's one floor down," said Besa. "Just off the hallway that passes through the front entry."

"Thank you," said Dickey, getting up to head downstairs. "See. You don't know everything, Miss...Don't-know-everything. I'm going to go do a little reading."

"Sure," snorted Margaret. When Dickey opened the door and disappeared down the stairs, Margaret asked, "Does that long hallway to the study go by the kitchen by chance?"

"Yes, it does."

"He'll be studying a pie pan or maybe a cake plate, but no books will be involved."

Besa chuckled. "Miss Maymi won't mind feeding him."

"Just remember, he has the appetite of a Titan."

Besa enjoyed the company, but stayed home longer than two weeks.

～

FINDING SYLVIE

Cyrus managed to scrounge some odd jobs at a few of Slim's other brothels. He used the money he made to buy some clean, non-raggedy clothes, and he'd also had a much-needed bath. When the Yankee came in from its two-day circuit up the Mississippi, he was at the docks. He didn't wait for the vessel to come to a complete stop and tie off. He sprang across the gap and raced below deck before anyone could say a word to him; he intended to get to cabin twelve as quickly as possible. It took him a minute because he had to count down. Reading wasn't his strong point, but he could count to twenty. When he got to the last cabin, and it was eighteen, he knew twelve was one level up. He started to get nervous as he got to thirteen. He stopped just before twelve, not knowing what he would say to her. But before he made up his mind, a tall man in a nice black suit walked past him. Cyrus's heart stopped for a minute, because it looked like Slim. He collected his thoughts in time to see that it wasn't, just as the man reached for the door knob of 12.

"Hey!" said Cyrus. "I wouldn't go in there," the lie he was concocting forming in his mind as he spoke.

"Why not?" asked the man, who had a smile just like Slim's. "I hear she's a lot of fun. But surely, she's too old for you, little man."

"I wouldn't go in there 'cause my daddy tracked my momma here. He's mad and got a gun. He ain't gon' shoot her if she come with us. But you don't wanna meet him." The smile left the man's face, and he backed away from the door. "Thank you, Sport. That was good information. And here..." The man reached into his pocket, pulled out his wallet and handed Cyrus a note. "For your trouble," he said, as he walked back toward the upper deck. Cyrus shoved the note into his pocket without looking at it and knocked on the door before some other man approached it.

"Who is it?" came Sylvie's voice. Cyrus was tongue tied

for a moment, because her voice sounded like their momma's voice.

"Sylvie, it's me," he replied. Sylvie didn't respond for a while.

"I don't know a Sylvie. There's no one by that name here," she finally said.

"Sylvie, you got our momma's voice. It's me, Cyrus. Please open the door."

"Go away, Cyrus. You can't be here. Slim will be angry if he finds you here. Go back to momma Stell's. She's supposed to take care of you. I made a deal with Slim. Please, Cyrus!" She was crying now. "You can't see me like this. Please go back."

"They ain't no more deal, Sylvie. I'm not at momma Stell's no more. And Slim is...Sylvie, Slim is dead." The door cracked open. As Cyrus walked in a strong smell of alcohol hit his nose, and Sylvie lay on the bed with the covers over her head, crying. Cyrus approached the bed and tried to pull the sheet back.

"Don't, Cyrus," she said, still crying. "You can't see me like this."

"But I know what you look like, Sylvie. I ain't scared of what you look like."

"I don't have any clothes on, Cyrus. Slim took them so I couldn't leave."

"That scalawag!" said Cyrus. "I'm glad he's dead!"

"Don't say that, Cyrus," admonished Sylvie. "It's not nice to say that kind of thing."

"It wasn't nice what he done to you. I came to get you outta here."

"Where are we going?"

"I don't know," said Cyrus. "But we gotta go. Before—"

A knock came at the door.

"Who is it?" asked Sylvie, before Cyrus could stop her.

"Time to change your sheets, Silver," came a woman's voice.

"That's just Lizzie," said Sylvie. "She comes and cleans the rooms."

"Why she call you Silver?" asked Cyrus.

"That's the name Slim gave me. He said it was best if I didn't tell people my real name."

"That make sense to me," said Cyrus. "That's the one nice thing he did."

"Let her in, Cyrus. Lizzie is sort of like my friend."

"Oh, and I got an idea how to get you outta here," said Cyrus.

"What kind of idea, Cyrus? What are you going to do?"

"Don't worry. I got good at this at momma Stell's. Let me do the talkin'."

Cyrus opened the door and let the girl in. She wasn't much older than Sylvie, and when he saw how slender she was, he knew his plan could work.

"Hey," said Lizzie when Cyrus let her in. "Who this boy here be?" The girl was a tall, slender, dark-haired Cajun, by her accent.

"Hello Lizzie," said the boy. "My name is Cyrus. I'm one of Slim's runners from his brothel over on St. Phillip. I'm supposed to take Sylvie over there to Slim. But she doesn't have any clothes. Do you have a dress she could borrow, and also a pair of shoes? It's kind of chilly out tonight."

Lizzie looked suspicious. But Cyrus had another ace up his sleeve. He pulled the note the man in the hall had given him and said, "I have a little money I can pay you with. Slim wanted us to take a cab over. How much for the dress and some shoes and some bloomers?"

"Tha's a fifty note! I ain't got no change for that. I give

the dress, shoes and bloomers for five. Tha's a fair price." Cyrus was stumped for a moment, then Sylvie spoke.

"Isn't there a cashier in the casino? Slim mentioned it once."

"I'll get change," said Lizzie, taking the note. "I'm not no cheater." She took the bill and left the room, but was back about half an hour later with a dress and bloomers that Sylvie was very pleased with, along with the shoes. She handed Cyrus the change. He handed her two notes back.

"For your trouble," he said.

"Thank you, Mr. Cyrus," said the girl, pleased with the transaction. "I'll have the room nice and clean when you get back, Silver!"

"Thank you, Lizzie," replied Sylvie, as the girl made her exit. "Step outside while I get dressed, Cyrus."

The boy did so without comment. He was too busy pondering their next move. They needed a place to go after this. He didn't want Sylvie walking the streets, because one of Momma Stell's people might see her and try to take her back.

Then he realized there was only one place he could go.

"Okay. You can come in, Cyrus," said Sylvie. When Cyrus walked in and saw his older sister, he realized that she wasn't a girl anymore; she was a woman. And with the dress he'd bought from Lizzie, she looked respectable.

"Come on, Sylvie," he said. "Let's get outta here before somebody else comes."

"But where are we going, Cyrus?"

"I have a friend I met over the last few months. We going over there right now. Just grab a bag, so we'll look like people gettin' off a boat after a trip. That one over there will do. We just need somethin' to carry."

"But that's Slim's bag!" cried Sylvie. It was a black doctor's bag sitting in the corner beside the armoire.

"I know he ain't gon you mind borrowin' it, Sylvie. We just need somethin' in our hand, okay? Let's go."

She snatched up the bag and Cyrus hurried her up the passage-way toward the main deck. Just as he'd hoped, there were taxi-for-hire waiting at the dock. Cyrus went up to one and opened the door for Sylvie.

"But where are we—"

"Just get in, Sylvie, while I pay, okay?" She still looked unsure, but decided to trust her brother, since he had gotten them this far. When Cyrus climbed into the carriage, she asked him again, "Where are we going, Cyrus? And where did you learn that fancy talk you used on Lizzie? You don't talk like that."

"It's somethin' called a bluff. One of the gamblers that used to come to Momma Stell's taught me it. He said when you want somethin' from people, you got to sound like somebody they can trust. The money brought it all together. They believe you ain't lyin' if you show 'em money."

"I noticed you've gotten a lot taller, little boy," said Sylvie. "You'll be taller than me soon."

"I'm almost ten, and I stopped bein' a boy around eight and a half. I didn't have a choice. I'm sorry I wasn't there when he took you. I'll try to make up for it."

"I'm sorry, too," said Sylvie, pulling her brother into a hug. "Cyrus, how did you find me?" When she looked down at his head leaning on her bosom, she saw that her brother was asleep. She could only imagine what he'd gone through just to get to her. And she'd had no idea if she would ever see him again. But there would be time to make up for that. She would never leave him again. She'd often rocked him to sleep when he was a baby, so holding him now felt very comforting. No matter what, they would face what came together. When the carriage stopped and she looked out the window, she knew there had to be a mistake.

"Cyrus, wake up," she said, shaking him. "The taxi brought us to some strange large house!"

Cyrus woke up yawning and looked out the window. "Wow!" he said. "It looks pretty much like I thought it would. Let's get out and see if she's home."

"See if who's home, Cyrus? Who lives here?"

"This is the person who helped me find you."

"But how did she know where I was if I've never met her?"

"I'll tell you later. Let's go meet Miss Melponte. She offered me a job once. Hopefully, it's still available."

Cyrus and Sylvie walked in on one of The Graveyard Club's after-school gatherings. They were all very happy to see the brothel boy again, and meet his sister Sylvie. Dickey was dumbstruck at the sight of her.

"Ugh," he managed. "Would you like some pie?"

"Dickey," said Margeret. "Close your mouth before something flies into it. And maybe offer her a chair, so she can sit down and eat pie."

"Oh, yeah," said Dickey, pulling over one of the parlor's wheelback side chairs. Once Sylvie was seated, he went over to the large apple pie that Miss Maymi had made for the group that evening, and cut her a large piece. "Thank you, handsome," replied Sylvie, accepting the pie. "You're so sweet."

Dickey looked like he might faint, he was so flattered.

Sylvie started eating the pie while still holding on to Slim's bag.

"Why don't I put that away for you?" offered Dickey, accidentally grabbing the clasp, which caused the bag to pop open and spill its contents at Sylvie's feet. Shockingly, the bag was full of one-hundred-dollar notes.

"Oh, my," said Margaret. But Cyrus's quick mind spat out a statement almost instantly, as he gathered up the notes and put them back in the bag.

"It's the inheritance Slim left Sylvie," he said in his bluff voice. "We were hoping you could suggest a place where we could put it." Sylvie didn't refute the story and decided once again to follow her brother's lead.

CHAPTER 13

DICKEY'S SECRET

One evening while Dickey rode Constance home from school, he made a left on Ursulines Avenue, and at the corner of Ursulines and Dauphine, an aroma made him come to a stop. "Oh, my goodness, Constance!" he said. "Can you smell it? That is the most amazing thing I've ever smelled."

Constance gave a little whinny. "Yes. Of course, Miss Maymi's is better, but whatever this is, we should at least investigate."

They turned up Dauphine and about half a block from the corner stood a pretty little building in the shape of a giant macaron cookie, with the delicate outer cookie and the cream in the middle. It was lemon colored, Dickey's favorite flavor, so naturally he wanted to stop and go inside. The shop was named Mimi's Sweets and Treats.

Dickey's only problem was, Constance didn't want to approach the little building; she tried to keep walking and wouldn't give Dickey her head.

"What's the matter, girl?" Dickey asked. Constance shook her head, like she was actually saying no. "Come on, girl. All I want is to go in and take a look. We won't stay long. I promise."

But Constance wasn't having it. She reared a bit when Dickey tried to force her head around. "All right. I get the message. You must be tired. Let's get you home. I can come back tomorrow. I'll let you rest that day. I've been riding you too hard lately. I'll bring someone else tomorrow."

He took the mare home and put the feed bag on her. As he rubbed her down, Constance was still trembling.

"Why are you so tense, girl?" asked Dickey, stroking her muzzle. "We're home now. I promise I will not take you back to the sweet shop. I'll ride someone else tomorrow."

And true to his word, he rode a brown gelding—named William. The shop was on a residential street with a number of other family dwellings, but when he arrived, there were no other patrons inside. And a sign in the front window said, "Free samples!"

Dickey got excited when he saw that, and quickly tied up William and went inside. As he entered, he saw a beautiful blond girl a little older than him going into the back. She wore a red day dress, and a gold medallion hung around her neck.

"Excuse me for a moment," she said with an amazing smile. "I'll be right back. Help yourself to any of the samples."

Dickey couldn't believe his luck. The sample tray was full of every kind of sweet he could want. Cookies, little miniature cakes, sweet rolls, lemon-flavored macaron cookies. Even maple and pecan glazed eclairs—which also had a praline filling. He'd never had anything like that before. Not even from Miss Maymi. The girl who went in the back never came out again, and Dickey gorged himself on the samples. She'd said for him to help himself. He ate so much that he wasn't able to finish off Miss Maymi's cake after the meeting that evening.

"Are you dying or something?" asked Margaret, seeing the kitchen assistants take the remainder of the cake away.

"Margaret!" said Besa. "That's a little harsh."

"Besa, we both just saw Richard O' Brien send back cake. Think about that for a moment."

"That is a bit strange for you, Dickey," said Besa. "Are you sure you're okay?"

"Yes. I'm just full," said Dickey.

"I have literally never heard Dickey utter such a phrase," said Margaret. "There is definitely something wrong with him."

Dickey looked perplexed and went over and stretched out on the settee.

"I don't know what the big deal is," he said. "I ate before I came."

Margaret went over and touched his face and neck.

"He's not running a fever."

"I said I ate before I came. Is that a crime?"

"And where did you eat that served enough to fill you up?"

"I'm not saying. It's my little secret." He then let out a satisfied burp.

Margaret went over to the dessert table and sat beside Besa, who was taking small bites out of her piece of cake, as if to make it last, and whispered into Besa's ear.

"You know, Besa, all you'd have to do is—"

"I'm not doing that, Margaret," replied Besa.

"How did you—So you won't read Dickey's mind, but you'll read mine?"

"I didn't have to read your mind, Margaret."

"That's the same thing."

"No, it's not. I already know how your mind works." Besa put a forkful of cake into her mouth. "Besides, Dickey deserves to keep his own secrets. He doesn't get many."

She didn't look at Margaret as she continued to eat her slice of cake.

"But he could be in danger! Could you look at me, please?"

"I'm trying to relax," said Besa, moving to one of the side chairs near the fireplace in the parlor.

"You know I can hear you, Margaret," said Dickey, putting one of the settee's pillows behind his head to make himself more comfortable. "It's good that Besa respects privacy—unlike some people." He closed his eyes as if to take a little nap.

"You're delusional!" cried Margaret. "She's already read your mind. She just won't tell me what she saw."

"Doesn't matter," replied Dickey. "Respecting people's privacy. Thank you, Besa."

"Thank You, Dickey," said Besa, handing her plate and fork to one of the kitchen assistants, who exchanged them for a cup of coffee.

"Oh, you two are just too much!" declared Margaret. "Butter guts over here is probably getting poisoned by some enchanted bakery that's also curbing his appetite. But we can't do anything to save him. Because we're protecting his privacy!"

"Margaret, please," said Besa. "Don't get yourself so worked up over this. Here. Have a cup of coffee." She handed her the extra cup off the coffee tray.

"No, thank you. I'd better be getting home. I'm getting a headache from all this."

It didn't help that most of the trays the kitchen assistants served with were either gold or silver. This was an influence from her mother. It made Margaret feel a bit guilty. Because Besa didn't choose the life she had. She was born into it.

"Oh, I wish you wouldn't, Margaret," said Besa, putting her arms around her dear friend. "It makes me think I've run you off."

"It's all right," replied Margaret. "Seeing all these cups and trays reminded me that I have to go home and help my mother clean up the dinner dishes."

She gave Besa a little pat as she pulled out of the hug and headed for the coat-rack in the hall to retrieve her thread-bare shawl. It was very cold in February, with the wind coming in off the gulf.

"I guess I should be going too," said Dickey. Besa was tempted to ask him to stay awhile, so she could pick his brain. But that would be too much like Margaret's prying.

DICKEY DIDN'T EAT MUCH at home that night either. "Are you not feeling well, Richard?" his mother inquired.

"Yes, ma'am. I feel fine," he replied. "I ate quite a bit before I got home today."

"Oh. Did Besa have another feast for the club this evening?"

"Yes, ma'am. Huge feast," replied Dickey and then headed up the stairs toward his room.

"No practice with Uncle Diego this evening?"

"No, ma'am. I'm just a bit tired," said Dickey. And as soon as his head hit the pillow, he was asleep.

THE NEXT NIGHT that Dickey came home and tried to skip dinner, his mother became so afraid for him, she started crying. "What is happening to my little boy? You are losing weight, so I made your favorite! You are starving yourself!"

~

THE CHILDREN at school noticed the difference as well. Dickey no longer ran and played, but sat down at the club's table and literally took a nap.

"Now, do you agree with me that something's wrong with Dickey, Besa?" asked Margaret.

"This is not our Dickey. Something is definitely wrong with him," replied Besa.

"It started with that secret place he goes to eat after school," said Margaret.

"Okay," said Besa. "It's time for prying. Why don't you follow him today and see where he's getting his sweets from?"

"I'm not sure that's what this is," said Margaret. "I've read some place that excessive fatigue is one of the signs of starvation."

"But that doesn't make sense, Margaret. This is Dickey we're talking about. And he's already told us that he's gorging himself at this secret sweet shop."

"I don't know what it is he thinks he's doing at this place, Besa. But I doubt it's eating."

~

MARGARET FOLLOWED Dickey as he took his usual route. He dozed off in the saddle, but the horse was familiar with the path. It went up Ursulines as Dickey had directed when he was awake, and turned left at Dauphine and carried him to the exact spot he had gone to everyday for the last week.

As the horse came to a stop, Dickey was jolted awake when he almost fell out of the saddle. He then dismounted his horse, tied it up and went inside the place he'd been keeping from Besa and Margaret. The strange thing was, Dickey had walked into emptiness, because where Dickey had entered was some kind of invisible void. Margaret landed quickly and stood on the spot, calling to her dear friend. But Dickey did not emerge from wherever he'd gone. And then she had a thought—even though she had no idea where it came from. She just knew this had something to do with the bishop.

MARGARET FLEW AS FAST as she could. So frantic by the time she reached the Melponte mansion, she didn't have the presence of mind to go through the sun porch that was always opened for her. She just landed at the front door, banging on it as she called Besa's name. By the time Besa and Felix opened the door, Margaret was in a panic.

"They trapped him, Besa! They trapped our friend! There was nothing there!"

"Margaret, please come inside!" But the girl cried so hard and hyperventilated so much she couldn't manage to stand.

"Felix," said Besa, "could you bring her up to my room?"

So the guardian scooped the girl up, carried her up the stairs to Besa's second-floor bedroom and laid her on top of the embroidered purple, black and green blanket—her father's colors—under the bed's purple, black and green canopy. Margaret curled up and just sobbed.

"He's gone, Besa! Dickey's gone!"

Besa asked, "Would you have someone bring us some tea, Felix?"

After the man left, Besa patiently listened as her friend cried. When the tea service arrived, the kitchen assistant placed it on the mahogany tea table. Besa offered her friend a cup with ample sugar—the way Margaret preferred it. The girl calmed a bit when she sat up and accepted the cup. "I'm sorry for crying on your bed, Besa."

"Margaret. Tell me where Dickey went when you followed him?"

Margaret took a sip of the tea, then set it down. "To the corner of Ursulines Avenue and Dauphine Street. He'd obviously been going there for a while, because he fell asleep in the saddle, but the horse knew where it was going and carried him to his destination."

"And where was that?"

"It was nowhere, Besa. I couldn't believe my eyes at first. But when the horse stopped, Dickey nearly fell off. That's what jolted him awake. He then dismounted, tied up the horse, walked to an empty space, and opened a door and went in. I landed and tried calling his name. But he never came out."

"But what would draw Dickey to an empty spot?"

"Food, Besa! He was going there to eat what was probably imaginary food—for the last week. That's why he's been so tired. He hasn't really been eating. He just thought he was. This was a projection. They used his appetite against him."

Margaret let Besa pour her a second cup of tea and also took a cookie off the tea service tray. "I think it has something to do with the bishop," said Margaret, dipping her cookie in her tea.

"But only a Magist could do something like this," said Besa, taking her own cookie. "The bishop is not fond of Magists."

"I know it sounds strange, Besa. I would say the same thing too, if it wasn't for the projection. It's too much of a coincidence not to see the bishop's hand in this."

"It doesn't really matter," said Besa. "We have to get him back."

"But why would the bishop do something like this?" asked Margaret.

"Technically, he didn't know," said Obsidia, standing beside the bedroom door. Besa and Margaret started and almost spilled their tea.

"How would he 'technically' not know?" asked Margaret.

"Because he knew something was going to happen, but they purposely didn't give him the details."

"How does she know all this?" asked Margaret, reaching for another cookie, but they were all gone.

"This is all she does," said Besa.

"It's not all she does," replied Margaret. "She also eats a lot. That tray was full of cookies."

"I'd better go," said the Seer, smiling.

"Wait a minute, Obsidia," said Besa, when the woman reached for the door. "Why would they take Dickey?"

"For the same reason they would've taken you, child," replied the Seer. "For your father's book."

She opened the door and went out. As Obsidia stepped out of the room, Felix stepped in.

"We will wait until morning," he said. "And if the boy isn't back, I'll go and inform his family."

∼

WHEN THE BUTTER boy didn't appear at the Melponte mansion the next morning, Besa, Felix and Margaret went to the O'Brien residence to inform his family. The judge wasn't home, so Margaret recounted the last time she saw Dickey to his mother, Sofia—who was crying by the time she finished.

"You say someone trapped my Richard? But who would do something like that?"

"We don't know yet," said Besa.

"Do they want money? My family has money," she said. "I would have to ask my father."

Sofia was a slim, short, beautiful woman. Her dark thick hair was coming undone from the braid she'd put it in, but her magnificent hazel eyes pulled you into her sorrow. She sat at the kitchen table, covered in flour from making the bread she brought to school for her youngest son. She ran her hands through her hair, and the flour gave it the appearance of being grey-streaked.

When the whole group had been back at the mansion about half an hour, there came a frantic knock on the front door. This time it was the judge, Dickey's father. The judge was a tall, pale Irishman. Dickey had inherited his blond hair.

"Good evening, your honor," said Felix. "Please come in." The judge took off his black top hat and the black wool frock coat he wore. His wool trousers matched the coat and hat.

"Thank you, Felix," said the judge, as Besa's guardian stepped back and allowed the man in.

"The girls are in the parlor," he said, leading the way. Unlike his son, the judge had never been to the mansion.

"I'm sorry this is my first time in your home, Miss Melponte."

"Please sit down, your honor," said Besa, directing him toward the settee.

"I should've come when father was—But a judge is not allowed even the hint of impropriety. And I—"

"I understand, your honor,"

"Can we dispense with the 'your honor'? Tonight, I am simply William O'Brien, concerned about his son. And while I am just a father, on my way over here, my prosecutor's brain was racing through all the connections. Thank you," he said to the kitchen assistant who brought him a cup of coffee. "I know you wouldn't say this to my wife, but is it possible the bishop had something to do with this?"

"Margaret seems to think so," said Felix.

"I think it was because of something Besa did to him in the courthouse that day," said Margaret.

"Yes. Everyone saw him run out screaming after he let you go, Miss Melponte."

"I would appreciate it if you called me Besa, Mr. O'Brien," replied Besa.

"Very well, Besa," replied the judge. "What made the bishop leave the court-room in that manner?"

"Because I used a technique called 'projection' to make him see the thing he was most frightened of—the creature that took his arm."

"Oh," replied the judge. "Then I understand why he was frightened. But why seek vengeance against me? I didn't attack him?"

"I don't think it was against you," said Besa, setting the piece of cake that was just delivered to her aside for the moment. "They took Dickey because they couldn't get to me."

"But how was it done? Dickey's not someone you can

just grab off the street. He would've put up a tremendous fight."

"They trapped him with his appetite," said Margaret. "He told us he had a secret bakery where he was gorging on sweets. So he didn't eat when he came here."

"His mother said he wasn't eating at home either—and was starting to lose weight."

"He was being tricked into starving himself."

"Good God!" cried the judge, looking stricken. "The poor boy."

"I followed him to an empty void. I watched Dickey go in, but he never came out."

"An empty void?" said the judge, perplexed. "But why would he—"

"It was a projection, Mr. O'Brien," said Besa. "The same technique I used to make the bishop release me. They used it to make Dickey believe he had found a bakery with everything he wanted to eat."

"I guess we'll wait for a ransom note to learn their demands," replied the judge.

"We have a pretty good idea we already know," said Margaret.

"Then what?" asked the judge, absently accepting a piece of cake delivered by one of the kitchen assistants. He then took a bite and his eyes light up. "What in the world kind of magic is this? My son has been kidnapped, but this is a delight! No wonder Dickey loved coming here!"

"He wants my father's book," continued Besa.

"Who wants your father's book?" asked the judge.

"The bishop. We think he has a Magist among his followers."

"Oh, yes. I'm sorry," replied the judge. "This cake has

me flustered. But the question is, will you give it to him for the return of my son?" he asked Besa.

"Yes, I will, Mr. O'Brien. It won't be much use to him, anyway. The Taafli will kill him if he tries to use it."

"It's good to know," said the judge, "that my son has friends like you. I guess I should be going. His mother is still very distraught."

"Thank you for coming, your honor," said Felix, following the judge to the front door.

"I don't always understand why some men do terrible things," said the judge, putting on his coat and top hat. "All this for some strange book. Please let me know if I can be of any assistance, Felix." Then the judge turned and headed toward his one-horse buggy, situated in front of the house. The horse pulling it was Constance. She dipped her head and gave a whinny.

"No. He's not back yet, Constance," said the judge. "But we have some good possibilities." He climbed into the buggy and the horse took off without any inducement from the reins.

The judge had had to suspend his cases for the day when he found out what had happened to his youngest son. The newspapers got the story soon after, and the headline

JUDGE O'BRIEN'S SON MISSING

was on the cover of that evening's edition

Michel usually the read the paper as he sat at his supper in the evening. But when he saw the headline, his stomach suddenly had no interest in food, and he was overcome with dread. The judge magistrate's son was a very close friend of the Melponte girl. This was well known throughout the city. So he carried the newspaper to the house in front of his, where his friend, the bishop, lived. When Michel walked in, Delacroix was just sitting down to his dinner. Father Guidry didn't say anything for a moment, just stood looking at the bishop.

"Good evening, Michel," said Delacroix. "Are you hungry?"

"Have you seen the evening paper, André?"

"No," said the bishop, watching the servant cut up his steak for him. "Is there anything interesting in it?"

Michel tossed the newspaper on the table next to the bishop's plate—so he could see the headline.

"Oh, my goodness!" said Delacroix. "Do they know who took the boy?"

"Do you, André? Know who took him?"

The bishop pushed back from the table. "Thank you, Evelyne. That will be all." He then got up and went to his study. Michel followed him there. "Are you implying, Father Guidry, that I could have kidnapped this boy?"

"Yes, André. I've watched you since you lost your arm. You've changed. I saw you try to strangle that girl in the court room, brazenly—in front of everyone. You literally justified it. Everyone saw this. So, yes. I believe you're capable of this."

"Where would I put him, Michel? Since you think me such a deviant. Where would I put a kidnapped judge's son? In my house, possibly? Because you apparently think I'm insane!"

"What I think doesn't matter anymore. I thought you were a good man, an honest, intelligent servant of God. Like you used to be!"

"Get out, Michel! Get out of my house!"

"I will be leaving soon enough, if this is your doing. I

won't just leave this house!" Michel slammed the door to the study and went back to his own residence.

BY THE END of the week, the bishop knew the truth: He was partially responsible.

"You took the boy?" shouted Delacroix, across the library in the borrowed house. "The judge's son? Are you insane? You were supposed to take the Melponte girl!"

The Shadows didn't look the least bit flustered by the bishop's fury.

"Our plan was to produce the best results as quickly as possible," replied the non-human Shadow in the middle. "The Melponte girl was not accessible."

"But what are you going to do with him?"

"After you receive your book, we can dispose of him."

"No! You will not! He hasn't seen you, has he? Tell me he hasn't seen you!"

"No. He has not, Your Grace."

"Good. The judge is a member of my congregation. And I couldn't look at him every Sunday, knowing I had his son murdered! He is not to be harmed. Do you understand?"

"Yes, Your Grace. We understand completely," said the Shadow in the middle.

"Where is he?"

"We have him safely hidden somewhere, Your Grace," said One. "It's best you don't know. There is talk going around that you might be responsible."

"I can't imagine how such talk came to be," said Delacroix, visibly angry at the Shadow's obvious attempt to intimidate him. "Then why don't you bring him here? If I'm going to be held responsible, I might as well guard his safety. Until we get the book, of course."

The Shadows didn't respond to that for a moment, as they clearly relished the advantage they had, controlling the boy and the bishop. "Did you hear me?" asked the bishop. "I said bring him here. Tonight."

"But what if he wakes and sees you, Your Grace?" asked the second Shadow.

"That is a chance I am willing to take. Deliver the boy to me tonight."

"As you wish, Your Grace," replied the first Shadow. "We'll bring him in a couple of days."

They all disappeared then.

"I don't know," said Denny. "Is it just me, or can we not trust them anymore?"

"No. It's not just you," replied the bishop.

A FEW MOMENTS LATER, a portal opened on the deck of an East Indiaman in the Newald harbor. The three Shadows stepped through. "Two," said the first Shadow. "Look down into the cargo hold there and see if our hungry friend is still asleep."

The cargo hold was quite a few feet deep, but the Shadow could see Dickey placed in the middle of the floor below the hold. "He's still down there, One," said Two.

"I think it's time we let the bishop know we don't answer to him. What do you think, Three?"

"I think you're right, One."

Besa and Margaret were sitting in the parlor, awaiting any information they might get on where to take the book. At about supper-time, Juan rushed into the parlor.

"Besa!" he said, "There's a message about Dickey on Night Rain!"

"What!" they both jumped up and ran to the stables. The horse was unsaddled, and on his left side was the message in white letters, "Bring the book to the eastern fields outside Marigny. Leave it there and the boy will be with you in an hour."

"That field is kind of large," said Margaret. "How will they find—"

"Let's go, Margaret!" said Besa.

Juan was very quick as he saddled up Night Rain for the girl. And just as Besa was about to mount, Margaret said, "We need to tell Felix, Besa. We shouldn't go out there alone. We need to be cautious."

"Okay. Then go get him," said Besa. "But hurry! We don't want it to get too dark."

Felix came racing out of the house and mounted a palomino Juan had ready for him. Margaret took flight toward the field, with Felix and Besa close behind.

"Did it say where we should leave it?" asked Felix when they got to the field.

"I think putting it in the middle would make sense," said Margaret. "I'll go up and watch what happens to it." They trotted the horses out to the middle of the field, and Besa pulled her father's book out of the saddle bag she carried it in, and sat it down in a spot on the ground. She then mounted her horse, and she and Felix backed away. They decided that backing off about twenty yards was the best course to take. When they reached about half that far, Margaret called from above:

"Besa! It's gone! It just disappeared."

"Good. Then it's done," said Besa. "We should go back to the hose and wait for—"

A portal opened in front of them and Obsidia stepped out.

"Besa! All of you must come quickly!" she said. "Dickey's in danger!"

~

THE PORTAL OPENED inside the Magist meeting chamber.

"Why is Dickey in danger? We gave them the book," said Besa.

"This is not a part of the bishop's plans," said Obsidia. "The Shadows want to punish him."

"For what?" asked Besa.

"That's not something I can see," said Obsidia. "My knowledge is what happens now and what will happen in the future."

"Okay. History lesson over," said Seuz. "We need a plan to get the boy out, Besa. They're holding him in a cargo hold on a ship in the Newald harbor. We have to be careful. The cargo hold is underwater. Portals don't do well underwater. We can get you on the ship, but you must try to revive the boy and find a way out of the hold."

"But can't we just rush them with some of the Dreids and rescue Dickey that way?" asked Margaret.

"There are a few tons of cargo suspended over the boy. If we try to rush them, they will just cut the rope. We need to move them away from the cargo hold and give Besa time to get Dickey out.

"I have an idea," said Margaret. When she told him, Septimius got really excited.

"Let's go!" he said.

~

A PORTAL OPENED in the library of the borrowed house. The Shadow named Three stepped out and approached the bishop as he sat behind the desk in the library.

"Here is your book, Your Grace." He set the book on the desk before the bishop.

"But where is the boy? You were supposed to bring him to me."

"The boy is of no more concern to you. You have your book."

"I knew we couldn't trust them," said Denny, pointing a pistol at the Shadow. The Shadow just looked at him and smiled.

"That is not a good idea," he said. "You're really just pointing it at yourself." And before Denny realized it, the gun was pointed at the side of his own head, and he was still holding it.

"You should probably put that down, Denny," said the bishop. "They don't die that easy."

"For some things we do," said the Shadow. "Like the boy, for instance. He will die very simply in a few moments."

"So, it's basically your plan to get me hung," said the bishop.

"No. You won't be associated with this. Although, it will be a bit of déjà vu."

"What does that mean!" yelled the bishop, as the Shadow disappeared.

~

In the next moment, Three stepped out of a portal on the deck of the East Indiaman.

"So he has the book, then?" asked One.

"Yes. The book is in the bishop's hands."

"Good. Now it's time to send him his déjà vu message. Raise the cargo a bit, Two."

A large load of wooden crates secured by netting positioned over the cargo hold, rose about twenty feet, as Two manipulated the boom.

Just then, the bishop came up from below decks and walked out toward the cargo hold. He wore his full vestments and his cross.

"You lying, scheming, sub-human trash!" shouted Delacroix. "I should never have trusted you!"

"I—Your Grace?" said One, shocked. "How did you get here?"

"Do you think you're the only ones who can use a portal? And I've brought reinforcements!"

Shadows started climbing up over the side of the ship. There were three at the helm, three at starboard and three at larboard.

"Oh, no, One!" said Two. They all look like us." He was right. They all wore black suits, fedoras and were white men with green eyes.

"We have you surrounded, One," said the bishop. "You can leave in one piece, if you give us the boy."

Two climbed down from the cargo boom. "What are we going to do, One?"

"What do you think you're doing, Two! Get back on the boom!" said One. "I have an idea. The bishop made a miscalculation."

～

IN THE MEANTIME, Besa was down in the cargo hold where Dickey was lying, fast asleep. The hold was crowded close around them with large crates and boxes. Besa leaned down beside him.

"Dickey," she whispered, shaking him a little. "Wake up. We need to get you out of here." Dickey just moaned and rolled over. "I didn't think about it, but I should've brought something to help you awaken." A plate of cake appeared on the floor beside her. Courtesy of Obsidia, probably. "Thanks, Obsidia," said Besa. She looked up as the cargo suspended from the boom swayed a bit, influenced by a gust of wind. "Come on, Dickey. We're both going to get crushed if you don't wake up." She took some icing from one of the slices of cake—caramel cake, Dickey's favorite and smeared it on his lips. "Wake up, Dickey." The results were promising. The boy licked his lips, but treated it as a dream and didn't open his eyes. "Dickey. Come on. This might be the last cake you eat if you don't get up," said Besa.

ONE FLEW QUICKLY to the bishop and grabbed him, twisting his one arm behind his back. "You forgot to protect yourself, Your Grace. Now who has the advantage? All of you just back up. Or I'll break his neck!" One shouted to all the Shadows surrounding the deck. They all started to back up. "We were trying to protect you, Your Grace, but by coming here, you will get all the blame. Although you do get to watch. Cut the rope, Two!"

That's when Margaret dropped down from the crow's nest and blasted two with a bolt that erased him.

"Who was that? Get over here Three and cut this rope!" shouted One.

"I don't think so," said the bishop, who turned into a white werewolf. But One was still behind him, and with a considerable amount of strength, shoved Septimius into the cargo hold. But the wolf was agile for his massive size. He sprang off the lip of the hold and hooked his claws into the cargo netting and climbed.

In the hold, Besa had pushed cake in between Dickey's lips. His eyes started to flutter then.

"That's right," she said. "Time to get up. They may be running out of tricks out there. Let's get going." Dickey rolled over...

"That's not going to help you, Septimius," said One. "Last time I heard, wolves can't fly. Cut the rope Three!"

But Three got intercepted by Margaret.

"Kill the little witch and cut the rope!"

"Nope," said Margaret, as Three flew toward her. "I'm not really a witch." She turned into a Dreid that swallowed Three in midair.

"Looks like it's just you and me, One," said Septimius, climbing on top of the cargo and guarding the rope.

"This is really stupid, you know," said One. "All this nonsense and you still haven't saved him."

"Get him!" Seuz shouted, and the Dreids closed quickly on One.

"I still win. Even if I die!" declared One. A Dreid erased him, but not before he got off a bolt that sliced through the rope, dropping Septimius and the cargo into the hold.

At that moment, Besa was relieved to see Dickey coming around. "That's good, Besa," said Dickey, still looking a bit groggy. "I'm really hungry." A lot more cake appeared. Dickey stuffed some of it quickly into his mouth, like it might disappear again.

"That's definitely from Obsidia," said Besa.

"That's good," said Dickey, stretching a bit. "She owes me quite a bit."

"Hurry up and eat your cake, Dickey," said Besa. "And also catch that!" She pointed up and Dickey shot up and to a massive twenty-foot-tall behemoth that intercepted the crates and pushed them out onto the deck.

"Whew! That was close," said Besa.

"Do we have any more cake?" asked Dickey.

"Help me onto the deck."

The massive boy picked her up and set her on the deck, where Septimius waited. Dickey soon climbed out of the hold as well.

A portal popped open on the deck.

"Yes," said Besa. "There's more cake right through there."

Dickey shrunk to normal size and moved quickly to the portal.

It took a week for Dickey to get back to his old hungry self. And for Margaret to lament not having a second piece of cake. "It's worth it, Margaret," replied Besa. "I much prefer him this way. Don't you?"

They were sitting at the dessert table in Besa's front parlor, the remains of a five cake four pie feast down to just one large slice of cake.

"I guess so," said Margaret, reaching for the piece of cake and watching butter boy erase it right before her eyes. "Just like old times," she grumbled.

CHAPTER 14

HOUSE OF THE RAVEN

The following week was the start of Mardi Gras, as well as the masquerade ball season. The Creoles held a number of exclusive balls for the children of upper-class families. This time of year was very tough for Besa, because she and her father often attended some of the Creole balls. Margaret initially thought going to one of them would be a great way to lift Besa's spirits. In the past, she'd created very ingenious costumes. But she mostly sat and cried in the parlor when Margaret tried to suggest an activity she might like to try. She finally agreed to attend the Mardi Gras parade, though. And Felix made sure to send Miss Maymi to accompany her. The parade was always a loud, boisterous affair. Pierre had often insisted they watch from the front seat of the carriage.

"Why don't we walk around a bit, Besa?" said Dickey.

"Be careful," said Margaret. "He smells food, and he'll leave us in a crowd."

"You are such a party-ruiner," replied Dickey. "I want to walk so we can look at some of the interesting costumes."

"I'm telling you, Besa. If we don't put a bridle on him, he's going to bolt at the first scent of a sweet roll."

"Let him go. If we hold him, he'll just want to go even more."

"I don't want to go without the two of you," replied Dickey.

"Oh, go on and go," said Margaret. "I can smell the sweet rolls from here, myself. Just remember to save at least a half of one for Besa and me."

"Okay," replied Dickey, climbing from the carriage. "If you insist."

He stepped into the moving crowd and was gone in a matter of moments.

"Don't worry," said Margaret. "He doesn't have a bad sense of direction. He'll make it back to us sooner or later."

"He'll probably be covered in sugar though," chuckled Besa. "But at least he'll have fun."

The Mardi Gras crowd was a sea of color, and Margaret was happy to see Besa smile a bit at some of the more fascinating designs on the costumes. They soon noticed a child —a little creole girl of about six, with her hair in a long braid and dressed in red. As she ran through the crowd, suddenly a flame erupted from the braid.

"Oh, my God, look!" said Besa. "She's going to—"

But then an even more amazing spectacle, a being that looked like they were composed of nothing but water, started to chase the fire child. The fire moved onto the child's shoulders. This water being was larger than the child but still not bigger than a ten-year-old. Margaret was happy that Besa couldn't take her eyes off the event. The fire child and the liquid being ran in and out of the crowd, and no one seemed affected by the blaze coming off the girl. At one point the girl stopped and erupted into a full-body flame, and the liquid slammed into her. The merge created a sizzling, boiling wall of steam. When the steam dissipated, a petite creole woman in an elegant red gown with red gloves that ran all the way up to her elbows and a large wide-brimmed hat adorned with a couple dozen roses stood smiling and waving at Besa. She then evaporated like a wave of heat into the roiling wall of color that was the Mardi Gras crowd.

"It is amazing what some Magists can do," said Besa, still clapping after the woman was gone.

THAT DICKEY HAD a nose for food was a given. He'd made good time going east with the crowd on Dumaine Street and had caught the scent of pralines and something else even more amazing that he couldn't name, so he picked up speed. And then something told him he'd better run, or it might all be gone by the time he got there. He took off, bumping into a twelve-foot rubber man wearing a coat of rainbows and a top hat that kept changing colors, bending him into the nearest storefront awning. He wasn't hurt though, because he sprang right back.

"Sorry," said Dickey, as he kept running. He rounded the corner on the four-story Furrier's Building on Bourbon just as something that looked like a large black-bird fell screaming from the fourth-floor balcony. Dickey, in full stride, shifted up to fifteen feet and caught it in his massive arms.

"Are you all right?" asked Dickey.

"Oh my God! You have saved my life, señor!"

It was a girl. And she'd said this in Spanish, which he could understand. Languages weren't really his strong point, but his mother, Sofia, was Spanish, and made sure he was fluent in the language.

"Turn around and run back in that direction! Or they are going to kill me!"

That's when three large men, also wearing black-bird costumes, came charging out of one of the doors on the ground floor of the Furrier's Building, brandishing swords.

"Please, my giant hero! Run!"

Dickey, looking like any other stretchy individual, raced through the crowd on his ten-foot legs. When he turned the corner on Dumaine Street, he shifted himself down to normal size.

"Oh! You are small, like me!" exclaimed the bird girl.

"We need to be less conspicuous," said Dickey. "So we can make it back to the carriage."

"You have a carriage?" asked the girl. "How convenient for us to get away."

"It's not really mine," said Dickey. "It belongs to my friend, Besa."

"Is Besa a countess, too?" asked the bird girl.

"I don't know what a countess is," replied Dickey. "But if it's some kind of royal term, then Besa is the closest thing I know to it. She lives in a mansion with servants."

"She certainly sounds like a countess. I want to meet her. And will she let me hide in her large house with servants?"

"Maybe. We just have to keep running to get there."

Once they got within sight of the carriage, Dickey picked up the pace.

"Hurry! We're almost there!"

When they reached it, there were two other people on horseback—a knight in full armor carrying a javelin and his squire. Dickey initially ignored them and hoisted the bird girl into the carriage, before climbing in himself.

"Dickey," said Margaret. "Who is this girl, and what are you doing?"

"No time to explain! We need to go! Someone is chasing us!"

"Besa leaned out of the carriage. "Please follow us Angeline and Simone!" she called.

"We shall, fair lady!" cried the knight.

Miss Maymi set the horses in motion. "Don't worry," Dickey told the girl. "We'll be safe soon."

"I didn't know you spoke Spanish, Dickey," replied Besa. "Who is this and what are we running from?"

"I don't know," said Dickey.

"That doesn't make any sense," replied Margaret. "Did she fall out of the sky?"

"Yes, she did. She was falling, and I caught her."

"You caught a falling bird girl?"

"Yes. And when I caught her, she told me to run back the other way."

"Is this red-haired one the countess Besa?" asked the bird girl.

"No, I'm Besa," said Besa. "Red-hair is Margaret. What's your name?"

"A beautiful ebony countess," replied the bird girl. "I am Countess Catalina Infante y Barbosa—at your service, señorita. I do not know the name of my champion, but he saved my life."

"His name is—"

"I am Richard Herrera O'Brien, countess," said Dickey. "At your service."

"Sir Richard, the brave," proclaimed the countess.

"What did she say?" asked Margaret.

"She called him Sir Richard, the brave," replied Besa.

"Oh, my goodness!" cried Margaret, rolling her eyes. "Tell her to stop that. There isn't enough room in this carriage for his swelling head. And ask if she speaks French."

Besa did so, and the countess replied, "Oui, mademoiselle, Margaret the bold."

"Wonderful," said Margaret. "He gets 'Sir Richard', and all I get is 'The Bold'."

"It fits you," said Dickey. "You are very bold."

"In that same light, I have another question, countess. What or who are we running from?"

"Shouldn't we wait until we get where we're going, before we start prodding her too much?" asked Dickey.

"Well, Sir Richard, we're going to Besa's house. Since this was her outing. I'm sure she'd like to know why we're leaving so soon."

"I would like to know that," replied Besa.

"Because I didn't fall out of the sky," replied the countess. "I was at a masquerade ball, and one of my uncle's lieutenants pushed me off the balcony."

"Why would your uncle want to kill you?" asked Besa.

"So I can't expose him for the murder of my father."

"Who is your uncle?" asked Dickey.

"Duke Ricardo Colon y Barbosa."

"But isn't he—"

"The Spanish ambassador," said Besa.

"Goodness gracious! You were supposed to bring sweet rolls, Dickey! What have you gotten us into?"

"I didn't know," he said. "I couldn't just let her hit the ground."

"I do not wish to be a burden, countess Besa. So, if you

will stop somewhere ahead, I will find my way back to the city."

"What?" said Besa. "We will not just leave you in the road, Catalina. You will be safe at my home until we figure out what to do."

"Thank you, countess Besa. You are as kind as you are beautiful," said Catalina, grasping Besa's hand and pulling it to her heart.

"And you are too precious," said Besa, smiling. "And please, you must call me Besa. I am not a countess."

And then they pulled into the stable yard of the Melponte mansion. Catalina caught her breath at the sight of it.

"What a magnificent castle, mademoiselle! You are no less a countess!"

"No, not a castle," said Besa, obviously flattered, and beaming, noted Margaret. If nothing else, this countess Catalina had lifted her friend's spirits. Now she would get to be a gracious host to her and the two creoles, which would take her mind off her father for a little while. One of the stable boys came and took possession of the carriage, and the knight and squire dismounted as well. Besa took them all into the front entry. Felix met them in the foyer.

"Is something wrong, Besa?" he asked. "You came back so soon."

"Yes and no," said Besa.

"Is this your father, Besa?" asked Catalina.

"Good heavens, no!" said Felix, looking flustered. "Who is this, Besa?"

"No. This is Felix, my guardian. Felix, this is Countess Catalina Infante y Barbosa, she is—"

"The Spanish ambassador's niece. She fell off a balcony. And good evening, Angeline and Simone." said Felix.

Simone gave a gracious bow but almost tipped over in her costume. Angeline came to her aid.

"That is amazing!" cried Catalina. "How did he do that?"

"Felix is Taíno, and also my behike. He knows literally everything."

"Everything that happens around you, Besa. Not really everything."

"Close enough," said Dickey. "Did you know I caught her out of the sky after one of the ambassador's men pushed her off the balcony of the Furrier's Building?"

"I do now, Dickey," replied Felix. "But most of what I pick up comes after you get into Besa's orbit."

"I saved her life," declared Dickey.

"Don't mind Sir. Richard, the brave, here," said Margaret, "We had to deflate his head a bit, so he could get through the front door."

"You're just jealous. Miss Red-head, the bold. I'm the hero, remember?"

"Oh, she'll change that title a little, once she gets to know you. Something along the lines of Richard the butter-headed chicken!"

"You take that back! You—red-headed meanie!"

Besa just shook her head.

"Can you two try to be more civil? We have guests. Angeline, if you want, you can take your sister upstairs to one of the bedrooms. The upstairs maids will help her out of her armor and find something you both can wear so you can come down to dinner."

The two sisters had surprised Besa, coming out of the crowd at the beginning of the parade on Dumaine after leaving a creole ball on Bourbon Street. They decided to stay and watch the parade with her, which Margaret now found had been a good idea for Besa's uplifted spirits.

"Thank you," replied Simone, still in character. "You are most kind, mademoiselle." A maid helped her navigate the stairs.

"I was trying to be good, but Margaret started it," said Dickey.

"And Margaret, please try not to bait him so much today. He did save Catalina's life."

"Okay. I apologize...Sir Richard. I mean, Dickey."

"I accept," replied Dickey, still eyeing Margaret suspiciously.

"That's better. Why don't we go into the parlor? Once Angeline and Simone find something to wear, we'll eat. I'm sure Miss Maymi is whipping us up something amazing. She is the best cook in the whole city."

And true to form, an hour and a half later, Miss Maymi showed up in the parlor with a three-course feast of chicken jambalaya, red beans, and rice and shrimp étouffée —with cornbread on the side.

"I'm sorry, Besa," said the cook. "This was the best I could do on such short notice."

"This is amazing," exclaimed Catalina. "I have never tasted such food. What kind of bird is this?"

"It is chicken, your ladyship," replied Miss Maymi, affecting a clumsy bow.

"You are an amazing chef, Madame Maymi."

"Thank you, your ladyship. I have coffee and caramel cake for dessert."

"Whew!" cried Dickey. "I can't wait!"

"Calm down, Dickey. Don't say it, Margaret."

"I'm not saying anything. I can keep my eye on my cake without saying anything."

"Besa," asked Catalina. "Is that magnificent-looking portrait above the mantel your father?"

Besa looked up at the portrait of Pierre and said, "Yes. That is my papa. I wish I could introduce you, but he is..." and she broke down in tears.

"It's okay, countess Besa," said Catalina, wrapping her in a hug. "I lost my papa, too."

"He's not dead. At least I don't think so," said Besa. "He's—"

"Wow!" said Margaret. "Here comes Angeline and Simone! Don't they look stunning!"

The two creoles had been given access to the Melponte family seamstress, who altered a few of Besa's day dresses. Simone was a little taller than Besa, being already sixteen. The girl had chosen a pale blue dress that was originally made by Madame Jarre, like all of Besa's clothes. She was stunning with her long neck and rich dark hair down past her ears, and deep blue eyes—she looked like the creole princess she was. Angeline was beautiful as well, having chosen a dress with colorful flowers. She was a beautiful, brown-eyed girl of fourteen like Besa, and smiled more naturally than the brooding beauty of her sister, Simone. The whole party moved into the large Melponte dining room. This was a beautiful room with mahogany floors, an oak three-leaf dining table with a gold sea turtle center piece. The chandelier above was composed of crystal and small seashells with gold trimming.

There were ivory statues of what looked like native warriors on pedestals all around the room. Angeline went over and looked at one of a woman warrior.

"Who is this woman," the girl asked. "She looks very strong and beautiful."

"That is Anacaona," said Felix. "She was cacica of the Taíno hundreds of years ago."

"Is that like a priestess?"

"No. That was chief. Time to eat," he said, when the kitchen assistants started bringing in the food on the service carts.

"This is the best étouffée I have ever tasted," said Simone. Father would definitely hire your Miss Maymi."

"He sure would," replied Angeline.

"Sorry. She's not available," said Besa with a smile.

"I am certainly not," replied Miss Maymi who brought one of the four cakes along with the other items being pushed behind her on the dessert cart. "Not on no plantation."

"Even if it wasn't a plantation," said Besa.

"Thas' right. Even if it wasn't, Miss Besa," said the woman. giving Besa a little hug. "Stayin' with my baby till the end."

The kitchen assistants brought in coffee, and two more caramel cakes, and a lemon cake for dessert. The cakes all had four layers and you could tell they were newly frosted.

"Wow!" said Dickey and tried to jump up. But Margaret grabbed him by the neck and pulled him back down.

"Down boy! We have guests. You are Sir Richard, the brave. Not, Sir Dickey, the greedy. Let the guests go first. There is plenty to go around."

"Yes, of course," replied Dickey, sitting down with his hands in his lap, while his left leg shook as if he were having a fit. But he managed to restrain himself until everyone else were served. Margaret was astonished at the amount of restraint he showed. And even when he did get a piece, it was generous, but not compared to his usual display of gluttony. When Miss Maymi came in to check on them, she was shocked there was still some cake left.

"Dickey," she said "Are you not feelin' well? They's still cake left. Didn't you like it?"

"Thank you, Miss Maymi," replied Sir Richard, the brave. "The cake was splendid. It complimented the coffee very well."

Miss Maymi went over to him and put her soft dark hand on his forehead and the side of his face.

"You not sick again, is you boy?"

"No, ma'am," replied Dickey. "I'm feeling just fine."

"I've never seen him this way," replied Margaret. "I was actually able to have a second piece for a change. That's never happened."

Dickey ignored Margaret, who was only trying to goad him.

"How was your coffee, countess?" he asked Catalina. "Angeline, Simone, shall I pour you all a little more?" said the Butter boy, carrying the pot around to them.

Margaret was having fun with the fact that Dickey was doing everything he could not to look at the cake.

"Somebody's gotta eat this cake," she said, getting up and cutting another piece. "Here Besa and everyone, let me cut you all another piece."

"Stop it, Margaret," said Besa. "You know you're torturing him."

"I'm not doing anything. There is just so much cake left. What are we going to do with it all?"

"You're just as bad as Mokheer."

"That is not fair, Besa! I am nowhere near as mean as Mokheer."

"So, you agree that you're being mean?"

"Maybe. But by comparing me to Mokheer, you're being cruel, too."

Miss Maymi and some of her kitchen assistants came and took away the dishes. "I guess I'm gon hafta fine somethin' to do with these here cakes," said the cook cutting her eyes at an obviously restrained Dickey. "I might hafta thow it out. Sho' is a shame," she continued, leaving the parlor with the remainder of the cakes.

"Why don't we go out and take a walk in the garden?" said Besa. "We can stretch our legs and chat a bit after that amazing meal."

"That is a splendid idea, countess Besa."

"I guess we'd better be getting back home," said Angeline. "Papa will be looking for his horses to be back in the stall before too long."

"That's true, Angeline," said Simone. "When we saw you at the parade, Miss Besa. I thought it would be good to spend a little time with you. So you won't forget us."

"I promise that we have not, Miss Dupard," said Besa. "You're never far from my mind."

"And your hospitality is a reflection of your beauty," said Angeline. "We will send the dresses back when one of Papa's servants retrieves our costumes. Good night." And they left by the front door heading to the stables.

All three of the girls got up to head out the side door that led to the garden. When they were half way out the door, Catalina noted someone was missing. "Oh dear, but where is Sir Richard?"

"He probably went to get more coffee," replied Besa.

"Yes, he probably is," said Margaret. "And maybe even helping Miss Maymi clean up the kitchen."

"Oh, he has such a big heart," replied Catalina.

"And a head and a stomach," Margaret whispered to

Besa. "Both of which are being stuffed with copious amounts of cake right now."

Besa shook her head and rolled her eyes.

"Just as bad as Mokheer."

"Is Mokheer an older brother?" asked Catalina. "Is he perhaps at one of the masquerade balls tonight?"

"I'm an only child. Mokheer is a nighttime member of our club."

"What is the name of your club?"

"We call ourselves The Graveyard Club."

"That is an intriguing name. What does one do in a Graveyard club?"

"We go out at night and raise the spirits of the dead," said Margaret. "Besa is our leader and president."

"But how is it done, this raising the spirit of the dead?"

"First of all," said Besa, "You've probably guessed that we're all Magists."

"I suspected as much, since Sir Richard grew in size to catch me, and then shrunk himself down so we could disappear into the Mardi Gras crowd. But what mechanism do you use to raise the spirit?"

Besa spent part of the afternoon explaining about the witching hour and how the Taafli does most of the important work, and how she discovered her power and what happened to her father.

"Your father was taken away, and now you're the only necromancer your family has left?"

"I hadn't thought of it quite like that. But I guess that's true."

"At least your father hasn't diminished your power, as my stepfather has mine. In my line, the patriarch is given dominion over all beneath him."

"What line are you?" asked Dickey, who'd rejoined the

group after helping Miss Maymi "straighten up the kitchen."

"My line is House of the Raven."

"Oh. So that's why you're wearing the bird suit?"

"She doesn't wear it all the time, Dickey. She was at a masquerade party," said Margaret. Catalina was a tall, raven-haired girl of fourteen. She was a bit more thick-boned, while Besa was petite. Besa's eyes were green with flecks of gold, and Catalina's was cobalt blue.

"And then I caught you. Now I get it."

"We're going to have to find you something to wear," said Besa. "You're my height, so I should have something that fits you."

"Are you staying with Besa tonight?" asked Dickey.

"She can, if she wants to," replied Besa, "We have more than enough room."

"Thank you, Besa. You are so generous. I will have to go home tomorrow. My mother, the Duchess, is probably beside herself with worry."

"But will you be safe when you get home?" asked Dickey.

"If only I could take you with me, my brave knight. But my uncle will not try to harm me directly. He would rather someone else do his dirty work. I will be safe with my mother."

"Felix will take you back to your residence when he takes me to school tomorrow. I would love for you to stay over tonight as well, Margaret. It will be a wonderful girl's evening!" Just then, Felix came into the parlor and said,

"Don't worry, Margaret. I've already received word back from your mother that it's okay for you to stay, and countess, you have a visitor waiting for you in the ballroom."

"A visitor," replied Catalina. "But no one knows I'm here."

"You are apparently mistaken."

The whole club escorted Catalina to the ballroom. When they arrived, something gave a cry and a large black bird came and landed on Catalina's right shoulder.

"Eduardo!" cried the countess. "What are you doing here?"

"When the guard decided to push you, I knew the boy was already coming. I made him come faster, so he could catch you."

"That was you?" asked Dickey. "That bird can do more than just talk."

"Your mother was worried, but I reassured her you were safe."

"Thank you, Eduardo. Let me introduce you to my new friends. Everyone, this is my mother's chief of security, Eduardo Elén."

"How can a bird be chief of security?" asked Dickey. Eduardo turned his head sideways to regard Dickey.

"The same way a boy can change himself into a giant, Mr. O'Brien," replied the raven. "I was bred for this. And I am not a bird. I am a raven. You could only hope to receive the kind of training I have, and it is wonderful to meet you, Graveyard club. I am sorry to hear of your father's confinement, Miss Melponte. Hopefully, he is returned to you soon."

"Thank you, Eduardo," said Besa, a bit teary-eyed at the mention of Pierre.

"Enjoy your evening with your friends, Catalina. The duchess will expect your return to the residence tomorrow."

And with that, the raven flew out one of the ballroom's open windows and disappeared.

"That is an amazing bird," said Dickey. "Did you train him, Catalina?"

"He's not a bird, Sir Richard. He's a corvid. He's almost two hundred years old. I couldn't possibly have trained him. He trained me, my mother, and my father."

"Eduardo is a fascinating creature. I would love to talk to him sometime," said Besa.

"He would probably bore you with stories about the Muslims and the conquest of Granada. He knows things most human don't even remember."

"I enjoy history myself."

One of Miss Maymi's kitchen assistants brought in rhubarb pie and the tea service.

"Miss Maymi thought you'd all like a snack before you went to bed," said the assistant.

"That pie smells amazing," said Dickey, moving toward the circle table where the girl had placed it.

"Easy, Sir Richard," said Margaret. "We still have a guest, remember?"

"Okay. I'll let all of you go first."

"It's almost time for the girls to head to bed, Dickey," said Besa. "Go on and get you a good slice before you head home."

"But why can't I stay over?" asked Dickey. I'm in the club, too."

"If you'd let us braid your hair and put bows in it and wear a nightgown, we'd love for you to stay, Dickey," said Margaret. "Although I don't know what Milicent might make of it."

"You're just trying to scare me away so you can have the last piece of pie."

"I would love to put bows in your hair, Dickey." said Besa. "But we won't have a night gown that fits you. But one of the scullery maids might."

"No way. I'm not staying," said Dickey. "I'll just take my pie and go."

"Okay," said Besa. "But you'd be missing out on all our girl stories."

Dickey sliced him a piece of pie, shoved it into his mouth and said,

"Goodnight. I'll see you all at school tomorrow!" And went out the front door toward the stables. After he was gone, Margaret said,

"That was amazing! I thought I was the mean one."

"I wasn't trying to be mean," replied Besa. "I just helped him decide."

"Oh, so that's what we're calling it?"

"Yes. Let's find you two some nightgowns."

It turned out to be quite an endeavor, because Besa had an extensive selection to choose from.

"These are wonderful, Besa," said Margaret, looking through all the night gowns. "I love all the colors and different fabrics." Besa's armoire was also carved with Taíno images, had mother-of-pearl handles, and was deep enough to hide all three girls in.

"How is it that you've never seen these, Margaret?" asked Catalina. "Have you not slept over before?"

"No," said Margaret. "I never have. I just realized how strange that sounds, and we've been best friends for more than five years."

"I'm so sorry, Margaret," said Besa, coming over and giving her friend a hug. "You know you're very dear to me. But it was never possible before."

"I understood, Besa."

"Was your father that controlling?" asked Catalina.

"Yes, he was," replied Besa.

"Then how were you able to be in graveyards at all hours of the night?"

"This all didn't start until after Papa was taken away by the Gendarmes."

"So there's nothing in your way now."

"No. Though I would prefer Papa were with us. Oh, how I miss him so!" and she sat on the floor in front of her wardrobe and sobbed.

"I'm sorry, Besa," said Margaret, reaching out and grasping her friend's hand.

"I didn't mean for it to sound like it was a good thing," said Catalina.

"I know. I just need to get used to this girl sleepover thing."

"Yes. We have some catching up to do," said Margaret, brightening a bit.

"Do you go to school with other children, Besa?" asked Catalina.

"That's how she met me and Dickey," replied Margaret.

"I envy you. The nobility is only allowed tutors. I am only close to Eduardo, and he only knew games that ravens played. They often ended with having your eyes pecked out."

"That doesn't sound like any fun," said Margaret.

"It wasn't. This is the most girl fun I've ever had. Outside of chatting and tea with my mother's courtiers."

"Outside of school, this is the first time I've been with girlfriends," said Besa. "I hope we do this more often, so we can all learn together."

"I'll make sure my mother knows how much fun I'm having," said Catalina.

The girls chatted long into the night, telling stories about school and Dickey's antics on the playground.

"You've known Mokheer since you were a small child?" asked Catalina. "And he only comes out at night?"

"Yes. He comes out just after the sun goes down, and helps protect us when we're on the site of one of our Graveyard Club cases."

"Protects us when he's not picking on or harassing Dickey," said Margaret.

"I'm glad we're discussing The Graveyard Club," said Catalina. "Perhaps the club can help me locate the body of Diego Montalbán, captain of my father's security detail. I was able to read the mind of one of my uncle's personal guards; and he revealed to me that Diego was the man who could name my father's murderer."

"You mean your father's body is somewhere in Newald?" asked Besa.

"This was his last posting. He fought in the war against General Napoleon, and came to claim the colony for Spain about ten years ago. He was supposedly killed in a duel. But that didn't make sense. My father was one of Spain's greatest swordsmen; he had never lost a duel. In fact, no one would dare challenge him. His skill was that great. But what also didn't make sense was his captain died in the duel as well. And what I learned from the mind of Raul Dejesus, was it had actually been an ambush."

"But if your uncle was suppressing your powers, how were you able to use them to find out so much?" asked Besa, pulling a bright floral night gown from the armoire and holding it in front of Catalina.

"Because the charm releases me when my uncle goes to sleep," said the girl, accepting the gown. "I just waited up late, and then I made sure to approach his personal guard.

It was dangerous, but something Eduardo said to me let me know that if there was a secret, Raul would be the most likely to know it. It proved to be true. And I was so excited, I got careless. One of the other guards spotted me near where Raul was sleeping. My uncle knew exactly what I'd done. And if I'd gotten this far, I wouldn't stop." Catalina watched as Besa tried a pastel pink silk night gown on Margaret, that had different color butterflies and flowers. "That looks so good on you," said the countess.

"But wouldn't your raven protect you?" asked Margaret, pulling the gown over her head and looking at herself in the armoire mirror.

"No. Eduardo is a part of my uncle's staff," said Catalina, sitting down at Besa's violet dressing table, so Besa could brush her dark raven hair. "He would be put to death if he goes against the ambassador. That is the raven's contract. They would let his subordinates kill him, and his next highest lieutenant would take his place in my mother's household."

"That seems kind of harsh." replied Besa, pulling Catalina's long hair into two ponytails and tying them with one yellow and one red ribbon. Besa then handed the countess coconut oil to rub on her face and arms. She seemed pleased with the texture and aroma.

"It is a part of raven society," said Catalina. "Betrayal is the same as death. They are very harsh with one another. They would peck his eyes out and pierce his heart."

"Oh, my goodness," said Besa, having Margaret sit at the dressing table to get her hair brushed. "Have you got an idea of where the captain's grave is located? I would like to help you if we can. Are you able to get out at night?"

"Once my uncle is asleep, I will be free," said Catalina, handing Besa a ribbon and helping her place Margaret's voluminous mane into a bun. "Then I will fly here as a raven."

"You can fly?" asked Besa.

"I'm House of The Raven," said the countess, rubbing some coconut oil on Margaret's arms and face. "We could all fly at one time. My mother said she could fly as well, when she was a girl. But they lose it once they get older. Can't you fly, Besa?"

"I would like to, I just…"

"She can fly," said Margaret, having Besa sit down at the dressing table, and binding the mass of braids with a couple of violet ribbons. "She just hasn't tried. She's still learning her powers."

"That's true. I haven't needed to fly," said Besa, choosing a cotton Taino design from the night gown selection, with coqui frogs, turtles and suns. "Margaret does well enough for all of us."

"Maybe Margaret and I can help you test your wings," said Catalina, as Besa had them all sit in a circle.

"I suppose so. If we have time. I am usually focused on the Taafli. Hopefully, your mother allows you to come back, because we'll need time to plan for your case."

"Dickey will want to be here too, if we're planning," said Margaret. "It wouldn't be fair to keep him out."

"You are so right, Margaret. The whole club will have input on the plan and preparing for the site. Hopefully Mokheer will come as well."

"I will ask my mother if I can come for a sleepover two nights from now," said Catalina. "She will be excited that I have found some upper-class girls my own age."

CHAPTER 15

THE BISHOP

The bishop had The Book of Taalu hidden in a secret compartment at the rear of his office desk, in his private chambers. He took it out now to stare at it. When someone knocked on the door, he threw the book back in and closed the drawer quickly, before going and opening the door. It was Father Guidry.

"André," said Michel. "Why is your door locked?"

"Because these are my private chambers, Michel," replied the bishop, ushering in his close friend. "And I have decided that I don't want someone just walking in."

"It was never that way before. I came to talk to you about something else. I suppose you heard that the judge's son has returned home?"

"Yes, I did hear about it. And I can assure you, none of the Shadows that were associated with me took part in any kidnapping."

"So I have your assurance that you had nothing to do with it?"

"I can assure you that though the boy had no knowledge of his captors, neither do I, Father Guidry! Please close the door when you leave. I have work to do."

"I'm sorry, André. I didn't mean to imply—"

"Out!" ordered the bishop. When Father Guidry closed the door, there was a Shadow standing in the corner.

"How did you get in here?" demanded the bishop. "I sent all of you out of here."

The man came and sat in the chair opposite the bishop.

"We both know that's not what you did, Your Grace."

"Get out!" said the bishop.

"Calm down, Your Grace. I was sent here to offer assistance."

"Assistance with what—another attempt to destroy me? Who sent you?"

"Someone who understands irony better than you do. I was sent here to offer assistance with the book you cannot open."

"Are you mad?" asked Delacroix. "I don't have any–"

"With this book," said the Shadow, waving his hand over the desk, which caused the drawer to pop open and the book to float out.

"What kind of—what are you?" demanded Delacroix.

"The same type of creature you sent out to kidnap the judge's son. And now you have what you've coveted. But if you try to open it, the entity will kill you. And you know that."

"How do you know what I know?"

"There's only one way to find out. It's sitting right there. Why don't you open it?"

"Are you some kind of demon?" asked Delacroix. The Shadow just laughed.

"I'm no more of a demon than you are. The one who

sent me here has the same goal as you do: holding the Dephii and his spawn accountable for their crimes."

"The who?" asked the bishop. "I don't know anything about a Dephii."

"The name may have changed, but the person's the same. It's still Pierre Melponte and his daughter. He has been rendered mute now with the Gendarmes assistance. But apparently not dead yet."

"What kind of help are you offering? And what will it cost me?"

"We will protect you from the entity when you open the book," said the Shadow. "That's why you wanted it, right?"

"And what will I have to do to receive your protection?"

"At this point, not very much, because although the Necromancer is incarcerated, he has not died. And could conceivably return. If or when he does, it will be your task to trumpet the evilness of him and his offspring. We want his world turned upside down. When he is weakened, he will be easier to eliminate. Do we have a deal?"

"Is there some kind of handshake involved in this transaction?" asked the bishop.

"It's more of a blood shake. It's the standard way contracts are signed where I come from. The Shadow produced a small wicked looking black knife. Delacroix bristled at the sight of it.

"You're not going to slit my palm open, are you?"

"Absolutely not. All it takes is a prick of your finger, Your Grace. We're not in the dark ages anymore."

Delacroix presented his hand, and the Shadow pricked his index finger. The blood flowed very quickly to his palm, and the Shadow produced a piece of parchment where the blood drops were collected. The Shadow pressed the bishop's hand down on it. Suddenly ancient-looking text that he couldn't understand spread out across the page. When the page was full, the Shadow told him, "You can remove your hand now, Your Grace."

The Shadow rolled up the parchment and placed it inside his jacket. "One last thing."

He waved his hand over the desk once again, causing the drawer to pop open and The Book of Taalu to float out.

"What do you think you're doing?" demanded the bishop.

"The book comes with me," said the Shadow.

"Wait a minute! I didn't agree to that!"

"Actually, you just did. But let me ask you a question: what are you going to do with it? Take it out and look at it every day, right? And keep the door locked? How long before Michel decides to come in and get your desk open and finds it? He knows about the secret compartment. And if he finds it, things will get bad, right?"

The bishop didn't disagree.

"But how will I access it when I need it?"

"Very simple," replied the Shadow, "All you have to do is hold out your hand and say, 'The One Who Knows, please send me the book'. Try it now so you'll know that it works."

Delacroix stretched out his hand and said,

"The One Who Knows, please send me the book." And that's when he saw the extent of the protection he'd agreed to, because when the book appeared in his hand he was suddenly enclosed in a sheath of shadow. "

Wait a minute, said the bishop, "What is this?"

"It's your protective shield," replied the Shadow. "Lay the book on the desk and open it."

"I don't know. Are you sure this flimsy bit of shadow will protect me?"

"If we wanted to harm you, Your Grace, we wouldn't

have just signed a contract with you. Please, just open the book and you'll see what I mean."

The bishop opened The book of Taalu. The Taafli floated out immediately, possibly hoping to find the Necromancer safe and free. Instead, it floated around the room for about five minutes and then returned to the gateway and the bishop, with a trembling hand, closed the cover.

"I—that was—I can't believe that! It didn't even see me. That was amazing!"

"The Shadow cloak makes you invisible to the entity. So now, you can use the book without fear of injury."

"This is a great gift you've given me!" exclaimed the bishop. "How will I ever repay you?"

"Don't worry. That will be taken care of in good time. And there is one more thing I must warn you about."

"What's that?" asked the bishop.

"The Shadow cloak is not an inanimate piece of clothing like a robe or a coat. It is a living entity, so be careful not to overuse it, because your human body will change if you do."

"Change how?" asked Delacroix.

"The longer the cloak stays, the more it becomes you. Until eventually…"

"I will completely disappear," said the bishop,

"Good, then you understand. But I know you'll be fine, Your Grace. Because you are a smart and careful man. So just close the book and the Shadow will go away." And with that, the Shadow walked through the wall of the bishop's private chambers and disappeared. Delacroix closed the book, and his cloak and the book disappeared as well.

CHAPTER 16

THE WARRIORS

Michel knew that there was a strong possibility that what the bishop had just told him was a lie. He had thought he could resign himself to this reality, that powerful men often lie, usually to those they are closest to. But this was different. This was not some incidental lie told to a few parishioners at a service, or a picnic on Lake Pontchartrain. This was a subversion of all that was holy, and godlike, a monster's lie. The lie of death. Michel had known André longer than anyone other than Jesus. He watched him practice lying as a child, and had always caught him and called him on his lies. The fact that he had not tried to save his friend and call him on this one spoke to the death of his friend's Christian conscience, and his own loss of faith. There's just death after this. His own, for sure. Because he wouldn't allow his old friend's new evil to destroy this community and this church. He wasn't sure what he could do, but he wouldn't allow fear to keep him idle. His first suspicion was that André had not really dissolved his Shadow force. The judge's son's kidnapping proved that. Michel cried and prayed all night after he read the news. Cried because his wonderful, strong friend had died. This new man was simply the old Delly, with all the anger, but without a child's consideration. The young Delly identified with all the kids he knew, even the ones he beat up. Especially the ones he beat up. He'd known that all his classmates came from difficult backgrounds. That any cruelty he inflicted was nothing compared to what their mother or father would dish out when they got home. Better an ally than an enemy. That was the old Delly. But this new one scared Michel. This new one sent forth monsters to commit crimes. But if he didn't try to stop him, who would? He didn't have to, though. He had a very comfortable life waiting for him if he decided to hang up his robes and his convictions. But his conscience would suffer, as would his soul. He had a duty to stand in the gap between good and evil. He had no expectations. Because the reckoning would ultimately come for him, too. But he would stand by his heart—if a bit weak. It was a muscle, and muscles could be strengthened with effort and determination. He would start now. He had proven that in the face of blasphemy and evil, he could be a force. And if such were to raise its head again, he would be ready with his outrage and his teeth, clawing and kicking to beat it back. But first, he would need to take action.

Following André was the most direct action he could take. That couldn't be done in the clothes he wore. Where would he find regular clothes? He had no idea, but he knew someone who would: Father Alexander. The young priest had come to the church from a family who'd owned a theater troupe. Even Father Alexander couldn't escape his theater roots; he had the best voice of all the clerics in the parish, and so the bishop placed him in charge of the boys' choir. He had even managed to produce a very good

Christmas program, along with a production called The Betrayal of Christ. Father Guidry waited after choir practice and followed Father Alexander into the small office the church provided for the choirmaster.

"Good evening, Giles," said Michel, closing the door behind him as he came into the cramped little space. This placed the very observant priest on high alert.

"Good evening, Father Guidry," replied the young priest, sitting on the front of his tiny desk. "What can I do for you?"

"I-uh-was wondering if you had access to any costumes, like regular clothes?"

"You mean, like non-cleric? street clothes?"

"Yes, like street clothes?"

"Have you looked in the donation box? There are usually some things in there."

"Yes. I've looked there, but nothing fit me...I mean, the man I need them for?"

"Why would you need regular street clothes, Father?"

"If you must know, I'd like to walk around the city sometimes. Without being noticed."

Father Alexander crossed his arms and furrowed his brow as he considered what Michel had just told him. And then it came to him:

"You're going to follow the bishop."

"You—how dare you! You are a presumptuous young man, Father Alexander!"

"I know. I've been told that before. But I was in the sanctuary a week ago, Father, when you tried to beat that vile man to death with his evil book. I had the task of holding you back. You weren't just angry at Von Boutin. You were also angry at the Shadows for bringing that man into the sanctuary, and the bishop for allowing that ceremony to take place. I can still hear the soul of that man screaming. We've all noticed the change in the bishop, like someone else is wearing his robes. But if you're going to try and stay hidden while you trail him and his Shadows, you're going to need more than street clothes. You're going to need wards too."

"I will not defile myself with—"

"Some of the Shadows who follow the bishop are not human. They can read your mind from half a mile away. Which means you aren't going to get very far trying to follow the bishop. And there are Magists in my family."

"Are you Magist, Giles?"

"I don't need magic to see where this is going. You're the bishop's closest friend, and it is only natural you'd want to save him from this."

"You've just proven that you aren't a Magist, and can't read minds. I'm not trying to save him."

"You're definitely going to need more than street clothes and wards to stop him. You're going to need some help."

"Are you volunteering, Giles?"

"Yes. And don't be surprised if I'm not the only one. It's our church, too."

WITHIN A WEEK, Father Alexander had recruited their version of the Shadows. And for the moment, all of them were non-Magist. They even had their own special meeting place.

"Why do we need to leave the chapel?" asked Michel.

"For the same reason the bishop sent his Shadows

away. To keep their plans and activities secret," replied Father Alexander.

"I don't want us to be called Shadows," said Father Guidry. "That name has bad connotations."

"Then what will we call ourselves?" asked Father Alexander.

"Why do we even need a name? I'm not trying to compete with André, I'm trying to stop him," replied Michel.

"We can call ourselves 'The Stoppers', then."

"That just sounds ridiculous. We're just Christan warriors. We don't need a name."

Father Alexander just smiled then.

Oh, good heavens! I just gave us a name, didn't I?"

"Yes, you did," replied a satisfied Father Alexander.

The Warriors held strategy meetings at the rear of a downtown theater, which was owned by one of Father Alexander's uncles.

"I knew we'd get you back in the theater some kind of way, Giles," his uncle told him.

"We're just going to hold a few prayer meetings in one of the rehearsal rooms, uncle Jacob."

"Shouldn't you be doing it at the chapel?"

"Not everyone will come to the church."

"All right, nephew. You don't have to tell me what you're doing."

"Bless you, uncle. I love you."

"Just make sure you saints lock up when you leave."

The initial corps of Warriors numbered only ten because, for some reason, the older priests were still loyal to the bishop. Recruitment was a slow and complicated process since the bishop hadn't done anything that was overtly evil, and he'd gotten rid of that bizarre group called the "Shadows". That had actually bolstered the morale of all the deacons and priests in the diocese and chapel. Father Alexander was also instrumental in outfitting their present corps of Warriors with wards to shield their thoughts. They were also cautioned never to confront a Shadow directly, because they weren't fighters. Just Christian warriors seeking justice.

CHAPTER 17

THE GRAVE OF CAPTAIN MONTALBÁN

The next day at school, Dickey was very excited about the coming meeting with Catalina. He was even able to take a break from his play with the third years so he could sit down and listen, but the children could be heard behind him, urging him to hurry back to the game.

"Dickey," said Margaret. "Why don't you play with kids your own age?"

Dickey thought about that for a second.

"Okay, Margaret. Are you up for a game of hide-the-Mandrake?"

"Ew! No!" cried Margaret. "That is a stupid game. Why would I want to play something like that?"

"That's why I don't play with kids my own age. It's the third year's game, and I want to play it."

"Dickey let's go!" said a seven-year-old sorcerer, who'd thrown his arms around his neck and was trying to climb up his back.

"Just a moment, Bartholomew. Are we done here?"

"Go on, Dickey," said Besa.

"Yeah. Those Mandrakes aren't going to hide themselves," snapped Margaret.

Dickey stuck out his tongue as he gave the little sorcerer a piggy-back ride toward the other group of children.

"He is such a dunderhead!" grumbled Margaret.

Besa looked at her and laughed

"Why are you so hard on him?"

"Because he never wants to sit with us," pouted Margaret.

"Margaret. You know that Dickey is the youngest in his family. His brothers are much older, so he never got to play with anyone when he was smaller."

"I guess I never thought about it like that."

"We just need to let him be himself; and the children love him."

They looked around and saw that the game had devolved into a raucous pile of arms and legs, with Dickey at the very center. He finally pulled himself free and came back over to the table.

"Okay. The game's over," he said, breathless. "So, we meet at Besa's in two days. Is Mokheer coming? He's not coming, is he?"

"He's in the club too, Dickey," said Margaret.

"I thought he quit?"

"He did not quit," replied Besa. "He just has to make up his mind about a few things."

"As long as he behaves himself."

"The question is: Are you going to behave yourself?" replied Margaret.

"What are you talking about? I'm always in control of myself."

That's when the little sorcerer stuck his head up past the edge of the table, giggled and tossed a Mandrake plant in Dickey's lap. The thing let out a screech that sent Dickey diving toward Margaret, knocking her off the bench.

"Get off me! You dunderhead!" cried Margaret,

"We might need someone to keep an eye on both of you," chuckled Besa

"Get off me, butter head. Before I hit you with a sparkle!"

"You'd better not!" said Dickey, scrambling away. "Those things hurt!"

When the gong signaling the end of recess sounded, Dickey took off for the school building before Margaret could make good on her threat. The third years were right on his tail, like this was all a part of the same game.

"Something just occurred to me," said Besa. "Dickey is going to make a great father one of these days. He really loves children."

"What is that supposed to mean?" snapped Margaret. "Why are you telling me that? I am not marrying him! I don't care what you and Mokheer say!"

"The lady doth protest too much, methinks," replied Besa, as she walked to the side door into the school.

"And I hate Shakespeare," growled Margaret.

BESA SPENT most nights studying with Felix and on her own, as well as having a one-sided conversation with her father. She felt sure her grandmother heard and would hopefully convey it to him.

"I've met a new friend, Papa," said Besa, sitting on the bed in Pierre's room. "Her name is Countess Catalina Infanta y Barbosa." Sometimes she cried. It pained her to think she might never see him again. "My club and I are helping her." But it fueled her desire to help Catalina discover her own father's killer. "Her uncle—the Spanish ambassador—may have killed her father."

And though Besa knew it would violate one of Pierre's unspoken rules, she started searching his library for old maps from the time Spain controlled Newald. It didn't take long for her to find something. Pierre's maps showed the Spanish plans of the city which also included burial sites that had been renamed by the French. She knew Catalina would want to see these maps, so they would have some places to search for Captain Montalbán's grave. There were three particular sites at the base of the levee right behind the Destrehan Plantation. She knew Pierre had done an enchantment ceremony at the owner's house. This was a ceremony to which Felix accompanied her father.

The owner's residence was already haunted, and the structure was heavily warded. There were so many ghosts wandering through the massive old Spanish house that Felix had a hard time judging who were the living and who the dead. There was also the St Peter Street cemetery.

When Catalina came back for her second visit to the Melponte mansion, she had an unexpected companion: Eduardo. She pulled up to the stables in an embassy carriage, and was carrying her own garment bag. When she stepped out of the carriage, she told the driver, "I will be ready to return in the morning, Teofilo."

"Yes, my lady," he replied and pulled away.

"I'm so glad you could return, Catalina," said Besa, who'd come out to meet her carriage. "Dickey, Margaret and Mokheer should be here soon."

"Wonderful," said Catalina. "Eduardo, are you here yet?"

The raven fluttered out of the oak tree next to the stables.

"I have been here fifteen minutes waiting for you," said the raven, landing on her right shoulder.

"I'm sorry. The carriage can't compete with your wings."

"Good evening, Besa." said the corvid. "I'm happy to see you again. Don't worry, I have a reason for being here."

"When Eduardo heard what we were planning, he decided to help," said Catalina.

"I can't wait to hear your ideas, Eduardo," replied Besa.

"Raven aren't much for ideas," said Eduardo. "Although I did think of something that will help."

"Let's go into the house. I'm sure Miss Maymi will have a treat for you."

"I prefer cracked corn, even crackers will do," replied the raven. When they got into the house, Besa informed one of the servants that one of their guests would be a raven.

When the rest of the club arrived and came into the parlor, Dickey saw Eduardo and said, "You are a thick billed raven."

"That is quite impressive, young man," replied Eduardo. "Did you do a bit of reading about ravens?"

"I did, actually," said Dickey. "It turns out, my grandmother kept quite a few corvids, but they didn't speak."

"Only Dickey would end up a bird expert," replied Mokheer.

"And who is the ghost expert?" asked Eduardo.

"I am not a ghost!" replied Mokheer. "I am an unspecified security entity."

"Really?" said Besa. "This is the first I've heard of it."

"Now that we know what we all are, we should probably get down to why I'm here," offered Eduardo. "But I suppose madam president should introduce the idea."

"Thank you, Eduardo," said Besa, standing up. "We are trying to locate Captain Montalbán's grave site. I discovered some old maps in my papa's library, showing the Spanish plans for the city. But what we need is a way to pinpoint a specific grave and know who's in it. Eduardo has offered his special skills in accomplishing that task."

"Yes," said Eduardo. "I, and a group of my soldiers, will retrieve the ledger of births and burials from the diocese archives."

"Wait a minute," said Mokheer. "How are a bunch of bir—ravens, going to get inside a locked archive?"

"Mr. O'Brien," said Eduardo. "Please explain."

"Thank you, Eduardo, I will," replied Dickey. "Corvids are smarter than birds and a number of other entities, apparently," said Dickey. "The archives of the diocese have large rafters that can be accessed by knowledgeable corvids."

"And unlike other species, the soldiers in my regiment read very well and won't have any difficulty locating the specific ledger and transporting it here," replied Eduardo.

"The diocese has maintained very detailed records for over a hundred years," supplied Catalina. "The French and the Spanish all have the same religion."

"And unlike humans, ravens can read in the dark," said Eduardo.

"Wow!" said Margaret. "When are we getting this book?"

"As soon as my contact on the ambassador's staff confirms the year of the captain's death," said Eduardo. "I should have that information by tomorrow night. The book will be here three days from then."

"And I will be here as well," said Catalina. "My mother is encouraging me to get out of the official residence more often. She also likes that you have security Dreids protecting you."

"I guess we're done," said Mokheer. "Time to go."

"Good night, Mokheer," said Besa. "See you in four days."

~

THE LEDGER ARRIVED on the evening of the fourth day, right after Catalina dismounted from the official carriage. Dickey and Margaret soon followed, but unfortunately, Mokheer didn't show.

"Where is your unspecified friend?" asked Catalina.

"He's probably just late," said Margaret.

"He's not much for entrances," replied Dickey. "Other than sneaking up on me."

"It doesn't matter," said Besa. "The ledger still has to be returned tonight."

"That is correct," replied Eduardo. "My contact on the ambassador's staff confirmed that Captain Montalbán perished October 10, 18_, approximately ten years ago. So that will be the place to start."

They took up stations in the library, on top of the tables with a lamp and room to open the large book. After about an hour of perusing the entries,

"This might be it," said Besa, pointing to an entry about midway into the page.

"Let me see," said Margaret, using one of the magnifying glasses in the library. "I can't read this. What language is that?"

"That's Arabic," said Besa. "But I don't know why an entry in this ledger would be written that way."

"Let me take a look," said Eduardo. "That is definitely Arabic, Besa," replied the Corvid

"But why would someone use that language in this kind of book?" Besa asked.

"This was undoubtedly done in anger. Apparently, the captain was a Moor, which means this was a curse."

"But he was a part of the duke's staff. Why would someone go to so much trouble for someone who was already dead?"

"It was important enough for someone," replied Margaret. "My father has spoken about practices such as this. Since the deceased was of the wrong religion, he could not receive absolution."

"This was something I've read about: A heretic burial," said Eduardo. "He was cursed before they put him in the ground. This notation in the ledger denotes a grave they don't want you to find."

"That sounds like something my uncle might commission," said Catalina.

"If he put this in place," said Besa. "It proves he has something to hide."

"I will understand if you don't want to do this, Besa," said Catalina.

"Yes, Ms. Melponte," replied Eduardo, "This grave will have a dangerous element attached to it."

"That has never stopped us before," said Besa. "

"But it should stop us, shouldn't it?" replied Dickey. "I mean, it's not like opening a crypt of some unknown person and being surprised. We already know something terrible is waiting!"

"You know that's not going to matter," said Margaret "Sir Richard, the brave."

"You just want to rub my nose in it, don't you?" Snapped Dickey.

"If she doesn't, I sure do," said Mokheer, materializing beside him. Dickey looked over at Catalina and slammed his hand over his mouth so he wouldn't scream.

"That is impressive, Sir Richard," said Mokheer. "You usually jump out of your skin when I do that. And if Besa's going, I have no choice but to go."

"Oh, my goodness!" cried Dickey. "Nothing says disaster like bringing our own ghost."

"He has a right to come, just like you, Dickey," replied Margaret.

"This is a very different situation, Margaret," said Besa. "Dickey has a valid point. I have my own personal reasons for wanting to help Catalina solve the mystery of her father's death. My own father is somewhere I can't reach due to laws I know nothing about. But I can't ask any of you to risk your lives on my behalf."

"What are you saying, Besa?" replied Margaret. "This club is the best thing that's ever happened to me. I wouldn't dream of missing this. I get to use my powers in ways I could never do in class. I go where you go!"

"Thank you, Margaret. I know we'll need everything you've got."

"I'm definitely not staying home if Margaret's going," replied Dickey.

"You just said you didn't want to go!" cried Margaret.

"If I don't go, who's going to protect you?"

"Protect me?"

"Yes. I can't let anything happen to you. You're my future wife!"

The only thing Margaret could do was sit down at the table and look stunned.

"That's the first time I've known her not to have a reply. Is that a good sign?" asked Dickey.

But Margaret did have a reply, she hit Dickey in the chest with a sparkle.

DELACROIX'S MISTAKE

One thing was for certain; the bishop wasn't idle during all this time. He was attempting his third enchantment ceremony with his new cloaked abilities. The human Shadows had managed to secure him a couple of corpses to practice on.

"Has this man been given absolution?" asked the bishop, when they showed up with his first corpse.

"Does it help that he died on his knees?" asked Denny.

"Was he praying?" inquired the bishop.

"No, Your Grace," replied Denny. "He got into a disagreement over whether the dice were loaded or not, and the man running the game stabbed him in the heart. Jackie knew him, and doubts the man ever set foot in a church."

"It makes sense that Jackie would know him," replied Delacroix. "Because I haven't seen him there in a number of months either."

"But I spend most of my time with you, Your Grace," replied Jackie. "Don't that count for something?"

The bishop didn't have the heart to tell Jackie that he doubted it would, given what they got up to.

∾

WHEN THE BISHOP attempted his second enchantment, he felt he'd gotten a grasp of the cloak's capabilities. He'd called the book, and once the cloak engaged, Denny opened the book's cover. But this time the Taafli did not come all the way out. He could see its glow but it seemed to loiter for almost twenty minutes just inside the cover; just floating but not rising. Denny was hovering at his elbow in case Delacroix needed some assistance. After about half an hour, the bishop whispered: "Can you see what it's doing, Denny. He took a quick glance.

"It's not doing anything, Your Grace. You want me to maybe close the cover?"

"Not if you value your life," whispered Delacroix.

When the Taafli finally emerged, it hovered around the library for an additional period of time, another half hour.

"We know you are here somewhere," it finally said. "Book thief." And then it merged with the waiting corpse. Delacroix's hand began to tremble as he realized the creature was hunting him. He was sweating so profusely inside the cloak that one of his eyes got blurry. Once the creature ascended from the corpse and returned to the gateway, and Denny closed the book, the man gave a cry, "Good heavens, Your Grace! Your eye!"

"Oh, it's just a little blurry from my sweating," replied Delacroix. "Hand me a handkerchief so I can wipe my face."

"But it's gone, Your Grace! There is no eye there!"

The bishop panicked and dashed toward the front foyer, like a man running for his life. But the front foyer was quite dark by that time. "A lamp!" cried the bishop. "Someone, bring me a lamp! I can't see my face!"

Jackie took the solemn task of revealing the bishop's face to himself. But he left quickly, knowing better than to stand and watch the great man's pain. When the bishop beheld his own face, he was so horrified he almost cried out. The place on his face where his right eye used to be was now a smooth blank spot. No empty socket, no scar, just smooth skin, as if his eye had never existed. Delacroix clamped his right hand over the empty spot and locked himself in the closest bedroom and held a pillow over his mouth to muffle his agonized sobs. Halfway through this sequence, he realized he had another problem: he had to hide his affliction from Michel and all the diocese staff. Not to mention the congregation. There was no way he could explain it—not truthfully, at least. He opened the bedroom door and shouted for Denny. "Will you please have someone go–" Denny was standing at the door brandishing an eye patch.

"Here you are, Your Grace."

"But where did you–"

"Matthews, one of our newest members, wears an eye patch."

"But won't he need it?" asked the bishop.

"He's just got a lazy eye," replied Denny. "He can keep it closed till he gets home tonight."

"Please express my gratitude to Mister Matthews." The bishop would've done it himself, but he didn't want to show his vulnerability.

During the third ceremony, the Shadows had located a man who inquired of the spirit whether he had slept with his wife. The spirit regarded the man with a very forlorn expression and replied,

"Thou hath taken my life over falsehood. I loved my own wife and knew not yours."

"But I was told that he did it. My friend Paddy said it."

"I forgive Paddy and so shall you," said the spirit and then receded back into the corpse.

"But Paddy is my best friend," said the man. "He wouldn't lie to me."

After the Taafli returned to the gateway and the bishop closed the book, he directed Denny to inform the Gendarmes about Mr. McBride's murder and where to find his killer.

"Will do, Your Grace," said Denny, grabbing Logan McDougal by his right arm and twisting it behind his back for good measure. "This way, you canker!"

HENRY MCBRIDE RECEIVED a quiet but solemn burial in the church graveyard.

"Was this man even a member of the congregation?" asked Father Guidry.

"He and Mary are recent members," said the bishop.

"Really, André? I am at the service too, and I don't remember seeing them."

"Do you believe I would make something like this up, Michel?"

"No, Your Grace, that is not what I believe. Your vision is obviously better than mine. Even with one eye?"

"Precisely," said the bishop.

THE ENTRY in the diocese ledger listed Captain Montalbán's site of burial at the St Peter Street cemetery.

"That won't be hard to find," said Dickey. "It's somewhere in Vieux Carré."

"I'm glad you're so enthusiastic for once, Dickey," said Margaret. "Tell him the rest, Besa."

"We're probably going to have to dig to get to this coffin. St Peter was not an above ground cemetery." Dickey's face dropped.

"And since we don't know what entity we may encounter, the wards will be crucial for this site, Dickey," said Margaret.

"Yes," said Dickey. "I gathered that from the fact that it's a cursed burial, Margaret."

"I'm glad you're paying attention. We can't afford any mistakes at a site like this."

"That's true," said Besa. "I have written up a list of mandatory supplies, and each of us must sign up for what items we want to be responsible for."

She passed the list around to the various members of those gathered. "What is a shoo-vel?" asked Catalina. "Is that a French word? I'm not familiar with it."

Dickey laughed.

"I doubt it's something you would have encountered, countess. There's probably not much digging in the nobility."

"You mean, like sticking something in the actual dirt?" asked Catalina.

"Yes. Exactly like that."

"And one other thing," said Margaret. "We shouldn't wear dresses for this case. We may need to do a bit of running. Especially since we don't know what entity we might encounter. Dresses aren't good for digging or running fast."

"I have a few pairs of knickerbockers I could let you borrow," said Dickey.

"Thank you, Dickey," said Besa. "If you bring them by tomorrow after school, we can have them tailored."

"Why would they need to be tailored? They fit perfectly."

"They fit you perfectly, Dickey. They would be a little big on us girls," replied Margaret.

"I'll see if I have any that are smaller."

"Look and see if you have some from when you were about eight," said Besa.

"Those will be really small."

"We'll also need shirts to go with the pants," said Margaret.

"I'll look," said Dickey.

"Anything you bring we can have tailored to fit us, Dickey," said Besa.

"What's left of the St. Peter Street cemetery is on the property of a house in the Vieux Carré," said Margaret. "Somebody will need to go look at the site and see if the house, or its occupants. will pose any difficulties."

"I will take that task," said Eduardo. "Since I will have no need for clothing or digging."

"You're not required to come, Eduardo," said Catalina.

"I will be escorting you, countess," replied Eduardo, "I would bring a human, but I don't trust humans. Present company excluded, of course."

"Of course," replied Margaret.

"Are you sure, Eduardo?" asked Catalina, "We may discover things about the ambassador you won't want to know."

"It's my understanding that the spirit you raise from this corpse must tell the truth?" asked Eduardo.

"That's how it works, yes," replied Besa." A spirit has no more reason to lie."

"That will be something to see, since live humans lie

almost all the time. Ravens never lie or contrive. We only provide a service. Truth will not bother me, countess."

"We of The Graveyard Club appreciate your assistance, Eduardo," said Besa. "Let's plan two weeks from tonight to embark on this case to help Catalina discover the truth about her father's death."

THE MOORISH HOUSE

Eduardo took his first reconnaissance mission to the property at the St Peter Street cemetery on the Monday of the next week and met the children when they had their usual congregation at Besa's house after school. And for his trouble, Miss Maymi provided him with a plate of freshly baked com bread.

"I am overwhelmed by your generosity, dear Miss Maym," he told the cook.

"Thank you," replied Miss Maymi and left quickly, like she was shy.

"She left so suddenly. I hope I didn't frighten her," said Eduardo.

"She spooks very easily," replied Besa. "She's afraid of the Cajuns at the French Market, so I don't know what she thinks of a talking raven."

The children sat and enjoyed the snacks the cook prepared. Dickey even managed to restrain himself with the cake Miss Maymi laid out; he only had three pieces—moderate by Dickey's standards.

"Now that everyone has been sated," said the corvid. "It is time I give my report to madam, president,"

"Madam, who?" asked Dickey.

"He's referring to Besa, Dickey," replied Margaret. "She is the president."

Eduardo sat looking at him.

"Are you done, Mr. O'Brien?"

"I...Yes, I guess I am."

"Good. The structure where the grave is located was very interesting. I have some experience with this, so I was excited to see such a building in this part of the world. The house is of Andalusian design, and what remains of the St Peter Street cemetery is enclosed at its center in a section of its courtyard."

"The graveyard is not accessible to the public?" asked Besa.

"Yes, it is very accessible. The courtyards of these type houses are open. Anyone can just walk in."

"But it's private property. How is it you are allowed to just walk in?" asked Besa.

"The house does not appear occupied. I flew into its center and was able to view a good part of it. No one lives there, though someone is maintaining the graveyard. It's almost as if the structure is there simply for people or corvids to look at it."

"But if we dig in the courtyard, that will be damaging private property," said Margaret.

"But the front door is open. All the rooms are accessible from the courtyard. This is not uncommon in Andalusian culture. Such a structure is there should someone need shelter. This was a common practice of the Caliphate of Córdoba. What good is a shelter if it cannot be shared?"

"Is this a raven's perspective?" asked Dickey.

"The Muslims of southern Spain had views similar to ravens, yes," replied Eduardo. "They valued justice, and abhorred betrayal, and they maintained major centers of learning and knowledge."

"I have never heard of Muslims," said Dickey. "You talk as though they are gone."

"They are," said Besa. "The Muslims of Granada were the descendants of raiders that came through the Strait of Gibran in the 6th Century. They had a major influence on Europe, they invented mathematics and coffee."

"Wow!" said Dickey. "What happened to them?"

"They were expelled by the Spanish crown in the 15th century."

"One of the worst injustices in human history," said Eduardo. "I am impressed, madam president. You are quite the scholar." Besa sat down and began to cry. "Did I say something to upset her?" asked the corvid.

"Her father was the reason she studied so hard. Calling her a scholar made her think about him," said Margaret.

"And he is still alive?" asked Eduardo.

"He is—I hope," said Besa, collecting herself. "I never know when that's going to happen, so I'm caught off guard,"

"I understand," replied the corvid. "And if you like, Margaret, we can fly to the Moorish house tonight, and you can inspect it for yourself."

"Thank you, I would like that very much," replied Margaret. "We can do it on my way home tonight."

The pants and shirts Dickey provided required extensive tailoring, most of them were at least four sizes too big for the girls. The Melponte's family seamstress made quick work of the task.

MARGARET GAVE Besa her assessment of the Andalusian house the next day at school.

"The raven was right. The rooms are all accessible from the courtyard. He neglected to mention there is a fantastic fountain in the courtyard. It's like some kind of monument. One lion, with a basin on his back. And I believe he's mistaken about it being completely deserted, because there is not a speck of dust anywhere in it, Besa. And someone is leaving fresh fruit every day, I believe, because none of it is rotten. It's almost like some kind of offering."

"An offering to who or what?" asked Besa.

"I don't know, but it was always placed in a large receptacle, like the size of a washbasin."

"That sounds promising," said Dickey in between various games with the third years. "Is there anything else in there to eat?"

"Dickey, you've already gotten in trouble like this once. You shouldn't go to a strange house and eat that food," replied Margaret. "We don't know who it's there for."

"According to Eduardo, it's there for anyone."

"I don't know if we can rely on a raven's idea of possession."

"Yes, I suppose you're right," said Dickey.

"There is only one grave in the graveyard, and it is very well maintained. Just like the house. It has a very expensive-looking headstone, and doesn't look more than a month old, like someone just replaced it."

"Who replaces headstones in a graveyard?" asked Dickey.

"Possibly a caretaker," replied Besa. "That would explain the fruit and the clean house."

"The thing is, I felt a presence there, Besa. I have a sense for that. But it didn't seem malevolent."

"That's strange," said Besa. "We should definitely tell Catalina, to see if she still wants to proceed with this."

~

But Catalina didn't hesitate. "I still want to explore the grave on this site."

"Are you sure Catalina? Margaret sensed there was a presence there."

"Are you afraid?" asked Catalina.

"Absolutely not," said Besa.

"Yes, let's go," replied Margaret. "Before Dickey goes there, eats all its food, and makes it mad."

The seamstress delivered all the altered pants and shirts they would need for the dig. Once all the shovels and sundry other supplies were gathered, the expedition would take place three days later. They also decided to ride their own horses rather than take one of the carriages.

CHAPTER 18

DICKEY'S PLAN

They arrived at the site a little after midnight, along with Catalina, with Eduardo perched on her right shoulder, following just behind them on a white mare from the royal stables. And just as Besa researched, it was a large square structure with a wonderful Andalusian scalloped arch over the single-entry point with what looked like an ebony wood door covered in golden metal rivets. The structure itself was painted a dark rust color.

"That's strange," said Margaret. "There was no door here when I came by a few days ago." Eduardo flew at the door and landed on the little wood ledge above it. He took a moment to examine the door and flew back to Catalina.

"Those are definitely solid gold rivets," he declared.

"We are going to have to get the door open if we want to get inside," said Besa.

"It'll have to be one of you," said the raven. "My strength does not work on doors."

"I'll do it," said Catalina, dismounting. "Let's go, Eduardo."

When she went up to the door and tried to push on it, it

disappeared. "I don't know if that's good or bad," she said. But Eduardo just flew straight in. "Wait a minute, Eduardo!" cried the countess.

"Come on in, countess," said the raven.

"All right. I'm coming," said the Catalina.

"Wait a minute, Catalina," said Besa. "It's best we all go together."

"There's a lamp!" said the raven's voice. "So you won't have to worry about light."

"Hey!" said Dickey. "Does anybody else smell that? Someone's baking bread!"

He dismounted quickly and was about to go inside, in search of the wonderful smell.

"Wait, Dickey!" said Besa. "Don't get trapped like that again. We all go in together."

"But it's wonderful, can't you smell it?"

"I don't smell anything," said Margaret. "Which means something is trying to lure Dickey in. Not that it takes much."

"I agree," said Besa, something wants to separate us."

"Yes, stay with us, Sir Richard," said Catalina. "We'll need your courage."

"Don't say anything, Margaret," said Besa. "That's how she sees him."

"Okay," said Margaret. "But she might be disappointed."

Once everyone had dismounted, they moved toward the structure as a group.

When they entered the foyer past the entry, the walls were decorated with a green and ruby floral tile along the bottom half of the wall. The top half was a fresco, with a scene of warriors fighting lions and demons and a dancing red figure. The pattern was repeated along the hall. The first room they got to there was a honey-combed arch as they entered the large airy space with very little furniture, mostly large rugs. The tiles on the walls were minimized a bit and the scenes of battle and dance took over the surrounding walls.

"Wow," look at that ceiling!" said Dickey. "It's like stalactites of some kind, but more even.

"It's a work in progress," came a booming voice that seemed to fill the room. The kids all started. Lounging in the far corner was a creature of myth: A giant red djinn engaged in a feast that would've fed a small brigade. The djinn was in the form of a large man of about nine feet, his shirt-less upper-body was covered in strange lit tattoos and a ruby the size of a grapefruit draped his neck on what looked like a silver chain. He was also reclining on an invisible couch that hovered about a foot above the marble floor.

When he moved his arm to reach for a piece of meat or fruit, Besa noted the metal bands around each of his wrists. His striking eyes had an almond shape. Besa thought they had a beautiful intensity, possibly aided by the tiny flame flickering just behind the irises. They marked him as a creature from a different dimension. His decorated brown skin would be what most people noticed, but his most terrifying feature was the plaited braid of fire draped over his powerful chest,

"I tried sending you an invitation, Dickey," said the djinn. "But you were slow to respond."

"Besa wouldn't let me," said Dickey.

"Shame on you, Miss Melponte, forcing me to slog through this feast alone."

"What is your name?" asked Besa.

"Names are kind of tricky in our line of work. You can't go handing them out to just anyone."

"But you know ours," replied Besa.

"Yes. That was easy enough. Who else would the countess find to help her locate the captain's remains?"

"Then if we can't know your name, what do we call you?" asked Eduardo.

"Let me see," said the djinn, tapping a rapier tipped finger on his chin. "You may call me Muhammad. After the last Muslim king of Granada."

"That was tragic, said Eduardo. "Were you there?"

"I was. And I don't know why I brought it up, because it's kind of depressing."

"Why are you here?" asked Besa.

"I'm here because I'm bound to this structure. I don't get many visitors, and none of them can usually see me. But after midnight, everything comes alive."

"I hope you don't mind Muhammad," said Catalina. "But we must dig up the captain's grave."

"I heard about those ridiculous shovels. I can't let you dig holes on this property. I'm here to protect it."

"Muhammad, will you please grant us access to the captain's grave?" asked Besa.

"There is a reason why you're the leader, Miss Melponte. You are a wonder, even without your Taafli engaged. I will definitely grant you access. But you must know it is cursed. Which is kind of silly when you think about it, because who goes around fiddling with remains? But someone saw you coming, Miss Melponte."

"It was probably my uncle," said Catalina.

"Possibly, but the first curse is a real doozy. So make sure to keep your eyes open. Oh, and hold on to this, Dickey." A sword materialized out of thin air before Dickey's eyes, and he pulled it out of the air.

"It's weighted to my hand."

"All he's going to do is trip over it and stab himself," said Margaret.

"You underestimate Sir Richard's courage, Miss Claiborne. Oh, and the ghost boy has arrived."

"I beg your pardon," said Mokheer, appearing next to Dickey. "I am an unspecified security entity. Wow! I've seen it all. A red djinn in Vieux Carré. Are we fighting it, or what?"

"Please," said Muhammad. "I could've killed you all before you got off your horses. I rarely have visitors and never entertainment. But if he's not going to help, I can keep ghost boy up here with me."

"You will not touch me, bottle boy," said Mokheer. But the djinn simply moved his hand and Mokheer was plastered to the twenty-foot stalactite ceiling.

"That is amazing!" said Dickey. "Can you teach me how to do that?"

"But he needs to come down," said Besa. "He's a part of The Graveyard Club, too."

"No, he doesn't," said Dickey. "He's fine right where he is."

"And Muhammad, you mentioned keeping Mokheer up here with you," said Besa. "Where is the grave located?"

"That is an excellent question, Miss Melponte. The body is in the ground but not touching the ground."

"How is that even possible?" asked Margaret.

"Because the body is inside a water sealed vault."

"But how are we getting into a water seated vault?" asked Catalina.

"It's sealed, but it's not locked," said the djinn. "I can provide you with a passageway down to it. But I can do nothing about the obstacles."

"Please open the pathway for us, Muhammad," replied Besa.

"Besa, are you sure?" asked Margaret. "He just said the first obstacle might kill you."

"It helps that I know that, Margaret. Obstacles never stopped us before. We made a commitment to Catalina."

"But I don't wish to see you harmed, countess Besa," replied Catalina.

"If I feared such things, I would not be here, Catalina. We are here to help you, and that is what we will do. So, Muhammad, please point us to the location of Captain Montalbán's grave so that we can get started."

"As you wish, madam president," said the djinn with a gracious bow and disappeared. "Meet me in the courtyard, please," echoed his voice.

As they moved through the house Margaret noted, "Why is there no furniture? Where would people sit?"

"This is a typical Moorish house," replied Eduardo. The Moors evolved from the Berbers, who moved about the North African desert in tents, with camels as pack animals. They used rugs and pillows as furniture. When the Moors took control of Granada and the south of Spain, the pillows and the rugs moved inside their fixed residences."

"Thank you, Eduardo. You are a wealth of knowledge," said Besa.

"And you must find a way to protect your chest," said the corvid.

"My chest?" asked Besa.

"Yes," replied the corvid. "The curse must know that if it can stop you, the expedition will not proceed."

"By driving a stake into your heart, it will neutralize the Taafli," continued Catalina. "I got that out of the guard's head. But at the time, it didn't make any sense to me."

"Thank you for sharing that, Catalina. I will be careful."

"This is a magnificent courtyard, Muhammad," said Besa, when they finally reached the central courtyard. "This marble is kind of unusual. The fountain is beautiful." The fountain and the courtyard were made of the same type of marble.

"Thank you, Miss Melponte. You have a good eye for art. The owners had the marble imported from Macael, Spain. I sort of copied the fountain from the palace. It is obviously not an exact replica. But it is a taste of home," said the djinn, as he hovered over a grass plot right next to the wall of the courtyard. "This property was purchased by the captain's family a few years before his death," said the djinn. "This whole area was renovated and the vault for his body was placed here. That was before I was bound to the site. The marble and the statue were a gift to me."

"Show us the pathway, please, Muhammad," said Besa. The djinn waved his hand and the ground split open, presenting a series of steps that descended into the dark.

"That looks promising," said Margaret.

"No, it doesn't," said Dickey.

"And while I cannot travel with you—too much water down there for a djinn—I do have a gift for Margaret." He produced a sturdy-looking oil lamp out of thin air and sent it floating toward the young witch.

"I know you usually make your own light, but there aren't any branches down there. "

"Thank you," said Margaret. "This should be helpful."

"As long as you keep it above your waist, it will stay lit. Good luck. It's been nice knowing you."

"That's a rather morbid send off," said Mokheer.

"I'm not being morbid. Djinn live a thousand times longer than humans."

"I see your point."

"No more time to chat. Off you go."

And so, The Graveyard Club descended into the depths toward the vault. The trek wasn't a short one; they walked for about five minutes, which meant this was the first mausoleum that was in the gulf, versus trying to stay out of the water. And then Dickey looked back up the stairs.

"Wait a minute, did that djinn close the hole? I see darkness up there."

"I'll go up and look," said Eduardo.

The raven took off, but was back in a few moments. "The opening is still there, Mr. O'Brien. It's just that the night is rather starless right now?

"If you would like me to hold the lamp, Margaret, I won't mind," said Catalina.

"Thank you," said Margaret, handing her the lamp. "I'm assuming we're going toward a wall. At that point, I might need my hands for casting."

"It won't be long now, Margaret," said Besa. "I sense the wall coming up."

Ten seconds later, they were at the entry point into the vault.

"Okay, everyone. Please ward yourselves up," said Besa. "I believe the first obstacle will be triggered when we open the door." Catalina and Margaret both slid charms around their necks. All except Dickey.

"Where's your charm, Dickey?" asked Mokheer.

"I didn't bring one," replied Dickey. "I thought we were digging someone up, not climbing down into an underwater chasm!"

"Then I'd better stay in front of you."

"What good will that do? Things just go right through you."

"That's true. But I can usually slow down the big stuff."

Then Besa opened the door, and the opposite wall shot out, pushing Margaret, Dickey and Catalina with Eduardo, into the left corner, sealing them in concrete, and leaving Besa and Mokheer alone.

"Besa! Get down!" said Mokheer. He saw it before it started. Sharp metal rods erupted from the wall straight at Besa. Mokheer was fast enough to dive in front of her, but they went right through him. When he turned around, he couldn't believe what he saw. Besa had somehow stopped the rods. It wasn't just that she was moving them, like bending the light around them. But the only light she had was the light he gave off.

"Can you make the lantern rise, Mokheer? I need a little more light."

Mokheer made Margaret's lantern rise above him. Besa quickly took the light, wrapped it around the rods, turned them and sent them back into the wall from which they'd come. She then pulled the wall away from Dickey, Catalina and Margaret and pushed it back to the right side of the room. After she'd done all that, she collapsed to the floor.

"Besa, are you okay? Can you go on?" asked Mokheer,

"That was quite wonderful, Miss Melponte," came the djinn's voice echoing down the stairs. "You do not disappoint!"

"I'm okay, Mokheer. It just took a bit out of me. Let me rest for a few moments."

"But Besa, what was that?" asked Mokheer."

"You seem to know everything about my powers. I was hoping you could tell me what it was."

"I—I've never even seen anything like that?"

Finally, Margaret got to them.

"Besa, what happened? It was fast. Did you pull the wall away from us, Mokheer?"

"Nope. It was too fast for me. If it wasn't for my insubstantial state, I would've been back there too."

"But what happened? Besa got us out?"

"She did a lot more than just pull the wall away."

"How did she do it?" asked Catalina."

"With light," replied Mokheer. "What the rest of you didn't see was when the wall shoved you away, the back wall shot twelve metal rods directly at Besa. I tried to jump in front of them, but they went right through me. But Besa didn't need me. She stopped it all on her own."

"With light?" asked Margaret. "But there wasn't much light in here. Not after I dropped my lantern."

"She didn't need much. She took the light from me to freeze the bolts and then used the lamp's light to rope them together and sent them back into the wall. Then she used it to grab the section of wall that was covering you and pushed it back on the other side of the room."

"Don't you mean the Taafli was doing this?" asked Dickey.

"No. I don't mean the Taafli was doing it! It was Besa by herself!"

"But that doesn't even sound like magic."

"It didn't look like magic either. It was more like something that was a part of her."

"Will everyone please stop talking about me like I'm not here? And help me stand up. We need to get going."

"Go where?" asked Dickey. "Besa, you aren't thinking about continuing with this?"

"I don't know what it was I just did. But it is apparently

still inside me. If I need to, I will bend the light again. Do you still want to do this, Catalina?"

"Yes, countess Besa. But only if you are uninjured."

"I promise, I am unhurt. Just a little fatigued after the whole light bending episode. I'll revive soon. And if anyone wants to leave, I'll understand."

"I'm not leaving," said Dickey.

"Thank you, Dickey."

A pitcher and a glass appeared on the ground beside Besa.

"An elixir to restore you, Miss Melponte," came the djinn's voice from above. Besa picked up the glass and took a sip.

"Oh, my goodness! This is amazing. What's in this, Muhammad?"

"A little of this and a little of that. The djinn has made it for millions of years. The power you put out probably overwhelmed your young body. I don't recommend doing it too many more times."

"Thank you, Muhammad. I feel restored already."

"Can I try some, Besa?" asked Dickey, approaching the pitcher.

"Dickey!" admonished Margaret. "You can't eat just everything. You didn't just bend light."

Besa finished the glass.

"Okay. I'm done, Muhammad. You can take it away."

The glass and pitcher quickly disappeared. Dickey looked disappointed. "It wasn't like anything you would normally eat, Dickey."

"But what did it taste like, Besa?"

"The closest thing I can think of is stars."

"But was it a good taste or bad?"

"You need to let this go, Dickey," said Margaret. "We need to get going!"

"That's true," said Besa. "Catalina is counting on us."

"Thank you, Besa," replied the countess.

"The door is open. We might as well go in," said Mokheer. "Why don't I just go first from now on?"

No one disagreed. The stairs were a little different in the second section. They were metallic. They didn't look old, so it was obvious they'd been produced by some kind of magic. The rest of the room—that they could see with the help of Margaret's lamp–was rather dirty, in line with being underground, while the steps were spotless. The steps took them to a staging area that looked out over a chasm that they couldn't see the bottom of, even with the help of Margaret's lamp. But on the other side was another metal wall and a doorway, and right below it, possibly a recessed bridge or gangway.

"I guess this is where you come in, Margaret." said Mokheer.

"But you can just float over," replied Margaret. "You're supposed to be going first, remember?"

"You have a point," replied Mokheer, and he floated over the gap and into the doorway.

"This is just as I feared," said Mokheer, looking at some things on the other side of the door. "The mechanism will require someone to physically manipulate it to get the bridge to extend."

"All right," said Margaret, going back and attaching the lamp to the railing on the stairs. "I guess you can't send an unspecified person to do a physical person's job."

She stepped out over the chasm to fly toward the open doorway, but suddenly something disengaged from the wall. It looked like some type of giant metallic bug and made a beeline for the young witch.

"Margaret! To your right! Look out!" cried Besa. Margaret turned just in time to see the thing and to strike and destroy it. But it slowed her progress, which made her vulnerable to the next two. She managed to get those, too. And then three more came. Mokheer was able to help with one of those.

"Can you see where they're coming from?" yelled Mokheer. "She will have to land soon!"

"It looks like some kind of vent that's spewing them out!" said Dickey.

There were some rungs along the wall, not far from the vent.

"I have an idea." He took off his sword and handed it to Besa.

"Dickey," asked Besa. "What kind of idea? What are you going to do?"

"I have to close that vent, Besa, or Margaret will be hurt."

"But what if you get hurt?"

"Besa, do me a favor, if you will please?"

"What?" asked Besa, not liking the sound of this idea.

"Make my right-hand sticky, so when I hit the wall, I will stick long enough to grab a rung on the wall."

"But what if it doesn't—-"

"Please, Besa. She's getting tired, and I won't let her fall."

"Okay," said Besa. "But we'll have to do your knees, too."

"I need you, Mokheer and Margaret, to do something

for me," said Dickey. "Don't destroy all of this next group. The vent spews out more when you destroy them all. Give me a chance to get into place."

"Sir Richard, what are you going to do?" asked Catalina.

"My idea is to smash and seal the vent. We just need enough time for Margaret and the rest of you to cross."

"Please be careful, my hero."

"This is something I can do," said Dickey. "I'll be as careful as I can. I'll roll up my pants a little more. My mother will kill me if I mess up these pants."

The word went out: don't kill all the bugs right away. This, of course, required Margaret to do a bit more dodging than fighting. It was more difficult now that she was tired, but Dickey didn't intend for her to have to do it for very long.

"Okay. I'm ready," said Dickey. Once Besa had conjured and applied the adhesive, the rest of the club had destroyed all but the last two bugs when Dickey shifted himself to a slightly less massive, but still huge nine-foot behemoth, took a little running start and vaulted onto the wall, grabbing one of the rungs. It didn't feel as solid as he would've liked it to, but he didn't have time to worry about that. He needed his bulk and Titan strength to smash and seal the vent. He moved up the rungs quickly, made it to the vent, smashed it shut with a massive stone fist and slapped on the magic sealant. Then it was done. "Kill the last ones and go in quickly, Margaret!"

"But, Dickey!" cried Margaret. "How will you get down?"

"Oh," replied Dickey. "I...uh."

The wall decided for him. The rung snapped under his weight and he fell into the unending abyss.

"Dickey!" they all screamed. But Catalina had an idea of her own and quickly plunged in after her hero.

"What are you doing, Catalina?" cried Besa.

"I believe I know what she is doing," replied the corvid.

"Sacrificing herself?" asked Besa,

"Her power transforms to the giant corvid. It will not be easy, but she is trying to catch him."

"Shrink yourself, Sir Richard!" They heard the girl cry. Margaret was so distraught she nearly fell in too, trying to look into the emptiness.

"Please, you butter head," said Margaret, as tears poured forth. "That was a terrible plan, Dickey. But please, please come back up."

"Margaret, I'm sorry," said Besa, who was also crying. "I should have stopped him. I–I don't know what to say..."

"It was his idea, Besa. I'm usually there to quash them, though. Mr. Wolf Sneakers wasn't going to come up with a great plan."

Margaret was laughing and crying. "Oh, please, please Dickey, come back up!"

"That's just great!" said a squeaky voice that sounded a lot like Dickey. "I fall into one stupid abyss and all anyone can talk about is my worst ideas?"

A five-foot raven rose up out of the darkness, clutching a two-year-old sized Dickey.

"Oh, Catalina!" cried Margaret. "Please, please bring him over here!"

"Margaret," replied baby Dickey. "You have a strange look in your eyes. Don't you get any ideas. I'm not really a baby!"

Catalina winged into the doorway, dropped baby Dickey into Margaret's waiting arms, landed and then laid down on the floor and took a short nap, while Margaret kissed and generally just mauled baby Dickey.

"Margaret, can you just stop!" cried Dickey. "I need to change back to my normal size!"

"No," said Margaret. "I want to hold you like this a little longer."

"Wait a minute!" cried Dickey. "Besa is still trapped on the other side of the abyss! We need to go check on her!"

That pulled Margaret back to reality. She went to the door and looked out.

"Besa. I guess I got carried away when I thought we'd lost him."

"I understand, Margaret," replied Besa. "I was afraid, too. Give him a kiss for me."

"Okay," said Margaret, turning around to deliver the request.

"Don't even think about it!" said Dickey, now at his regular size. "Slobber time is over! We need to engage the bridge so Besa can cross."

"That's true," said Margaret.

"And we must never speak of this incident again!"

"All right, Dickey," replied Margaret, still looking disappointed at the loss of the baby. They finally started to focus on the large metal wheel they hoped would extend the bridge across the gap, that would provide them a way back as well. When the bridge started to fully extend, a hand rail was a part of its structure. When the bridge was halfway across the abyss, Eduardo, who was situated on Besa's right shoulder, asked, "Why don't we take a running start and meet it, Besa?"

"Is that what a raven would do?"

"That is exactly what a raven would do," replied the corvid.

"Unlike Catalina, I am not part raven. I will wait until the bridge gets here."

"I understand," said Eduardo, taking a running start and winging to the leading edge of the thing. "But you are missing the adventure of it!"

"I am already in the middle of the adventure. I don't need to hurt myself to enjoy it." When the bridge connected the divide, Besa took tentative steps to gauge the structure's stability. The rail was a good guide along her path, and she didn't find any gaps or weak sections, and so quickly made her way into the open doorway where the rest of the expedition awaited her.

"Welcome, madam president!" cried the raven. "So glad you could finally join us."

Once she arrived, she went straight to Dickey and gave him a big hug.

"Oh, god! You're not going to slobber on me, too!"

"No. I will leave the kisses to Margaret. You must promise to be careful, Dickey. I want us all to leave here together. "

"I do as well. I'll do my best, Besa."

"And here is your sword. I made sure I didn't drop it."

Dickey took it and buckled it around his waist.

CHAPTER 19
MARGARET'S FOLLY

They made a survey of this new section, which had a series of doors and metal stairs leading up to other sections, but Besa decided that they didn't go where they needed to go.

"We need to continue going down. Whichever door or stair that lets us do that, that's the one we take." That turned out to be the third door in a wall of doors.

"I will take the lead," said Mokheer.

It took them another five minutes to reach the bottom of the stairs, and once they did, it was a lush area of ground covered by a tightly manicured field of grass; and even more amazing was the sky above, filled with stars.

"Aren't we underground?" asked Margaret. "Why is there a sky?"

"And a huge moon," replied Dickey.

"I think the moon's here so we can see that," said Catalina, pointing across the field of grass, where they could all see was a large wooden casket, situated on four granite rocks at each corner, and guarded by three armored skeletons. One wielded a spear, the other a spiked mace and the last a saber.

"This is going to present some problems," said Mokheer.

"Not if we approach it correctly," said Eduardo. "These are Moorish spirits. You can tell from the star inside the moon emblems on their armor. We will need to fight them separately for us to have a chance."

"I call the spear," said Margaret.

"Margaret?" said Dickey. "What are you–"

"Shut Up, Dickey. He just said we have to separate them."

"Yes. I call the mace," said Besa.

"Besa, wait," said Mokheer. "You're not a fighter."

"If you know so much about my powers, Mokheer, then tell me what I am."

"I–I can't," said the unspecified security entity.

"Then I'll find out for myself," she said, moving out toward the mace wielding spirit. "Besa, be careful!" cried Dickey.

"The sword's yours, Dickey," said Besa.

"Oh! I guess you're right," said Dickey, taking his sword off his belt and moving toward the sword wielding spirit. But the corvid landed on his shoulder.

"Hold for a moment, Mr. O'Brien. Let the first two members do battle before you start."

"But shouldn't I be fighting those other two as well?"

"They have chosen based on their skill. You would not survive all three. You are familiar with destreza, I take it?"

"Yes," said Dickey. "My uncle had me train in that style and three others?"

"There is more to you than meets the eye, Mr. O'Brien.

You will need to be creative, since you don't have a dagger with your sword."

"I can do that. I have some idea?" said Dickey.

"We shall soon see," said the corvid, as he winged out onto the field between the first two spirits poised before Margaret and Besa and said some words to the spirits.

"I have no idea what he just said," replied Margaret.

"He said the witch goes first," translated Besa.

"All right!" said Margaret, launching herself upward. "Let's go, bonehead!"

"What?" said Dickey.

"Not you, Dickey!" cried Margaret. She was surprised when the armored skeleton went up with her. It then executed a type of spin move and drove the spear into her face. She dodged left, just in time, but the skeleton had another surprise and landed a blow across her right shoulder when it spun and flipped the spear.

"Ow!" cried Margaret. "This is going to get embarrassing. I need my own stick. Whalem mowey!" The stick came just as the spirit brought his own slashing toward the top of her head. Margaret got hers up in time to block it. "Hah!" cried Margaret. "Witches are good with sticks!" But the spirit had another surprise. It grabbed her stick, snatched her forward and head butted her. This knocked Margaret unconscious and sent her plummeting to the ground.

Dickey and Besa raced toward the spot where Margaret would hit the ground.

"Besa, we need to slow her down and then catch her!" said Dickey.

"Just shift and jump, Dickey. I'll use a gust of wind to push you up so you can catch her. I'll have something soft waiting when you come down."

Dickey shifted and in the next step vaulted himself

upward. A boost from Besa's air gusts gave him enough altitude to reach Margaret, cradle her in his arms and then drop back down. He and Margaret landed on something soft and Dickey scooted off the thing that looked like a gigantic mattress. "This was fun!" said Dickey. "Can you make something like this for the schoolyard?"

"Please focus, Dickey. We're trying to save Margaret's life."

"Oh, sorry."

They spent the next few moments trying to revive Margaret. Besa finally conjured a small vial and waved it under her nose. Margaret jolted awake.

"Ew! What is that?" she asked.

"Essence of goat musk," said Besa.

"It smells awful!"

"I needed you to wake up."

"My head is killing me! Oh! Did I win?"

"Hardly," said Dickey. "It's still waiting for you right over there."

Margaret's vision was almost double, but she could make the thing out pacing at

the edge of the field "This was really stupid of me."

"Do you want me to finish for you? asked Dickey.

"No, I can finish it. Just help me stand up."

You just said you'd been stupid," replied Dickey.

"Please help me to my feet, Dickey."

Dickey gave her a hand up and stood beside her shoulder in case she toppled over.

"I meant I was stupid for trying to fight this thing with a stick! Come on, bone head!" she said, gesturing at the spirit. It turned and charged at her with its spear point extended, intending to run her through.

"Margaret," said Dickey. "You might want to mo—"

When the thing got within 6 feet, Margaret waved her hand and cried "whagom!"

The skeleton's head popped up into the sky. "Let me borrow this for a moment, Dickey."

She removed his sword from his belt and split the head in half when it came down. "Teach you to head butt me."

She handed Dickey's sword back.

"Okay. I'm dizzy. I need to sit down."

Dickey caught her as her knees buckled and eased her down to the ground.

"Keep an eye on Besa, Dickey. I'm going to take a nap."

Dickey managed to maneuver a small portion of the giant mattress for her to lay her head on.

"I hope you have a better plan than Margaret did, Besa."

"I do, too," replied Besa, moving toward the mace wielding spirit. At that moment, her chest glowed with a golden light and the Taafli blazed out to buzz around her head. "Besa," said Violet. This is not the wisest choice you've made."

"I don't have to be asleep for you to engage?" asked Besa.

"It's obvious that you are well past that stage in your development. I am simply here to make sure you don't die. Or we don't die, at least."

Besa was suddenly covered in a white gold, linked armor around her chest and at her knees. In her left hand was a shield, and in her right a gleaming sword, its blade composed of light.

"That's a nice sword," said Dickey "I'll trade you."

"I don't think you can touch that element, Mr. O'Brien," said the corvid.

"He's right, Dickey. It's only made for me."

She took another step toward the mace wielding spirit.

"Keep your shield up, Besa," said Violet "Just let it wear itself out."

But the spirit wasn't planning to just whale away. It clearly had its own plan. It bobbed and weaved as it flailed at Besa's impenetrable shield. But then it did something unexpected and whipped one of its fleshless legs out and took Besa's legs out from under her. She landed hard on her behind and her shield went flying, the mace would have crushed her head if she hadn't rolled. Now the sword was gone, but it wasn't far away.

"Besa, please pick up your sword!" cried Violet.

"Oh, shut up!" said Besa, bobbing and weaving with the spirit. "You're as bad as my papa, Violet. Wrapping me up to protect me. I don't need a sword. I am a sword!"

When the spirit swung the mace at her face, she caught the spikey ball in her right hand and jerked it off the chain. The skeleton seemed confused for a moment, and it didn't like look in Besa's blazing eyes. But before it could turn and flee, Besa flung a spikey ball of light that shattered its skull and the skeleton disintegrated.

"Hurry up, Dickey," said Besa, walking past him to go sit by Margaret. "We need to get this done."

"Bravo! Madam president!" said the raven, "Did you know she could do that?" he asked the Taafli.

"No," said Violet. "I knew that one day she would learn it. But not this soon."

"She doesn't know how she did it either," said Mokheer. "Just like the rods."

"I can't explain those either," said Violet.

"Somebody better start explaining something to her," said the corvid, "Before she peels back the fabric of time!"

"I certainly couldn't help her with that," replied Mokheer. The Taafli didn't say anything. It just blasted back into Besa's chest as everyone sat waiting for Dickey to complete his challenge. Dickey was over doing his stretches and practicing his lunges and thrusts, when Margaret's eyes popped open.

"Oh my god, Besa! Dickey's got a plan! Help me up. We have to talk him out of it!"

"Oh, yes we do!" replied Besa, getting up quickly and pulling Margaret up too.

"Dickey," said Margaret approaching her friend in the middle of his warmups. "What are you thinking?"

"Thinking?" asked Dickey. "I'm thinking I need to warm up."

"What she means is what's your plan?" said Besa.

"Basically, my plan is to get through his defenses and exploit his weakness."

"See, I told you, Besa. He's going to get himself killed."

"I am not. There are things about me you don't know, Margaret. I happen to train with swords every day. I will not be a pushover."

"Dickey, listen to me," said Besa. "That thing has probably killed more people than you've eaten cakes."

"What!" said Dickey, suddenly shocked. "That's not possible. I've eaten hundreds of cakes."

"Dickey, we studied the crusades, remember?" said Margaret. "That thing is at least five hundred years old, which means it probably fought in battles where it killed a hundred people that looked like you every half hour. You're not going to defeat it with your sword training. You saw what happed to me when I tried to stick fight with one of them."

"So, any plan you have, get it out of your head," Besa told him. "Or we will be carrying your body out of here."

"Do what we finally did," instructed Margaret: "Use your advantage."

"Okay. I've got it," replied Dickey.

Eduardo flew to the middle of the field. "Warmup time is over, Mr. O'Brien! It's time to cross Swords!"

"I've gotta go. Wish me luck," said their blond hero, as he trotted out to the center of the field.

"You think he's going to—"

"I don't know," replied Besa. "I wish we hadn't brought him. I don't like him doing this."

"Swords up!" commanded the corvid, so Dickey and the spirit crossed swords.

"Ready, go!"

And in just a split second, the spirit flicked its wrist and his blade slashed right across Dickey's neck.

"Oh!" cried Margaret, as Dickey's head was off his body. But then she realized that Dickey's head wasn't there. He'd shrunk himself just that quickly and scampered between the skeleton's bony legs, slashing at its shin bone as he went past. The spirit then chased tiny Dickey around the field, mostly hacking at the ground as Dickey quickly skirted away.

"This is getting kind of ridiculous," said Margaret. "But it's better than what could've happened."

"That's true," said Besa.

Finally, Dickey flitted between the granite rocks situated to the right of the field.

"I think I see the plan," said Margaret.

"Thank goodness, me too," replied Besa, as the skeleton raced into the rocks in pursuit of him. And then they heard a crack! Like a rock splitting. The next moment Dickey trots out of the rocks carrying what's left of the skeleton's crushed skull.

"Bravo! Mr. O'Brien!" cried the raven.

"I have to admit, that was quite the show, Dickey," Mokheer told him. "You had me worried there at the beginning, when that thing tried to take your head off."

"You were worried about me, Mokheer?" asked a surprised Dickey.

"For a moment. But then I could see where it was going."

Margaret ran up and smacked him on the arm.

"You scared the dickens out of me!"

"What? I did what you told me to do!"

"Yes, you did."

"Then can I maybe get one of those baby kisses?"

Margaret's hackles rose as sparks shot out of her fingertips.

"You're pressing your luck, butter boy!"

"Dickey, I can't believe you asked her something like that," laughed Besa.

"Perhaps if you shifted back into a baby, Mr. O'Brien," suggested the raven.

Margaret spun around and glared at the corvid, like she might rip its wings off.

"Don't try to help me, Eduardo," replied Dickey.

"You are still my hero, Sir Richard," said Catalina, coming up and giving him a hug. "Thank you, countess."

"Let's get over to the casket," suggested Besa. "So we may complete this leg of Catalina's case. Dickey, please check to see if the lid can be removed."

"Use the end of your sword Dickey," suggested Mokheer. "In case there is a surprise." Everyone turned and looked at Mokheer, for making such a considerate suggestion.

"On second thought, Dickey," said Margaret. "Let me levitate it from here while we all stand back."

The lid levitated and sure enough, a scimitar-like blade whipped out of the casket but flew harmlessly over their heads.

"Thank you, Mokheer, you saved my life," said Dickey."

"I'm just being practical. I can't very well tease you, if you don't have a head. Not that there's much up there. And they'd probably make me carry it!"

"We most definitely would." provided Margaret.

"Thanks anyway, Mokheer."

"Since we've sprung the trap," said Besa. "We should take a look at what we have here."

It was an interesting sight, Captain Montalbán had been very well-preserved and was a very tall, very dark man. When Besa saw his face, she screamed, "Papa!" and fainted. Luckily, Dickey caught her before she hit the ground.

When Dickey laid Besa down in the grass, Margaret and Catalina went about trying to revive her.

"But Besa's father doesn't look that much like Captain Montalbán," said Catalina.

"That's true," said Margaret. "It must have been something about his size and skin color that set her off."

"I hope she wakes up soon. We've come too far for this to stop us."

"If nothing else, the Taafli will bring her around," replied Margaret, and in that next moment, Besa's eyes opened and she sat up.

"I'm so sorry, everyone," said Besa. "But it was like my heart stopped when I looked at the captain."

"Are you going to be okay, Besa?" asked Mokheer.

"I'll be fine. Just give me a few moments and we'll get started."

She was true to her word and was soon standing over the corpse of Captain Diego Montalbán, as the Taafli buzzed around her head.

"This is a new development," observed Dickey. "You don't have to be asleep to invoke the Taafli?"

"Not anymore. The Taafli explained that my advanced skills make it unnecessary."

"I like it. She'll be less vulnerable this way," replied Margaret.

"Let's get started," said Besa.

When she finished her chant, the Taafli descended into the corpse, causing a white eminence to emerge from the flesh.

"Oh, my goodness," said Catalina. "It is so beautiful."

"Please step up and ask your question, Catalina," directed Besa.

As Catalina collected her thoughts at the bottom of this impossible grave...

ON THE OTHER side of the city, in the library of the large borrowed house of a supporter, the bishop made ready to perform his own enchantment ceremony.

He had cloaked himself in shadow and then called the book, but once it arrived and Denny opened the cover, no Taafli emerged. In fact, the item appeared to be a regular book. This was an embarrassment, because a well-to-do member of the congregation had submitted the corpse of their beloved, but secretive, father for this ceremony. Apologies were extended and the bishop and a few of his most trusted lieutenants retreated to the parlor so Delacroix wouldn't lose his cool in front of this important congregation member. Finally, the bishop held his hand out and was about to scream his command, when the Shadow appeared and said,

"We don't know what happened."

"This is not my book!" cried the bishop.

"The book you received is the same book you gave us. We have no need of it. Are you sure the Necromancer is locked up? Perhaps he's found another way to call the entity?"

"He is no longer a factor. And if he had escaped, he would probably try to reach his residence," said the bishop.

"And we've kept a presence near his residence, ready for his possible return," said the Shadow.

"We obviously can't get as close as these creatures," said Denny. "But we've been watching too."

"We know the book is a gateway," said the Shadow. "It may be possible that someone else has access to the entity. Someone who obviously has priority over you."

"The only one I can think of is the girl, his daughter. We must find a way to stop her," said the bishop.

"You mean kill her," said the Shadow.

"If that's what it takes. She has no right to it. It's mine now!"

"The One who knows will set the Shadows to searching," replied the Shadow, and then disappeared.

"We humans will keep our eyes peeled too."

"Thank you, Denny. I know I can count on you,"

Meanwhile at the bottom of the grave...

~

"Captain Montalbán," said Catalina. "Can you name the man responsible for my father's death?"

"There is more than one name in that deed, countess. But my name must be added to the list. Duke Barbosa was assassinated by greed and jealousy. I was offered gold and an elevation to the rank of nobility."

"But that can only be conferred by royal decree," replied Catalina.

"I was assured that once the deed was done, the Earl of Paladin would make sure the decree went through smoothly."

"The earl of Paladin is my uncle," the countess told Besa. "Can you tell us how it was done, captain."

"Once the duke's vessel lay at anchor and we'd reached the shore, I received a message that the earl and a small party were trapped by a large contingent of French troops. This was a lie. I then led the duke into the actual trap on the shore of lake Pontchartrain. When we arrived at the earl's position along the lake shore, a flotilla flying the French flag was firing upon their position. The duke, myself and six men reached their position without drawing extra fire."

"'What has happened? Did they not surrender?'" asked the duke.

"'We came upon this small party possibly attempting a sneak attack or sabotage,'" replied the earl. "'There is also a landing party firing from the western levee there.'"

"I sent my six men to attack that position, leaving the duke alone with me and the earl of Paladin. It was then that the earl stood up in the middle of the battle, and I handed him my pistol."

"'What are you doing, brother?'" asked the duke. "'Get down, or you will be shot!'"

"But the earl just pointed my pistol at his brother and said,

"'All that is yours is now mine, brother.'"

"He shot the duke in the heart, and to top it off, he took his brother's pistol and killed me. I was the only one who deserved to die that day."

And then the spirit receded back into the corpse as the Taafli emerged and re-entered the gateway that was Besa. It was Catalina's turn to sit down and cry for a moment.

"Is the truth so heartbreaking?" asked Besa. "You were right about your uncle."

"It isn't the truth that hurts. It's that I still can't prove that my uncle killed my father."

"I fear your father will never receive justice," said Besa

"That is what I fear, too," replied Catalina.

"Don't fear, Catalina," said Dickey. "We'll just have to find a way to make him confess."

"That, I assure you, will not be an easy task," said the raven.

"But my case is done," said Catalina. "You fulfilled your promise of helping me find the captain's body. There's no need for you to put yourself in further jeopardy."

"I'm afraid it's not that simple, countess," said Margaret. "Her intent was to help you name your father's killer. And to do that, we will need a confession."

"But my uncle wouldn't hesitate to kill all of you."

"But if we stop, do you think he won't try to kill you again?" asked Dickey.

"Yes. He'll keep trying because he knows I won't give up until I expose him as a murderer."

"Then that decides it. We have to find a way to expose his crime."

"I think I have a way that we can do it," said Besa.

"We're going to need the assistance of someone I know. And Catalina, you will have to sleep-over on another night."

"I will inform the duchess," replied Catalina.

"And Mokheer, please ask my grandmother to meet me in my dreams tomorrow night."

"I will see what I can do," replied Mokheer. "Can we please get ourselves out of this grave?"

They made their way out of the world of the cursed grave faster than they went in and made it to the horses. But after Catalina mounted, a man dressed in a raven's costume, carrying a sword, ran up and pulled her off her horse; and as he reared back to run her through, an up-sized Dickey crossed swords with him. Thus began a furious battle as the raven man slashed and parried, hacked and chopped, but Dickey's sword was more than a match for him. The man had not come alone. Two other ravens rushed out of the Shadows to help their compadre dispose of the talented boy swordsman and the ambassador's niece. But Margaret wasn't having it.

"No fair triple-teaming!" she cried, subduing them both and then snatching them up and flying them to the open grave and dropping them in. "Muhammad, would you close this for me?"

"Wait a minute, Margaret," said Dickey, finally disarming the attacker, then shifting to fifteen feet to snatch him up and toss him over the Andalusian house toward Margaret. "You forgot one!"

Margaret caught him and dropped him in. "You can close it, Muhammad."

"With pleasure, Miss Claiborne!" And the djinn sealed the entryway to the cursed grave.

"You did that sword proud, Mr. O'Brien," complimented the raven. "All that training came in handy."

"If no one else is going to," said the countess. She ran over, threw her arms around Dickey's neck, and gave him a big kiss on the lips. Which made him turn beet red. "No offense, Margaret," she said. "But Sir Richard really deserved that."

"Why would I be upset?" cried Margaret, who went over and punched Dickey in the arm.

"Ow!" cried Dickey. "What was that for?"

"For looking so smug! With your sword training!"

Then she glared at Besa, who was grinning from ear to ear.

"Shut up, Besa! I'm going home!" And she took off over the trees and out of Vieux Carré.

"Why was she so mad?" asked Dickey. "I didn't do anything."

"Yes, you did, Mr. Hero swordsman. Let's all get out of Vieux Carré," said Besa.

WHEN DICKEY RODE his horse into their stable to put bag a on him and rub him down, Francis was lurking in the corner, and dived on his unsuspecting little brother from behind. Dickey didn't even think twice, she shifted, grabbed his brothers arm and flipped him over his head. Luckily the older brother landed in some hay. "Oh, Francis," said Dickey. "It's you. You caught me off guard."

"Yes!" cried Francis. "And I am telling mother you used your strength on me!"

But then it occurred to Dickey. This wasn't in the house.

So, when Francis tried to get past him, stronger Dickey caught him by the back of the shirt and threw him into the corner of the stable. "Mother said I couldn't handle you in the house, Francis. This is not in the house. And furthermore, neither is uncle Diego's." He walked over to his older brother and lifted him up. "No more of sneaking up on me, hitting me in the back, or choking me. Or when we leave the house..." He grabbed Francis and rammed him into the back of the stable. "Ow!" cried Francis. "Help! Dicke—" Dickey put his hand over his mouth, and slammed him into the wall again. "That's what going to happen every time you do that. You understand now? I won't bully you, but I will hurt you if you try anything." He punched his older brother in the gut, taking the wind out him, leaving him gasping in the straw. "That's what that feels like by the way. I owed you that one. See you at dinner." He walked out of the stable to his family house.

WHEN BESA GOT HOME, she went her to father's room.

"I'm alright, Papa. I know I might've scared you. But it came out well. We're not done though. I love you, good night." She blew him a kiss. This was something she'd never done before he was taken away. But a lot of things had changed. Felix was still her official guardian and protector—along with the Magist council, of course. She now also had to keep the household books and make sure the servants received their wages. This was something her father had instructed her in. Felix kept possession of the household keys, but she still had her duties as the sole heir. She just never expected to perform them until she was much, much older. Her papa had been very successful in his occupation. Because of the Melponte estate, she would never need employment to support herself.

WARRIORS

The Warrior's tasks were mostly very boring. It generally consisted of walking around downtown Newald, hoping for a sighting of the bishop's carriage. They'd already had a close call when one of the Shadows noticed a man lurking near the bishop's compound. Three of them surrounded him. And though they didn't hurt him, they pushed him back and forth between them, while yelling that he needed to find a different place to congregate. After that, Father Phillips was afraid to go out surveilling for a while. Michel understood. He was just thankful they were the human Shadows and knew they weren't supposed to be near the bishop's residence either. The encounter reminded them how dangerous this task could get. They had to be aware that while they watched and tried to keep tabs on the bishop, they needed to be careful that they weren't being watched themselves. The bishop wasn't hard to find; he still conducted mass, did the occasional confession—mostly with wealthy parishioners, helped out in the Sisters of Mercy food mission once a week, and rode out to give spiritual council to various slaveholding, but extremely wealthy donors to the chapel and rectory construction fund. Nothing unholy or destructive about these pursuits. It was the evening endeavors that Michel and the Warriors were concerned about. After nine o'clock nothing good occurred in the mind of men and Shadows. One of the Warriors who was sitting on a downtown bench got a lucky break when a large man in a dark blue hat and cape rode by on one of the horses owned by the diocese. The Warrior had just enough time to get to his own mount and trailed the bishop to a very large house in Vieux Carré. Someone neglected to inform the bishop that if he were going to hide his identity, he needed to start with his mount. And as the Warrior hid himself a distance away and observed the house with a long glass, all the Shadows in black suits and hats soon made an appearance.

"This was a great find, Father Nelson," said Father Guidry. "This is the place where all the evil and unholy plans are laid. I will have to find a way into those meetings."

"But, Father Guidry," said Father Alexander. "That's too dangerous."

"That may be true, Giles. But I am no better than Daniel. Someone must go into the lion's den,"

"Then let some of us come with you, Father."

"I don't fear André. His soul may be corrupted, but he still has some care for me."

THE HELP WANTED signs posted in Vieux Carré solved the dilemma for them. And it struck Michel as a bit brazen. Surely the bishop had not conceived such a spectacle. The event was billed as an evening of: Mystical wonder that offers a glimpse of life after death.

"What does that even mean?" asked an unsettled Father Phillips.

"It means our beloved bishop has come completely unhinged," replied Michel.

The Warriors took down all the posters they could find throughout Vieux Carré, to make sure that as many Warriors as possible accompanied Father Guidry to this event. And as if to make their attendance even easier, all guests and wait staff would wear masks.

"I will caution all of you," said Father Guidry. "When the time comes, I must be the only one to remove my mask. This will be between myself and the bishop. We don't know what type of ceremony this will be. But I have an idea it will involve some unholy book the bishop has acquired since he moved his evil headquarters out of the diocese. Be prepared and follow my lead. All of you will very likely still be priests after this evening. I will not."

"But Father, why ex-communicate yourself?" asked Father Milton. "If the bishop is truly corrupted, we will need your leadership."

"I know, Father Milton. But I know the church will not support me after I challenge the bishop. I have been a priest too long not to see where this is going. If it's a choice between myself and the bishop, they will choose the bishop. I've already prepared myself. But this fight isn't going to end here, because these Shadows and their influence aren't going anywhere—and neither am I. Let's go and take the first shot across their bow."

There were now fifteen Warriors, but only six got hired along with Father Guidry. The event took place in the house's massive library, and when Michel saw it, he thought they could've gotten more Warriors in. He didn't see the bishop yet, but a corpse was laid out on a broad table in the center of the room. Michel had to restrain himself, because he knew the poor man probably hadn't received absolution. The best he could do at the moment was say a prayer for his soul. Such a strange, evil display this was. He wondered if the spectators gathered here knew that the bishop was responsible for this sordid affair. But it looked like things were about to start...

CHAPTER 20
THE AMBASSADOR'S DREAM

Unlike Besa, Catalina had a much less picturesque existence when she entered the official residence. When she got to her room, her bed clothes were laid out neatly and the covers on her bed pulled back, and a note had been placed on her pillow, with a dagger stuck in it. She pulled the dagger out but would let Besa read the note. She knew who left it. The dagger was emblazoned with her uncle's initials. He had taken to leaving her threatening notes, so she had a basic idea of what this one said "Catalina," asked Besa, when she handed her the note "Why is there a hole in it?"

"Because it was attached to my pillow by a dagger."

"I know you have breached the grave," read Besa, "The next grave shall be your own."

"That is the usual tone of all his secret notes."

"How can you sleep knowing he means you harm?"

"I have no choice. It's my home. But Eduardo has provided me with one of his soldiers to guard my room, and a ward on my door that will slow down anyone trying to breach it."

"Would your mother not believe you, if you informed her of what he's doing?"

"I will not tell my mother about this. He won't harm her as long as I don't bring her into it. But if I lost my nerve and sought her help, she would be his enemy. And I cannot protect her."

"I understand," said Besa.

"What are we going to be doing tonight?" asked Catalina.

"It's something Margaret, and I learned about in Magist school: Dream manipulation. But we need someone with more experience. That's why we'll need my grandmother to join us."

"She is skilled at this dream manipulation?"

"Yes. She took over my dream without me even realizing it. The fact that she can even be in my dream is an incredible feat in itself. I will ask her to teach us how it's done. My class has only ever covered the basics of dream walking. We will need something much more powerful. Hopefully she won't give us a lecture about the dangers of what we have to do. Though that seems to be the main job of our elders. We will wait for Margaret to arrive, and our little dream party will be set."

Once Margaret arrived, they did all the things girls have been doing at sleep-overs for the past three hundred years, probably. Hair was braided, secrets were shared and snacks were consumed. When it was time for bed, Besa told Catalina:

"Margaret and I will guide you through your first dream walk. We shall lie down shoulder to shoulder."

"Is that how it is always done?" asked Catalina.

"No. This is only because this is your first walk," said

Margaret. "Once you learn control, you will be able to move into anyone's dream like crossing the street."

When they laid down, Besa and Margaret held Catalina's hand, to ensure they all entered the dream together. But to Besa and Margaret's surprise, the landscape they entered into was not the bayou or the boat.

"What in the world has happened?" asked Besa.

"This is not the normal setting for the dream?" asked Catalina.

The land they'd come into was thick jungle with mountains all around. They were at the beginning of a trail that led up the mountain or deeper into the thick jungle.

"Don't be afraid, little ones," said a tall, dark, beautiful woman wearing a vibrantly colored pagne and a tignon head wrap of the same color. "This is my doing."

The woman was coming down the well-worn trail out of the mountains.

"Grandmother!" said Besa, running into her grandmothers loving embrace. "Where have you brought us to?"

"First, you must introduce me. I have seen Margaret. Come here girl and let me put my hands in that lovely red bushel of hair you have." Margaret came and received a hug and a kiss on the forehead. "You have been such a dear friend to my Besa. As a child, my only friends were the animals in the jungle."

"That sounds exciting and dangerous," said Catalina.

"And who might you be, young lady?

"Grandmother, this is countess Catalina Infante y Barbosa." At which point, Catalina executed a perfect curtsey.

"My goodness," said Grandmother. "I haven't seen someone do that since the archbishop visited the island."

"This is Haiti, isn't it, Grandmother?" asked Besa.

"Yes, it is, child. I thought you might like to visit my side of the world for a change."

"Felix described it to me, but this is the first time I've seen it up close."

"Besa, this is incredible," said Catalina. "Then you are a sorceress, Grandmother?"

"It's been a while since I've heard that, but yes. That's what some have called me."

"I can't imagine the kind of power this must have taken."

"You are here because my granddaughter and her friend are holding your hand."

"Is this what you meant by dream manipulation, Besa?"

"Yes. This is exactly what I meant."

"What I'm doing right now is holding a bridge open that you can come through. It's something that requires a bit of practice. It's easier because you have all agreed to be here. But what you're going to attempt, Besa, is a bit more complicated."

"You're reading my mind again, Grandmother," Besa admonished.

"I'm in your dream, child. What did you expect me to do?"

"Since I can't read your mind, it's not courteous for you to read mine."

"Children have gotten so complicated these days!" exclaimed Grandmother. "All right. I will no longer mention what I read in your mind. Will that do?"

"No, Grandmother. I would like you to not do it."

"I'm sorry, little one. That is not possible. I have knowing, which means I receive the thoughts of all my living children. Once you reach knowing, you can shut your thoughts off from others. But enough about this. Let's go sit down so we can discuss your intentions."

She led them further up the mountain to a large cave, laid out with pillows to sit upon, along with food and water refreshments.

"But this is a dream," said Besa. "Why would we need food and water?"

"Because your mind is not perceiving this as a dream, which is why you can receive my hug as well as eat my food and drink water."

"She's right, Besa," said Margaret. "I find I am quite thirsty, and a drink of water would be quite refreshing."

"I'm feeling the same way, Besa," replied Catalina. "I also find I am quite famished. This dream is amazing, and I would like to learn how it's done."

"All right," said Besa. "I have to admit that it feels like I've been walking all day."

They all sat down around the fire Grandmother had made and accepted wooden bowls full of a rich stew with pieces of some type of meat and seafood. "What kind of meat is this?" asked Catalina. "I've never tasted anything like it."

"That is a sea turtle," replied Grandmother. "They mate and lay their eggs here on the beach."

"I can't wait to learn how to do this. This is an amazing power."

"Me too," replied Margaret. "And this stew is amazing. I didn't realize I was so hungry."

"In your mind you are," replied Grandmother. "That is the realm where the dream really exists. But be careful, because just like you can taste, you can also cause great harm to yourself and others."

"Can someone really die in a dream?" asked Margaret.

"If your mind perceives a wound grave enough, it could put you in a sleep that was as deep as death."

"Is there a way to protect yourself from such an incident?"

"The same way you would in the waking world: Stay away from dangerous situations."

"Catalina doesn't have an option to stay away. If you've read my mind, then you know that if we don't help her, she will be dead in the waking world. So please, Grandmother. Help us save our friend."

"I suppose I should blame your father for setting you on this path."

"I'm on this path because Papa chose to share a small part of himself. And at the moment, that's all I have."

"Besa, why take these dangerous paths?" asked her grandmother. "I spend all my time worrying and being fearful for you."

"All I want is to protect those I love, and who love me," replied Besa.

Grandmother covered her face and sobbed.

"Oh, please no, Besa. Please, no. Are the women in our family doomed to this fate? Never a child, and always pursued by forces bent on our destruction?"

"I don't know what you mean, Grandmother. This is the life Papa left me with. And it is only now I am able to have friends and feel like a person with others to spend time with."

Besa could hardly control her sorrow as Margaret embraced her.

"It's okay, Besa. We're here with you now."

"Yes, countess, Besa," said Catalina, grasping Besa's hand.

"I can't control if forces are pursuing me. But I won't be like Papa, and fight them alone!"

"I agree, child. I suppose I had better teach you about dreams before you decide to look elsewhere."

"Thank you for helping us, Grandmother.

"The first thing you will need is a powerful anchor."

"Would that be like the anchor on a ship?" asked Margaret.

"Very much like an anchor on a ship. Only this will be the person with immense power. Someone who can create the dream and hold everyone inside it. The rest of you will be arms flowing out of the anchor. The arms are important, because they will need an amount of power too. You will be important when influencing and interacting with those whose dreams you want to tap into. You will draw power from the anchor so that the dream can maintain its fluidity. You will also need markers set out, so you don't get lost in this world you are trying to create."

The girls spent that night and the next, learning how to manipulate dreams from Grandmother.

"Your grandmother is amazing, Besa," said Margaret. "I never knew dreams could be this powerful."

"You have such a remarkable family," said Catalina. "We are lucky to have you as a friend."

"I am the lucky one," replied Besa. "I don't know how I would've managed without all of you. I know my life isn't normal compared to other people, but I wouldn't want a different life."

"Me either," said Margaret. "And I'm practicing the techniques we learned in my sleep."

"I'm working up to it," replied Catalina. "I want to sneak into my uncle's dream."

"Be careful that you don't change anything," cautioned

Besa. "Not without an anchor to give you a clear escape route."

"I won't touch anything. I just want to be in there to see all that he is conspiring."

"I'm practicing on my brothers. Their dreams are all about girls and moving away from home. Nothing treacherous though."

"I have to practice on the scullery maids," said Besa. "Felix's dreams are locked tight. I'm sure Felix would be shocked to know that one of the kitchen assistants has a crush on him."

They had a very good time talking and laughing about all the dreams they'd snuck into. By the next week, they had Dickey included in the sleepover at Besa's. They'd all laid on the floor in Besa's room, holding hands with Besa at the center, anchoring their adventures. And in usual Dickey form, there were huge quantities of food and sword fights with everyone from Napoleon to Genghis Khan.

"Dickey, for Pete's sake!" said Margaret. "Can we do anything else in your dream besides eat and fight?"

"If you've noticed, I am usually saving you in my dreams."

"I saw that," said Besa. "It's so sweet that he dreams about you."

"Stop it, butter head. It's getting embarrassing. I'm never going to be trapped in the belly of a whale fighting a bunch of pirates with you! We're supposed to be practicing."

"You practice your way, and I'll practice mine."

When the snacks showed up, everyone was famished. They'd taken an early session so they could warm up for their midnight excursions.

"Tonight, we must practice distance," said Besa.

"Catalina, was Eduardo able to steal an item from Juan, the stable boy?"

The countess pulled a cap out of her garment bag and held it up like it was the crown jewels. "Wonderful," said Besa "Tonight we will be practicing with our very own Juan."

"I sure hope he likes pirates," said Dickey.

"And cake," replied Margaret.

"What's wrong with cake? Everyone likes cake."

"Not as much as you. The reason those pirates fight so hard is to get out of your cake dreams."

"Then how about if I just do 'marry Margaret' dreams?"

"You do that, and I'll hit you with so many sparkles, you'll have holes in you!"

"It just so happens, we will only be watching during Juan's dreams," said Besa. "We need to know how well we can work from a distance. Grandmother said that is the real test. If we can cast across a wide space, then we will have a good weapon to help us with this case. And then maybe we can see some of Dickey's marriage dreams."

"Besa!" cried Margaret. "You have such a cruel streak in you!"

"I don't mean to be cruel. I'm just curious. But first, let's get to work."

Juan's dream was very fascinating. In them, he was a talented bullfighter and did some sword fighting in his spare time, and the woman he was married to was Besa. They were both great horsemen, riding some of the most spectacular horses anyone had ever seen. Some of them were breeds that did not exist in the real world, Andalusian Palamino's, or quarter horses crossed with white stallions and pintos. Besa was an accomplished swordswoman in her own right. But the part that Margaret enjoyed the most was they kissed every time they mounted a stallion. Soon, it became too much for Besa, so she ended the dream.

"Why did we stop?" asked Margaret. "I was just starting to get the hang of this distance dream!"

"I'm sure you found me kissing very entertaining," said Besa. "We will do this a few more times to get more practice in. After a while, we can start to move little things to see how much of an impression it makes on the dreamer. Now we need to get some sleep ourselves. Dickey, your room is just down the hall on the other side of Margaret's."

"Wonderful. Thank you for your hospitality, Besa."

"Just don't snore too much, mister," said Margaret.

"Just so you know, I will be practicing kissing you in my own dream. In case you want to join me there!"

He ran out the door before Margaret could act.

"I'll definitely go as a dragon. See how he likes kissing that!"

"Good night," said Besa. "Sweet dreams."

Margaret just shook head and rolled her eyes, but left without responding.

"They're perfect for each other," said Catalina. "She is fire and he is fun."

"I'm glad you noticed that, too."

The dream practices got more intense over the next week, and Catalina did her best to stay two steps ahead of her uncle's henchmen. But they wouldn't dare attempt an attack while her mother was present. For the week of their final practice, she told her mother that she'd been having bad dreams and requested to sleep in the duchess' chamber.

"Of course you can, my darling," replied the duchess. "It will be like you were a small child again. Right after your father died. You had bad dreams then, too."

"Thank you, mother. I'm hoping they will go away soon."

They got very proficient in the dream practices. Juan woke up one morning to find himself sitting in a boat on the bayou, screaming commands at a ship full of Spanish sailors, as they repelled British sailors trying to board the Spanish galleon he commanded.

"How did I get all the way out here?" The stable boy asked the trees and insects around him. Besa and the club made sure to leave a paddle in the boat, and his horse tied close to the shore.

"That was a good practice, everyone," Besa told the whole group. "Dickey, your grasp of a British accent was uncanny."

"I managed to pick it up watching the British Ships unload cargo in the harbor. My father also has a good ear for voices. His angry Scotsman has us in tears at the dinner table."

"I thought you did a beautiful job creating the whole crew that tried to board Juan's ship," said Catalina.

"I agree," said Besa. "And let's not forget Catalina impersonating me as Juan's wife. Everyone was amazing. But now we need to prepare for the real case to come. Catalina will smuggle Margaret and I into the embassy as new kitchen help. And Dickey will come through the stables as a new member of Antonio Marquez's staff, with a personal recommendation from the countess, of course."

Eduardo had the floor plan for the ambassador's residence.

"I have studied these plans very closely for the last few years. The architect must have been afraid of a possible attack or maybe a war, because every room has some type of hidden wall in the event an escape was needed. Even the prison cells at the western wing of the complex have special crawl spaces installed in the ceilings."

"But why would they give prisoners an avenue of escape?" asked Dickey.

"It depends on who the prisoner was," replied the corvid. "Most of the spaces are unknown to the ambassador and his staff."

"But I know them," said Catalina.

"How did you learn about them?" asked Dickey.

"When you have a raven for a playmate, you learn some very unusual things. Like the secret room where your uncle is hoarding gold he's stealing from the Spanish crown, or how to get out of any room, no matter where you are in the building."

"That must've been fun."

"It would've been. If I'd had other children to play with. But try playing hide and seek with a raven that knows all the hiding places."

"Oh, yeah. I see what you mean. Kind of one-sided, huh?"

"And when they catch you, they peck the devil out of you!"

"Was I that harsh?" asked Eduardo. "I thought you enjoyed our games. "

"I did, Eduardo. I just needed other children to join us."

"Let's set up the new game we will be playing in a week," suggested Besa.

"You have more than enough children to play with now, countess," said the corvid.

For the next week, Eduardo taught the graveyard club all the secret rooms in the official residence. Besa noted that the ambassador's bedroom was closer to Catalina's bedroom than Juan's quarters in the stables were from Besa's bedroom.

"We won't have any problems with the distance, at least," said Margaret.

"This should be pretty easy," said Dickey.

"That's not the way you plan, Mr. O'Brien," said Eduardo. "The strategy needs to account for the unexpected."

"How can you plan for something if you don't know what it is?"

"By considering all the possible outcomes of the situation you are going into. For instance, what will you do if all of you are discovered and captured?"

"But that's not possible. No one will know what we're doing; even if they see us."

"That's what Eduardo is trying to explain, Dickey," said Catalina. "Anything is possible with magic. And my uncle has magic, too."

"We have to consider it, Dickey," said Besa. "So, let's talk about it. What can we do if we are separated?"

"We'll need something to keep us all connected," said Margaret. "Like a charm or some kind of token."

"It would also need to be made of some kind of special material that could hold our connection to one another," said Catalina.

"I think I have something," said Besa. "I'll go get it."

She left the room and went upstairs, but was back in a few moments, clutching a dark wood box. "This should do the trick," she said, sitting the box on the circle table in the parlor. When she opened it, everyone understood.

"Chess pieces," observed Dickey.

"They're made of ebony. My papa had these custom made. Everyone, please take one, and I will bind us all together, so that if we are somehow separated, we will still have our connection and the dream will hold up."

They each chose a chess piece and Besa uttered a charm,

"I, as the anchor, call these tied as one across space and time."

All the pieces emitted a little glow. "Make sure you're not separated from your link," instructed Besa. "Hide them somewhere on your body."

They all agreed, and they even had a test run to check the viability of the connectors. They all worked well.

WHEN THE NEXT WEEK CAME, Besa and Margaret were outfitted with kitchen help clothing, but Besa had never worked in a kitchen.

"What is the best way to stay busy in here?" she asked Alexis, one of the kitchen assistants trying to show her the ropes.

"Are you planning to help out a bit, Besa?" asked Grace, a kitchen assistant who was just two years older.

"No," said Besa. "We are giving a play at school, and my part is the kitchen assistant. I just want to play my part right."

"Will there be a prince to dance with like in Cinderella?" asked another assistant whose interest was piqued.

"No," said Besa. It's just something we're doing in our class. It won't be put on in public."

"Oh," said the girl, looking disappointed.

"She only wants to see the ones with kissing and dancing," whispered Alexis.

Margaret didn't need any extra training. One of her

nightly chores was helping her mother prepare dinner and then clean up the kitchen.

ON THE DAY of the event, Besa and Margaret rode their horses to the stables and none other than Dickey took their mount—under the watchful eye of an older, more experienced, stable boy.

"Ain't no need to be smiling at 'em," said the stern-faced Esteban. "They're only the kitchen help."

"Yes, but I think the redhead likes me," replied Dickey.

"In your dreams, horse boy!" snapped Margaret.

"Margaret, what are you doing?" whispered Besa. "Please stay focused."

"Oh, sorry."

They entered the kitchen at the rear of the facility. The first person they encountered was an angry-looking, tall, broad woman by the name of Consuela.

"I am Miss Consuela. You are to call me Miss Consuela. Do you understand?"

She was standing in the middle of the doorway, and it was clear she wouldn't let them pass until she had their assent.

Yes, Miss Consuela," they both chimed.

"I didn't quite hear that!" yelled Miss Consuela. "Speak up!"

"Yes, Miss Consuela!" cried Margaret and Besa.

"Good!" declared Miss Consuela. "Let's get your hands in some hot water."

They were marched to a large metal tub filled with dirty pots and pans.

"I need these done in less than an hour, or you won't get paid for the day. Get to it!"

The room was filled with activity. There were women of all ages working around the room, at several large tables where vegetables were being chopped, with meat and poultry laid out and prepped for roasting or baking.

"Be careful," said a woman in a bloody white apron. "That crazy cow likes to scald the new ones. So she won't have to pay you when you don't finish in time."

"Then why even try to finish?" asked Margaret.

"Because if you don't, you're out the door," said another woman, walking by with a large pan of chopped vegetables.

"Then we'd better get to it," said Besa, dipping her hands in the scalding water. "Wow! This is hot."

"Don't worry. I'll cool it down just a little," said Margaret.

"Not too much," replied Besa. "The point of this is for us to be very uncomfortable. Everyone is obviously watching."

"Ow!" cried Margaret. "This is hot!"

"Don't worry. Keep trying, Henrietta. We really need the money!"

They kept up this exchange of complaining while still working in the scalding tub. Margaret was obviously the best actress at complaining, so Besa just followed her lead. They finally got the pots done, but weren't really doing very much scrubbing. The implement for scrubbing was purposely inadequate. The pots were finally clean almost two hours later, which various other workers in the room made clear was the usual standard. You wouldn't get paid, but you'd still have your job. And right on the second hour, Miss Consuela came by and was pleased at the quality of their work.

"You girls have done a fine job. You are not going to get

paid, but I have some other tasks that will keep you busy the rest of the day. Do you want to stay?"

"Yes, Miss Consuela!"

"Whoa! No need to shout. I'm standing right here. Let's find you some vegetables to chop."

Unfortunately, Dickey was having a bit more trouble with his initial assignment of mucking out the horse stalls. He couldn't seem to heave the chips into the adjacent stall without hitting his trainer in the face with it. The further away Esteban stood; horse chips still landed on his head. Soon Dickey was reduced to collecting any pile left by horses moving through the stable yard into a big wooden bucket. Esteban made sure he was at least fifty yards away as Dickey performed this task. He was also not allowed near the pitch fork in the hay stall.

In the meantime, Catalina stayed in her room while her mother and some of the courtiers promenaded along the levee like the wealthy Creole families. Catalina was making use of some of the secret passages to get around the official residence without being noticed. She sensed her uncle's guards were searching for her. Eduardo had warned her as well that if they got their hands on her, the duchess would never see her again. Besa and Margaret were getting on well within the back room of the kitchen. Once Miss Consuela saw that they caught on quickly, she threw more and more tasks their way. By the time they made it to the butter churn, their day was over.

"I am very impressed with the way you too work together. And your hard work will be rewarded by more hard work tomorrow. Good night girls. See you bright and early in the morning. Oh, and before you go, Mr. Rojas has a reward for you in the royal dining room. It's right through that door on your right. Hurry up. It's getting late. Time to close up."

The door took them through the main kitchen, where the evening cleanup crew had already begun scrubbing down all the floors, walls, and counters where the food was prepared. Margaret got through the door first and saw a familiar sight: Dickey sitting at a table wolfing down plate after plate of pastries, and then she saw that the room was full of guards. Margaret froze, and then a guard went over to Dickey and pointed a flintlock pistol at his head. "If you do any magic, the boy is dead."

This came from a tall, blue-eyed man with a short beard and a sword at his waist.

"I am commander Rojas, captain of the ambassador's guard. The ambassador sensed you were here. But what sealed it was your gluttonous friend here. He was the worst stable hand Esteban had ever seen. But don't worry, you won't be here long. As soon as we get our hands on your nosey little countess, you will all be disposed of."

Besa had a thought that made her heart race a bit. Felix would be coming to her aid soon and might get hurt. She needed a way to warn him to stay away. They were prepared for this. They took them all down to the jail in the eastern wing of the complex and locked them in two cells.

"Please make yourselves comfortable before slaughter," said the guard, who locked them in. "I would have something brought for your last meal, but the kitchen is closed. The pudgy one ate most everything, anyway," said the man with a laugh and slammed the cell block door behind him.

"Don't worry, young ones," said Eduardo, fluttering from a crevice in the ceiling to land on Besa's right shoulder. "These are not very good guards. They are lazy. No one will check on you once they lock you in."

"Thank you, Eduardo. That is good to know," replied Besa. "This is obviously a minor setback."

"No thanks to mister terrible stable boy, here," said Margaret.

"I didn't do anything," replied Dickey. "I've never worked in a stable before."

"It's okay, Dickey," said Besa. "We're all new at these tasks. Hopefully, they don't find Catalina. And Eduardo, please fly toward my residence and tell Felix to stay away. That I am in no immediate danger."

"Right away, madam president," replied the corvid. "I shall return soon."

He got through the bars at the top of the window and was off.

ELSEWHERE IN THE STRUCTURE, Catalina got wind of the servant's talk about how the guards had captured some French spies trying to come in through the kitchen and stables. She'd heard those terms before in reference to a man suspected of trying to seduce the duchess. The official story was he was a spy, but the gossip was a lot more accurate. The man had been her mother's lover. But the ending was tragic, because he was never seen again. Catalina believed the man was fed to the crocodiles and alligators of the swamp. A fate Commander Rojas probably had in store for her and the rest of The Graveyard Club. But they had plans too. She would stay hidden and play her part when the time came. The ambassador was eager to get this over with. He even broadcast a charm that only she could hear:

"Be careful, little niece. Tonight will be the end for you.

I don't care what I have to do. You will not wake up in your bed tomorrow."

That scared her a bit, but would not deter her from her true course. She found the center section that connected all the secret rooms and sat down on the floor to wait for midnight, when everything would start. As the evening wore on, she heard the guards rushing down the halls, searching every room and then slamming the doors. Her uncle's prediction would come true: she would not wake up in her own bed tomorrow. Soon Eduardo found her in the central room.

"The plan appears to be coming along well, and the minister of the royal treasury will be here in the morning for a breakfast meeting with the ambassador. And coincidentally, he served with your father in some of the many battles against General Napoleon."

"Thank you, Eduardo. That will be helpful. Do you have any crackers hidden in one of these crevices? I haven't had lunch or dinner."

The corvid disappeared into the walls and came back with a small package wrapped in string.

"These should satisfy you."

"But I gave these to you for your birthday, two weeks ago!"

'The package's smell is sweet," replied the raven. "I don't enjoy sweets as much as you."

"Thank you. You are very generous."

She tore into the package like the hungry child she was. The package was empty in a little over five minutes.

"I wish I had more to offer you, my lady. But you would not enjoy raven food."

"Thank you, Eduard. I will manage until morning."

The other members of The Graveyard Club only got bread and a cup of water.

"For your last meal, and none of you are making it to breakfast," said the cell block guard.

"Would you happen to have any butter to go with this?" asked Dickey.

"Dickey, really?" asked Margaret.

"What? The bread is dry. My mother would be unhappy if she knew I had dry bread for my last meal!"

"But you–"

"Let it go, Margaret," said Besa. "It doesn't matter."

"I will see what I can do," said the guard.

"Are you going to eat your bread? If not, I want it."

"Here you go, Dickey," said Besa, tossing hers over to him.

"Thank you, Besa. You are always so generous."

"You can have mine, too," said Margaret.

"Never mind. I think I have enough."

"Should I just toss it on the floor and step on it?" she asked, motioning to do so.

"No, wait! Don't waste it. Then I'll take it."

"But said you didn't want it."

"I changed my mind. I do want it, okay?"

"Margaret, I know you're just bored," said Besa. "Why don't you lie down and sleep for a while?"

THE CAPTAIN of the guard was just then delivering unhappy news to the duke.

"Have you located her?" demanded the ambassador.

"I am sorry to inform you, Your Grace, that we have not

found your niece, and the duchess' carriage has just returned to the stables. Should we kill the three others?"

Duke Barbosa was a tall, elegantly handsome man with green eyes that were like a knife if he looked at you a certain way. "Did I tell you to kill the other three?" The guard backed up at the tone. "She is up to something. I can sense it. I want all of them together. So I can torture it out of them. And then we kill them. All of them! Keep looking. Or I might have a new captain of the guard by morning!"

Captain Rojas' face went pale at the implication.

"Yes, Your Grace. We will find her."

He turned and left the room quickly.

ON THE OTHER side of town, the bishop was getting ready to do another enchantment ceremony. He decided to try an earlier time, since the previous times when he'd used the book, the Taafli had appeared. On this night, he had invited a total of twenty spectators. All of them were required to wear masks to shield their identities. The less they knew about each other, the less likely they might be informers or even spies. The evening had a show-like air. The corpse was that of a convicted murderer. Delacroix wasn't altogether comfortable with the tone of the evening. Even though it was his idea. The serving of alcohol was Denny's touch, and the bishop grew a bit dismayed when the servers—also masked–appeared to charge each patron taking a drink, a fee. He would've objected, but he was already into his preparation. He called the book, and when it appeared, Denny stepped up as the dutiful assistant and opened the cover. The Taafli ascended and flitted about the room. They had already discovered there was no danger to others if they did not interfere with the book. The Taafli entered the corpse, and the white eminence ascended. The first unexpected thing that happened was the spectators began to clap. This had a jarring effect on the entity, because it looked toward the crowd in fear and confusion. The second unexpected thing that happened was a server nearest the bishop reached over and snatched the book out of Delacroix's hand and then tossed it across the room to someone who ran toward the front of the house. Then the snatcher took off his mask, and it was Father Guidry.

"I am the one who knows, André!" cried Michel. "I know that you are a thief, a liar and a criminal!"

"What have you done, Michel!" bellowed the bishop. Right then the spirit receded back into the corpse, and the Taafli rose and searched for the gateway.

"I have done justice, is what I've done," replied Michel.

"You must return the book at once, Michel! Or you have killed me! Please, my friend!"

"It is not your book, André!"

"But if it doesn't return to the book, I will be trapped in this darkness! Please!"

Michel suddenly realized his mistake and took off after the book. When Michel left, the Taafli hovered in front of the bishop.

"We know that voice." chimed a thousand voices. "And now we know what you have done. Come out. Come out and die! "

FORTY-FIVE MINUTES LATER, someone knocked on the front door of the borrowed house. When the Shadow answered it, they found the book of Taalu on the front stoop, with a note to the bishop. The book was quickly delivered to Delacroix, and the Taafli returned through the gateway. During his extended time in the cloak, Delacroix lost most of his left foot and a section of his right ear.

"Your Grace, we have to do something different," said Denny "That cloak is more dangerous to you than the Taafli."

"You're right, Denny. That would've been the end of me, if Michel hadn't brought the book back. Where is he? Did he come back?"

"No, Your Grace. But he left a letter attached to the book."

"Let me see it! Why were you keeping it from me?"

"I'm sorry, Your Grace. I was waiting to see if the cloak left you with eyes to read it."

"I clearly do have my eye left. Let me see it."

"*Dear André,*" the letter began. "*I did not intend to cause you harm when I took the book. I was just so angry that you had become secretive and untruthful. You have changed so much since your attack. But to discover the level you have descended to was too much for me. I am telling you now, I will not be at the residence when you return home this evening, and I am leaving the priesthood. There is no way back from this path you've taken. I pray that God will protect me on the course I've taken and forgives you once you reach the end of yours.*"

Sincerely

Michel.

The bishop looked stricken but refused to shed a tear in front of his Shadows.

"Bring the carriage around, Denny."

"Is it bad news, Your Grace?"

"Please, just do what I tell you, and bring the carriage around!"

Delacroix pulled the carriage up as close as he could to Michel's residence and limped quickly inside. The place was clean and organized. Michel had obviously been planning this for a while. He hadn't had many clothes. He hadn't needed any, but all of his books were gone. Delacroix went to the priest's room, sat on the bed, and cried, "Michel! Michel! Michell!" and then laid down and wept.

Besa and the rest of The Graveyard Club were also preparing to lay down for the night. She couldn't link hands with Dickey in the cell across from hers, but he still had his connecting ebony chess piece, so he held on to that as he laid down on the cot in his cell. Besa and Margaret took to the cell floor, hands linked. They quickly located Catalina.

"It's time to come out of hiding, Catalina," Besa told her. She was standing in the hallway outside of Catalina's bedroom. Dickey soon joined them. He had a plate with half of a caramel cake that he was eating.

"What are you doing, Dickey?" asked Margaret.

"This is my dream, so I'm having a piece of cake."

"It's actually Catalina's dream," said Besa. "And we need to help her make it as real as we can."

"Okay, I'm ready," said Dickey, flipping the cake over his shoulder. Catalina soon emerged from her room, wearing a sword at her waist and a small breast plate.

"My mother told me she kept one of my father's swords hidden where no one could find it. But my raven, who studies blueprints, found it. It's my dream to wear it in battle."

"I have my sword too," said Dickey, brandishing the sword he'd received from the djinn. Besa had recreated the sword of light she'd received from the Taafli, along with the linked armor and shield.

"Where's your weapon, Margaret?" asked Dickey.

"Let me see now," said the young witch. "Where would I—Oh! I've got it!" and she was suddenly clothed in the armor of the Moorish spirit, complete with his spear. "I'm ready."

"I should've gotten me some armor, too," said Dickey.

"All right, Catalina," said Besa. "Time to go wake them all up."

Besa and Margaret stationed themselves outside the doors to the guard's quarters, while Dickey located the quarters of commander Rojas.

"On Catalina's signal. We all go as one. So let us know, Catalina."

"Okay, now!" cried the countess as she kicked open the duke's door, ran in and ripped back his covers. "You are a coward and a murder, Duke Barbosa! I seek justice for my father! I challenge you to single combat!"

And then she heard the bomb Margaret flung into the guard's quarters go off. The impact surprised the ambassador.

"What are you up to, girl?"

"Nothing. I just brought my friends along."

She ran up and slashed him across the cheek.

"That is convenient," replied the duke, grabbing his own sword. "You can all die together!" and he lunged, trying to stab Catalina in the neck. But she was too quick, parrying his lunge and stepping aside. He momentum took him into the hall, but she slashed his arm as he went flying by, landing on his face.

"You will die for that!" he cried, getting up and charging at her.

"Not like that I won't," said the countess, "Quit stumbling around. Stand up and fight!"

He took a swipe at her head and she ducked under it.

"Stand still so I can kill you!" demanded the ambassador.

"I don't know how much sword fighting you've done," replied Catalina, keeping herself just out of his reach. "But it doesn't work like that. But you wouldn't know that being a coward."

"We'll see who the coward is. Stand and fight me like a man!"

At that, the countess crossed swords with her uncle and nicked him on the cheek. "If I were a man, you'd be dead already," she said, striking and parrying so ferociously she drove the duke back into his bedroom. That's when he realized he was overmatched.

"Guards, someone help me! I'm being attacked!"

Catalina just laughed at his urgency. "Yes, let them come and discover you've been bested by a child, and a girl at that!"

Besa, Dickey and Margaret were having a much closer battle with the guards and Commander Rojas. The commander was obviously a better swordsman than his boss. He and Dickey exchanged several cuts and slashes on their faces and arms. While Besa and Margaret had their hands full with a room full of guards, Catalina sent Besa a message.

"Besa! My uncle has given up. He's such a coward. Please send him something to give him courage."

"Drive him toward the bed," replied Besa. Catalina charged her uncle, while slashing and stabbing at his face. He retreated backward and fell onto his bed, where his hand landed on a loaded crossbow, with a quiver full of arrows. The duke grabbed the crossbow and shot at the countess, who ducked in time and fled the bedroom. The duke also grabbed the quiver of arrows and gave chase.

"Where are you going, my little niece? Who's the coward now?"

Catalina conveniently dropped her sword as she ran.

"Oh look. You seem to have forgotten your sword. Don't worry, I'll bring! it to you!"

She made sure to duck back and forth across the hall, allowing the duke to expend more and more of his arrows.

"I hope you never led men into battle," said the countess. "You have terrible aim, most of your men would've been killed by you!"

"Maybe you should come closer. My aim is much better up close."

Catalina dashed out at just the right time. The duke caught her across the shoulder with the sword. Catalina cried out as she fell through a door and landed in the room where the sun was just coming up.

"That's more like it," said the duke. "Closer is always better for killing."

"Is that how you killed my father?" asked Catalina. "Up close with a sword?"

"I am not a fool, child. No one could challenge your father with a sword."

"Then how did you kill him?" asked Catalina, tears falling as she dodged around the breakfast tables.

"That was easy. I waited for his back to be turned and then shot him through the heart."

"Why? He was your brother!"

"Because he had everything as first born and I had nothing!" said the duke, lunging at her around the table. "Now, it's your turn my nosey little niece."

"My mother will know," said Catalina. "I left her a letter in case I died."

He had her cornered with her back against the wall.

"It won't matter. She'll be dead too in a month. I've already found her replacement! Die, little niece!"

He brought the sword down, but it was blocked by something. It was another sword. It struck his sword, and he was pushed back. He landed hard on a table and was jarred awake, and saw he was in the breakfast room, and the swordsman who'd blocked his strike was the minister of the royal treasury. Standing right behind him, with a look of utter shock, was the duchess, along with half her courtiers.

"What happened?" asked the duke, getting up quickly. "How did I even get here? I must have been sleepwalking."

The treasury minister leaned down and picked up the duke's sword.

"That didn't look like you were dreaming and this is not dream blood," said the treasury minister, holding up the ambassador's sword. "You tried to kill that child, and confessed to murdering her father, who was a better man than you could ever be. Gendarmes! Take him to his own jail!"

The minister's royal guard picked the duke up off the floor and escorted him to the jail, that Besa, Dickey and Margaret had already vacated. The official residence's physician saw to Catalina's wound. It was not as bad as it could have been, were the duke better with a sword. But the countess would wear the scar as a badge of honor, that and the legion of merit, which the duchess had the privilege of pining on her daughter.

~

As was expected, Felix waited nearby with the carriage to take Besa, and the rest of The Graveyard Club, home. It wasn't until a week later that Catalina pulled up to the mansion in the embassy's official carriage. She made sure to time her visit, so that everyone was there. Except for Mokheer, of course.

"That is a very nice medal, countess." observed Dickey.

"Thank you, Sir Richard. I received it for bravery, and because I was injured in the pursuit of justice."

"Wait a minute. I was injured in the pursuit of justice too. Can I get a medal?"

"Dickey," said Besa. "No one was supposed to know we were there, remember? We were just piggybacking onto Catalina's dream, remember?"

"Besides, you weren't really injured," said Margaret.

"It sure felt like I was injured; and I was hungry!"

"That's part of the reason why I'm here," said Catalina "My mother would like to invite all my friends to dinner tomorrow at the official residence. And, as an added bonus, Sir Richard will meet the royal pastry chef and take a tour of the pastry-making suite and the pastry vault."

"Oh, my goodness! He will never–"

"Shut up, Margaret. How long do I have?"

"How long do you have where?" asked Catalina.

"How long do I have in the vault?"

The kitchen assistants were just delivering the cakes to the parlor.

"I'll take those," said Dickey.

"What do you think you're doing, Dickey?" demanded Margaret.

"I'm getting some practice in for tomorrow," replied Dickey, slicing into the first cake. Everyone just laughed, including Margaret.

When the raven showed up, he had a question for madam president.

"I have been considering something," said Eduardo, in between bites of the cornbread Miss Maymi always had ready for him. "I believe the countess and I have proven our mettle in courage and intelligence, so it is time to consider us for membership in your Graveyard Club."

"Eduardo!" cried the countess "How presumptuous of you! We did not discuss this."

"What is there to discuss? The facts are as obvious as my black feathers."

"He's right," said Margaret. "I say we vote on it."

"But first we need to ask a question," said Besa, "Do you want to be in our club, Catalina?"

The countess started to cry.

"You don't understand, countess Besa. From the first day we met, I never wanted to be parted from you. When I'm with you, it's like I can do anything. Of course, we want to join you!"

"Then let's take a vote," said Dickey. "I vote yes!"

"So do I," replied Margaret.

"Me, as well," said Besa. Mokheer appeared next to Dickey, but Dickey didn't even flinch.

"I hope you weren't forgetting about me," he said "I have a say in this, too."

"Well," asked Dickey. "What's your vote?"

The entity seemed to think for a moment.

"The countess and her talking raven? Hmm. She did save Dickey's life. But that raven can be a bit of a—just kidding. I vote yes, too."

"Then it's official," said Besa. "We welcome countess Barbosa and Eduardo Zelén as the newest members of The Graveyard Club!"

Suddenly there were a lot of people clapping. The kids turned around and found Miss Maymi, the kitchen assistants, the scullery maids, Felix and his upstairs and downstairs. staff, and the stable master and his staff. The entire Melponte compound applauded these additions to their young mistresses' life. She still cried.

"What's the matter, Besa?" asked Margaret, pulling her best friend into an embrace. "I thought you were happy?"

"I am. I was just thinking about Papa. I hope he would approve."

"I hope so, too Besa," replied Margaret. And ironically, the whole thing had been orchestrated by the raven. Which was why Miss Maym and her staff prepared a feast to mark the occasion. The celebration lasted the rest of the evening, and Besa also took time to go upstairs to Pierre's room and share the news with her father.

By the end of the next week, a ship with the king's guard came to extradite Duke Barbosa back to Spain, so he could face the king's justice for the murder of his own brother. There would soon be a new Spanish ambassador, but the duchess and countess Catalina were allowed to remain in Newald for an indefinite period. She had found great community and friendships within the upper-class Creole families and her own core of courtiers.

Catalina was trying to convince her mother to allow her to attend sister Gerard's with the rest of her new friends.

CHAPTER 21

THE DEATH OF AUGUST GLAZIER

Within a week, the raven petitioned Besa for the next adventure they would embark upon. That's when Besa informed Felix that the club would reach out to the two creole girls, Simone and Angeline, and let them know The Graveyard Club is ready to start.

"I don't think that is a good case for you, Besa," replied the behike. "Dupard is a very powerful man. Creoles don't tolerate anyone meddling into their families."

"I appreciate your opinion, Felix, but the request came from within his family."

"You're going to do this no matter what I think, aren't you?"

"Yes, we are. We will fulfill the request."

The next week, Eduardo took off for the Dupard plantation, with a note from The Graveyard Club to set up a time and a date to meet, so they could discuss their case. The raven spent half the day searching the property for any sign of Angeline. He finally spotted the dark-haired girl sitting on the back veranda of a massive Spanish-style house. She was sitting next to a younger black child on the porch swing. The raven landed on the arm of the chair and said,

"Do not be alarmed, Angeline Dupard. I bring word from Besa Melponte and The Graveyard club."

Angeline wasn't afraid; she was excited

"A talking bird," noted the black child.

"Your message is attached to my left claw, please remove it."

Angeline did as the corvid instructed and removed the small bit of note attached to Eduardo's claw.

"Are you in the club, too, Mr. Crow?" inquired the girl.

"I am not a crow. I am a raven. And in answer to your question, yes, I am in the club. The countess and I are the newest members. I have to go. Good bye, Angeline Dupard. I will return tomorrow for your response," and the raven was off.

The response directed them to a beautiful one-story house in Vieux Carré.

When Besa knocked on the door, a black woman answered.

"Are you Antoinette Dupard?" asked Besa.

"Yes," replied the woman. "Are you mademoiselle Melponte?"

"Yes, ma'am, I am."

"Please come in, necromancer."

With a gracious nod Besa followed her to a neat, well-appointed front parlor, that was furnished with some of the very same pieces located in the front parlor of the Melponte mansion, including a red velvet tufted chesterfield sofa. Two matching scroll chairs, and a mahogany whatnot cabinet in the corner with a number of interesting-looking nick-nacks. And above the marble fireplace a magnificent landscape showing a scene of a lone Cajun fisherman in his boat. "You must excuse the mess," said the woman, "Nora hasn't gotten to this room yet."

Antoinette a tall, beautiful coffee-with cream colored woman had a very regal manner as she gave Besa a tour of her beautiful abode. "This is another Auguste. He enjoyed landscapes as well as portraits." They were already on the tenth painting by her son when they reached the sitting room. "I hope you don't mind," said Ms. Dupard. "I've had Celeste make some of her lemon cookies to complement our tea. Please have a seat," ushering Besa to oak settee with what looked like an ebony wood circle table. Besa obliged. Both the cookies and tea were of good quality.

"Why did everyone call your son, Glazier instead of his first name, Auguste?"

"That was his idea," replied Antoinette. "The master he studied came from France, and all the artists he admired only had one name. I was a bit irritated by the idea at first until he explained it to me. Do you want any more cookies?"

"No. I'm pretty full from the tea."

"Then let's go sit out in the garden. There's good shade, and I want to get away from all these paintings. They make me miss him too much."

The breeze was very nice in the garden, which was also well appointed with stylish cast iron wheel back chairs and a cast iron circle table. Once they sat down, Besa asked her, "Why didn't your son leave the Dupard property with you?"

"Miss Melponte, I know you can read minds, among all the other things you can do. Don't you already know all this?" Besa just smiled.

"I think it's rude to read someone's thoughts without their permission."

"That's very considerate of you. Auguste didn't leave

because I couldn't pay for him and myself. My son's value was more than I could afford, given his talent."

"Can you tell me what you know about Clément Dupard."

"I know that he killed my Auguste." she said.

"That's not what I meant. I need to know everything you can tell me about him. We're going to have to trespass on his property for this case."

"But I thought Angeline and Simone invited you."

"Will that matter to him if he catches us?"

"Absolutely not. So, you'd better make sure you don't get caught. Trespassers usually disappear if they catch them. Le Borge is a world within itself and Clément lord and master of it all."

Eduardo had already given them the preliminary reconnaissance report. Le Borge was six hundred acres, and Dupard had his own private army protecting almost every inch of it. The army consisted of a total of two hundred men broken into five groups of forty. Each group was responsible for maintaining a section of the property. By this method Dupard ensured he never had a runaway. These men had autonomy to do whatever they wanted when they caught someone. This often-involved torture, murder and any number of unspeakable acts. Le Borge held more than fifteen hundred slaves, and the Seventy-five overseers were not included in the small army. Though they didn't hesitate to use it to strike fear in any rebellious or organized group. But the most interesting fact about Le Borge, was it wasn't an enterprise utilizing brutality. The slaves were well cared for, sometimes over fed, and wanted for nothing. Auguste was an example of this policy. He'd been provided a first-rate education, and when his talent presented itself, the best masters were found to help develop it. The boy had been raised with the Dupard children, just as his mother before him had been allowed to flourish and grow into the refined women that greeted Besa.

"Why do you think Mr. Dupard might've harmed your son?" asked Besa.

"Because of Simone. You only had to see the look in that girl's eyes when she looked at Auguste, to know he was doomed. She was in love with him. The Dupard's come from French nobility. They are proud of that. I tried to warn Auguste that his relationship with the girl could never be more than a childhood crush. But he felt that becoming a famous artist would be the key to acceptance within the family. I suppose I'm partly to blame for whatever happened to my son."

"Why do you say that?"

"Because I didn't explain how the world worked. That no matter how talented he was, he wasn't any different from Clément's prized thoroughbreds. He spent a lot of money to pamper them too, but they were just animals to Clément, and even with all the preening, Auguste was still just a slave."

"And you are what is called a Voudon?"

"Yes. When I discovered I had a talent for calling the dead, and sending hexes, I knew I couldn't stay in that church-centered household. It's a good thing I inherited this house from Arnas Dupard, Clément's father, when I did. He left it to me in his will, so Clément couldn't take it away from me. Otherwise, I wouldn't have had anywhere to go. But he got his revenge by keeping my son."

"Was there a way to purchase his freedom?"

"I offered to give him the house back, but he refused, saying it should be his already. That's how much he holds a grudge. I don't know what Simone and Angeline are planning to do, but if it involves going against Clément or embarrassing him in some way, you should not do it. I don't care what they're paying you."

"We don't do it for money. They just want the truth."

"What good is the truth? It won't bring Auguste back, and you will be lost to your own family."

When Besa had been at the house for about 45 Minutes, Simone and Angeline finally arrived, both a bit excited and breathless as Besa and Antoinette returned to the front parlor.

"Thank you for meeting us, Ms. Melponte!" They both took their places on the main couch next to Besa.

"Antoinette, fetch us some tea and lemon cookies," commanded Simone.

Antoinette just sat and looked at the girl.

"Stop it, Simone," said Angeline. "She's not one of our servants. If you will tell me where the tea is, Miss. Antoinette, I can go and fetch it."

Antoinette rang a little bell on the side table next to her. A young Afro-Creole girl came in answer.

"Please brings our new quests some tea and cookies, Celeste."

"Yes, ma'am."

Once the tea and cookies were consumed, Besa asked, "Where is Auguste's body located?"

"It's in an unmarked grave at the back of our family cemetery," replied Angeline.

"How do you know that, girl?" asked Antoinette.

"Because one of the men in Captain Trudeau's militia is sweet on Simone."

"He is not sweet on me!" cried Simone. "If you tell people that, father will have something done to him."

Angeline just rolled her eyes. "Like I was saying. One of the militiamen told Simone that he helped bury Auguste."

"Did he tell you what they did to my son?" demanded Antoinette. "Did he tell you that?" Simone began to cry. "No, he did not, madame. I loved him, too!"

"Yes! That is why he is in that grave! I need to go lie down," she said, rising. "Nora will see all of you out," and she exited the room.

"Do you know the schedule of patrol for the militia?" asked Besa.

"I never thought we would need such a thing," replied Angeline.

"We will fabricate a plausible reason to be on your property," said Besa. "But before we can approach the cemetery, the coffin must be taken out of the grave, and we will need the militia's patrol schedule."

"Benjamin would tell you that, wouldn't he, Simone?"

"If I ask him, he will," replied Simone, still a bit sniffly.

"Good. We will also need some kind of map of your property. Will three days be enough time to get it all together?"

"Yes, that should be plenty," replied Angeline.

"Then I'll send Eduardo out in three days to retrieve it."

"Thank you, Miss Melponte," said Simone. "It's time we got home, Angeline."

Each of the groups took off in opposite directions.

~

"BESA, A MILITIA?" said Felix, when she climbed in the carriage. "Don't you think this is getting a little out of hand?"

"We'll have the patrol schedule and a map of the property soon."

"So, you have just decided and don't want to talk about it?"

"I would love to talk about it. But first, let's talk about why Papa hid everything from me for so long."

"You have become a bit too clever, young lady."

"You don't have to help if you don't want to, Felix."

"You know very well I can't let you go on something like this alone."

They rode the whole path back to the mansion without uttering another word. Besa requested that her dinner be brought to her room.

THE NEXT DAY AT SCHOOL, Margaret asked:

"Besa, how are we going to get past a militia?"

"How many men?" asked Dickey, sitting down next to Margaret.

"Don't you have a Sprite or something to chase?" asked Margaret, snarkily.

"Nope. I thought it would be best to hear what Besa found out."

"That's very mature of you, Dickey." replied Besa.

"Yes, it is," said Margaret, putting her hand on Dickey's head and feeling around his neck.

"Cut it out. What are you doing?"

"I'm just making sure you're not coming down with the black plague or something."

"Stop it," he said, brushing her hands away. "I can be mature if I want to be. I just don't always want to be. Like one day, I will make a very mature hus—"

"Don't you dare say it, Butter boy!" growled Margaret, her hands raised to cast. "Because I'll make sure you get the black plague, right now!"

"I wouldn't try her, Dickey. She looks serious," chuckled Besa.

"You are so sensitive."

"Back to what we were discussing. There are two hundred men in the militia. But if we plan well—as we did for Catalina's case, we'll be fine."

The raven picked up the map and the patrol schedule from Angeline three days later.

"I have an idea of how we can get on the property," said Catalina, munching her tea cake and sipping her tea.

"Okay. What is it?" asked Margaret.

"We will need to be invited."

"That is not going to be easy to pull off. You mean, like being invited to a party?"

"No. I mean, we will have a legitimate reason for being on the property."

"Oh! I know exactly what she means," replied Dickey.

"Oh, no. This is starting to sound sketchy," said Margaret.

"Give him a chance to make his point," replied Besa.

"Thank you, Besa. All we need to do is make a delivery, say, from the market. It could be a load of apples, or something."

"That's a brilliant idea, Catalina and Dickey," said Besa.

"But that actually makes sense," said Margaret, completely stunned.

"That's right!" cried Dickey, who got up and did a little jig. "Stuff that in your Wolf Sneakers!"

The implications of Dickey having a good idea were almost too much for Margaret.

"Are we in some kind of dream?" she asked. Dickey leaned over and pinched her. "Ow!" cried Margaret.

"Nope," said Dickey. "This is all real."

The plan was laid out. They would enter the property hauling a wagon full of apples from native sellers at the French Market. Angeline and Simone would convey this message to the militia, which would get them past the perimeter. Four of the baskets would not be all apples, of course. Felix volunteered to drive the wagon, which saved them from asking someone else. He looked as native as anyone at the market. He might as well help, thought Besa, since he insisted on coming. The patrol schedule showed that a group of forty militiamen patrolled the northeast region of the property approximately every forty-five minutes. That was plenty of time for an enchantment. Especially if the casket, or whatever means they had used to bury the body, was already dug up. Angeline sent a message by Eduardo saying that the best night to come was on the twenty-fifth, since that was the start of harvest. The slaves usually held festivals and engagements, and there were usually one or two groups planning an escape. They'd also had an auction recently, selling off a few incorrigibles. These types of events often spurred escape attempts, which kept the militia busier than usual.

THE GRAVEYARD CLUB laid out their plan for the site.

"We will need a good lantern to light the area," said Besa. "Can we count on you for that, Dickey?"

"Yes, I have a very reliable oil lantern. But shouldn't we be concerned that the patrol will notice our light and come straight to us?"

"Eduardo will keep watch from above and warn us if a patrol is coming our way," said Catalina.

"Margaret also has a spell she developed for just such a situation," said Besa.

"What does it do, Margaret?" asked Dickey.

"It holds light in, so it stays confined to only the immediate area."

"That sounds amazing. I can't wait to see it at work," said Catalina.

"To hopefully see it at work," said Margaret. "I've been trying to work the kinks out for the last three weeks."

"But you never told me about this!" complained Dickey.

"I never get a chance. You don't sit with us at recess."

Dickey looked over at Besa.

"She's telling the truth, Dickey. We talk about a lot of things during recess."

"All right. I get the point. I'll spend more time with you at recess."

"I'll believe that when I see it."

"You just watch. I'll sit down for three whole minutes!"

"Wow! I don't know how we'll get through all that time together."

"Give him a chance, Margaret. If he sits there for too long, every eight-year-old witch, warlock, and wizard will be climbing over us to get to him."

"Oh, yeah. I forgot about that. You have a deal, Dickey. Three it is."

FELIX WASN'T happy about having to wear one of the tattered outfits favored by the native apple sellers, but he bought that and an apple wagon, making sure he looked the part of a hapless apple seller. The natives had told him that the clothes were important. People didn't buy as much if they looked too prosperous. They wanted to feel like they were doing them a favor by buying their apples. Angeline and Simon were going to meet the wagon, because they needed a place to hide until midnight, when the enchantment would take place. One of the large barns at the eastern edge of the property had been made ready with blankets to sleep on, along with food and water. Four of the apple baskets were set up with a top tray to carry the apples, while the bottom section concealed one of the four club members. Dickey's basket looked like it might be too small for him until Catalina reminded him to shrink himself.

"Oh, yeah. Thanks, Catalina."

Once Dickey was installed in his basket, the inserts were placed and the apples piled on top of them.

Felix got underway. Eduardo flew ahead to check the status of the militia and whether they would be an impediment to entering the gate into the property.

"So far, everything looks clear," reported the raven, when they'd gone halfway. Felix didn't respond, intending to maintain his role as the silent, barely literate, apple-selling native. When they turned up the road leading to Le Borges's gate, Eduardo reported, "Angeline and Simone are waiting to receive us. At this moment, they are alone."

"Thank you, Eduardo," came Catalina's voice from one of the baskets.

"It would be best if you did not speak, countess," replied the raven. "Not until you reach your destination."

When the gate was in sight. "Not long now," said Felix.

"And the girls are still alone." They stopped, and the gate was unlocked and swung open.

"Thank you for bringing us our apples, Mr. Ta-po," said Angeline. "If you will follow us, we'll lead you back to the house." Once the gate was closed and locked, the wagon took off again. A testament to the size of the Dupard property, they rode for more than half an hour before coming to a stop.

"Everyone will be safe in here," said Simone. The tops of the baskets were removed, and the kids found themselves inside a vast barn.

"We made sure we took you to the lower eastern barn," said Angeline. "It's only about half a mile from here to the graveyard. We'll meet you there at midnight. There are blankets, food and water waiting for you up the ladder on the second level."

"Thank you," said Besa. "I'm sure we will be quite comfortable."

"Thank you, mademoiselle," replied Simone. "You don't know what this means to us. I only wish we could have had you in the house."

"We understand," said Margaret. "Our cases usually occur in unusual circumstances."

"Yeah. This is the safest we've ever been," said Dickey, picking up an apple and biting it. "Wow! These are good apples."

"Dickey!"

"What? I'm starving."

"We learned of your sweet tooth from Eduardo, Mr. O'Brien," said Angeline. "There is cake up on the second level as well."

"What?" said Dickey, jumping over the side of the

wagon and clamoring up the ladder. "He's fast," chuckled Simone.

"You should see him eat cake," replied Margaret.

"I'm not going to eat it all, Margaret!" replied Dickey.

"Sure, you won't."

"Thank you for your hospitality," said Besa. "We'll eat and get some rest before midnight."

The Creole girls made their exit, and Besa, Margaret, Felix and Catalina made their way up the ladder to the second level, hoping Dickey had kept his word. The second level was laid out like a large open bay flat, with an area for sleeping, including blankets and pillows, with water basins placed on stacked bales of hay so they could refresh themselves before bed. But the most amazing setup was the feast the girls had had brought up the ladder. There were three kinds of meat, bread, potatoes and a rich vegetable soup. All of it was laid out on a tablecloth with place settings on linen. They'd stacked bales of hay for the table, and five smaller bales of hay for their seating. The lamp sitting in the middle of the table made it all very cozy and enticing. But of course, there was already someone who'd gotten there before them. Dickey's plate was piled so high with food, it threatened to tip over.

"Oh, Dickey," sighed Margaret.

"What? There's plenty more. Look over there."

Where Dickey pointed looked like a small bakery. There were pies, cakes and custards in soufflé dishes.

"Oh, my," said Besa. "How are we ever going to eat all this?"

Margaret snorted.

"Have you forgotten who we have with us?"

"Oh, that's right," chuckled Besa. "I am rather hungry,

though. We might as well sit down while we still can." They'd even included a plate of cornbread for Eduardo. The time was just after seven—dinnertime. Once everyone had eaten their fill, the girls camped out in the far eastern corner of the loft, while Felix went down the ladder to check on the horses and make sure the barn door was still secure. While Dickey took care of the considerable number of leftovers, Catalina had a question:

"Is it always this quiet right before you start? This is obviously my second case. But is it always this quiet?"

"No. Usually something is coming at us," replied Margaret. "Or, coming at Besa."

"I definitely expected more resistance than we've gotten," said Besa.

"It's making me a little uneasy," said Margaret.

"I'd prefer not to be caught off guard," said Besa.

"Speaking of being caught off guard, look who's coming," said Margaret.

Dickey had piled cake and pie on three different plates and was delivering them to the three ladies of The Graveyard Club.

"I was thinking you girls might want a snack before bedtime."

"Thank you, Sir Richard. This is very generous of you."

"A bit out of character for you, isn't it?" asked Margaret, accepting her plate.

"My character has always been genuine. Even if you refused to see it."

"Thank you, Dickey," said Besa. "Just what we needed."

"You're welcome, madam president," and he strolled back across the loft without giving Margaret another look. He was satisfied to see Felix at the table, finishing off his own plate of sweets. "Do you need me to go down and keep an eye on the horses for you, Felix?"

"No. They've been watered and settled into a stall. Go get some rest, Dickey."

~

FOUR AND A HALF HOURS LATER, the behike roused the boy Titan and the rest of The Graveyard Club from their sleep.

"The midnight hour has arrived. Time to go, everyone."

They all climbed down and piled into the wagon.

"We must still be on our guard. Without the girls, the militia is still a threat."

Angeline and Simone met them at the gate leading into the cemetery. As they approached the excavated grave, a large group of armed men were stationed around it.

"Uh-oh," said Dickey. "Looks like we'll get a fight after all. But Felix's instincts were to protect Besa and her club. He made the horses do a wide turn to make a run for it. But it wasn't going to happen. Another group of armed men blocked their path.

"Nobody's going anywhere, chief," said an angry-looking man leading the group. "I'd just as soon shoot you for trespassing. But Mr. Dupard would like a pow-wow."

The wagon turned back and proceeded toward the grave. When they got there, Besa saw a familiar face: Antoinette. The tall, brown-skinned woman didn't look any too pleased to be among the attendees. She was standing next to a well-dressed man on a tall, exquisite black horse. Besa could tell from his piercing blue eyes that this was Clément Dupard, Angeline, and Simone's father.

"I trust you all et and slept well?" asked the man when the wagon came to a stop.

"Yes sir. Quite well," replied Dickey.

"Good," said the man, dismounting his horse and passing the reins to one of the militiamen. "We can get this business over with."

"I don't know what this has to do with me," complained Antoinette. "I am being kidnapped here!"

"Settle down, Netta. This has everything to do with you. You have sown the seeds of discontent within the hearts of my own children. And if you weren't my father's favorite, I'd have you strung up. I'm still considering it. So, don't give me anymore sass. If I'm not mistaken, sir, is that Duchess Barbosas' daughter among your little group?"

"It is, sir," replied Felix.

"Oh my. This has gotten crazier than I could've imagined. I had dinner at the official residence not three nights ago. Good evening, countess."

"Good evening, señor Dupard," replied Catalina. "What are we doing?"

"I think I'd better let my two discontented offspring tell us that."

Everyone turned their attention to Angeline and Simone. They were hesitant at first, and then Simone made a gesture that Angeline should speak for both of them.

"Papa, Simone and I were both heartbroken when Auguste disappeared without explanation."

"But I told you he went away by choice."

"That makes no sense!" snapped Antoinette. "Why would my son leave without a word to those he cared about?"

"Why would I lie to my own children?"

"Because you had something done to him!"

"I expect that from her. But do you two really believe I would harm someone I raised, like my own son?"

"We didn't know what to think, Papa. But Antoinette was so sure."

"And then Gerard told us where they buried the body," said Simone, almost in tears.

"He told me about that. I agreed to let him tell you. It still doesn't explain what the countess and her little group are doing here."

"The negro girl's their leader," replied Simone.

"Her name's Besa," corrected Angeline.

"It still doesn't explain their presence on my property and in the family graveyard."

"She can supposedly speak to the spirits," replied Simone.

"What? How much did you two pay them for this?"

"She doesn't accept money, Papa?" said Angeline.

"I would hope not! This is what you and your sister spend your time doing? Mother Mary. Since you've gone to the trouble of having the body dug up. We might as well see what this spirit-speaker can do. This way for your demonstration, Miss. Besa." When Besa moved to the front of the wagon, the militiamen were still crowding her path. "Step aside, gentlemen. Henri, help the young lady down."

A very large man wearing sergeants' stripes on his sleeve stepped up and plucked Besa from the wagon and placed her gently on the ground. "Is there anything you need, Miss Besa?"

"First, I will need the top taken off the casket," replied Besa.

"Off with the top, men!" commanded Dupard. A chisel and a mallet were located, and short work was made of the lid sealing the casket. "Miss Spirit-Speaker, what else do you require?"

"That the rest of my club be with me?"

"All right! The rest of her club, come this way!"

When the big man stepped up to reach for Margaret, after removing Catalina from the wagon, she simply floated over him and landed next to Besa.

"Oh, Magists!" declared Dupard. "This should be interesting."

The Graveyard Club approached the casket as a group, with Margaret looking daggers at anyone who looked like they might interfere. By the time Besa reached the corpse, her eyes were ablaze, and she had begun her chant. When the Taafli emerged from Besa's chest, everyone got quiet. The Taafli merged with the remains and a white eminence rose and regarded those present. The spirit looked to have been about Sixteen.

"Why has thou summoned me?" it inquired. As usual, those assembled were either shy or afraid to approach.

"Someone must ask it a question," said Margaret. "Or it will recede and not return." Finally, his mother, Antoinette, came forth, tears streaming down her face.

"Auguste, my heart. You were taken from me too soon. Tell us the terrible things Clément Dupard had done to you!"

"Dear mother, thou art balm to my wayward soul. There be not charge to lay on this man. He doth clothed me in the raiment of a son. The finest of the learned he doth bring. Warm thy heart, beloved blood, Twas not his hand quickened my demise. None but my own."

"Oh!" cried Antoinette and almost fainted, but Dupard gallantly stepped up and caught her, and she leaned her head back against his chest. A gesture so casual, you could imagine it repeated from the days of their childhood. "But why, my son?" she cried. "Because I knew not the world, mother. I lived as a pampered lamb.

See my life before, on the day the world of men, Dupard, laid bare for me,"

We are suddenly swept into a vision of a large luxuriously appointed room, its walls covered by a vibrant meadow filled with birds nesting in plum, apple and various other fruit trees. We see baby foxes playing with baby rabbits, while raccoons play tag with bear cubs on a deep green carpet of grass sprinkled with sunflowers. Multicolored butterflies lit upon these. This scene was laid upon a canvas of gold that covered the whole wall. It was only a wall in a room of dark mahogany tables and leather-gold-buttoned upholstered chairs. But that was not the scene. There was a boy standing before the chairs on a rich Persian carpet suited for a palace. Because surely this tall, creamy mocha-colored boy was a prince. He was beautiful, from his hazel tinted with blue eyes to his noble nose and strong forehead and evenly spaced eyes. Those eyes were focused on another work of art, as the boy worked to re-create the landscape of magnolia and cypress over dewy grass with the morning sky a heavenly blue and the sun just pecking through the trees.

"That is absolutely magnificent, Auguste," said Clément Dupard, who stood behind him. "Your gift has truly blossomed."

"Thank you, father. I'm still learning."

"Your skill has really taken a leap over these last five months. Master Matier was worth every penny."

"I agree, and he has made me an offer that I need to discuss with you."

"An offer? That sounds promising. Let's sit over by the window."

There were two exquisite looking chairs of dark wood with carved Egyptian stylized arms and cream-colored calf skin covering the upholstered back and seat. When they set down, a beautiful dark-skinned girl of about fourteen delivered a tea service along with a plate of cookies. She cut her eyes at the boy and offered a smile, but he never even looked at her.

"Thank you, Marie," said Clément. The girl executed a slight curtsey and left the room quickly. Clément poured himself some tea and helped himself to a cookie. "Tell me about this offer you've received." The boy sat musing for a moment, as if the offer were too much even for him to comprehend. "It's okay, son," said Dupard, placing a reassuring hand on his shoulder. "You've worked hard for it. Tell me what it is."

"Master Matier has granted me an apprenticeship to train with him at his studio in Paris. It's a standard three-year apprenticeship. And Jean said that my work is already quite advanced for my age, and that within a year I will be able to sell some of it. Isn't that wonderful, father? And I will be nineteen when I return, and Simone and I will be married—with your blessing, of course."

Dupard was very quiet now. He got up with a sigh and went to stand gazing into the cold fireplace. "Mother Mary. Please give me strength," he prayed out loud."

"Is there something wrong, father? If you are worried about my expenses, Jean will allow a small stipend, and I will live in the loft above the studio. So there will be little cost to you."

Finally, Clément turned and looked at the boy, and his face was a mask of anguish. The boy rushed over to him.

"Father, are you ill? Please let me help you to your chair. Shall I go and retrieve Dr. Martinique?"

"No, Auguste. I'm not ailing. At least, not in a way that Giles could remedy. My pain is in my heart because of what

I must reveal to you. Sit down, please." The boy obliged. "Tell me something, Auguste. How many times have you been into town?"

"Only twice, as I recall. Once with you, and another time with Miss Gertrude."

"Do you remember what it was like?"

"I didn't much like it. People looked at me strange and when I spoke or smiled at them, they didn't speak or smile back. And they called me jigger. 'Stop looking at me, jigger! Where'd you steal them clothes from?'"

"It's been about eight years ago. You must've miss-heard them. They weren't saying jigger."

"Then what were they saying?"

"It doesn't matter. My point is, we've always protected you from that. It's why you've never gone back."

"Protected me how, father? I don't understand."

"We've protected you from the world."

"What? But that doesn't make any sense. The world's here with you, Miss Gertrude, Angeline, and Simone. With all my teachers and my paints. This house—with the slaves and Drakens. That is the world, father. Not those people in town who refused to smile and called me strange names."

Dupard let out a sigh as he put his face in his hands.

"Okay. Just listen for a moment. When my father died, in his will he bequeathed your mother a house and her free-dom. And I de–"

"What? Why would Pawpaw need to bequeath my mother her freedom? Didn't she already have her freedom? I thought only slaves needed to be given their freed—My mother was a slave! But that would mean that I am..." He couldn't say it. Every part of him, this cream-colored prince, could not get his mind around the reality that Clément just laid at his feet. So instead, he fled out of the house. He ran across the yard toward the massive cane field not more than one hundred yards from the front yard. There were people out there in that field, toiling mightily in the sweltering heat. And they were slaves, just like Antoinette, his mother and him!

"No!" he yelled at the slaves. "I'm not! I'm not!" He ran past the fields as some of the slaves who saw him smiled and waved. Even in their sweltering toil, they were glad to see him. Why shouldn't they? He was just like them. He had to run faster, had to get away from these smiling fools. Smiling when they didn't have their freedom. He ran past the fields farther up the road that was adjacent to the cane field. He'd never really run before, at least not this far. But his stamina was fueled by panic. At the end of the road was one of the numerous barns littered about the large property. He didn't know this because he rarely left his work room. "His" work room was obviously a joke. There was nothing on this property that was his. Not even—especially, not himself! He found an old wagon horse in the barn, but no wagon. He also found an old saddle, so he threw it on the mare and mounted it. This was better. He felt more like himself again. But where would he go? Maybe he should go find Simone and ask her to run away with him? That was ridiculous, though. Why would Simone need to run away? She could come and go as she pleased. No one would call her jigger if they saw her in the street, or inquire whether she'd stolen her clothes. And if he left the property, they would probably ask him where he'd stolen the horse, because it would be stolen. He turned the mare east, toward the interior of the property. By now his father, or master, probably had the militia out looking for him, and he had no expectation that the mare could outrun them, or run at all, for that matter. He kept moving, hoping to stay ahead of them. But where was he going? he asked himself, and what would he do when he got there? All good questions that he didn't have the answers to. He just didn't want to be caught by the militia. He'd heard stories about their brutality with escaped slaves. Even though he hadn't escaped—since he hadn't left the property. If he did escape, he'd want to go someplace where he wouldn't be a slave. This was insane. Such a place didn't exist in the real world. It only existed in his mind. He was lost. His whole life, everything he'd learned, those who pretended to care about him—was all an elaborate lie. He finally came to a wooded area. When the mare got through it, there was a small lake on the other side. He wondered if this was the edge of the property. He didn't know because he'd never been to the edge of the property. He'd never needed to. This might be one of the many lakes within the boundary of Le Borge. He decided to treat it as though it really was the end. He dismounted and sat down along the shore of the lake to consider what he might do next. The sun was starting to set as the day was about to end. This made him panic a bit. Because when the sun came up this morning, he still had his whole life before him. The life of someone who was still free. He didn't want that life to end. But once the militia caught up to him, it would definitely be over. He couldn't let them catch him and bring him back as a runaway slave. To see everyone in the house and in the fields watch as he bent under the weight of his new bondage. He couldn't bear the look in his love's eyes. The pity and embarrassment were smothering him right now. The lake. That was the answer. It would get rid of all the pain. The militia couldn't get him in the lake. He wouldn't have to give up his world, the world where he was still a prince, where no one questioned ownership of his clothes, called him strange names, and wasn't happy to see him. He took off his shoes and his shirt. He might need them again, no sense getting them wet, and waded out into the water. It was surreal, but just before he went under, he would've sworn he heard his mother screaming, "No! No! My baby. My baby. My baby!"

~

Antoinette buried her face in Clément's shoulder. "You could have let him go, Clément! You could have let him go!"

"Let him go where, Netta? I never held him. I gave him everything. I wasn't going to hold him back. But the world– we'd always protected him from it. I didn't want him to go without knowing what it would be like for him."

"I go now, mother," said the spirit and receded back into the remains. The Taafli ascended and merged with Besa, who went and sat on the back of the wagon to regain her strength.

"Are you tired, Besa?" asked Margaret.

"I am. This was the longest ceremony we've ever done."

Clément came over to the wagon to speak to Besa.

"I owe you my thanks," said the landowner. "You have saved my family with this ceremony. My daughters can go on with their lives knowing their father was not responsible for their dear friend's death. What can I offer you in payment?"

"Your solemn word that you will never speak about what you've seen here. Margaret has already set a charm among your men. That will make it seem like an unspecified dream."

"It's time to get home now, Besa," said Felix. "You are due for some much-needed rest. And you can have the apples, Mr. Dupard. They really did come from the market."

"I'm sure my cooks will find something to do with them?

"Some apple pies, perhaps?" suggested Dickey.

"If that's what you would like, Mr. O'Brien. Come by Wednesday of next week and they will be ready."

"Dickey!" said Margaret.

"What? I shrunk myself to fit in a basket of apples. I deserve a pie!"

CHAPTER 22
THE CASE OF HENRY TOOMEY

Two days after Dickey returned to the Dupard property to retrieve his two apple pies:

"You wouldn't believe the crust on those pies. It was so good I could've eaten it separately and saved the filling for last. It had a light dusting of su—"

"Dickey, you've described it fifty times over the last two days," complained Margaret. "You enjoyed the pies! We believe you. Let's talk about something else."

"I agree," replied Besa. "Margaret was just telling me about a woman at her father's church, whose husband has recently disappeared."

"Maybe she made terrible pies." Margaret stood up with an evil look in her eyes. She wasn't rolling a charm, but Besa knew she was contemplating something terrible. "What was that about the pies again, Dickey?" she snarled.

"I–I wasn't talking about a pie, babbled Dickey, backing away.

"I could have sworn I heard you mention a pie."

"I wasn't doing that. I was talking about the pie—I mean, the guy that disappeared."

"It might be best if you went and chased something, Dickey," suggested Besa.

"Good idea," he replied, and bolted toward the tower on the far side of the playground.

"You ruined that for me. I had something special planned."

"I know what you had planned, and I couldn't let you turn the future father of your children into that."

"I am not going to dignify that with a reply, madam president."

"Good. Tell me more about the missing Mr. Henry Toomey."

"Alice and Henry are an usher and a deacon in my father's congregation. I talk to her often when I help gather up the hymnals at the end of service, and she told me that Henry left two days ago heading to Algiers to pick up supplies for the store and hasn't been back since. She said she could understand if there'd been a hurricane and the roads were flooded, but he's usually back in two days."

"Is she thinking something might've happened to him? Could he be hurt somewhere?"

"She went to the Gendarmes, but they won't consider him missing until he's gone two weeks."

"But that doesn't make sense. If he's lying somewhere hurt, he could die in two weeks."

"She did say there was another possibility, but it was too crazy for her to consider."

"How crazy?"

"She says it's possible that some woman took him."

"What would make her think that? Maybe he went willingly?"

"I asked her that too, but she said while Henry was an attractive man, he's never even looked at another woman.

I've seen women pass him notes during service. He just gives them to Alice."

"But what woman does she think might've done this?"

"She told me about a woman who walked into their store one day and froze when she saw Henry.

"'May I help you, ma'am,'" Alice asked her. Henry was working in the far corner, installing some new oak shelves they'd had built.

"'Emile?'" said the woman, who was white. "'Emile, I cannot believe it!'" She ran and threw her arms around Henry. "'Emile, my love. I have been searching everywhere for you!'"

"'Madam, please,'" replied Heary, pushing the woman away. "'You have me mistaken for someone else. My name's not Emile, it's Henry.'" He used the shelf he was holding to give him separation from the amorous stranger.

"'Lady, this is my husband,'" said Alice. "'You've made a mistake.'"

"'It's your mistake,'" replied the woman. "'I've been with this man more than two hundred years.'"

"'Madam, that is just insane!'" cried Henry. "'No one could live that long.'"

"'Florence, please go inform the Gendarmes that there is a madwoman escaped from the asylum,'" Alice told one of the shop assistants.

"'I will show you how mad I am, fool. He has a small mole below his right ear.'" Alice's mouth just dropped open. "'He is also missing the little toe on his right foot.'" Alice looked at Henry in confusion. He just shook his head and said,

"'Trust me, Alice. I don't know her.'"

"'Miss you'd better leave before the Gendarmes get here,'" Alice told her.

"'I don't care about the Gendarmes!'" cried the woman. "'They have no power over me.'"

"'Then who does?'" snapped Alice, just to be sarcastic. The woman just smiled.

"'You wouldn't know him. He was one of the gods of this world. I can't say it out loud, or we'd all be dead. But I can write it.'" She produced a pencil out of nowhere along with some ancient paper.

"'I'll go now,'" she said, after leaving a word written on the piece of paper on the counter. "'But I'm not leaving this world without Emile. I don't care what I have to do,'" and she strolled back out into the street.

"Did she tell you what name the woman wrote?"

"She couldn't read it because it was a language she didn't recognize. But she gave me the paper. I told her that if anyone could know what the word meant, it was you." Margaret pulled the ancient parchment out of the leather valise she carries to school and handed it to Besa. "Oh, this is Aramaic. Some of the books in Papa's library are written in this language."

"I knew you'd know. So what does it say?"

"She was right not to speak it aloud. This is the Druids name for the god of death."

"I don't know much about the Druids, but I bet this doesn't bode well for Alice getting her husband back."

"We haven't studied them yet, but Papa has books about them. They were a race of ancient seers, and even they commanded that this name not be spoken aloud, or destruction will rain down upon the race of men."

"That is not helpful, Besa. I can't tell that to Alice."

"Then are you suggesting we should take this case?"

Margaret sighed, put her hands in her red mane and her elbows on the table. "I don't know. I mean, I know we don't do this kind of thing, but she's afraid, and no one else is trying to help her."

"Don't pull your hair out, Margaret. We can try to help her. The least we can do is try to find out who this woman is."

"Yes! That's true. Thank you, Besa."

"I think it's time to send Eduardo on another reconnaissance mission."

BESA HAD Felix take another detour off their route from taking her home, to the small elegant house in Vieux Carré. Antoinette opened the door before Besa knocked.

"I had a dream you'd be visiting today."

"I hope you didn't mind. Dreams are usually quicker than a note."

"Come in. I've had Celeste make one of her coffee cakes."

"You are too sweet. I don't want to be an imposition."

"I know you don't. But it would have been bad manners not to, since I knew you were coming." She rang a little bell.

Celeste entered carrying a tea service along with generous helpings of a delectable looking brown-sugar and pecan coffee cake.

"I'd better not tell Dickey about you, because he'll be over here every day."

"I'd welcome any member of your Graveyard Club. I owe all of you a great debt."

Antoinette passed Besa a cup of tea and a slice of cake.

"We were happy to be of some assistance. I know too well how it feels to have something terrible happen to a loved one, and not understand why."

"How is your father, Besa?"

"I..."

Besa was overcome for a moment, and Antoinette wrapped her in a hug.

"It's okay. You don't have to be invincible."

"I'm fine," said Besa, pulling out of the hug. "I don't really know how he is. Hopefully, he's still alive. But that's about it. I would give anything to have him back."

"I know, Besa. Everyone in the Magist community is hoping for the same. What brings you here today?"

Besa took out a pencil and a piece of paper and wrote a name on it. "Do you recognize that name?"

Antoinette raised her eyebrows in surprise. "Where did you get this name, child?"

"A strange woman walked into the shop of a close friend and tried to claim her husband. When my friend threatened to call the Gendarmes, the woman said this was the only power she answers to. She was obviously a Voudon."

"We're all familiar with the un-named god. Did she tell you, her name?"

"No, but she was a white woman. Are there any white voudons here in Newald?"

"None that I know of. The majority of us are former slaves. Are you sure she wasn't a high-yellow who was mistaken for white?"

"I don't know. But I suppose that's a possibility. Since she was trying to claim a man of color as her love."

"Was she able to claim him? Is that why you're asking?"

"We don't know, but he hasn't returned home in over a week, and our friend is worried."

"Your only other option is the Magist Council."

"Oh, yes. I happen to know the president."

"What? You've met Septimius Seuz? That's impossible!"

"No. I did really, Thank you, Antoinette. I'll go and see him."

"Septimius doesn't see people. How do you know him?"

"I had breakfast with him the other morning. He wasn't a monster then, just a beautiful man."

Besa gave Antoinette a hug and left before she could close her mouth.

THAT NEXT EVENING at the mansion, Eduardo gave a report on his latest reconnaissance mission:

"I followed a blue creature to a structure at 57th Rue Royale. It was a nondescript building, and late at night. The creature was in a hurry. Not a lot of blue beings on the streets during the day. And as I watched and waited, other unusual looking creatures arrived. Not everyone was a creature, but that structure is definitely some type of gathering place."

"Thank you, Eduardo. You have been very helpful."

"GOOD EVENING, YOUNG ONE," said the massive, man-ox who opened the door when Besa knocked. "May I help you?"

"Hello, Lucius. You are looking well today. I would like to address the council, please."

The man-ox stepped back without a word, and allowed the girl to enter, and just before she entered the meeting hall, the creature said, "Your father was a dear friend. Hopefully he returns to you."

"Thank you," replied Besa, and stepped into the

meeting room. The first member she encountered was Obsidia, who seemed to have been hovering near the door in anticipation of the girl's arrival. Besa looked at the woman and something happened with her eyes that struck the seer momentarily speechless.

"Good evening, Obsidia," said the girl, with a smile. "Yes. I do believe the black pearls highlight your eyes very well. I would like to address the body, please."

"Absolutely," the seer was finally able to say. "Follow me and stay close."

She led Besa to the speaker's spot etched in the middle of the floor.

"In the name of Saturn!" cried Tarum. "There's a child in the chamber! What do you mean by this, Obsidia?"

The seer stood up, "This is–"

"I can speak for myself, thank you, Obsidia. My name–"

"Is this someone's idea of a joke?" interrupted Tarum. "A child is not sanctioned to speak to this body."

"Shut up and let her speak, Tarum," growled Seuz.

"Good evening, Mr. President. When will we see you for breakfast?"

"Don't you recognize her, Tarum? We've had dinner with her a few times over the last month."

"What? The little girl with all the food?" cried Tarum. "But she looks so different. That explains why I'm so hungry all of a sudden," he said, getting up and pacing a bit.

"Tarum," said Seuz. "Please let the child speak. We have our own meeting."

Besa just stood watching the man, or whatever he was. She'd never really looked at him before, and realized his eyes weren't those of a human. They were more reptilian. And she was glad not to be alone with him.

"Where's my dinner, child?" he asked, moving toward her.

"I'm sorry?" said Besa

"Tarum," said Seuz, getting up from his chair. "Back up."

"Why, she's such a cute, edible little thing," replied the vice president, his grin very wolf-like. I can't believe how hungry I am. I could just swallow her whole." He moved quickly toward the speaker's spot, as if to do just that. But when he got within six feet of where Besa stood, she put up her left hand and the council vice president found himself flattened between two sheets of light.

"I don't know what you are," said Besa. "And frankly, I don't really know what I am, either. But I do know that I don't like the thoughts in your head, and I'd like you to be quiet for a moment while I ask my question."

She turned to address the members.

"First of all, I would like to apologize for the intrusion, Mr. President. And with your permission, I would like to proceed."

"Please do so," replied Seuz.

"Thank you. Members of the council. I am so happy to be with you once again. You know my group, The Graveyard Club. You also surely know that we have helped a few citizens over the past few months. I am seeking your help in locating a Magist woman who entered the establishment of one of our non-Magist friends and tried to claim her husband. He is a loyal, good man, but has not been home for two weeks now."

"But isn't this a matter for the Gendarmes?" asked someone sitting behind the third rib.

"He is a free man of color," replied Besa. "The same

police that won't look for a Magist, will also not look for him."

The assembled mumbled or growled their agreement to this fact.

"But how can we help?" asked Tovar, the fanged, hairy woman behind the fourth rib.

"The woman left a piece of parchment that listed the name of her god," replied Besa. "Would someone of you look at it and tell me if you recognize the handwriting or possibly the paper?"

"Obsidia, if you would pass the item around so everyone has a chance to see it, please?" directed Septimius.

When Obsidia took the paper from Besa's hand, she froze. "She is not a white woman," said Obsidia. "And she's old. This man belonged to her before."

"What?" said Besa, incredulous, "How is that possible? He said he didn't know her."

"He doesn't. Not in this life. His memory isn't continuous like hers is. He's lived a long time too."

"I don't know how I can explain this to Alice. She'll be heartbroken."

"But she's breaking the rules with his retrieval," continued Obsidia. "The life he has, is the life he belongs to."

"She made reference to having to find him before. I will not say this to his wife. This is her life with him, and now we must bring him back to her."

"Miss Melponte," said Seuz. "If this woman is immortal, or partially immortal, she could be quite powerful. I would tread cautiously."

"Thank you, Mr. President. We will take that into consideration. Can someone sniff this paper and tell me what part of town it came from?"

Everyone looked to Septimius for guidance. The council president sighed and shook his head a bit. He wasn't surprised the girl had ignored his warning—stubbornness must run in her family—but he was still miffed about it.

"Jeyda. Would you do the honors, please?"

Jeyda, who was almost the size of Lucius, stood up in the rib cage and made his way to the speaking spot and accepted the parchment from Besa's hands.

"My prayers are with your father, Miss Melponte," said Jeyda.

"Thank you," replied Besa. Jeyda took a couple of whiffs of the parchment, then tasted it with his tongue.

"Hmm," said Jeyda. "I would start your search in the areas of Royal and Bourbon. I hope that narrows it down for you."

"Thank you, it does. And thank you, Mr. President, and members of the council for allowing me to speak," and she moved toward the door.

"We are here whenever you need us, Besa," replied Seuz. "Please be careful."

"We will do our best," said Besa, and was out the door. Once she was on her horse and a good distance away, the sheets of light released Tarum.

"So that is how it is then?" said the angry vice president. "Everyone just stood by and allowed her to do that to me!"

"Calm down, Tarum. You know the rules. No one is allowed to approach when a speaker is on the speaker's spot. And you allowed your animal instincts to get the best of you. You're lucky her Taafli didn't fry you."

"She won't be so lucky the next time I meet her."

"Something tells me it will be you who won't be lucky."

Tarum didn't reply to that but gave an evil eye to the

rest of the members and stalked out of the meeting chamber.

EDUARDO TOOK the task of scouting the buildings between Royal and Bourbon, searching for anything that looked unusual. It took three days of constant vigilance before he spotted something he found very peculiar. A large Creole man was walking very slowly up Bourbon Street and leaving a place that sold meat to humans. He carried several paper-wrapped bundles, but he dropped half of them and just kept walking. The raven often observed humans when they bought food; they were usually very fastidious about getting all of it home, and when they dropped something, they usually picked it up. The raven followed the man for a few blocks until he arrived at a house with a red roof. The man banged on the door while letting out a guttural howl. The door was opened by a woman who was not a person of color.

"Leopold!" cried the woman. "Where is the rest of the food?" She snatched the packages from him, which made him roar and howl even more. "Shut up and close the door!" she commanded, which caused Leopold to slam the door. Eduardo reported this whole strange incident to the club once they assembled after school.

"That is kind of bizarre," said Margaret. "It could be nothing. Just like the last two leads."

"We're running out of houses on this block. I'm hoping this will be the one," said Besa.

"Besa, we also haven't talked about how we're going to get her to release Mr. Toomey, said Dickey. "Are we prepared to fight this lady?"

"I'm hoping it doesn't come to that, Dickey. Because if there is a battle, Mr. Toomey could get injured. I'm hoping to reason with her."

"I don't know how that's going to work," said Margaret. "Adults don't usually listen to children."

"What if she thought you were his daughter?" asked Catalina.

"That is a brilliant idea, countess!" said Margaret. "Besa. You will have to dress down."

"What is the matter with my clothes from Madame Jarre? But not all my clothes come from Madame. Some of them are custom...I see your point."

"We also need a Plan B, if she suddenly figures it out," offered Eduardo. Plan B basically came down to everyone coming together to help Besa escape.

"We don't yet know what this woman's powers are," said Catalina. "So just be careful, countess Besa."

"I can do that. Margaret, let's chat for a moment, please."

Margaret followed her up to her room.

"Is there a problem, Besa?" asked Margaret.

"No. I just need a potion."

"What kind of potion?"

"I'm too tall for a small child. So, I will need to shrink, like Dickey. Have you a potion for something like that?"

"I kind of do. I'll need to rework it a bit."

"How long will that take?" asked Besa.

"About three days. That's not a lot of time, Besa. This potion won't be strong."

"It won't need to be that strong, Margaret. A few hours will do fine."

"Okay, Besa. It will work for a while. But I won't have time to test it like I like."

"It only needs to work for a little while until I get Henry back."

"Okay. I'll get on it," said Margaret.

~

THREE DAYS LATER...

"Hello," said an eight-year-old girl in a plain calico frock. "I'm looking for my mama. She works here in the kitchen."

"I'm sorry," said Dickey. "We can help you find her. What's her name?"

"Her name is Maymi."

"Miss Maymi? But I thought she didn't have any children?"

"She doesn't, Dickey," said Margaret. "This is Besa."

"What! But she's so small. How did you shrink yourself like that, Besa?"

"It took a bit of work from Margaret's potion. I appreciate how much skill it takes, Dickey. But we don't have the time it would take me to learn it."

"Where did you find the plain-looking dress?" asked Catalina.

"The seamstress had it in her rag pile. It fits perfectly; don't you think?"

"You look so real; Dickey was about to start a game of tag with you," said Margaret.

"I was not! You're just making things up again!"

Besa just shook her head.

"This shouldn't take long, but try not to harm each other while I'm away."

"Okay. If I turn him into anything, I'll turn him back when you return."

"You'll what?" asked Dickey, getting up and moving behind the big tufted chesterfield couch in the parlor. "You—you wouldn't dare! Just try it and see what I'll do!"

"As a rock or a toad, you won't be able to do much," chuckled Margaret.

"Margaret," said Besa. "Swear to me that you won't do anything like that."

"I swear. I was just thinking out loud."

"All right. I'm a bit tired. Dickey, please reach over and ring the bell for our bedtime snack."

THE NEXT EVENING, before suppertime, Besa, dressed as a little girl named May, walked up the street and approached the red-roofed house. She was already crying when the woman opened the door. "Is my papa, Henry, here?" she asked. "I miss him so much."

"Aren't you a little dear," said the woman, taking the child into her arms to comfort her. Emile–I mean, Henry, come out here," said the woman. When Henry came out, Besa conveyed a silent message that she was there to rescue him.

"Henry, is this your child?" asked the woman.

"Yes, she is," said Henry." She's my little May," he said, kissing the child on the forehead."

"Papa, I've missed you so much. Why did you leave me?"

"I–I didn't," replied Henry. "I—I"

"It was my fault," said the woman. "I stole him away." She was crying too. "I didn't realize he had a child who needed him."

"Then can I take him home now?" asked little May.

"Yes. Of course, you can. I didn't mean to be so evil. We were just about to have supper. I wouldn't want him to go hungry."

The woman produced a hearty three-course meal, along with wine for her and Henry and a cup of sweet milk for little May.

"A toast," said the woman, holding up her wine glass: "To fathers reuniting with daughters. Henry touched glasses with the woman, and so did May. Then they all chugged down their drink. May was last and then decided not to be rude and chugged hers too.

"Even when they are fake daughters," continued the woman.

Besa soon realized her mistake. Her head spun and her heart raced. She jumped up from the table to run toward the front door, but her legs wouldn't move. It was like something was holding her down.

"Don't worry, child. You aren't going anywhere," said the woman. "Who are you anyway? Emile can't have children."

Besa felt like she was sinking. She dropped back in her chair and started to lose consciousness. It was surprising because it had never happened to her like this before. She laid her head on the table, and she was out.

"I wonder who sent her?" said the woman. "I'm going to make sure she never goes back. Leopold! Come and take this child—who has started to change–to one of the bedrooms. This is a much older child. Where could she have from? Hurry up, Leopold! Before she grows much bigger!" Leopold finally appeared and slung Besa over his shoulder. "Daargh!" he said. "In the bedroom on the other side of mine, of course. And don't you damage her. We may be able to get some money for a child who can change her shape like that."

BESA HAD SOMEHOW BEEN PLUNGED into a strange dark world with a moonless sky that was almost black with very few stars. The ground she stood on was grass-less and soft, like it had recently rained. In the distance ahead of her, she made out what looked like some kind of hedge, and began moving toward it, hoping that a way out of this dark realm might lie on the other side of it. Then she heard the thunder of a herd of some kind, as the ground began to shake. She knew it was coming right at her. It was obvious that she'd better get to those hedges before it trampled her. She took off running, but something—a few things—flew past her and landed on the ground, blocking her path. There were three of them. They were black like the landscape, but were outlined with a red light, possibly an internal fire, their eyes were also red. They were each the size of a giant bull mastiff, and then they all sprang at her at once. Her armor engaged quickly and her sword took the head off the first and a blast of light from the Taafli blinded the second, and Besa speared the third on her sword. The Taafli erased the second, which gave Besa time to keep running toward the hedge. She didn't know what that herd was, but had an idea it wouldn't be anything good, judging by the first three creatures out of it.

"You need to run faster, Besa," said Violet. "That herd is gaining on us!" They had more than a hundred yards to go and knew they wouldn't make it. Suddenly she was snatched off her feet and was flying as the herd surged under her.

"I've got you," said Violet. "Don't look down. You don't want to know what those things are."

And as they approached the compacted green mass of the hedge, Besa saw she'd made a mistake.

"That isn't a hedge."

"I can see that," replied Violet. "But it's the only refuge we have against that mass of beasts down there."

The Taafli placed Besa at the beginning of the maze. Once she was inside it, the noise of the mass of monsters on the outside completely disappeared. Besa began to make her way toward the other side of the maze, when she rounded the first turn a thing that looked like a combination bear and giant praying mantis, rushed at her. Luckily her sword morphed into a spear and she flung it at the thing without much time to aim. It wasn't moving when she ran by it.

"We have to think strategically before we enter a turn in here," said Violet.

"That I agree with," replied Besa, "But I don't think we should stay in one place too long. I want to get through this thing. I have a feeling that's our only escape from this horrible place."

"I believe that too, Besa. But we will have to keep fighting to do that."

"Better one or two in here, than a whole herd out there. Let's keep moving forward."

WHEN BESA DIDN'T RETURN after three hours, the kids could only think something had gone wrong. Now they had to make a plan to try and rescue Besa.

"We don't need a plan," offered Dickey. "I'll just run down there, snatch the roof off and get Besa out."

"I don't think so, Dickey," replied Margaret "Besa is the most powerful person we know."

"Exactly," said Mokheer. "And if the woman has over-powered her in some way, we need a safe way to find out what she's capable of. I'll go and take a look and report back what I find. Eduardo, would you lead me to the location?"

"Absolutely," replied the corvid. "Let's go now."

The corvid and the unspecified took off toward the red-roofed structure.

"It is not hard to find among all the surrounding structures with dark roofs."

Mokheer did not waste any time entering the front part of the house and working his way through each room. He finally found Besa unconscious and chained to a bed in the second bedroom.

"Besa, wake up. We need to get out of here."

He could easily manage the chains, but there was no way he could carry her. He left to report what he'd found to the rest of The Graveyard Club.

"Whatever the woman did, Besa's now chained to a bed in one of the back bedrooms."

"Does she look injured in any way?" asked Margaret.

"No. But she is unconscious."

"Like in a dream?" asked Dickey

"Yes, that's what it looked like."

"Okay. I have an idea," said Margaret. "But we're going to need a few things."

~

IN THE MEANTIME, the woman had put out a call for anyone interested in a shape-shifting child. Quite a few parties showed up, but few could deal with what they found. On the evening of the second day, two black-cladded individuals knocked on the door of the red-roofed house.

"We understand that there is a special child you want taken off your hands?" the first one asked, when the door opened.

"Yes, come in. You two don't look like much," said the woman, jaded after so many refusals.

"I don't see how it matters what we look like," said the first one. "We're here to relieve you of something you don't want."

"You'll want to have a look at her first."

"Why? Is something wrong with her?"

"If you can't handle her, I don't want to waste my time, like the others."

"What happened with—"

"Just go look at her and see!" snapped the woman. "She's in the second to the last bedroom. Watch out for the thing that comes out of her chest."

"What thing that comes out of her chest?"

"It killed my Leopold. Pulled his spirit out and I couldn't revive him!"

"Was your Leopold possibly already dead?" asked the second Shadow.

"What if he was? That's my private business. Go look at her!"

The Shadows disappeared heading toward the bedroom. They were back in less than a minute. "We will definitely take her," said the first Shadow.

"I don't believe you," said the woman. "You see that glow she's putting out? It melts through that chain holding her to the bed, but doesn't burn through the bed like it knows that it shouldn't. What is that?"

"That is something we can take off your hands, in less than two hours."

"But how are you going to touch her? The last fool that tried, it turned him to ash."

"We have a device that will let us move her without touching her."

"Is that so," said the woman, looking more hopeful.

"Yes," said the second Shadow." We can have it here in less than two hours"

"Can you, now? Then go and get your device. I want this strange child out of my house."

The Shadows headed toward the door. "We will be back in no tim—"

"Wait a minute, gentlemen," said the woman. "There are a few other things you will need to bring back with you. Namely, two hundred pieces of silver coin, and transportation for myself and my friend out of this city."

"Agreed," said the first Shadow. "We shall return in less than two hours."

Meanwhile, in the maze, Besa and Violet had fought their way through half of it. Besa had lost count of the number of monsters they'd killed, but she was starting to notice an unsettling trend: The farther they'd gone into the maze, the monsters had doubled. Which made their movement more difficult. "We need to rethink our strategy, Besa," said Violet.

"I didn't know we had a strategy," replied Besa. "I'm just trying to survive and you're helping me."

"We need to do better than that. I have an idea to help us move faster."

"I'm game."

"I will fly you toward the front half of the maze."

"Sounds simple. Let's try it."

But when Violet tried to lift Besa into the air, a type of net knitted itself above them, preventing them from getting off the ground.

"It sounded like a wonderful idea. Do you have any others?"

"Not at the moment. That was my best one."

"We can rest here for a good while and then move on to the next monster."

"That is not really a better plan, Besa."

"It's worked so far."

"I was hoping my plan had worked and I wouldn't have to tell you that something is coming behind us. You can't hear it yet, but I can. It sounds like the herd of creatures have made their way into the maze."

"Since we are exchanging bad news. I would like to say that I am tired, and I don't know how much longer I can do this."

"Besa, I know that. That's why I was trying to get you out of here."

IN THE MEANTIME, back in the waking world, the Shadows arrived driving an undertaker's hearse, that carried some type of glowing mechanical device.

"What is that contraption?" asked the woman, standing in her doorway.

"It's an air agitator," said the first Shadow. "It energizes the air around an object or a person and allows them to be moved without touching them."

Right after the hearse pulled up to the red-roofed house, a large covered wagon rolled a little further up the street and stood about twenty yards away. It was driven by Felix wearing a black suit, along with a top hat and beard. Inside the large wagon was the rest of The Graveyard Club, all laid out side by side, holding hands. Eduardo was there as well, sleeping on the countess's chest. Once the covered wagon stood at the proper distance, Felix dismounted and trotted over to the undertaker's hearse, making sure no one in the house was watching. He fed the two horses each a carrot to calm them and then quickly unhitched them from the hearse and led them away to the next street over, where Juan took possession and delivered them to the nearest livery.

BESA AND VIOLET had now fought through two more levels of the maze. Besa had somehow taken an injury when a giant creature with a snake's head and a lion's body had leapt out of the green wall of the maze and caught her from behind. Violet killed the thing, but it bit through the armor protecting her shoulder. Violet was at this moment frantically trying to draw out the venom because Besa's arm was paralyzed.

"How did it get a bite through? My armor is impenetrable."

"It is, usually. But this is a strange world."

"And I can hear that herd of monsters coming behind us. I'm scared, Violet. How are we going to get out of here?"

Violet didn't want to tell her that they were scared, too.

But the worst part was, they believed the beast that attacked Besa was a part of the herd coming behind them. Once the venom was out, Besa could move her arm again, but Violet wasn't sure how much fighting she could do, and they didn't think she could survive another venomous bite.

~

AT THE RED-ROOFED HOUSE, the Shadows had arrived with a horse-drawn hearse, and the two hundred pieces of silver the woman demanded.

"She's your problem now," said the woman, after accepting the small, heavy dark trunk the Shadows brought. She'd counted up to a number and then did a reasonable guess that it would add up to 200. She handed them the key to the lock on the girl's wrist. "You may not even need it if she's melted the chain's again."

But the chains were still intact, as Besa wasn't glowing as brightly.

"Hurry. Let's get the device while she's a little weaker."

Meanwhile, the club was having no luck breaking through the barrier into Besa's dream.

"I don't understand," said Margaret. "We've practiced this fifty times, but nothing seems to work. Anybody got an idea?"

"You know my idea," said Dickey. "She's right over there. Let's just go and get her!"

"We have to be careful, Dickey. There're Shadows there now," said Margaret.

"Shadows or no Shadows, I'm not leaving here without our Besa!" He was climbing out of the wagon when Felix rushed back to it.

"Something's wrong! We need to get Besa out of that

dream! I feel her getting weaker. Everyone lay down. I'll act as your anchor. They did as Felix directed. They all grasped hands, and the behike pushed them into a deep sleep; and with Felix anchoring, they soon broke through the barrier into Besa's dream.

~

"Wow! This is dark. I can barely see."

"It doesn't matter. We're in a dream, Dickey. Give yourself night vision," said Margaret.

"Oh, yeah. That's much bett—look out!"

They all ducked as six creatures flung themselves at them. Dickey snatched up his sword and killed two, while Margaret erased two more with some kind of super sparkles from her fingertips. Catalina had conjured a crossbow that shot arrows of blue fire, and incinerated two creatures at once.

"That's a great idea, Catalina," said Dickey. "I wish I'd... Oh, yeah. I hope Besa doesn't mind if I borrow this," and his sword became Besa's sword of light. They spent the next ten minutes slicing through a barrage of monsters.

"Wait a minute. Dickey, hold your sword up," said Margaret. "There's something in the distance. And if I know Besa, that's where she went."

"It won't be easy getting there. Not with what's in front of us," said Dickey."

There was a sea of monsters between them and Besa's green maze.

"Anybody up for some cake? We're going to need the extra energy."

"I don't think this is the best time for dessert, Dickey. If something's happened to Besa, we need to get to her as quickly as possible," said Margaret.

"Yeah. But fighting always makes me hungry."

"Let's get through all this and make it to that bushy thing, and we'll see."

"Has anyone seen Eduardo?" asked Catalina. "I know he was sleeping with us."

"It'll have to wait. Here they come!" said Margaret, as a wave of monsters charged toward them. Margaret cast a charm that hobbled the front line, which meant the second line tripped over them and laid waste to the whole charge. They were disorganized already, but hobbling the first group allowed the kids time to pick off a good number before they could re-group.

"Oh my god! what is that!" said Dickey looking up.

"A dragon?" replied Margaret.

"We're going to have to retreat," said Catalina. "We can't fight all these things and a dragon, too."

"But we have to get to Besa," replied Margaret.

"Why don't you just fly over them, Margaret," said Dickey. "You both can. I'll stay here and hold these off."

"Absolutely not, Dickey!" said Margeret and Catalina together. "That is a terrible plan!"

"It's here now. You're both stuck!"

"Greetings!" boomed the dragon.

"Wait a minute," said Catalina.

"Greetings! My Graveyard Club compadres!" said the dragon.

"Eduardo?" replied Catalina.

"Yes, my countess. Please make room, so that I may land."

"Okay, let's give him some room," said Margaret.

Eduardo was at least twenty feet long, not including his

tail, which was about 14. But for some reason, the monsters chose the occasion of the dragon's landing to mount another attack.

"Eduardo, lookout! They're charging!" cried Catalina.

"Don't worry, countess," said the corvid. "I shall make us a little room."

The dragon inhaled and laid down a two-hundred-yard wave of flame. It gave the kids some room, but it also showed them that the herd of monsters was much bigger than they'd imagined. Because there were still thousands left.

"We'll have to fly over them. Otherwise, we'll never get to Besa in time," said Margaret.

Back at the red-roofed house, Besa's light had almost gone out.

"Looks like we won't need the agitator after all," said the first Shadow.

"Good. Let me whale on her a bit, for what she did to Leopold," said the woman.

"No. If you damage her, we're taking back the silver," said the first Shadow.

"Then get her out of here!"

One Shadow reached for Besa's legs, the other reached for her shoulders, but a powerful blast hit both of them, knocking them against the wall.

"Looks like she still has some fire left in her," said the first Shadow. Which was what Mokheer hoped they would think. But he couldn't keep this up all night. He hoped Besa woke soon.

THAT PROBABLY WASN'T GOING to happen, since the situation inside the maze had not improved. Violet had a barely conscious Besa to protect and a small army of motivated monsters to hold off.

"You will have to climb on my back," said the dragon.

"But how are we to—?"

"I will lay down my head, and you climb on my neck, right behind my ears. The wind from my wings won't bother you there."

They clamored over the dragon's head and stationed themselves behind his massive ears. "Okay, is everyone comfortable? asked Eduardo.

"Yes, hurry!" said Margaret.

"Then we're off!" said the dragon, taking to the sky.

"Oh, no," said Margaret, when they got over the green bush. "It's a maze. How are we going to find her in all that?"

"I can fly down a little closer to get a better look," offered Catalina.

"Okay. But be careful. We don't know what surprises that thing holds."

Catalina changed as she dived off the dragon's neck and glided over the top of the maze.

"Besa, show yourself!" she said. "We're here trying to find you!"

After about five minutes of calling and searching, she finally noticed a little light about three levels down from the end of the maze. She dipped in closer to get a better look.

"Countess, be careful," said Violet.

"Hey! I found them!" cried Catalina, turning around to tell the rest of the club. Suddenly, a vine whipped out and snared one of the countess's claws. "Help! I'm caught!" she cried.

"Oh, no!" cried Dickey. "Eduardo, if you will go a little lower, I'll jump down in that bush and chop it away with my sword."

"No. Don't do that, Dickey. That's not a regular bush."

"I cannot allow it to harm my countess," said Eduardo. "Let me try something."

He released a fireball that hit in the spot just before where the countess was trapped and it burned away a large section of that wall, which released Catalina. The wall started to recede a bit, as if it was dying. They got a good look at Besa and Violet's position then, along with the creatures that were attacking them.

"We need to land Eduardo," said Dickey. "There's room with the wall burned away."

The dragon didn't hesitate, and soon the club was on the ground, in the middle of the battle.

"Reinforcements are much appreciated," said Violet. "If you will see to Besa a moment," said the Taafli. "I will help clear away some of these nasty creatures."

It struck and evaporated three at once. But it was obvious that it and Besa were weaker.

"We need to get Besa out of here," said Margaret, holding her friend's head in her lap. "It's like her light's going out."

"I happen to have something special I've been saving for just such an occasion," said Dickey. He pulled a small silver flask from his front pocket. "Here, give her some of this."

"What is that?"

"Something I made. She'll recognize it!"

"I'm not poisoning my friend. Where did you get it, Dickey?"

"From Muhammad, okay?"

"From the Djinn?"

"Yeah. We've become friends. I go to have dinner with him sometimes. He taught me how to make it."

"Dickey, are you serious?"

"She's my friend too, Margaret. Give it to her!"

Margaret took the flask and held Besa's head up and gave her a sip.

The effect was immediate. Besa opened her eyes and sat up.

"Wow!" she said. "Where'd you get that?" She took the flask and had a big swallow.

"You sure you're okay?" asked Margaret.

"Yeah. Did you make this?" asked Besa, handing the flask back.

"No. It was Dickey."

"What? The Djinn gave you the recipe, Dickey?"

"Yes. And no, I haven't tried any. He made it very clear that it wasn't meant for me. But if I do, only under horrible circumstances. He said you'd understand."

"I do. Let's get out of this maze and out of this terrible dream!"

Violet's light had tripled, which meant he could evaporate 20 monsters in one blast of light. The club had an over-abundance of fire power with a dragon and an energized Taafli at their disposal. They quickly pushed their way to the end of the maze.

Besa woke up from her nightmare as they attempted to remove her from the bed. A third Shadow kept Mokheer busy.

"Besa!" cried Mokheer when she sat up, eyes blazing. Violet sprang from her chest and erased the Shadow harassing him. The second one disappeared. The third one that had put a hand on Besa, she managed to freeze in place. She got up and was examining it closely. It couldn't move, but she made sure it could speak. Besa walked around it quietly as she gazed at it.

"What are you doing?" asked Mokheer.

"Just getting some information."

"But Besa, it's dangerous. Let it out of here."

"Be quiet, Mokheer, while I think of some questions. Oh! what is your name?"

"I am called five," replied the Shadow.

"Are there more of you?" asked Besa. "How many more?"

"Only The One Who Knows can answer that."

"Is that where you were taking me, to The One Who Knows?"

"No. I was taking you where they wanted you to be."

Felix came into the bedroom.

"Besa, that's dangerous. What are you doing?"

"I'm trying to find out some things. Were you a part of the group that kidnapped Dickey?"

"No," said Five. "That was one, two and three."

"Do you know where my father's book is?"

"Yes. I know where it is."

"Please have it brought here. Can you do that?"

"Besa!" cried Felix. "Wait a minute. You go too far."

"If you can, please have it brought here."

Five stuck out his hand and said, "The One Who Knows, please send me the book. And the book of Taalu appeared in the Shadow's hand. Besa quickly confiscated it and handed it to Felix.

"You must let it go, Besa. You don't know where this will lead."

"Yes, I know. But I can't just let it go. Because where it goes, I may have to follow one day. So Besa reached up and touched the Shadow's chest. When she did the Shadow's eyes lit up. "I now bind you to me, Five. When I need you, I will say, Five, come to Besa. You may go."

The Shadow quickly disappeared.

"Besa, what was that all about?" asked Felix. "Why would you do something like that?"

"Half the time I don't know how or why I do something. But I believe The One Who Knows has all the answers I'm looking for, and one day I will have to meet him."

"But that isn't something you should want, Besa."

"What I want is my father back safely, and to know what he was hiding from me."

"All that may cost you your life," replied Felix. "A child shouldn't have such pursuits."

"I wish I were a regular child that didn't need them. But I'm not. Let's get Henry home to Alice. I find I'm having a craving for cake. A huge piece."

Dickey, who'd followed Felix into the bedroom, just smiled, while Margaret cut her eyes at him.

CHAPTER 23

GOD OF THE DEAD

Felix escorted Henry out to the covered wagon. But as Dickey and Besa were about to go out the door, the woman blocked it.

"You must think this is some kind of game, child. You come and invade my home, kill one of my men, and take the other. You aren't going home smiling to eat cake! Hasaam balagma desuticata yasaam!" She threw up her hands. "Now, you lose one!" The ground began to shake.

"Besa, let's get out of here," said Dickey.

"Besa!" cried Margaret. "Where are you?"

"We're here in the house!" replied Besa.

"But it's not there anymore!" cried Margaret.

"Dickey! Push the roof off and climb out!"

But that's when the floor split and Dickey got sucked down. When Besa looked at the women, she was sinking, too.

"Oh, no you don't!" said Besa, grabbing the woman's arm. "I'm not letting you out of my sight! Where did you send my friend?"

"The same place you sent mine. To the land of the dead!"

"You will bring him back!" said Besa, placing a hand of light on the woman's face, which made her scream.

"I just heard your name when you screamed," said the girl. "You are Agasia."

"No! You have no right to use my name!"

"Now that I know it, I can use it whenever I like!"

"You're an evil child. I should've killed you when I had the chance!"

"It's not going to help you now, Agasia; evil witch. Where did you send my friend?"

Agasia was struggling, but she couldn't refuse a question with her own name.

"Ugh! He is with my lord, God of the dead!"

"Then we shall go and bring him back."

"You can't make me! I won't go back there!"

"Agasia, we go to the god of the dead." Then Besa repeated the charm the woman used to send Dickey through the gateway, and the floor shook while Agasia trembled with fear, cried and fought, but Besa held her fast. When the floor split, she jumped in and pulled Agasia down with her.

IT WAS PROBABLY MEANT to be a drop, but Violet made sure to slow Besa's descent. The atmosphere got hotter the further down they went. Agasia had no Taafli to slow her descent, so she dropped like a stone, screaming all the way down. Besa heard a splash below her.

"We will land on the shore, Besa," Violet told her.

But as they came to it, it wasn't really a shore as you'd expect. It was ringed by torches of blue fire and strange horned beasts with tusks coming out of their mouths, brandishing swords and spears lined the edge of the shore. And as individuals landed in the black body of water and swam toward the shore, the monstrous guards dragged them from the water and flung them toward a crowd of individuals already congregating and kneeling before a throne composed of pearl-like bones; and on the throne sat an entity with eyes the color of moonlight but had no specific shape. Its form shifted between earth, wind, fire, and mist. It held a scepter of blue fire.

"Come!" boomed an impossibly big voice. "Kneel before thy god and accept thy fate!"

Besa saw Agasia among their number, prostrate before the throne, pleading to be returned to life. The Deity dismissed her with a wave of his scepter that burned the hair from Agasia's head.

"But I did not mean to return!" screamed the Voudon, as the beast guards snatched her up and tossed her into a lake of fire to the left of the throne. Agasia shrieked as a monster rose up from the fiery depths. It was a massive three-head thing that matched Agasia's shriek and then swallowed her.

"I hope that's not what happened to Dickey," said Besa.

"I don't think so," replied Violet. "The beings kneeling before it are already dead. We must be careful. It requires your acceptance before it can keep a living soul. We will not be offering that."

The Taafli placed Besa on the throne room floor and she approached the throne by walking past those who were kneeling. The entity flicked its scepter of fire and three guards charged at them. The Taafli sent a flicker of light in their direction; and the beast guards evaporated, leaving only armor, helmets and shields in their place. When others attempted to avenge their comrades, the deity flicked his scepter, and they stood down. "Who are you?" came a voice from all around them. "I have heard of this power."

"We are not here to give tribute or to kneel," said Violet. "We seek the living boy sent here by that woman your fire creature just swallowed. You cannot hold him, and you know that."

"You dare come into my throne room, destroy my guards and then make demands. You will kneel and offer tribute, or die!"

"She will not kneel to you Hèlfṁṁ." The deity startled at its own name. "I have a similar lake at my disposal. It's called knúúkliu!"

"My father and all my brothers perished in that lake!" cried the deity.

"Yes. My kind have been fighting your kind since the beginning of time."

"Speaking my name makes you an enemy, Talyum. So that is how you will be treated. The being you seek is chained to the Dèmolrú. If she cannot survive it, both her, the boy and you, Talyum, will die. Then you will kneel!"

"We don't like this, Besa," said Violet. "The Dèmolrú is a vicious trial."

"Why? What does it entail?"

"You are chained to the back of a monster, and you have to answer a riddle while the thing tries to throw you off."

"What? How hard are the riddles?"

"How hard are the–Did you hear what we said?"

"I'm not bad at riddles, Violet."

"It's not just the riddles, Besa. It's the answer. You must find a way to get the monster to hear your answer. And it's doing everything it can to tear you to pieces before it hears it."

"If we don't do this, what other options do we have to get Dickey back?"

"We would have to kill about fifty thousand beast guards, subdue the god of the dead, and force him to send us back to the world of the living. Oh, and we'd still have to get Dickey away from the Dèmolrú."

"Do you have a plan for how we might be able to do all that?"

"No. I'm not a great planner."

"Then we go with the monster," said Besa.

THEY PLACED Besa inside a small steel cage and then chained the cage to the back of a reptilian monster the size of a castle.

"This will definitely make it more difficult," said Besa. "And where is Dickey? Have you located him yet?"

"I think he's close. But I doubt he's conscious," replied Violet.

"My next question is more practical: Where are this thing's ears? I definitely need to know that."

"I'll go out and do a little test," said Violet. They flew out of the cage and fluttered around the creature's head, and emitted a piercing high-pitched sound that made the castle-sized beast slam its claw to the sides of its head.

"Now we know," said Violet. "I also saw Dickey chained to the beast's chest."

"Thank you. That's good to know."

WHAT ARE we going to do, Felix?" asked Margaret, as they stood on the spot where the red-roofed house used to be.

"You can go home, Margaret. But I have to stay," replied Felix. "This is the last place they were, and I must hope they will return here. If not, I'll have to inform Judge O'Brien that his son is missing again."

"I can stay for a while, too. I don't have to be home until tomorrow night. This was a sleep-over night."

"You can't just stay out here, Margaret. Why don't you go back to the house and get something to eat?"

"I'm not really hungry."

"Has something happened to Sir Richard and countess Besa?" inquired Catalina.

"They never came out of the house," replied Eduardo.

"Please," said the behike. "There is nothing you can do. Everyone, please go back to the house?" But not one of them moved.

"Something must have happened to Dickey," said Margaret. "Besa's probably trying to get him out of whatever it is. Are you getting anything from her, Felix?"

"No. The last thing I heard from her was a chant, and now it's like she's not in this world anymore."

"You mean, like she's dead?" asked Margaret. "That's not possible. Her Taafli wouldn't let her die. You must be getting the signal wrong, or something's blocking it. Do you remember the chant?"

"Chant? What are you talking about?"

"You said the last thing you heard from her was a chant."

"It was the chant that opens the doorway to the land of the dead," said Obsidia, who just walked into the yard of the missing house. Margaret startled at her sudden appearance.

"Good evening, Obsidia," said Felix. "What did you see?"

"I saw enough to make me come down here before something terrible happened. The woman was bitter at the loss of her lover and sought to punish Besa by sending the boy to his death. But the boy isn't dead, and neither is Besa."

"It always worries me what you don't say, Obsidia. Besa's not safe, is she?"

"No. The god of the dead condemned the boy to Dèmolrú, and Besa must give the monster the answer if she is to save him."

"By the ancestors! She's strapped to the back of that thing!"

"What is the Dèmolrú, Felix?" asked Margaret.

"Something no fourteen-year-old should attempt."

"That doesn't tell me anything."

"It doesn't matter, Margaret. You can't help her."

"Will you tell me, Miss Obsidia?" asked Margaret. Obsidia glanced over at Felix to make sure he didn't object. When he didn't, the seer explained about the riddles.

"That doesn't sound that bad," said Margaret.

Felix only shook head.

"As always, Obsidia, you leave the important parts out." Felix told the young witch the rest.

"What?" cried Margaret, sitting down hard on her bottom. "Has anyone ever survived this trial?"

"Two individuals," replied Felix. "One of them was Hercules."

"Oh my god! Can we get down there and maybe try to help them?"

"The best you'd do is get yourself killed, or be trapped in some other dangerous ordeal."

BESA WAS ALREADY CONSIDERING her options as they strapped her into the cage on the monster's back; and devised her own little plan.

"That doesn't sound like a very good plan, Besa," said Violet.

"First of all, Violet. Stop reading my thoughts. It's very rude."

"I don't think that counts as reading your thoughts. Since I'm a part of you. How do you know it will come?"

"I don't. But you don't have a better plan. Besides, it just has to give Dickey a sip."

"You'd better call it now, before all this gets crazy."

Besa closed her eyes and chanted, "Five, come to Besa!"

It took only a moment, and the Shadow hovered outside Besa's cage.

"Your wish is my command, Mistress Besa. Shall I free you from this cage?"

"No," said Besa, "I want you to go to the boy chained to this monster's chest, find the silver flask in his front pocket, and give him one sip."

"As you command, Mistress, Besa."

The Shadow took off toward the giant monster's chest. Dickey looked mostly dead, since they had no idea if he'd already gone through the trial, but hadn't been able to participate due to near death, unconsciousness or both. But when Besa heard a loud gong sound, she knew it was about to start. She could tell that they weren't outside in the elements, but in some kind of giant chamber. She did have a second part of her plan, but needed Dickey to be conscious and hopefully free to carry it out. If it could even work. When the gong sounded again, she knew they were out of time.

She then noted that this chamber had another function: as an auditorium This trial would have an audience composed of the God of death himself, wavering and shifting in a seat almost at eye-level to Besa's cage. He wanted to watch his enemies die. If Five could get Dickey to wake up, they would give him a show he would never forget.

"And now," boomed the gigantic voice. Five returned to Besa's cage.

"I have done as you commanded, Mistress Besa. The boy has taken a sip, and he is awake."

That's when Besa realized she'd forgotten something.

"Five, please go and tell the boy that Besa says get her off this monster's back." Five took off again—Everywhere I go, I look the same. And even though I'm everywhere, I've never moved. What am I?

The monster suddenly began to shake, and its roar was the sound of a hundred elephants. It began to paw and scratch at Besa's cage on its back. The cage held up for now. Besa didn't have to stay in the cage, but she needed Dickey to come to her so they'd be able to leave this world together —if her idea worked like she hoped it would. The monster was slamming itself against the rocks inside the chamber. It was coming un-glued trying to dislodge the cage. Besa couldn't imagine anyone surviving this trial under normal circumstances. She hoped Dickey wouldn't have any trouble—"

Somebody stop the boy!" Besa heard the booming voice shout. "Don't let him—something huge and white flashed past the cage. And then she was pressed up against it. Then she heard,

"I'm a tree!" it screamed in a massive booming voice. And then her cage was inside something huge and white, and then a massive eye looked at her.

"Besa, are you okay?" inquired the giant.

"Yes, Dickey."

"The elixir wasn't bad," boomed giant Dickey. "It had kind of a sweet taste."

"Dickey, focus! I need you to jump," said Besa.

"Jump where?" boomed Dickey.

"Straight up!" said Besa. "Just take a running start and jump as high as you can. Like when you caught Margaret. Now go!"

Luckily, he thought to stuff Besa in his front pocket, or she would've been shaken dizzy by the revolutions of his pumping fists. When Dickey sprang into the blackness of the dead sky, Besa told Violet to: "Push him higher!"

"Push him where? What are we doing, Besa?"

"Just push him!"

Dickey picked up speed as the Taafli added more thrust to his ascent.

"What now?" asked the Taafli.

"I need you to broadcast my chant, Violet," Besa told the Taafli.

"Broadcast it where, Besa? And something is coming after us?"

"Oh, no! Let me start!"

Besa began Agasia's chant that opened the doorway to the land of the dead. Once she was finished, Violet sent the chant out into the blackness above, and then Besa heard a screech and something flew at them from Dickey's right. Violet erased it before she got a good look at it. Not that she wanted to see it. Just as she finished that thought, some other hideous winged thing came flying in on Dickey's left.

Besa sent a blast of light into it, and it dropped. She was starting to doubt this would work, and then something landed on Dickey's back and wrapped an arm of some kind around his neck. Besa knew she couldn't kill it without killing Dickey.

"Violet! Get it off!" cried Besa. It was choking him, probably hurting him.

She wanted to cry, but this was not the time for it.

"Please, hold on Dickey." And she could feel the thing trying to pull them backward. "No! Get it off him!"

"Besa, look up!" said the Taafli. There were stars.

"How did we get—stars!" cried Besa. "Give him another boost, Violet!"

The Taafli obliged, and they shot through the opening, as if they were headed for the moon. The thing on Dickey's back didn't care for moonlight. It let out a screech and turned to dust. Gravity took over, and they were falling back to earth, to the land of the living, to their frie–

"Violet, please slow our descent!"

"You really didn't have to tell us that, Besa. We're falling too," said Violet.

And then Dickey began to shrink and Besa popped out of his pocket.

"I'd get rid of the cage, Besa. Otherwise, we're going to land on him with it."

"Oh, that's right," said Besa. She popped the lock on the cage and kicked it away. But she didn't drop like Dickey. She just floated down, and just before she landed, she hoped Margaret had laid something out for their friend to land on. But then she realized that she didn't know how to land either and ended up smack on her bottom. She looked up and there was Margaret standing with her usual smirk.

"It's not that easy, is it?" she asked.

"No. Where's Dickey? How's he doing?"

"He's fine. He's got cake. Felix had Miss Maymi bring food while we waited for you to come back."

"I'm glad you had confidence in me coming back. Because it wasn't a sure thing. Is that Obsidia?"

"She tried to come and warn you."

"She has a huge piece of cake!"

"Are you hungry, Besa?" asked Margaret. "The food's over at the covered wagon. Dickey's over there too."

Besa got up and hurried toward the covered wagon.

WHEN BESA GOT HOME, she went straight to her father's room and sat on his bed again.

"I'm okay, Papa. I know it didn't look good for a while. But we're fine. Dickey is safe and Henry is back home with his wife. Goodnight, Papa. Hopefully you are sleeping. I love you."

Acknowledgments

As authors we don't always have a good safe harbor where we can land after we finish a book. We often look crazed and a little desperate. I'm not kidding. These were my safe harbors.

My dear friend Myra Hofer, who read everything I finished and handed her.

Toronto Science Fiction and Fantasy Writers. There are over a thousand of these people. No way I've met them all. But I've met some of them, and they're pretty cool.

David F. Shultz. Man! I was in a Facebook group after I finished my second novel, looking crazed and desperate, and Dave threw me a lifebuoy. I have never been to Canada, but I will someday, and I know exactly where I'm going: To Toronto! Okay, we may not get past the border right now... but things won't be like this forever.

Jacqueline Thorpe (Jackie) Wonderful Sci-Fi author, and the person I...sort of attached myself to. What can I say. I like women writers, and Jackie is so patient and friendly. And like most Canadians, she manages to tolerate obnoxious and anxious people from across her border.

Jaime Babb: You know how you think you're a writer and then you meet a writer who is really like: OMG! This is a "writer"? And I am so glad this is not a contest! She is so sweet and humble, and very talented. And she read my book!

Jeff Butler. I only know Jeff from the meeting. But what I

grasped in that interaction showed me that I wanted this guy on any team I put together. He's very solid, and his opinion mattered a great deal, by their very tone and substance.

I'm on team Canada!

ABOUT THE AUTHOR

K.M. Harrell is a veteran of the United States Air Force, and the eldest of five siblings. Four girls and himself. They were and are a close-knit southern family. He hails from Louisiana, in the United States of America. He has written most of his life. The Graveyard Club: The Death of Diamond Slim is his second novel. His first is: Nyira and the Invisible Boy. A semifinalist in the 2018 Publishers Weekly Booklife Prize. He can be reached at: graveyardclub.net

www.ingramcontent.com/pod-product-compliance
Lightning Source LLC
Chambersburg PA
CBHW070756120726
47910CB00001B/186